SKULL MAZE

NYRA JAE

ISBN (Paperback): 978-1-7638564-1-7
ISBN (ePub): 978-1-7638564-0-0

Cover Design by Dave Leahey

Maps by Dave Leahey

Typography by Lorna Reid

Edited by Oren Eades

Published by Shadow Print Books

First Edition

TSTHARN
Forest of Darkness
Skull Maze
Turnback Forest
Tampoc Lake
Grassy Plains
Keyp Marshes
Keyp
Rocky Greenlands
Rivers Tor
Ground Thern
Shadow Fang Guild
Deserts of Whaern
Zairedrein
Comtun
Jarnda
Lorhaven
Whispering Wood
Sky Thern
Mountains of Thern
Smarb
N
S
W
E

ONE

Shadow Fang

A deep rumble reverberates through the thick stone walls of the Shadow Fang guild, dislodging fine dust from the beams in Peren Naïlo's room. The atmosphere has been oppressive for hours, charged with the looming threat of an impending storm.

Lightning finally cracks, splitting the sky outside his small window and illuminating the thick stone walls for a heartbeat, the flash and bang startling Peren awake from his deep sleep. Pressing a hand to his head, he groans in pain, the vivid memories of the previous night's revelries flooding his mind, making him wince.

A soft knock at the door precedes the opening creak. A young novice pokes his head in and sees the look of pain on Peren's face, and his own lights up in a mischievous smile. "You're late for the ceremony," the boy says, unnecessarily loud.

The sound cuts through Peren's skull like a blade. The novice doesn't wait for a reply, slamming the door behind him with a laugh that echoes in the hallway. The crash makes Peren wince, bile rising in his throat.

Trying to roll out of bed like he has for the past ten years,

Peren misjudges how far to roll and crashes onto the cold stone floor with a bone-jolting thud. Cursing under his breath, he stays on his hands and knees for a few moments, the cool stone against his palms a small relief from the heat simmering beneath his skin. The oppressive humidity clings to him, thick as a cloak, as though the very air in the room refuses to let go.

With effort, Peren struggles to get to the chamber pot before emptying his stomach with a violent heave. The sour stench fills the small room, making his eyes water. Seeing the vomit rise to the top, then overflow the rim, frustrates Peren, showing how little he can handle alcohol compared to his human companions.

Taking his time, he manages to get to his feet, fighting to keep his stomach from turning as the room sways around him. His legs feel weak, and the pounding in his head intensifies with every movement, but he grits his teeth and steadies himself.

Despite the pounding in his head and the disquiet of his stomach, he fights to regain his composure. Moving over to the wash basin, he cleans himself before dressing carefully in a dark tunic, breeches, leather boots, and leather gloves, all from his chest. Each movement sends the room spinning, making him stop regularly and move at a snail's pace.

Glancing in the mirror as he creeps past, he sees beyond the glamour that conceals his true nature. He sees a very young orphaned elf, standing six feet tall, who would be eighteen in human years. The illusion changes his horizontally slanted, almond-shaped magenta eyes into human-looking, almond jasper brown. It also transforms his pointed ears into rounded human ones.

Looking deeper into his eyes, he can see the tiredness lurking within, along with uncertainty as to this journey and final quest. With a sigh, he shakes off the moment of introspection, hardening his resolve.

His mind clears enough for the realisation that he is late for the ceremony. Rushing to the door, he buckles his weapon belt, unsheathing the well-made but unadorned dagger he has had all his life. Picking up his saddlebags, he clumsily opens the door and hands the waiting novice the bags to take to the stables.

Grabbing his dark hooded cloak from a peg next to the door as he pulls the door shut, he takes one last look around the room he has spent many years in. As he turns away and shuts the door, a sense of never returning sends foreboding icy pinpricks down his spine.

Forcing that morbid thought out of his mind, he heads down the maze-like corridors and flights of stairs, finally making his way towards the courtyard.

In front of the wall stands a tall old man garbed in all black from his hooded cloak to his shoes. Unable to see his face due to the hood, Peren strides up to him with his usual confident swagger. Kneeling before the man, he waits impatiently to be addressed after being forced to endure a four-year wait for the "overconfidence and lack of maturity" that bristled in his bones, even though most didn't get to this point till their mid-twenties.

A booming voice pulls him out of his simmering frustration, speaking loudly enough for all to hear despite crashing thunder that breaks the silence. "Peren Naïlo, initiate of the Shadow Fang guild, welcome."

When the man indicates that Peren should speak, he says, "I, Peren Naïlo, initiate of the Shadow Fang guild, present myself for the honour of receiving permission and blessing to attempt the final test and become a master of this infallible guild."

The booming voice erupts again. "Rise, Peren Naïlo, initiate of the Shadow Fang guild. As the current high Master, I hereby give you permission to attempt the final test: entering the Skull Maze. By plucking and retrieving a single bud of the Broaf flower that only grows in the middle of this maze, you will have shown yourself worthy of the title—Master. Do you, Peren Naïlo, agree to uphold the code of this guild, never to reveal your true identity to anyone who is not a member of this guild?"

Rising from the ground, Peren says in a loud, clear voice, "I do."

The guild's wizard, Ordan Vixel, steps forward, pulling from his sleeve a beautiful, ornately made dagger with unusual carvings down the blade. The high master speaks again in his booming voice. "I, high Master of Shadow Fang, present you, Peren Naïlo, with the Shadow Fang dagger, permitting your name to be added amongst these great names of past and future."

Peren stretches out his left hand, presenting the palm to the wizard. Muttering an incantation, the wizard slices Peren's palm open, forcing him to grit his teeth against the pain momentarily, the blood making the carvings on the blade of the dagger glow.

Continuing to chant, Ordan pulls a rag from his sleeve and wipes the blade clean. Sticking his finger on the wound, coating it in blood, the wizard turns and walks up to the wall, writing Peren's name below the previous entry of Cartlan Stracs.

Peren casts his eyes up at the wall containing many names, pausing to read some of the names that survived this quest. Only his friend's name stands out, one among the many carved to the wall. Despite the nearly ten-year age gap, they were closest of friends. Peren smiles bitterly inside at the memories of them growing up together despite their physical age, along with the mischievous pranks they used to pull on people and the different punishments that resulted from them.

Clawing his way to the present, he gets caught up in the last and most painful memory of Cartlan alive: seeing him off on this very quest only a few months before. He remembers how the masters would talk about how he was one of the best students the guild had ever seen. And now, that well-trained and highly skilled friend was dead and lives on only in memory.

Steeling himself as tears spring into his eyes, Peren refocuses on the ceremony, thinking, *That's all I would need. I would be nicknamed 'the Weeping Initiate' or something worse.* Taking all his emotion and shoving it down deep inside, he focuses on the chanting.

The wizard finishes writing Peren's name on the wall, and as the incantation concludes, the blood stops glowing, and only a few smudges remain on the wall. Turning back to Peren, Ordan pulls out another clean rag from his sleeve and ties it around Peren's sliced hand to stem the bleeding. With a flourish, he deftly pulls Peren's dagger out and, turning away, starts another incantation, binding Peren to the dagger to put a handicap on his elven abilities.

As this happens, the high master's voice booms out. "Fare you well, Peren Naïlo, initiate of the Shadow Fang Guild. May your weapons be ever sharp and your aim ever true. May the gods guide your hands and protect you from evil."

Ordan deftly slides the dagger back into Peren's sheath without anyone else noticing. Peren gives a slight nod of understanding to the wizard, as he spoke to him a few days ago as one of a small group who knows his true identity. Bowing before the high master and wizard one last time, he turns to see the novice leading his horse, Mercy, out of the crowd, fully tacked, with saddlebags already attached. As he mounts Mercy, a young, gentle, grey palfrey, the crowd parts, leaving him a clear path to the gates.

Gently heeling her ribs, he heads for the gates. With each step forward, he can feel the eyes of his fellow guild members upon him. Approaching the gates, he feels a surge of anticipation mixed with unease, the weight of the impending journey ahead settling upon his shoulders like a heavy cloak.

As he reaches the gates, the entire guild echoes in one voice, loud enough to be heard over the thunder, "Fare thee well! May your weapon be ever sharp and aim ever true."

Passing through the threshold, he leaves behind the familiar confines of the guild courtyard, stepping into the grand expanse of the world beyond.

The path ahead stretches out before him, winding its way south towards the distant horizon, where his destiny awaits. He takes a deep breath, steeling himself for the challenges that lie ahead, his resolve unwavering as he sets out on his quest to become a master of the Shadow Fang Guild.

Despite the road ahead being fraught with uncertainty, he pushes forward with determination etched into every line of his face. The wind howls, whipping his cloak backwards, trying to tear him from the horse. Mercy's echoing footsteps on the cobblestones are whipped away by the wind. Despite the chaotic whirlwind of thoughts and emotions, one thing remains clear: he is prepared to face whatever challenges come his way, for within him, the strength of his convictions and the fire of his ambition burns bright.

Setting off at a trot, they head down the road, which quickly transitions from even cobblestones to packed dirt, towards the farms that supply the guild with its food. Not ten minutes into the journey, the heavens open up, and great sheets of unending rain pour down on them both, soaking through Peren's clothes in minutes. Thunder rumbles overhead, echoing through the countryside, while jagged bolts of lightning streak across the dark sky. Feeling the cold, he leans down closer to Mercy, trying to soak up any warmth radiating from her. With the angle of the rain blinding him every time he opens his eyes, he has to blink constantly to see at all, struggling to see more than a few paces in front of them. Within minutes, the road becomes a small river, forcing them to slow, lest Mercy trip and break a leg.

Time seems to stretch endlessly as they trudge through the downpour, Peren's thoughts consumed by the discomfort of wet clothes clinging to his skin and the relentless pounding of raindrops against his hood. Thunder booms overhead, while lightning flashes illuminate the landscape in brief, stark bursts. The chill is seeping ever deeper into his bones, sapping his strength with every step, despite the heat he pulls from Mercy. He longs for the warmth and comfort of shelter, the relentless downpour offering no respite. Desperation gnaws at him as he searches for any sign of refuge amidst the storm.

As they pass by the fields that dot the countryside, Peren's spirits sink further with each passing moment. Thunder rumbles ominously in the distance and lightning streaks across the darkened sky, casting eerie shadows over the sodden ground. The rain shows no mercy, intensifying with each passing hour and transforming the road into a quagmire of mud and muck. Mercy's hooves squelch loudly with each step, her movements becoming increasingly laboured as the weight of the sodden ground slows her progress. Peren's own muscles ache from the constant strain of guiding her through the treacherous terrain, his clothes heavy with water and clinging uncomfortably to his skin.

Finally, through the curtain of rain, Peren spots a dim light flickering in the distance. Thunder rolls overhead, its deep rumble punctuating the relentless patter of raindrops against the earth. With renewed hope, he urges Mercy forward, determined to reach the source of the light before nightfall.

As they draw closer, the outline of a farmhouse emerges from the gloom, its silhouette barely visible against the backdrop of the storm. Lightning flashes overhead, briefly illuminating all in stark relief before plunging the world back into darkness.

With a surge of relief, Peren guides Mercy towards the shelter of the farmhouse, his heart pounding with anticipation. Thunder echoes through the night air, reverberating off the walls of the farmhouse as if in greeting. As they approach, he calls out for assistance, his voice drowned out by the roar of the storm. He hopes the inhabitants will offer them refuge from the tempest, their kindness a beacon of hope amidst the chaos of the storm.

The farmhouse door swings open, revealing a welcoming glow from within. Peren's heart lifts at the sight. Thunder rumbles overhead, punctuating his sense of urgency as he guides Mercy towards the shelter of the entrance.

Standing in the doorway is a wiry woman of perhaps mid-thirties, her expression one of genuine concern mixed with kindness. Her eyes, framed by lines of hard work and hours in the sun, hold a warmth that seems to chase away the storm's chill. A weathered hand from years of work points to Mercy and then the barn. Waving, Peren leads her off. He hangs everything out to dry as he does what he can to rub her slick coat down.

Dashing from the barn back to the house, Peren stands shivering at the door and knocks. When the door opens after what feels like an eternity, lightning flashes, flooding everything in a bright white light before plunging the threshold into stark shadows. With a grateful sigh, Peren steps into the main room, the warmth of the blazing, crackling flames comforting him from the cold, miserable weather outside. Moving close, he hangs his cloak near the fire to help it dry. Despite his protests, the woman makes him change into dry clothes, hanging the wet ones up to dry. Thunder continues to rumble in the distance, rain pelting against the windows as the farmhouse keeps the weather at bay.

Waking up with the dawn, Peren finds the storm has eased, replaced by a soft drizzle that patters gently against the windows. Stretching his stiff limbs, he rises from his makeshift bed, feeling refreshed despite the trials of the previous day.

Moments later, the farmhouse is a hive of activity, the family having breakfast, then going about their morning chores with cheerful efficiency. After putting everything on the landing, Peren starts making his way to the barn, his boots sinking into the squishy, deep mud with each step.

Walking inside the barn, Peren sees Mercy standing there patiently, her coat glistening. Leading her out of the barn all saddled-up, he waves goodbye to the family as he heads back to the road.

As Peren and Mercy venture forth, the landscape around them has undergone a drastic change. Puddles of rainwater dot the muddy road, reflecting the gray clouds that still linger overhead. The air is heavy with the scents of wet earth and vegetation, and the distant rumble of thunder serves as a reminder of the raging storm.

Leaving the muddy river of a driveway, they turn onto a slightly less muddy road. Each time Mercy puts her hoof down, the mud pulls at it, making each step noisy and challenging.

To avoid risking a broken leg for his horse, Peren keeps a slow pace.

Time slowly passes, with Peren clinging to his horse, shivering from the cold wind, which makes it almost impossible for him to keep the cloak closed enough to huddle in. Despite having the hood up, he is chilled to the bone as he keeps Mercy moving. Every now and then, he reaches out to pat her neck and speaks soothingly in her ear.

Stiff from staying in the same position for hours on end and fighting to keep the cloak wrapped around him as much as possible, he realises he can't keep this up for much longer. When the sun finally starts to get low in the sky, he keeps his eyes open and starts to look for another farmhouse to beg for shelter.

Eventually finding a small farmstead, Peren follows the treacherous path up to the house. He quickly finds his request for succour only minimally met. The man, who looks to be near his second or third century, is willing only to allow the use of his barn. Peren settles in for a cold dinner with Mercy. Putting her in a stall with some hay, he climbs to the loft and hunkers down to get some sleep.

Climbing out of the hayloft, stiff from the ride yesterday and the fitful sleep, he wipes his eyes clean of grime, looking out and noting the muted colours of the morning. Sighing tiredly, he saddles Mercy, ensuring she's prepared for the day ahead. After a quick breakfast, he leaves the barn and steps into a dull grey world, where pinpricks of muted sun shine through.

The first thing that he feels is the gale-force winds snapping back his hood and cloak, the biting chill cutting right through his bones. Fighting the flapping fabric, he struggles to wrap the cloak around him. Mounting Mercy and fighting the cloak again, he heels her forward, her hooves sinking into the chilly, muddy ground with each step.

They move forward, the wind in their face as they continue to head south. Deciding they can't keep this going against such a strong wind, Peren begins to keep his eyes out for any form of shelter.

At first, he doesn't believe his wind-crazed eyes as the ruins seemingly appear from nowhere in the haze of the horizon. Eyeing the ruins sparks a fleeting glimmer of hope.

Getting close a couple of hours later, they make their way towards the ruins. As they approach the shelter, it becomes evident that it was abandoned many years ago and left to the elements. Parts of the roof have collapsed and most of the walls are in shambles. Fortunately, after a few circuits, Peren is able to find a small section that is relatively protected from the howling wind.

Looking around and not finding any way to start a fire, he is forced to go back and huddle with Mercy, taking any heat radiating from her body, settling in for a very cold night ahead. Relieved that there is no rain, he eventually succumbs into a fitful, tiring sleep.

Waking bleary-eyed, Peren sighs in relief, as the wind is more a gentle breeze than a strong gale like last night. As time passes, he feels his mood improving as more sunlight pierce the clouds.

After breaking their fast, Peren re-saddles Mercy and mounts her once more, setting off towards their destination. Despite the thinning clouds and the brightening sun, the ground beneath them remains a quagmire of sticky, squelching mud, so Peren is forced to maintain a slow pace, guiding Mercy carefully to prevent her from slipping and risking injury.

The ground firms up as the day continues, so Peren takes advantage and urges Mercy into a faster pace.

As the sun dips below the horizon, Peren finds that he is

struggling to keep his eyes open, so he looks out for somewhere to camp for the night. Eventually finding a small copse of trees, he camps down for the night. Able to start a fire, he relishes in the warmth from the flames and a good hot meal. As the night takes over the sky, he drifts off into a peaceful slumber, lulled by the crackling and warmth of the flames.

Moving on in the morning, both Peren and Mercy are well-rested. The hours pass by in a blur. Mercy, for the first time in days, gallops freely, finally able to stretch out and run at her best speed. Peren lets go of the reins, letting her have her head and neigh in delight, truly enjoying being able to move at a fast pace once more.

By early afternoon, they arrive at a cobbled T junction. To the right, in the far distance, lies Lorhaven, the capital of Thaloria, whose direction is opposite from Peren's destination. He guides Mercy to the left, and they continue moving towards the Whispering Wood.

As the afternoon passes, they travel swiftly down the road, Mercy's hooves clacking against the stones as they fly across the landscape, passing mostly meadows and fields. As the sun sets, they stop for the night and make camp.

The next morning, they both rise early, eat quickly, and break camp. Mounting Mercy, Peren feels a stiff breeze that sends shivers of foreboding down his spine. As they travel across the flat, almost barren landscape, they pass copses of trees and more fields. The hours pass as slowly, as does the view in the distance, and Peren finds himself employing all the tricks for impatience that he has, eager to get to his destination.

Eventually, a fork becomes visible in the distance, and Peren reins in Mercy to decide which fork to take. Opting to take the time to have something to eat and let Mercy rest and graze, he sits on a grassy knoll, munching on some mushrooms he found in a grove of trees a few feet away.

Looking to the left of the fork and into the distance, where he imagines the haunted Whispering Wood resides, he feels an ominous chill running down his spine. When he looks to the right and into the distance to where he imagines the town of Smarb, the ominous chill disappears.

He weighs up the alternatives between the two forks. If he takes the shorter route to the left, he realises that he will possibly be facing multiple different packs of Brooders. But to the right, there is only safety and boring dull fields, which would add months to the journey, if not longer. Not wanting to take longer to complete this quest, he is positive that any reports on the Brooders are based on the overactive imaginations of superstitious men and women.

Making up his mind, he drops the mushrooms that he picked up and wipes his hands clean on his breeches. Steeling himself for the journey ahead, he guides Mercy to the left fork.

Peren and Mercy travel for another day and a half before suspicious haze becomes noticeable on the horizon. As they slowly follow the road toward the haze, he realises that the haze is growing in both width and height alarmingly fast.

Jaw going slack at the sheer size the Whispering Wood is becoming, Peren feels a sense of awe. Mercy whinnies and slows, jolting him out of his trance. Regaining control, he urges her back into their previous pace.

He struggles not to stare in awe at the growing forest, his brain on overdrive trying to process the sheer size of each tree. Feeling small, he panics for a moment before he gets a grip on it.

The closer they get, the more uneasy Peren feels as he cranes his neck back to try and see the top of the trees, thinking, *If the information about the sheer size of the trees is accurate, could it be possible that the reports on Brooders are accurate?*

Quickly calling to mind all he knows about Brooders, he tries to find a mention of any weaknesses.

In the heart of the Whispering Wood, where the ancient trees loom like giants and the air hums with the whispers of unseen spirits, the Brooders reign as silent monarchs of the shadows. Towering like spectres amidst the colossal trunks, their forms are a testament to the merciless challenges of the forest's depths.

Each Brooder stands taller than a large stallion, with sinewy muscles rippling beneath its taut, impenetrable hide, its movements graceful despite its monstrous nature. Their sleek forms glide through the underbrush with an eerie silence, their movements as swift as the flicker of moonlight through the leaves. Agile as cats and swift as the wind, they are the apex predators of this ancient realm.

Their faces are grotesque symphonies of terror, with mouths that resemble the gaping maws of sabre-tooth tigers, lined with rows of serrated teeth that gleam with deadly intent. But it is the two fangs that protrude from their jaws, dripping with a venom so potent it could paralyse the largest of all beasts, that strike the deepest fear into the hearts of those who dare to cross their path.

From these fangs, the Brooders' toxic venom is so insidious that even the hardiest of souls quails at the mere thought of its touch. A slow-acting poison, it creeps through the veins like icy tendrils, rendering its victims helpless as it slowly shuts down their systems over the course of agonising days.

Brooders' eyes, like orbs of burning flame, betray a sensitivity to light that speaks of a life spent lurking in the shadows. They gleam with an otherworldly intelligence, a chilling reminder that these creatures are more than mere beasts—they are cunning predators, finely attuned to the rhythms of the forest and the movements of their prey.

But perhaps most terrifying of all is the Brooders' hide—

a marvel of natural armour that mocks the efforts of would-be conquerors. It repels blades and arrows with stunning ease, rendering even the most valiant warriors impotent against its formidable defences.

No Brooder has ever been seen hunting alone. They hunt in lethal, well-coordinated packs, prowling the forest together, wreaking devastation on all in their way. It is said that only a handful of all the tens of thousands who have faced them have lived to tell the tale, their encounters etched into their souls as nightmares that never fade.

Driven by an unquenchable need to avenge fallen pack mates, Brooders are relentless in their pursuit of those who harm them. If you kill one, the pack will track you down and kill you, no matter where you are or where you go. They will follow your scent across any distance, their vengeance as certain as the rising sun.

Encountering a Brooder is like coming face-to-face with the god of nightmares—a living embodiment of fear and suffering. And for those unlucky few who find themselves in their path, the memory of the Brooders will linger like a curse, haunting their every waking moment with the spectre of impending doom.

Peren's resolve to advance toward the Whispering Wood doesn't diminish, despite his nagging worries. Even with the unsettling atmosphere and Mercy's evident unease, he forges ahead, enticed by the prospect of time saved. However, as he pauses to listen to the whispers that seem to permeate the forest's edge, a fleeting sense of relief washes over him upon realising they're merely the natural sounds of the wind. Yet, beneath his attempts to rationalise, a lingering feeling of dread persists, akin to a shadow lurking just beyond his sight. Despite his efforts to dismiss it as mere paranoia, the forest's aura continues to weigh heavily on him.

With a wry chuckle, Peren steels himself, preparing to venture closer to the entrance of the Whispering Wood, guided only by the dim light filtering through the towering trees and the rhythmic beat of Mercy's hooves.

TWO

THE WHISPERING WOOD

Entering the Whispering Wood, Peren is engulfed in a disorienting darkness, his vision completely obscured. Halting Mercy, he patiently waits for his eyes to acclimate to the opaque surroundings. During this unsettling moment, a notion flits through his mind: *The total darkness only adds to the ominous atmosphere of this place.*

As seconds stretch into an unnervingly long wait for clarity, a fleeting doubt tugs at him, tempting him to consider retracing his steps. Yet, just as he teeters on the brink of hesitation, his eyes gradually adjust, revealing a murky expanse merely a few strides ahead before succumbing to the impenetrable gloom.

Gazing upward, unable to discern the tops of the trees, he focuses on soothing Mercy, who is grappling with the complete inability to see. Knowing that she is so intimately attuned to him, he works on sending her calming energy. Leading her forward, he guides her into the dark void.

Turning his attention from keeping Mercy calm, Peren focuses his thoughts on more hopeful prospects: returning from this quest in record time, being the youngest and fastest. Not only does it help Mercy to stay calm, but it also gives a major boost to his own confidence.

Being so focused on the guild's response to his heroic skills, he loses track of time. The hours slip by unnoticed, only broken by the gnawing of his stomach, a reminder of the need for food. Rummaging around blind, he finally finds something to chew on, all the while completely focused on the forest floor in front of them for anything that would cause Mercy to stumble and break a leg.

As time passes uneventfully and the forest remains eerily quiet, Peren's confidence steadily grows, allowing him to entertain the notion that perhaps the tales of predators lurking within these woods are merely folklore, exaggerated to deter the fainthearted. He ponders the possibility that the foreboding reputation of the Whispering Wood is nothing more than a cautionary tale spun to dissuade children from venturing into its depths. With a growing sense of reassurance, he offers Mercy a comforting scratch on her neck, eliciting a contented prance from the mare in response to the familiar gesture of praise.

Sensing more than seeing that the sun is setting, and not having anticipated how swiftly night descends on the forest, he momentarily panics, jumping down and hastily setting up camp before his little bit of grey disappears. Just as his vision fails completely, he manages to settle down, his heart still racing from the frenzied activity. With a gentle pat, he reassures Mercy, who stands by his side, sharing in his silent apprehension, before exhaustion claims him, pulling him into a restless slumber amidst the shroud of night.

Startled awake by the suffocating darkness, Peren immediately panics. He calms down as his senses adjust to the surrounds and the memories come back as to him—entering the Whispering Wood, almost completely pitch-black. With a deep breath to calm his nerves, he reassures himself that it's merely the early hours of dawn, not the ominous depths of night. Swiftly, he fumbles for the provisions he packed, his hands searching in the darkness for sustenance both for himself and for Mercy, his loyal companion in this eerie journey.

After both he and Mercy have consumed their meagre breakfast and the necessary preparations are made, Peren notices a subtle change in the darkness surrounding them. The oppressive blackness begins to recede slightly, replaced by a faint greyness that extends a few feet ahead, reminiscent of what he observed the day before. It's a small but significant shift, offering a glimmer of hope that daylight may eventually penetrate the dense foliage of the Whispering Wood. With renewed determination, Peren tightens Mercy's saddle, preparing to resume their journey through the enigmatic forest.

Settling into the saddle, Peren's senses sharpen as he hears a low, guttural growl emanating from what seems like a considerable distance away. The sound sends Mercy into a frenzy, her panicked whickering and whinnying reverberating through the forest. Instinctively picking up on the horse's fear, Peren momentarily feels his own panic rising within him.

In a reflexive response, he allows Mercy to bolt forward a few paces at a gallop before firmly reining her in. With a determined effort to suppress his own fear, he focuses on calming her, soothing her with gentle words and reassuring strokes along her mane.

Drawing on his senses, he sends them out to detect the presence of any creatures nearby. With a concentrated effort, he mentally scans the forest, attempting to discern the location and number of these mysterious entities lurking in the darkness.

His heart quickens as he detects the presence of six Brooders hunting him with predatory intent. With a sense of urgency, he realizes they are closing in on him at an alarming speed, sending an icy shiver down his spine.

Urging Mercy to move faster, he breathes in quickly, hoping to outpace the rapidly approaching threat, despite the danger of the uneven ground and lack of vision. The tension mounts as he focuses on maintaining their pace, knowing that the slightest misstep could have dire consequences.

Peren's mind races as he considers his options. Retreating is out of the question; some of the Brooders are already closing off that route. With their superior sight in the darkness, attempting to outrun them on foot would be futile.

The chilling reality sinks in: he's left with only two viable choices.

Standing his ground seems foolish against such formidable adversaries, but the alternative is equally grim. Resolved to maximize his chances of survival, he opts for the riskier option: fighting on horseback. It's a gamble, but with Mercy beneath him, he hopes their combined agility and height will tip the odds slightly more in their favour.

With a steady hand on the reins and his weapon at the ready, Peren braces himself for the imminent clash.

He maintains his focus on the encroaching pack, his senses keenly attuned to their movements. Urging Mercy forward at as fast a speed as he dares, he endeavours to put as much distance between them and the advancing Brooders as possible. Every stride of Mercy's hooves is a heartbeat closer to safety, yet with every passing moment, the relentless pursuit of the predators looms ever nearer.

With grim determination, Peren tightens his grip on the dagger, already poised for the impending struggle. As he surveys the oncoming threat of the Brooders, the small blade in his hand feels almost insignificant compared to the size of the creatures bounding toward them. Yet despite the overwhelming odds, he refuses to give up, only willing to go down fighting, his resolve burning in his eyes as he prepares to face whatever fate awaits.

Sensing the Brooders gaining ground, Mercy wickers nervously, her pace quickening in response. Peren strains to gather any information he can about their potential weaknesses, but to his dismay, his efforts yield no discernible advantage. With a sinking feeling, he realizes that their foes have no obvious vulnerabilities, leaving him to confront the harsh reality of their impending encounter with grim determination.

The hairs at the back of Peren's neck stand on end as the pack draws nearer, their excitement echoing through the dense forest. With his hearing muffled by the thick trees, he struggles to pinpoint their exact locations.

Muscles tensed, Peren braces himself for the impending confrontation, resigned to the grim reality of facing the Brooders head-on. Though unable to rely on his senses in the conventional manner, he draws upon his elven instincts, honed through years of training, to evade fatal blows.

As the Brooders close in on their prey, a palpable sense of fear emanates from Peren and Mercy, fuelling the predators' excitement as they anticipate their imminent kill.

Suddenly, rounding a thick tree trunk, the lead Brooder catches sight of its quarry just a few paces ahead. Yelping eagerly, it surges forward, drawn by the scent of fear permeating the air. With a ferocious leap, it launches itself into the air, claws outstretched and jaws agape, ready to pounce upon its prey.

Reacting with lightning speed, Peren twists his body in a desperate attempt to evade the predator's deadly descent.

Within a heartbeat, he realizes his mistake—underestimating the Brooder's speed by a fraction of a second. With a surge of adrenaline, he manages to move faster, adjusting the trajectory of his dagger just in time. With a swift thrust, he drives the blade upward, piercing through the roof of the creature's mouth and into the soft, vulnerable tissue of its brain.

As the Brooder's life is abruptly extinguished, a gush of blood spurts forth, drenching Peren's hand as he withdraws his arm from the creature's maw, panting heavily in the aftermath of the intense struggle.

As the lifeless body of the Brooder crashes to the forest floor with a resounding thud, Mercy is startled, spurred into even faster motion by the sudden commotion.

Meanwhile, the next Brooder in line approaches cautiously, pausing to sniff and nudge its fallen comrade, emitting mournful noises in a futile attempt to rouse it. Once it realises that its kin is truly dead, a spine-chilling howl of grief echoes through the forest, sending cold shivers down Peren's spine.

With ground-rumbling, ominous growls and fierce leaps, the Brooders bound after their prey, driven by a thirst for revenge. Swiftly closing the distance, one of them veers off the track and disappears into the dense foliage of the trees.

Peren is torn between keeping his focus on guiding Mercy safely through the treacherous terrain and staying vigilant about the Brooders' movements. He knows whatever they're planning cannot bode well, and his heart races with apprehension as the chase intensifies.

Suddenly, out of nowhere, the Brooder that veered off into the forest emerges from the trees, launching itself through the air and crashing into Mercy's right flank. As it makes contact, Peren's leg is pushed against her side, assisting in shattering her ribs. Splinters of bone are sent through her chest, piercing and cutting her organs and severely bruising his leg.

He leaps out of the saddle just in time to avoid having his leg crushed and pinned under Mercy as she crashes down on her left side, sliding into a tree and stunning herself as more ribs break. The Brooder lands nearby, narrowly missing her by inches.

Rolling unsteadily to his feet after landing on the ground, Peren manages to keep hold of the dagger, taking in the dire situation.

With the Brooder now positioned between him and Mercy, whose life is quickly pooling on the ground, Peren is forced to act swiftly. He taunts the Brooder, diverting its attention away from his beloved horse.

The Brooder, recognizing Peren's scent from its sibling, responds with a menacing growl. Assessing the situation, it realizes it must deal with this smaller threat before it can enjoy the larger prey. Cautiously, it moves closer to Peren, sizing him up.

As the Brooder approaches, Peren shifts his weight to favour his good leg, bracing himself for the impending attack.

Meanwhile, the rest of the pack creeps up behind him, preparing to strike while he is distracted.

When the Brooder in front of him moves forward as a distraction, the one directly behind him seizes the opportunity to launch its attack. Peren manages to duck and roll away just in time, though not without crying out in pain.

As he rises to his feet, he realizes he is now surrounded by the rest of the pack. With a sinking feeling, he understands that his chances of survival are zero. Nevertheless, he adopts a fighting stance, prepared to fight to the end.

Refusing to let the Brooders dictate the terms of the fight, Peren goes on the offensive and charges at one of them. Caught off-guard by his sudden aggression, the Brooder sidesteps, narrowly avoiding the dagger aimed at its neck. In a reflexive response, the creature swipes at Peren, who manages to evade the attack by leaping away just in time.

Unwilling to relinquish his advantage, he lunges forward once more, this time driving the dagger deep into the Brooder's eye and into its brain, killing it instantly.

As the creature collapses to the ground with a sickening thud, Peren is drenched in a foul mixture of vitreous humour and brain tissue, causing him to gag involuntarily. Fighting back the bile rising in his throat, he swiftly turns his attention to the next assailant, determined to press on despite the overwhelming odds.

Anticipating the next Brooder's move, Peren braces himself as the creature charges at him, its claws slashing through the air with deadly intent. With lightning-fast reflexes, he manages to evade the lethal strike, narrowly escaping certain death.

Undeterred by his injuries, he moves with remarkable agility, closing the distance between himself and the Brooder in an instant. With a swift and precise movement, he thrusts his dagger through the back of the creature's jaw and into its brain, ending its life in an instant.

As he withdraws the dagger, blood oozes down his arm from the fatal wound, adding to the grisly scene unfolding before him. Despite the pain and the overwhelming odds, Peren remains resolute, his determination to survive undiminished.

The last three Brooders spread out, launching a coordinated attack to overwhelm him. Unbeknownst to them, his elven reflexes are far superior to those of a normal human.

Despite moving slower due to his injuries, he narrowly avoids their onslaught. Even with his impaired mobility, he strikes decisively, eliminating another Brooder with a precise stab to the neck, spraying blood in all directions.

With keening cries, the remaining two Brooders converge on him from different angles, their claws swiping at him simultaneously. Peren, grimacing in pain and quickly running out of energy, leaps and dodges their attacks, improvising a desperate move. He hurls his dagger towards one of them, the blade cutting through the air until it lodges itself between the eyes of the nearest Brooder, burying itself deep into the creature's skull.

Landing on his good leg, Peren hobbles over to retrieve his dagger, momentarily focused on the task at hand. However, he's caught off-guard as the last Brooder swipes at him with a vicious strike, sending him flying through the air. He slams into a tree with bone-crunching force, the impact jarring his entire body. Collapsing to the ground in a crumpled heap, he gasps for breath and struggles to fend off the encroaching darkness, his vision blurring as he fights to stay conscious.

The Brooder approaches cautiously, wary of the dangerous creature it has just attacked. After a few moments of caution, seeing Peren motionless, it moves in closer with the intent to finish him off and feast on his flesh.

Just as Peren manages to push back the darkness, he rolls instinctively toward the Brooder, narrowly avoiding its snapping jaws. Continuing to roll beneath the creature, he positions himself under its belly, out of its line of sight.

The Brooder snaps its jaws shut on empty air, momentarily confused. It looks around, searching for its elusive prey. Growling in frustration, it leaps backward, anticipating Peren's next move. Landing several feet away, it scans the area for any sign of movement, only to catch sight of a blur darting toward one of its dead pack-mates.

Limping as fast as his injured leg allows, Peren grits his teeth against the searing pain, reaching the downed Brooder with the embedded dagger in its skull. With a swift tug, he retrieves the weapon just as the surviving Brooder launches itself at him, driven by instinctual aggression.

Aware of the imminent threat behind him, Peren spins around as the Brooder hurtles through the air with its jaws gaping wide. With adrenaline-fueled precision, he throws the dagger underhand, each moment seeming to stretch into eternity as it flies toward its target.

In that suspended time, a darkly humorous thought crosses his mind: *What if the handle hits the Brooder harmlessly and falls to the ground?*

With a desperate roll to the side, Peren braces for impact. The dagger strikes true, but it's the hilt that connects with the Brooder's forehead, causing it to stagger upon impact. Shaking its head in confusion, the creature searches for its intended prey amidst the chaos of the forest floor.

Peren steadies himself, waiting for the dizziness to subside before doing anything. Spotting the dagger nearby, he moves swiftly, his movements fuelled by urgency and adrenaline.

As he grabs the weapon and whirls around, the Brooder locks eyes with him, leaping forward with deadly intent. Acting on instinct, Peren hurls the dagger once more, his aim unwavering despite the exhaustion and pain.

The blade finds its mark yet this time, burying itself deeply in the Brooder's forehead. With a final thud, the creature crashes lifelessly to the ground.

Exhausted and relieved, Peren sinks to the ground, his chest heaving as he catches his breath. He is jerked out of his daze by Mercy's distress, and he pushes through his own fatigue to reach her side as quickly as possible.

With Mercy's life hanging by a thread and quickly disappearing, Peren's desperation drives him to attempt the impossible. Placing his trembling hands on her body, he begins a rhythmic chant, channelling his healing energy, delving deep into her tissues and organs, knowing that he is left bedridden when he heals a minor cut. Despite his own exhaustion and the enormity of the task, he refuses to let her die. Casting aside the doubts that plague him with determination and focusing, the adrenaline and stress of the recent battle coursing through his veins, he is able to channel more of his healing abilities than normal.

As he probes Mercy's injuries, he's met with the daunting sight of extensive damage and signs of internal bleeding from the shattered ribs. With grim determination, he locates the worst-affected areas and begins the painstaking process of healing.

Drawing upon every ounce of his special ability, he works to expel the toxins and repair the damage, causing Mercy to react with cries of pain. Each agonized sound she makes pierces Peren's heart, but he pushes through, knowing that his efforts are her only hope for survival.

Lost in his relentless efforts to save Mercy, Peren loses all track of time as he pours every ounce of his being into her healing. Despite the overwhelming challenge and his own physical and emotional strain, he continues to work tirelessly, refusing to give up on his loyal companion.

Only when he loses focus and the risk of making a fatal mistake becomes too great does he reluctantly pause, knowing that pushing himself further could undo all his progress and cost Mercy her life.

As he finally allows himself a moment of rest, fatigue washes over him like a suffocating wave, dragging him into the embrace of darkness.

Rousing sometime later, he initially feels disorientated and drained, as if he had only gone to sleep moments before, and is wracked with a gnawing hunger that demands attention. In the enveloping darkness of the night, he fumbles for food, finding solace in the meagre rations of hardtack. With hands trembling from exhaustion, he hastily consumes what little nourishment he can find, ensuring that Mercy too receives her share of the scant provisions.

Then, with a renewed sense of purpose, he returns to keep healing Mercy, understanding that her survival hinges on his unwavering dedication. Ignoring his own exhaustion and discomfort, he channels his abilities again, delving into her body to mend her injuries.

Guiding his energy to where it's needed most, he repairs damaged organs and bones with painstaking precision, extracting splinters that torment her and cause her distress. Each movement of his hands is a symphony of empathy and determination, his focus unbroken despite the weariness that weighs heavily upon him.

After lifting his hands off Mercy a few hours later, feeling emotionally and physically drained, he has something to drink, watering Mercy too. He looks down at his injured leg to determine why it is causing him so much discomfort; he's unable to determine the colour in this void, but he guesses that it is heavily bruised.

Waking up from a short rest, he focuses his gaze on a standing horse. It takes a moment for him to process what is different, then the memories come flooding back. Getting to his unsteady legs, he stumbles over to Mercy, checking to see how she is healing. He heaves a sigh of relief when he sees that she is recovering nicely.

Knowing he has the opportunity of a lifetime, he sets his sights on extracting the poison sacks from the Brooders. Hobbling over to the nearest one, he opens its mouth and is shocked at the true size of its fangs. Identifying the venom sacks, he works on the left one first, gripping it firmly. However, in his determination, he accidentally applies too much pressure, causing venom to leak out, nearly getting it on himself in the process. Reacting instantly, he jumps back, landing awkwardly, and checks himself to ensure he did not get any venom on him.

Being more cautious this time, he tries again, locating the smaller sack. Carefully reaching out, he grabs it as gently as he can, ensuring not to squeeze it too hard this time. Managing to avoid further venom leakage, he proceeds to cut out the sack, exposing the venom duct. Deciding to keep this attached as well, he cuts out a length of the tube.

After inspecting the removed venom sack, Peren notices there is still plenty of venom inside, as it is about the size of a medium melon. To prevent any further leakage, he ties up the tube securely and packs it into one of his saddlebags, rearranging the contents to accommodate it.

Moving on to extract the venom sack from the other side, he repeats the process, being careful not to apply too much pressure until after the tube is securely tied. Once he has both venom sacks secured and stowed away, he turns his attention to his own needs and finishes off the last of the food from his bags.

Looking over to the carcasses, Peren makes a decision for survival. Moving swiftly over to the same Brooder he took the poison from, he carefully makes an incision on its side and extracts some meat to replenish his supplies.

Despite the unpalatable taste, he takes bites while working on gutting the massive beast, separating the edible organs from the inedible ones. Struggling to swallow each mouthful of raw meat, he decides not to push his luck and focuses on the task at hand.

Pausing for a moment, the raw meat still in his mouth, Peren remembers the dagger's unexpected effectiveness.

Confusion washes over him as he stares at the weapon, wondering how it managed to pierce the Brooders' supposedly impenetrable hides so easily. If the reports on the forest and the creatures have all been accurate, then why would the detail about their hides be any different? Standing there confused, he decides it's better to accept this without questioning it.

Realizing that if the hide is as impenetrable as the reports say, it presents too good an opportunity to pass up, Peren sets to work skinning the Brooder. Hours later, after meticulous effort, he manages to skin all but the face, leaving him with a single large piece of Brooder hide. He carefully packs away the massive hide as best he can, ensuring it is secured for transport.

Still feeling forced to consume the raw meat, he stops before he becomes too nauseous, bunking down for the night before the little grey void of light disappears.

Waking up as the greyness materialises slowly, he knows he has been really pushing his luck. He needs to get a move on if he is to get out of there safely. Both he and Mercy are still recovering from the damage that the one pack of Brooders caused.

Taking a brief respite, Peren acknowledges the precariousness of his situation, aware that he has already pushed his limits. Satisfied with Mercy's healing progress and the absence of visible distress, he gathers the remaining meat, stowing it carefully in a pouch. His fear rising, he quickly mounts Mercy, urging her deeper into the darkened forest while gently guiding her with a touch to her ribs.

Reluctant to pause in the forest, Peren maintains a relentless pace, urging Mercy forward until the final moments of daylight each day, healing her as much as he can, then resuming their journey at the earliest hint of dawn, still forced to consume the raw meat. This routine persists for the next five days, with Peren determined to cover as much ground as possible.

As he's setting out on the fifth day, Peren's apprehension mounts as he hears the ominous sound he has been dreading: a low, guttural growl echoing through the forest. Without needing any prompting, Mercy quickens her stride, her movements more fluid and assured thanks to Peren's healing.

Focusing his senses outward, Peren grimaces in despair, realizing the dire predicament they face. *One pack was enough to nearly end us, and we were fresh and uninjured,* he muses with a sense of resignation. *There's no way I can take on another pack, let alone fifteen or twenty.*

Pressing Mercy to increase her pace despite her energy draining, Peren feels a sense of urgency gnawing at him. Though he longs to stop, the looming danger propels them forward relentlessly.

As they draw nearer to their escape from the forest, Peren's sense of dread intensifies. It becomes clear that confrontation with the Brooders is inevitable in the dense expanse of the Whispering Wood.

With the Brooders closing in at an alarming rate, moments stretch agonisingly into minutes. Peren can almost sense their hot breath on his neck, igniting a familiar sensation he loathes: fear. Taking a steadying breath, he channels his apprehension into a more potent emotion: anger. Determination floods through him as he resolves to push forward no matter the odds, prepared to face whatever challenges lie ahead. If they aim to bring him down, he vows to take as many of them with him as he can.

The eerie howls and growls of the Brooders echo through the forest, sending a chill down Peren's spine as adrenaline courses through his veins while he prepares for the inevitable upcoming confrontation.

As they round a bend, Peren's focus is so fixed on the

imminent threat that he's oblivious to the subtle shift in the surroundings. It's not until Mercy lets out an excited neigh that he notices a change—the darkness is beginning to recede slightly, replaced by a faint glimmer of light.

Hope flickers within him at the prospect of visibility, but it's short-lived. In a heartbeat, a Brooder closes the gap with alarming speed, shattering any sense of relief.

Glancing back for a fleeting moment, Peren's heart sinks as he witnesses five Brooders closing in on them rapidly. A sense of dread washes over him as he realizes the gravity of their predicament—if these Brooders catch up, they're dead.

Amid his internal turmoil, Peren's senses snap to attention just in time to catch sight of a Brooder hurtling toward them through the air, jaws agape and claws poised for the kill. Reacting swiftly, Peren flips out of the saddle with practiced agility, delivering a well-placed kick to the Brooder's nose, knowing that if he kills this one, he will have to kill more. The force of the impact deflects the creature's trajectory, causing it to land awkwardly and stumble forward, its momentum carrying it until it comes to a sudden stop, momentarily stunned by the un-expected blow.

As he lands back in the saddle after delivering the kick, Peren's heart sinks as he sees another Brooder touching down squarely in their path ahead, blocking the exit. Despite the overwhelming sense of defeat weighing on his shoulders, Peren braces himself, urging Mercy to press onward. Though every instinct screams for her to turn away, Mercy's unwavering trust in Peren compels her to continue toward the looming threat ahead.

Snarling at the pair of them, the Brooder moves forward, unwilling to wait for its prey to come to it. Knowing their only chance of survival is to divide and conquer, Peren leaps from the saddle and lands in a roll, swiftly regaining his feet and sprinting past Mercy as she nears the advancing Brooder. Making threatening gestures, he grabs the creature's attention, then dives behind a nearby tree as the Brooder changes course, lunging at him.

Emerging from cover, Peren spots Mercy just a few paces from the exit. With adrenaline coursing through his veins, he vaults back into the saddle, and they break into a full gallop, racing to escape the clutches of the Whispering Wood.

The midday sunlight momentarily blinds Peren as Mercy bursts from the forest at full speed. Quickly pulling back on the reins, he manages to bring her to a complete stop. Shielding his eyes from the bright sun, he takes a moment to appreciate the clear, bright day before glancing back at the forest's edge.

He watches as multiple Brooders reach the forest's edge, growling in frustration at the loss of their prey, having to move back as the sun hits their eyes. Noting the dark-brown hue of their hides for the first time, he sees that they resemble the trees of the Whispering Wood.

Smirking at them, he turns his attention back to the road ahead.

After washing himself and his clothes, Peren inspects his dagger, surprised to find it as sharp as ever. With meticulous care, he cleans the blade of any remaining traces of Brooder fluids, then rinses the large pelt to remove some of the odour before laying it out to dry in the sun alongside his clothes.

As the sun begins to set, Peren dons his clean clothes and returns the pelt to Mercy's back. Remounting her, he gently urges her forward, setting off toward Comtun as the sun dips behind the trees.

THREE

COMTUN

Arriving after the sun has completely retreated below the horizon, as if tactically running away from the encroaching darkness, they enter a gloomy and eerily quiet town. The only sound is Mercy's dirt-flaking shoes hitting the cobblestone road. Peren looks around in confusion, wondering where everyone is. It's not so late that everyone should be in bed asleep, yet the entire town seems deserted. Continuing down the street, he passes a few houses, boarded-up and abandoned. In others, faint light seeks escape from the edges of boarded-up shutters and doors.

As he moves further into the town cautiously and on guard, a wave of foreboding flows through Peren, making him shudder and shiver as if from the cold. Continuing down the street, he eventually comes across an inn: the Eyeless Boar, according to the sign. He hops off Mercy and starts to lead her towards the stabling area when suddenly, he feels bile rising up, accompanied by a deathlike stench wafting over him.

He turns towards the direction from which it seems to be coming—to the right, perpendicular from the way he came. Doubling over from the increase in stench and nearly emptying his stomach of all the food he ever ate, he feels like he will faint.

Managing to swallow the bile back down, he struggles against the constant urge to vomit, despite breathing through his mouth.

As he peers down the road, trying to make out what is causing that awful sick dread, the door to the inn flies open, revealing a portly, well-rounded middle-aged man in a white apron, wringing his hands in fear. As he waves Peren over, he calls out, "Sir? Quick! Hide before they come! Quick, now, inside!"

Peren starts at the sudden noise and whirls to face the innkeeper, confusion heavy in his voice as he struggles to ask with the stench making him gag, "What are you talking about?"

Before the innkeeper has a chance to explain, they both hear a click-clacking noise on the cobblestones. With a face as pale as death, the innkeeper replies, "I'm sorry, too late now." He slams the door shut, barring it from the inside.

Left standing bewildered at what just happened, Peren shoves the thought aside as the click-clacking increases in volume. Turning back in the direction of the noise, he notices now that there are lots of little bobbing red dots materialising out of the darkness, bouncing in time with the click-clacking.

Unsheathing his dagger cautiously, Peren keeps peering at the unusual sight with knotted brows. As the creatures near, he can make out more and more detail, his stomach churning as he recognizes them from a picture in a book about dangerous creatures: Spliganders. In the books he's read about them, these extremely ugly, revolting, nocturnal rodent-like creatures are fox-sized, with long needle-sharp fangs and claws and saliva filled with a necrotising bacteria that infects any bite and slowly rots the body from within. There is an antidote, but it must be administered within the first forty-eight hours, or you have to amputate that limb.

Now not only hearing but seeing row upon row of rodents, Peren curls his mouth into a snarl. He's still wounded, with next to no energy from healing Mercy and the hard traveling. Even though the Spliganders are easy to kill, the sheer number of them makes it overwhelmingly impossible to kill them all. Knowing he will have to fight them, but wanting to keep Mercy safe, he leads her a couple of streets away, finding an abandoned building with a large boarded-up front door. Forcing his way into the building, he pulls Mercy along behind him and sets about reboarding-up the building to protect her the best he can. Finished with her protection and knowing the Spliganders won't stop when faced with prey, he readies for the longest fight of his life.

Peren, already weary, expends his dwindling energy, moving like an elf—after a quick look to ensure no one is watching—as he leaps from the house to confront the approaching Spliganders. Ignoring the pain in his stiffly healed leg, he dives into the fray. His dagger slashes through the air, decapitating the creatures with precise, fluid movements. Amidst the chaos, the sickly stench of decay assaults his senses, intensifying his discomfort as he battles on.

In the midst of battle, Peren manages to sever one of the Spliganders' paws, causing a spray of black, sticky blood. When he attempts to wield it as a weapon, the claw radiates intense heat almost instantly, forcing him to drop it, wincing in pain, remembering the restrictions that the wizard Ordan placed on him. Seizing the advantage, the rodents close in, attempting to breach his defences. Ignoring the smoking pain in his left hand, Peren twirls and blocks their attacks, fighting back with diminished speed and strength.

As the battle wears on, his exhaustion deepens, his reactions slowing down from weariness. Despite his fatigue, he continues to fend off the relentless onslaught of Spliganders. Gradually, they close in, forcing him to manoeuvre with dwindling agility to prevent being flanked. In a vulnerable moment, one of the creature's leaps in and bites him under his right arm, injecting its necrotising saliva into his bloodstream.

Wincing in pain, Peren swiftly dispatches the rodent with his left hand, the mingled red and black blood dripping to the ground. Though battered and increasingly fatigued, he presses on, fighting back against the horde. As his exhaustion mounts, he fails to notice when the Spliganders begin to retreat.

Collapsing to his knees, Peren gasps for breath, oblivious to the lightening sky and the shocked reactions of the townsfolk emerging from their homes to find the street littered with dead Spliganders, knowing that the bacteria-infested saliva of the creatures threatens to rot his body from within.

Hearing the townsfolk start unbarring their doors, Peren, still covered in sticky black blood, quickly moves over to the inn. As the door is opened, he strolls in, head held high. Stopping in the middle of the common room, he takes in the innkeeper, the largest-bellied man he has ever set eyes on. Fighting back a yawn and the need to lie down, he demands, "I will be requiring a stall for my horse and a room for myself." A look of confusions passes over his face as he finally realises that they are all gaping and gawking at him. Looking down at his arms and body, he chuckles, "And a bath, too, while you're at it."

Doing his best to hide another yawn, he turns, looking for the stairs. Heading towards them, ignoring the protests from the innkeeper, the wave of black that he had been struggling to keep at bay breaks, crashing over him.

The last thing he sees before the blackness is the floor rushing up to meet him.

Waking with a start, Peren jumps up from the bed, his

hand instinctively reaching for his dagger. Instead of his hand finding the reassuring grip of his weapon, it grasps nothing but empty air. Confused and suddenly distracted, he knocks over the person standing nearby, landing on top of them with a snarl, ready to strike. To his horror, he realizes he's pinned a young girl beneath him, her rich, enchanting amethyst eyes wide with fear and her dark hair sprawled out beneath her.

Shock and guilt wash over him as he registers her terrified expression and the cloth in her hand—it's stained with blood from cleaning him up. With a rueful smile, Peren apologizes, scrambling to his feet as he extends a hand to help her up. But before he can speak, the girl's eyes widen in realization, her cheeks flushing crimson as she takes in his state of undress.

Embarrassment floods through Peren as he becomes aware of his own nakedness, and as he's moving to cover himself, his cheeks blaze with embarrassment. With a mumbled apology, he retreats to the bed, feeling the weight of his injuries as pain courses through his body. The wounds from the recent fight throb relentlessly, each one a reminder of the harrowing ordeal he endured.

Lost in his thoughts, he barely notices the arrival of an old woman, her hunched form supported by a gnarled walking stick. "Ah, you're finally awake, are you?" the woman croaks, her sharp gaze scrutinizing Peren. "You seemed touch-and-go for a while."

Peren meets her gaze, his nerves on edge as he braces for questions. The woman's words catch him off-guard as she continues, her tone tinged with suspicion. "You're healing faster than anyone I've seen, and unusually, too."

Internally freaking out over her scrutiny, Peren attempts to defuse the tension with a joke, flashing the woman a cheesy, arrogant grin despite the pain coursing through his body.

"Magic," he replies with forced nonchalance, hoping to deflect any further inquiry.

The old woman's response is to mutter, "Kids." It's accompanied by an eye roll and a shake of her head. Without hesitation, she presses a cup against Peren's lips, instructing him firmly to drink.

Forced to swallow or risk drowning, Peren chokes down the liquid swiftly, feeling its effects kick in almost immediately. A wave of drowsiness washes over him, his eyelids growing heavy.

The old woman removes the cup and sets it on the tray before rising from her seat and heading to the door. As she crosses the threshold, Peren struggles to form one last coherent question, his words slurred and barely intelligible. "Who... are... you?" he manages to croak out before succumbing to the sedative's grasp.

Upon waking, he feels remarkably better. Surveying the room, he takes in its cozy atmosphere illuminated by sunlight filtering through the window. Judging by the angle of the light, it must be mid-morning or mid-afternoon. The furnishings are simple yet welcoming: a bedside table, a three-legged stool, a chest, and a few hooks near the door. On the bedside table rests a tray laden with food—bread, cheese, some cold stew, a mug, and a pitcher of water. His stomach growls loudly at the sight, as if announcing to the entire town his hunger.

Moving into a sitting position, Peren winces from the stiffness and soreness of his repaired skin and muscles. He reaches over, moving the tray from the bedside table to the bed and then onto his lap. Wolfing down all the food and water as if he hasn't eaten or drunk in a week, he rests his head back against the wall, belching in satisfaction. Closing his eyes in bliss, he lets the food settle in his stomach before contemplating his next move.

Slipping out of bed, he moves the tray back to the table.

It's then that he realizes, with a blush, that he's still naked. Hastily, he rushes over to the chest, hoping to find something to cover himself up. Opening it, he finds unfamiliar clothing. His brows knit together as something triggers a memory at the back of his mind.

Suddenly, the memories flood back, and he recalls securing Mercy in an abandoned house before dealing with the Spliganders. He quickly slips on the clothing, rushing downstairs into the common room.

Just as he enters, a very young barmaid crosses his path. Noticing her too late, Peren plows into her, knocking her to the ground and sending her tray flying, spilling its contents over the customer she was walking to.

Landing on top of her with a thud, Peren hastily rises and extends a hand to help her up, sputtering out a murmured apology. His expression goes slack as his eyes take in her face, those amethyst eyes sending shivers of deja vu down his spine. Realising that this is the same girl he accidentally attacked earlier, he blushes bright red. Similarly, she blushes redder by the second, quickly pulling out of his grip and squeaking in shock before rushing into the kitchens, out of sight.

Peren's eyes follow her out of the room, taking in the surroundings. It's tidy, clean, and of decent size, with a bar at one end and a door leading to the kitchen.

Looking up from cleaning a glass, the barmaid's gaze zeroes in on the source of the crash. She sees her little sister, bright red and rushing to the kitchens, leaving a very embarrassed, blushing young man, and her eyes pause for a second as she appraises him from head to toe. She likes what she sees—the lithe, graceful body and beautifully delicate features—before shifting her attention to the girl rushing into the kitchen, redder than a ripe tomato at peak harvest time.

Noticing that a customer is covered in food and the tray is upended on the floor, she sets the glass down and rushes around the bar to the scene of the disaster. Moving up to the customer, she apologizes profusely and tries to clean him up as best she can. All the while, he sputters forth curses and complaints.

Coming to his senses, Peren quickly moves over to the customer and offers profuse apologies for the mishap. He insists on paying for the upturned, ruined meal and offers to cover the cost of a replacement as well. Dropping down onto his haunches, he joins the barmaid in gathering the scattered food and items onto the tray, apologizing to her for the mess. Despite her graceful understanding and acceptance of his apology, he continues to assist her in cleaning.

As they work together, their hands inadvertently touch while reaching for the same thing, causing them to pause and finally look into each other's eyes. In that moment, Peren's mind goes blank as his brain misfires completely, his body feeling as if it's turning to goo. He is overcome with a sense of blissful pleasure as he gazes into her beautiful, large, round, liquid amber eyes.

Feeling overwhelmed by all the sensations, feelings, and thoughts flooding back to him at once, he watches as the barmaid's cheeks flush with embarrassment. Returning to his body, he becomes aware of his surroundings once more. Realizing that he has been staring, he quickly averts his gaze and apologizes, his eyes taking in the rest of her features. He notices her perfectly sized, slightly upturned nose, her masterfully sculpted prominent cheekbones speckled with tiny freckles, and the contagious smile that brightens the room, all framed by beautiful, luscious, long, light-auburn hair.

When Peren is partway through cleaning the mess with

the barmaid, a big, rotund, balding man of middle years emerges from the kitchens. His apron strains at the seams as it attempts to contain his ample girth, and his large hands grip a wooden spoon with a sense of authority. Despite his intimidating appearance, there is a weariness in his eyes, hinting at the challenges of managing the inn.

His voice booms through the room, commanding attention and respect from patrons and staff alike. He carries himself with an air of confidence, but there is also a hint of warmth beneath his gruff exterior, suggesting a deeper concern for those under his care.

With a stern expression, the innkeeper stalks over toward Peren and the barmaid, his heavy footsteps echoing on the wooden floorboards.

As his feet come into view, Peren looks up and sees the largest-bellied man ever. Gawping at his bulk, he is yanked to his feet. Despite being shorter, the man puts his face in Peren's and, spittle flying out of his mouth all over Peren's face as he points to the door, demands, "I will have none of your kind in here causing trouble. Now git, 'fore I take this spoon to ya."

Struggling between amusement at the threat and feeling insulted by all the spit now dripping off his face, Peren's eyes narrow menacingly towards the man as he rises to his full height—head and shoulders taller than the innkeeper.

However, two things stop him from getting revenge on the man. Firstly, he hears multiple chairs scraping back as every male patron of the establishment rises in warning. Secondly, he remembers why he was rushing out in the first place. Fear overcoming his features, he rushes out the door, hastily wiping the spittle from his face.

Mistaking Peren's fearful look for intimidation, the innkeeper calls out after him, "And don't come back!" Turning to the barmaid, he asks with concern, "Are you okay? Did he hurt you too?" Anger clouds his judgment despite her protests.

As the innkeeper turns away, satisfied, the barmaid stands up and, defending Peren, says, "You got it wrong. I saw what happened after Gizle ran off. He came over, apologized for the accident, insisted on paying for the ruined meal and a replacement, then started helping me to clean up the mess."

Refusing to believe her, not happy about the way she is addressing him in front of all the customers, the innkeeper says through clenched teeth, "He already attacked her when she was assisting old Herb Mistress Marizbeth."

A look of horror overcomes every face in the room but hers, with most of the men gathering their things and walking towards the door. Stepping over and blocking the men, she says indignantly to the innkeeper, "He woke up to her wiping his forehead. He was in a strange place with a stranger standing over him. Anyone would react the way he did. She just got a fright from waking him up and him grabbing her with no clothes on."

Blocked by an irritated and frustrated young woman, the men all look between the innkeeper and barmaid multiple times. Finally, her glaring look and clipped responses wear down the innkeeper's rage to a chastened stubbornness. With a grumble of "He better not do it again," he stomps off back to the kitchens.

Waving the rest of the standing men back to their seats, the barmaid moves over to the mess and continues to clean it up.

Meanwhile, reaching the abandoned building as fast as he can humanly go, Peren instinctively checks his surroundings for any onlookers. Finding none, he uses his elven strength to pull the boards off the house and moves inside, only to be met with an overwhelming stench of horse excrement and urine.

Panicking further, he searches the house thoroughly but finds no trace of Mercy. Exiting the building and scanning the surroundings, he can't find any other evidence that she was there.

Rushing back into the inn, struggling not to move faster than is safe to, Peren interrupts the barmaid as she stands up from cleaning the mess, grabbing her arms in his urgency. Stiffening under his grip, she mutters something under her breath, clearly annoyed. Her reaction goes unnoticed. Peren is entirely focused on finding Mercy as, puffing from his rush, he asks, "Where... is... my... horse?"

Pulling out of his grip, the barmaid steps back and rubs the impressions he left on her arms, her gaze unwavering as she demands for him to repeat himself.

As Peren repeats his question, his brain puzzles out what the barmaid muttered earlier. Pausing for a second, hands held out placatingly, he adds, "Sorry about that, ma'am. I didn't mean to be so rough with you."

Grumbling an acceptance of his apology, the barmaid focuses on the question he asked her. Brows knotted together in deep concentration, she tries to think back and remember if there ever was a horse with him. Drawing a blank, she shakes her head and shrugs, saying, "Sorry, I know nothing about a horse." Seeing his crestfallen face and noticing his gaze turning glazy, she quickly adds, "I will go check with my father. I'm sure he will know more about your horse."

A short while later, storming out with the barmaid a step behind, the innkeeper gets in Peren's face even more than last time, stabbing him in the chest with the wooden spoon and emphasizing each word. "I. Thought. I. Told. You. Not. To. Ever. Come. Back!"

Looking down on him without flinching once, Peren demands, "Not until I get my horse back."

"Ain't got no horse. Now, bugger off, a fore I make you regret it."

Pushed to his very short limit and standing up even straighter, towering over the innkeeper, Peren speaks very slowly through clenched teeth. "After spending my time protecting this good-for-nothing town, you can't even look after a horse. You're lucky that I don't hurt you right here, right now, for your unjustified demands."

Affronted and taken aback by the gall of this boy, the innkeeper, dark-red in the face, raises his voice, sending missiles of spit pounding Peren's face. "How dare you act all innocent when you unjustly attacked my youngest daughter? Naked, no less!"

Incredulous at the accusation, Peren gets in his face, noses touching, and opens his mouth. He is interrupted by the barmaid, who somehow manages not only to squeeze in between them, but also push them both back a step, screaming, "Stop!"

Both males are so shocked at this they hesitate. The barmaid continues before either party can form a word. "We went over this, father. I'm sure it was an accident; I'm sure he didn't mean it, so maybe ask him first?" Turning to Peren, she asks, "Did you deliberately try to attack my little sister?"

Shocked at the question, Peren takes a step back in confusion. Brows knotted, he thinks back, trying to work out who the barmaid is talking about. Drawing a blank, he says, "I don't know who you mean, ma'am."

Taking his blankness for a façade, she clarifies through clenched teeth. "The girl you took to the floor in your room while she was cleaning your face."

Peren thinks back, confused for a couple of moments more, before realisation hits, his mouth making an O. Bowing from the waist to them both, he says, "I am so sorry for scaring her like I did. I assure you, it was an accident and without any malicious intent. I would like to apologize to the miss when she is ready."

Reluctantly and hesitantly, a very red-faced girl emerges from the behind and accepts his apology in front of the crowd that has gathered. Everyone calms down, and the atmosphere returns to normal once the innkeeper is able to see it from Peren's perspective.

Smiling and chuckling at his embarrassment, the innkeeper introduces them all: he's Torach, Norta is his eldest, and Gizle is his youngest.

Bowing again, Peren replies, "It is very nice to meet you; my name is Peren." Focusing on the innkeeper, he asks, "Is there any way to find out what happened to my horse?"

Innkeeper Torach sighs sadly, answering Peren's question. "Sorry, lad, but, as you might have noticed, we have a big infestation problem, and yer horse is most likely dead from them rats."

A look of confusion crosses Peren's face as the information sinks in. His shoulders slump in defeat, his eyes tear up, and a couple of tears make their escape. His mind races back to that first time he met her, the corner of his mouth curling up at the memory of a little Peren looking up to his master and complaining, "I don't need a horse; I can move faster and easier than with a horse."

The master crouched down on his knee and said to little Peren, "You don't have to like her, but she is a great cover for you, making it so people are less suspicious of you. If you're a lone traveller without a horse, people will look at you suspiciously, especially if you have travelled a long way." Looking down at the boisterous youngling, he added, "It will also mean you will be forced to only travel as fast as humans can move.

Plus"—he chuckled—"it will give you a reason not to rush into things headfirst."

Sullen, little Peren nodded in resignation, knowing he had no choice but to accept this unnecessary burden, chafing under the limitations imposed on him. Refusing to face the truth of his master's words, little Peren did his best to avoid looking after her, only doing so when under strict supervision of his master—so much that he was the worst rider in the entire guild.

One day, when he was forced to muck out her stall, sneaking out before he was finished, little Peren saw Mercy in the pen next to the stables. Poking his tongue out at her in hatred, he was suddenly rooted to the spot, staring in shock at what he was seeing.

Blinking and rubbing at his eyes, he looked again, brows together knowing that what he just saw was not possible. She stuck her tongue out at him. Not for a lick or a treat, but as if in response to him poking his tongue out at her. Shaking his head, thinking he was going crazy, he turned to leave. Taking a step, stopping at a wicker from her, he turned around, mouth open to insult her, but was left frozen on the spot, jaw hanging open, unable to believe his eyes at what he was seeing: Mercy was prancing sideways and spinning at the same time. Powerless to the feeling, Peren emitted a hearty chuckle at this, laughing all the harder as Mercy seemed to be encouraged by his laughter.

No matter how hard he tried to hate her or avoid her, she would constantly worm her way into his thoughts, his heart melting a little more each day.

He didn't realise it till today, but she has become a steadfast and reliable friend, a true companion. A sad smile tugs at his lips as the tears fall while he remembers his time with her.

Norta slips behind the bar and fills up a large mug of ale, putting it in his hands. Downing the ale in a single gulp, he hands the mug back. Struggling to get the words past the lump in his throat, he asks softly, "What about my saddle and saddlebags?"

"They would be with the bones of yer horse."

It takes moments for his words to sink in. Once they do, Peren's head lifts so quickly it looks like it went from facing the floor to facing Torach without movement. Eyes intently focused on the innkeeper looking hopeful, he asks, "Can you repeat that?"

Repeating slowly, confused Torach says, "With the bones of yer horse."

Peren's eyes light up at this revelation. He turns to the innkeeper excitedly, exclaiming, "When I went to find her, she wasn't in the abandoned house I left her in, so she must still be alive!"

Looking at Peren intensely, Torach asks, "You put your horse in an abandoned house?"

"Yeah, why?"

Turning to Norta with a chuckle, Torach remarks, "Well, that explains that mystery." Peren turns his attention back to the innkeeper, who is still astonished by the unusual circumstances surrounding Mercy's unexpected appearance in the house. "We were wondering how a horse magically appeared in the house, all barred-up like it is on the outside. She's currently in me stable eating everything in sight." Torach shakes his head with a mix of confusion and amusement.

Relief washes over Peren as he slumps into a nearby chair. Feeling calmer, his stomach decides that now is the perfect time to make its complaint by grumbling loudly. "Could I have another drink and some breakfast?" he asks sheepishly.

Flashing Peren a warm smile that lifts his spirits, Norta darts off to fetch his request. Meanwhile, Gizle rushes to assist the customer who had food spilled on him during the earlier commotion.

Turning to Torach with a curious look, Peren inquires, "What's the deal with all the Spliganders?"

Torach sighs heavily, his expression grave. "They just showed up one night, attacking and eating people. The local militia tried to fight back, but they were quickly overwhelmed. Only those who managed to barricade themselves in their homes survived. We sent a message to Smarb for help, but we're still waiting for their response."

Peren's gaze hardens with determination. "Does the town have a wanted board?"

Torach nods solemnly. "Yes, but most travellers passing through aren't equipped to handle one Spligander, let alone thousands of them."

"I'll accept the contract," Peren declares confidently.

Torach raises an eyebrow sceptically. "How can you deal with them when fully trained soldiers can't?"

A smirk plays on Peren's lips. "Because I can."

Shaking his head, Torach motions for Peren to follow him to the door. "You'd better go see the mayor if you're going to accept the contract."

After making sure that Mercy is ok and safe, Peren follows Torach's directions, making his way to the mayor's office, determined to take on the challenge of dealing with the Spligander threat.

FOUR

Contract

Entering the opulent municipal building, Peren is greeted by towering columns adorned with intricate gold designs. A weathered, elderly man with a long beard stained with ink looks up from his work as Peren approaches.

"I am here to speak to the mayor about this contract," Peren declares, placing the document on the desk.

The old man's eyes widen in surprise and confusion as he examines the contract and then looks back up at Peren. With a shrug, he gestures to wait and exits the room briefly.

Returning a few minutes later, the elderly scribe motions to follow him. Peren complies, following the man through the ornate corridors until they reach the mayor's office.

Seated behind a grand desk, the mayor, with his puffy face and thinning hair, eyes Peren curiously. "So, my secretary tells me you want to accept the contract for the infestation of Spliganders in my town?"

Peren confirms his intentions, introducing himself as Peren Naïlo.

"Mayor Jornstawn," the mayor replies, extending his hand for a handshake. Peren accepts with a polite nod. The mayor leans forward, a hint of amusement in his eyes. "So, you'd be wanting a burial plot too?"

Peren chuckles. "Maybe when I'm old and grey, but not anytime soon."

Amused by Peren's response, the mayor continues, "So, you think you can solve our infestation problem?"

Peren's confidence is unwavering. "I know I can."

The mayor laughs heartily, his jowls swaying with mirth. After composing himself, he regards Peren thoughtfully. "How can a boy do something that men cannot?"

Peren meets the mayor's gaze squarely. "That is my secret," he replies with a determined edge. "So, will you acknowledge that I have accepted the contract?"

The mayor hesitates, his jovial expression turning serious. "No," he says firmly.

The mayor's refusal perplexes Peren. "Why not?"

The mayor explains, "You're just a boy, and I won't have that on my conscience."

Peren's frustration simmers beneath the surface as he rises from his seat, leaning forward on the desk. "I. Am. Not. Just. A. Boy," he replies, his voice tinged with indignation. His resolve hardens. "I am offering to clean out this infestation for you without negotiating the terms of the contract, and you are refusing to let me accept?"

A tense exchange follows, and by the end, the mayor relents, granting permission to accept the contract. They sign the document, and Peren departs, determined to fulfill his mission.

After returning to the inn, he goes into his room and dons his intact clothes. Buckling on his dagger and rifling through his bags, he finds the pelt is starting to smell from being in the saddlebags too long. Putting it under his arm, he heads downstairs to find both Gizle and Norta working as the common room starts to fill up.

Deciding that the best way to ask a question is to sit at the bar and wait for Norta to come and serve him, he moves there and sits down, waiting patiently.

Instead of Norta, Gizle comes over and opens her mouth to ask what he would like to drink, but she goes bright red in embarrassment, causing Peren's cheeks to colour at the memory. Taking a deep breath and steeling her features, she stutters, "W-what would y-you like to d-drink?"

Looking away, embarrassed, Peren manages to keep his voice steady as he says, "Actually, I would like to know if there is a tanner in this town." She nods, unable to speak at that moment. Peren continues, "Could you please tell me where to find him?"

Gritting her teeth at being forced to speak to this person who thoroughly embarrassed her, she squeaks out directions to Tanner Jon.

Thanking her, Peren heads off. Following the directions Gizle gave him, he eventually finds the tannery, identifying it by the smell long before he sets his eyes on the place.

Entering through the chiming door, he is greeted by a shop front. Shelves and hangers on the wall contain many different hides, some made into clothing or accessories, but mostly stacked or hanging neatly. A woman in her mid-thirties who's standing behind a counter at the back of the store looks up and, with a very pleasant welcoming smile, greets him.

Moving up to the counter, Peren puts the smelly pelt on the counter and, after introducing himself, explains his plan for the pelt, asking if it might be possible.

Calling her husband in and introducing him as Tanner Jon, she sums up the request. Looking down at the hide, unfolding it and checking it over, the tanner turns to Peren with a frown. "What animal did you skin this off?"

"Brooder," Peren replies, pride building in his chest as he tries to answer nonchalantly. Feigning confusion, his brows touch at the pale look the tanner and his wife gives him, and he asks, "What?"

"It is not possible. Their hides are impenetrable. They hunt in packs, and if you kill one, the rest of the pack will track you down and kill you unless you kill the whole pack," explains the tanner.

Going over his battle with the packs of Brooders, Peren concludes that he only killed the first pack and deterred the rest. Turning to the tanner and his wife, he says to their relief, "You have my personal guarantee and word that there will be no repercussions pertaining to that hide."

Feeling and looking over the pelt again, Jon marvels at the quality and the light weight of the pelt. Assuring Peren that he will be able to turn it into leather, he says that he will be unable to do any more than that, as he doesn't have the quality of steel required to pierce the hide.

Frowning in confusion, Peren tells them it was easy with his dagger. At their incredulity, he pulls it out and hands it over hilt-first to Tanner Jon. After examining the blade, the tanner explains to Peren that he has never seen this type of steel before, and it certainly doesn't come from nearby.

The tanner hands the dagger back to a surprised and con-fused Peren, who looks it over before slipping it into his sheath with a dismissive shrug. Agreeing on the price, they shake hands, and Peren leaves the shop.

Arriving back at the inn, he slumps down onto a stool at the bar, this time getting served by Norta, for whom he turns on the charm. "You are looking mighty pretty today."

Pretending to giggle and flutter her lashes at him, willing her cheeks to redden, she shyly replies while looking at him through her lashes. "Thank you, kind sir."

He smiles smugly in return.

"How may I serve thee, sir?"

Peren asks for dinner and ale as the sun start to set behind the horizon. Just as he is taking his first few bites, everyone begins to clear out. Momentarily confused, he calls Norta over with a puzzled expression. "Why is everyone leaving?" he asks, confusion evident in his voice.

Norta replies incredulously, "They're going home to hide behind walls for protection against the Spliganders. I suggest you get settled for the night, as we'll be closing up shortly."

Realizing his obligation under the accepted contract, Peren rises from his seat and responds, "Oh, please excuse me, I must make sure I'm ready."

Brows knotted in confusion, Norta looks at him and asks, "Ready for what?"

As he heads out, Peren answers over his shoulder. "The mayor acknowledged my acceptance of the contract to cleanse the town of the Spligander infestation."

Having already determined that using his window will offer the safest option, Peren locks and barricades his door, ensuring that any potential intruders will be thwarted if they manage to breach his room.

Moving onto the roof outside his window, he squats at the gutter, observing the town as it locks up, shuttering and barricading everything in preparation for the night ahead.

The sun disappearing from the horizon is a clear signal to everyone, like that of a tolling bell. The air becomes thick with the stench of death, decay, and all things unholy. Peren gags at the overpowering smell and, unable to hold back, empties his stomach over the side of the roof with a wet splat. After finally purging himself, he dry-retches for several minutes until his nose begins to acclimate to the foul odour.

Meanwhile, the eerie sound of needle-like claws tapping and scraping across the cobblestone road sends spine-chilling echoes throughout the town. Soon, the Spliganders' beady red eyes emerge, red dots piercing through the darkness like a tale straight from hell.

Despite his stomach's persistent attempts to purge itself, Peren manages to control the reflex. Peering down to the street below, he observes the Spliganders as they amble past, climbing posts and swarming over roofs in search of prey.

Though initially struck with fear at the sight, Peren now feels adrenaline coursing through his veins, calming him and preparing him for the arduous battle ahead. Determined to prove his worth, he snarls at the creatures before rolling off the roof, crushing those beneath him as he lands.

Blood sprays in all directions as he stabs and slashes at the rodents closest to him, creating space by constantly manoeuvring in a circle to prevent flanking attacks. Falling into a rhythm honed by years of training, he allows muscle memory to guide his movements, anticipating attacks and countering with swift parries and strikes.

Leaping, rolling, lunging, and ducking, Peren utilizes every skill and ability at his disposal to evade the creatures' bites and scratches, but despite his efforts, the relentless horde continues to press on, crawling over their fallen comrades with no regard, focused solely on Peren as their next meal.

As the night drags on, Peren's energy wanes. He's shocked by the seemingly endless numbers of Spliganders, but nevertheless, he remains resolute, facing the relentless onslaught like an unyielding barrier against the inexorable wave of claws and fangs.

Moving swiftly to the side of the street to minimize the areas from which they can attack, Peren is taken by surprise as one Spligander squeals and drops down from the roof onto his head. Its claws dig in, and it reaches down with its fangs, aiming to bite his face.

Reacting instinctively, Peren stabs and slashes at the surrounding rodents as he manoeuvres back to the centre of the road. With a swift motion, he slashes the throat of the Spligander on his head, causing blood to gush down, blinding himself in the process. Cursing under his breath, he attempts to clean his eyes of blood, but his efforts are in vain as other Spliganders attack, latching onto his legs with their claws and attempting to take chunks out of his flesh.

Realizing the imminent danger, Peren utilizes his inhuman speed to remove the Spligander from his head, clean his eyes, and dispatch the rodents attached to his legs, albeit with some flesh missing.

Despite the blood streaming from each wound and the sting of sweat in his cuts and eyes, Peren presses on, redoubling his efforts to combat the never-ending tide of attackers. With dawn approaching on the horizon, he spares a quick glance skyward, feeling a surge of relief.

Dizzy from blood loss, he doesn't stop fighting, determined to take down as many Spliganders as possible. Gradually, he notices the creatures retreating, and as he looks around, he realizes that the sun is beginning to rise, signalling the end of the nightmarish ordeal.

Falling to his knees, panting and struggling to stay conscious from exhaustion and blood loss, Peren finally succumbs and collapses face-first onto a pile of Spligander carcasses, out cold.

As the inhabitants on the street begin to unbar and open up the buildings, they are greeted by a shocking sight: hundreds of Spliganders lie dead, their vomit-inducing saliva oozing onto the cobbles. Looking around, the townspeople see that everything is covered in a thick layer of black, viscous blood.

Near one end of the street lies an unconscious human figure, sprawled face-down and motionless. Norta, who is in the process of opening the inn, is the first to notice him. She cries out to her father, Torach, as she rushes over in horror. Gasping and covering her mouth with trembling hands, she assesses the scene, her heart pounding with dread.

Torach, alerted by his daughter's cry, hurries over, and together with Norta, carefully lifts Peren's limp body and carries him back to the inn. Calling out to Gizle, Torach sends her to fetch the Herb Mistress Marizbeth for assistance.

Arriving at Peren's door, they find it locked and barricaded from the inside. With no time to waste, they place Peren in another room and do their best to stem the bleeding and stabilize him until Marizbeth arrives.

A few minutes later, the Herb Mistress bursts into the room, promptly ordering everyone out as she takes charge of Peren's care. Hours pass in tense anticipation until she emerges from the room, looking weary, but with a faint hint of annoyed relief on her face. Torach and his daughters anxiously await her verdict, and with a subtle nod, she signals that Peren will pull through.

Waking up in a fog, Peren's memory slowly returns, flooding him with the events of the previous night. He panics for a moment before calming down, taking stock of his surroundings. His body is bandaged, and it appears recent, indicating he must have received medical attention today.

Throwing off the bedcovers, he notices he's once again naked. With a sense of embarrassment, he carefully puts on his tunic, mindful of his injuries. Moving slowly, he uses any nearby support to make his way down to the common room.

When he enters, the Herb Mistress scoffs at him, striding

over and chastising him. "If you weren't so injured, I would crack you over the head with my stick! Now, back to bed with you." She takes hold of him, guiding him back upstairs.

Back in the room, Peren reluctantly complies with the Herb Mistress's orders, stripping naked as she examines his bandages. She mutters to herself about his rapid healing before instructing him to get back into bed. Despite his embarrassment, he follows her instructions, reluctantly drinking a draught that puts him to sleep for a few more hours.

Looking out the window as dusk approaches, Peren senses the impending danger of nightfall. Feeling much better, he gets out of bed and stretches, noticing a pair of breeches on the stool. Grateful to avoid a repeat of the earlier embarrassment, he quickly dresses. Secretly wishing he didn't have to go out again and take the Spliganders' on, he heads downstairs, where he sees people clearing out to lock up against the upcoming attacks.

Norta notices him and gives a genuine smile of relief. Moving over to him, she asks, "Anything I can get you, sir?"

Feeling flattered by her attention and wanting to impress her, he immediately stands a little straighter, smiles back, and replies, "Just a light meal. Their stench doesn't seem to agree with my stomach."

The corners of her lips curling up at his quip, Norta curtsies and says, "Yes, my lord." She hurries off to the kitchen and returns with some bread and cheese.

Smiling in thanks, Peren starts eating, realizing how hungry he really is. Forgetting momentarily about the stench he will have to face, he clears his plate.

Leaving once he finishes the meal, he heads back upstairs and finds his room barricaded and locked. Remembering the previous night's events, he barricades the other door and heads out onto the roof, preparing for another night of work.

Looking down from his perch, he sees that the road has been cleared of all the dead Spliganders. He takes a moment to appreciate the hardworking townsfolk before finishing his preparations.

Better-prepared, he braces for the stench of his adversaries. As the sun sets behind the horizon, the foul odour hits him again, causing him to empty his stomach over the side of the building. Despite recovering a bit quicker with less in his stomach, he still grimaces at the unpleasant sounds and sights. The beady red nightmare eyes slowly emerge from the darkness.

Seeing the creatures drawing near, Peren leaps down and lands on the necks of two of them, killing them instantly. He swiftly dispatches others with his dagger, keeping his movements efficient. Remembering the lessons from the previous night, he stays in the middle of the street, preventing ambushes from above as he continues to fend off the relentless horde.

Keeping the Spliganders at bay with swift but precise movements, Peren remains vigilant, only shifting from his spot when necessary to counter their attempts to flank him or when their numbers swell. Despite the exertion and the foul stench filling his lungs, he stays focused and manages to evade injury this night.

As the sky begins to lighten, he watches as the creatures retreat to their lair. With a sigh of relief, he climbs back up to the borrowed room, unlocking and unbarring the door before returning to his own room to do the same. He strips off his smelly blood-soaked clothes before washing himself down as best he can. Collapsing onto the mattress, he falls into a deep sleep, exhaustion pulling him under before his head even touches the pillow.

Waking up some time later, he realizes it's early afternoon. He dresses in his spare shirt and original breeches before heading downstairs to the common room in search of something to eat, his hunger gnawing at him. As he's finishing off his meal, he is greeted by Mayor Jornstawn, entering the inn.

Moving with purpose up to Peren, the mayor envelops him in a huge bear hug, making him wince from his ribs being crushed as his mind races with a mix of emotions—pride, relief, and a hint of apprehension. The mayor's booming voice fills the room, congratulating Peren on his efforts in stemming the infestation plaguing the town. Despite the man's outward joviality, Peren can't shake the nagging feeling of being under scrutiny, a sensation that seems to intensify with each passing moment.

After ordering a round for everyone at the inn, Mayor Jornstawn pulls Peren aside to a private room, his scribe trailing behind. Peren's muscles tense as they settle around a table, the weight of the mayor's gaze heavy upon him. "I am so sorry to have doubted your word before," the mayor begins, his tone sincere, but tinged with lingering doubt. Peren forces a polite smile, though inwardly, he bristles at the reminder of their earlier interactions. As the conversation unfolds, he struggles to maintain his composure, his thoughts racing a mile a minute.

As the mayor speaks, Peren's mind races with frustration and determination. *Of course they're suspicious. How could they not be? But I can't afford to let them see through me.* He meets the mayor's gaze evenly, his own emotions hidden behind a mask of confidence. *I must keep playing this game—keep up the facade.*

Holding his hand out to the scribe, Mayor Jornstawn is handed a sheet of paper. After perusing the paper for a minute, he looks up at Peren, looks back down at the paper, then looks at his scribe, who nods, then turns his attention back to Peren with a look that is a mix of awe and shock. "It says here in the report I have in my hands that you dispatched well over two hundred of the critters over the last two days, which, to say the least, is an incredible feat." He pauses to give Peren another suspicious glare. "Which we are very grateful to you for." Getting up and giving Peren a forced friendly smile, Mayor Jornstawn continues, "Now, if there is anything you need, don't hesitate to ask for it." Handing the paper back to his scribe, the mayor leaves the room.

Peren sits there, struggling to calm the storm of emotions swirling within him. A sense of foolishness flows as he silently berates himself for overlooking the warning signs. Of course, suspicions would arise; after all, what he achieved single-handedly would challenge entire armies. Yet he knows he must convince them that he is nothing more than an exceptionally skilled human.

His thoughts drift back to the heated argument with his master just a week prior to his quest, the words still echoing in his mind. "Peren, you are too young and impulsive, even for a human."

Peren retorted, "But I'm not just a human, am I? I can do everything every master here can do, and better." The master's dismissive gesture only stoked Peren's anger, but losing his temper now would mean forfeiting his chance at this quest. With a deep breath, he swallowed his pride and bowed his head, his eyes seething with fury as he forced out an apology. "I am sorry, master. Please forgive my petulance."

The elder sighed heavily, pinching the bridge of his nose in weariness. "Peren, do you even understand that word?" His gaze bored into Peren's, despite their similar height, making Peren feel as though he was being looked down upon. With a firm voice and gritted teeth, he continued, "Do not disappoint me or make me regret this decision. You may go." Raising a finger to forestall Peren's premature celebration, he added,

"But you must promise me, and genuinely mean it, that you will keep your head down and not do *anything* that will cause any suspicion from any human out there."

Peren's eyes lit up, his mouth open in triumph, but before he could speak, the elder cut him off. "I don't want to hear it, Peren. I know you well enough that unless you are extremely vigilant, you *will* bring suspicions down not only on yourself, but this guild as well. And if that happens, I cannot protect you. Once you officially accept this quest, I am unable to shield you anymore. Your path is your own, but remember, we are in hiding."

Peren's frustration simmered as he struggled to contain his retort, but the elder pressed on. "No, I will not tell you why we are hiding. Just know that if we don't keep a low profile, there will be extreme consequences that will not only endanger your life, but also those of your friends. Not to mention, humans tend to act rashly out of fear of the unknown. Now, I will leave you to ponder your decision, despite already seeing your mind made up." With that, he turned and left Peren's room, shutting the door quietly behind him.

Seething with frustration at the truth in his master's words, bringing himself back to the present, Peren clenches his fists, his determination burning even brighter. He knows he must keep his head down and complete the task at hand swiftly. Once that is done, he resolves to slip out of town as quickly as he can.

As he moves back into the common room, Peren's mind remains troubled by his recent conversation with the mayor. Despite the celebratory mood around him, his unease lingers, casting a shadow on his triumph. He tries to hide his worries beneath the revelry, but the mayor's words weigh heavily on his mind, reminding him of the challenges ahead.

As he joins the festivities, Peren catches a fleeting glimpse of concern in Norta's eyes. Smoothing over his own worries with a practised smile, he shares rounds of drinks with the crowd before slipping away to prepare for the night's challenges.

Balancing on the edge of the roof outside his window, Peren braces himself for the inevitable onslaught of the Spliganders. The night air is thick with the putrid stench of their presence, a bleak reminder of the horrors lurking below. With grim determination, he leaps into the darkness, a lone figure amidst the swirling shadows, his movements swift and precise as he strikes down each threat.

After hours of relentless combat, Peren returns to his chambers, landing on the floor with a heavy thud. Before he can even register the exhaustion weighing down his limbs, his senses jolt him into action as a Spligander launches itself at him from inside the room. With reflexes honed by countless battles, Peren dives out of the creature's path, watching in slow-motion as the Spligander sails out the window into the night.

Moving swiftly, Peren slams the shutters shut just as another Spligander crashes into them, nearly knocking him back in the process. Regaining his stance, Peren braces himself for the rodent's heavy attack, only being forced back half a pace by its relentless assault. As the onslaught continues, he holds strong, his muscles straining with the effort.

After what feels like an eternity, the Spliganders' assault finally begins to wane. Peren maintains his guard for a few more minutes, ensuring the coast is clear before allowing himself to collapse to the ground, utterly exhausted. Gritting his teeth, he summons the last dregs of his energy to strip, clean himself, and crawl to the bed. Flopping onto the mattress, he can't keep his eyes open any longer and falls into a deep sleep, his body weary, but his spirit unbroken.

In the early afternoon, Peren wakes to jarring thuds at his door, his head throbbing in unison with the heavy pounding. With a grimace, he bolts upright, his senses assaulted by the relentless noise. Rubbing his temples, he stumbles out of bed, bleary-eyed and disoriented, his body protesting the abrupt awakening.

As he reaches the door, the noise continues, relentless in its persistence. With a sigh, Peren unbarricades and unlocks the door and is greeted by Norta standing on the other side, a tray of food in her hands. Despite his discomfort, he manages a weak smile, motioning for her to enter.

Norta steps into the room, her gaze meeting his with a mix of concern and curiosity. A moment passes where the sun seems to add to her radiance. The concern in her eyes overwhelms his senses.

Before either can speak, Peren is seized by a sudden impulse, closing the gap between them in a bold gesture. Their lips meet in a tentative kiss, surprising them both with its intensity. For a moment, time seems to stand still as they share this unexpected moment of intimacy.

As the kiss deepens, Peren's pulse quickens, his senses overwhelmed by the taste and feel of Norta's lips against his own. With a surge of desire, she responds in kind, their bodies pressing together in a silent embrace. With each passing moment, the world fades further away, leaving only the two of them lost in the heat of the moment.

Pulling back, glancing down and up his body, a blush rising in both their cheeks, Norta turns without a word and all but runs from the room, leaving Peren standing there bright-red and confused at what just happened. Worried that he did something wrong, he paces back and forth, trying to work out what he should do. Unable to come to a conclusion, he heads out with his dagger to do some practice, knowing it will help him to collect his thoughts.

When he comes back hours later and sits on his bed, reflecting on the events of the afternoon, Peren still can't work out what he should do. The whirlwind of emotions overwhelms any ability to think straight, especially since the kiss with Norta.

The fading light of the setting sun casts elongated shadows across Peren's face, jolting him out of his contemplation. With a start, he realizes how late it's become and swiftly rises from his bed, his mind snapping back to the task at hand.

Making his way to the edge of the roof of the inn, he settles in, his senses on high alert for any sign of danger. It doesn't take long before the foul stench of the Spliganders assaults his nostrils, causing him to lean over the gutter and empty what little remained in his stomach onto the ground below.

As the creatures draw nearer, materializing into their grotesque forms with every step, Peren braces himself for the impending onslaught. The sound of needle-like claws tapping against the stone sends a shiver down his spine, a detestable reminder of the battle that lies ahead. With steely determination, he prepares to face the night's horrors head-on, ready to defend the town and its inhabitants from the relentless onslaught of the Spliganders.

The assault on his senses intensifies as the Spliganders draw inexorably closer, their stench permeating the air. Despite the horrific situation, he finds himself in surprisingly good spirits, a sense of morbid contentment settling over him as he anticipates the impending battle.

With a snarl of pleasure, he leaps from the roof, landing amidst the creatures below with lethal precision. Moving with the fluidity of a seasoned warrior, he dispatches the Spliganders with swift and deadly blows, his movements blurs of steel and sinew. Black, viscous blood sprays everywhere as he plunges into their ranks, his confidence buoyed by the desire to impress the woman he likes.

However, his overconfidence leads him to take unnecessary risks, and he finds himself in a precarious position as the creatures close in around him.

Despite his incredible healing abilities, Peren feels the strain of his muscles and flesh stretching with each movement, affecting his reactions and making him more vulnerable to the creatures' attacks. As the battle rages on, he falls into a pattern, unwittingly exposing himself to the Spliganders' onslaught.

With a sharp inhale of breath, he feels searing pain as one latches onto his right calf, distracting him long enough for another to grip his left bicep and yet another to sink its claws into his left thigh. The creatures tear chunks from his body, their relentless assault overwhelming him.

Moving away from the horde, he is so completely focused on removing the attached Spliganders that he doesn't see the one sneaking up behind him. Hissing, it leaps onto the middle of his back, using its claws to latch onto his ribs, making it all but impossible to remove it. Screaming and arching his back in agony, tears spring to his eyes as he feels the creature's claws shredding his insides.

In a moment of lucidity, Peren realises how much trouble he is in.

Desperate to dislodge the Spligander clinging to his back, he resorts to desperate measures, slamming himself against a nearby post in a futile attempt to crush the creature. With each failed attempt, the Spligander's claws dig deeper into his flesh, severing vital organs and rendering him increasingly immobile. With morning still hours away, he can feel the Spligander already making parts of his body go numb as it tears its way into his spine.

Moments later, he hears and feels bones, tendons, and disks snapping and breaking as the Spligander manages to work on severing his spine. Fear cuts through his panic. Knowing he has moments before half his body is gone, he tries one last time to remove the Spligander on his back, managing to dislodge it, tearing through his vital organs.

Quickly removing the others as well, he focuses on moving into an abandoned house and barricading himself inside. Hoping that he will be found quickly enough, he succumbs to the peaceful dark embrace of unconsciousness.

As the sun comes up and the Spliganders retreat, Norta rushes up to Peren's room to confront him about the kiss. Banging on the barricaded door in a show of bravado, her initial feisty stance soon gives way to dread as her gut begins to clench in fear at the unsettling silence. Rushing down the stairs, she runs outside with her family close behind and starts to look among the piles of dead Spliganders.

Not finding Peren anywhere, in a moment of lucid panic, Norta begins to search the nearby abandoned houses.

Gizle's screams piercing the tense atmosphere brings Norta sprinting over as fast as she can. Taking in the sight before her, Norta screams in horror. In front of her, face down, claws sticking out of his back in a mess of blood as it leaks onto the floor, lies the man whose lips she can still taste and feel on hers.

Rushing over, the townsfolk take in the scene, some rushing off to get the Herb Mistress while others help carry Peren to the inn.

When the Herb Mistress arrives, she does a quick assessment. Disappointed and sad at his stupidity, she turns to those standing by with a crestfallen face. Most nod sadly and leave, knowing that Peren is either dead or about to be. Norta's hands fly to her mouth in horror, her head shaking as tears spring to her eyes.

Seeing her reaction, the Herb Mistress says comfortingly, "I'm so sorry, child. There is nothing I can do. He won't live much longer." As she sees a flash of a look in Norta's eye, she continues, her voice firm. "No, you would have to have gotten to him before he passed out, not hours later. There was and is nothing you can do to stop his fate." Beckoning Norta over to Peren, the Herb Mistress adds, "Spend what moments you have left with him now."

Tears streaming down her face, mouth opening and closing, unable to speak, Norta shakes her head, trying to compose herself as she turns to the Herb Mistress. "I will *not* give up on him yet."

Rushing over to the table, Norta begins to work on Peren, removing the claws.

Seeing the broken girl working on Peren, doing more damage as she removes the deeply embedded claws, the Herb Mistress shuffles over and, gently moving Norta out of the way, begins to remove the vile claws with quick and practiced movements.

Peren's eyes flutter open, confusion clouding his mind as he takes in his disembodied state. Shock courses through him as he gazes down at his own form, a sight for which he was wholly unprepared.

Before he can comprehend the situation, he is whisked through the air, suspended in front of the Wall of Remembrance. His name begins to etch itself onto the stone, glowing softly as each letter takes shape one after the other.

As the engraving starts on the last letter of his first name, he feels a distant tugging pulling him away from the wall.

Distracted by the sensation, he turns his attention in its direction, only to be suddenly thrust back into his body with a jolt. Gasping for air, he sits up abruptly, senses overwhelmed and body protesting painfully against the movement. Before he can utter a word, he chokes and gags on a vile liquid, numbing his body and mind as darkness descends once more.

After what feels like an eternity, Peren's eyes slowly pry themselves open, panic flooding his senses at first. In the darkness, he flails, seeking some semblance of reality. Calming down as he takes in his surroundings, he finds what appears to be Norta asleep by his side. Seeing her there sleeping acts like a soothing balm to him.

Thinking that the afterlife looks so real, he takes a closer look at her. Feeling confusion at seeing the exhaustion etched into her features, he can't follow any thread of thought as his mind fades, unable to keep him awake. He smiles softly before drifting back into slumber.

Waking up with bright sunlight streaming straight onto his face, Peren winces, moving his eyes out of the direct sunlight. The shutters closing brings him welcome relief. His eyesight adjusting, he finally makes out Norta sitting down beside him, tears running down her face as she smiles at him. Reaching out and tentatively touching his face, as if she is dreaming, her words penetrate the deep fog of his mind. "You're awake! Oh, thank Twileron that you're still alive. I was certain that he escorted your soul to Iinortria for judgement..." Taking a breath to continue, she opens her mouth, but nothing comes out as she chokes on the words. Tears stream down her face as he sees the fear in her eyes.

Hating himself for causing her fear, he smiles and says, "I met Twileron. Not very impressive, kinda imposing. When he saw me, his face paled because of my awesomeness. To avoid embarrassing him, I turned around, waved, and came back." Attempting to shrug, he continues, "It was a lame place, anyway."

Seeing this idiot trying so hard to make her smile after his brush with death, Norta's heart swells with tenderness, and laughter escapes her lips. His attempt at light-heartedness about such a serious matter moves her deeply.

Her laughter fills Peren with warmth, his smile brightening as he watches her eyes crinkle and light up. He is hit by an epiphany: this is the woman he will join souls with.

Seeing the look on his face, Norta becomes concerned and asks, "Why do you have that look on your face? Is everything ok?"

Quickly shifting his expression, he changes the topic. His throat drying out, he rasps, "How... long... have... I... been... out?"

Sitting vigilantly by his side, Norta tenderly assists him, offering water to soothe his parched throat. "One month," she whispers, fighting back her tears as she holds onto him as if afraid he might slip away once more.

He is so shocked by this revelation that his words slip out in a breathy whisper. "One month?"

Norta nods her head as Peren's mind races, trying to process this information. He recalls the scarily realistic dream of his name being engraved in the Wall of Remembrance and how it stopped abruptly as it finished his first name.

"A whole *month*?" His voice is filled with confusion and disbelief.

"After we carried you to the inn," she says, her voice trembling with anger, "Marizbeth refused to treat you. Said you were... were gonna—gonna..." Tears trickle down her cheeks as she relives that moment of despair.

Seeing Norta's tears and the pain in her eyes, Peren feels a deep ache in his chest. His anger flares at the emotional pain Marizbeth inflicted on Norta. He hates himself for being so helpless, for not being able to comfort her when she needed it most.

"Please continue," Peren says through gritted teeth.

Sniffling, she says, "So I started to work on you, refusing to let you go without a fight." There's a look of determination beneath her teary exterior. "She then moved me out of the way and began to work on you, with me assisting." Drawing in a breath, she continues, "I refused to believe that you would give up fighting too. I just knew it. No matter what people said, I wouldn't stop." Smiling down at him, she says, "And here you are, just as I hoped."

Peren just lays there in awe for a few moments, unable to speak. Finally finding his voice, he struggles to say, "I owe you a life debt."

Smiling down at him, she runs her fingers through his hair. "You owe me nothing. You came back to me. That is all I want." Her smile brightens as she adds, "One thing I did enjoy was feeding you and looking after you like I used to with Gizle. You looked so cute when you slept."

Peren's face goes bright red at this news. His mouth opens and closes silently as he imagines what it looked like.

A chuckle escapes her lips at the look on Peren's face.

Peren's face stills as it dawns on him that the Spliganders would have had free reign over the town while he was out. Words tumbling out, he struggles to make a coherent question. "The people, are they ok?" Norta looks at him with confusion until he asks, "Have there been any casualties?"

Gently putting her hand on his arm, Norta reassures him, "It's ok. The town hasn't suffered any casualties. Even all the animals were kept safe."

As he struggles to keep the facade in place, a feeling of panic washes over him. *What if she saw my true form? How am I able to hide it now? What will happen? Will she tell someone? Will I be burnt alive for not being human?* His mind racing as he tries to discern how exposed he has been. Scrutinizing her behaviour, he concludes that if that were the case, there would be a level of suspicion, and she would be asking direct questions as to his true nature. He's flooded with relief as he realises the glamour hasn't disappeared.

Without preamble, Marizbeth strides in, shoves past Norta, and addresses Peren directly, her words cutting like knives. "So, you live." She dismisses this miracle as being as unimpressive as someone eating. Turning to Norta and scornfully continuing, she points her cane at her. "All you did was condemn him to a life in bed. Hope you're satisfied." As she turns back to Peren, he sees the ugliest emotion that he could ever imagine in her eyes: pity.

Feeling his anger rise at her pity, he grits his teeth and opens his mouth. She continues, in a dreary, almost bored tone before he has a chance to suck air in for his retort. "Your spine is severed between your shoulder blades. Hacked away, more like. As such, the nerves to your arms have also been affected, which is why you will be paralysed like this for the rest of your life, in addition to the other very serious injuries. I hope you have a very peaceful short life."

Despite her trying to make it sound like a merciful blessing, Peren refuses to give up. Refusing to believe that this is it for him, he opens his mouth again to retort, but is cut off by Norta replying vehemently, "What do you mean, 'short?' I did not spend the last month keeping him alive just to lose him."

Whirling on her, Marizbeth points back at him as she replies forcefully, "Look at him. Who would want to live in his state? He will either stop eating and drinking to die or beg for the knife. He will be nothing but a burden"—she gives Norta a knowing look—"on you and any offspring you produce. It would have been a mercy to let him die while he was unconscious and weak."

Nodding to herself, proud of her argument, she leaves in a rustle of skirts, slamming the door shut behind her.

Norta looks down at Peren, teary-eyed, feeling her whole body has been gutted, berating herself mentally. *What was I thinking? Of course she is right. Peren will never be able to lift a single finger. I should just give him the knife when he sleeps. But how could I do that to him? This must be the man that will save Comtun. If so, then this is the man who I—I—I—*

Pausing for a moment, confused at where that thought came from, she follows that thread to a memory from when she was little.

A very old woman came and stayed at the inn for a while. The old woman had a magnetic air about her, something that little Norta was constantly drawn to, often leading her to getting into trouble with her father for not helping him with the chores and her baby sister.

Ever eager to learn, she would sit in the old woman's lap or next to her, bombarding her with questions. Loving the inquisitive nature of this little girl, the old woman would laugh at the speed and number of questions that came from little Norta. Unwilling to extinguish such a curious girl, the old woman always happily answered.

The last day of her stay, she always stayed with little Norta. As the woman said goodbye to her, feeling sad over this girl's future, she whispered, "You will find someone one day who takes your breath away. Someone you will love the rest of your life. Children will grow in your belly, and you will be happier than you have ever been up to that point."

Leaving her to contemplate what she said, the old woman thanked Torach and started to shuffle away. A thought dawned on Norta, and she calls out to the woman, "How will I know him?"

Pausing and chuckling over her shoulder, the old woman called back, "He will be the cure to the plague." Turning back to the road, she continued to shuffle away, ignoring the myriads of questions coming from Norta.

Norta is pulled from her memories as Peren vents, "Excuse me, I am here, you know! I can speak! I do have opinions and thoughts on this!" Fuming at the way the Herb Mistress spoke to Norta, he looks up at her, only to lose his anger in an instant. Looking into her eyes with gratitude for what she did, he says, "Norta, I meant what I said: I owe you my life. I know how hard it must have been making such an impossible decision, but I promise you, you made the right one. I would pick being a cripple over death any day, so thank you for not giving up on me and fighting for me."

Seeing the doubt on her face, he nods for her to sit on the bed, continuing, "You did the right thing, do not doubt that for a second, because I don't. You are amazing and incredible for standing up for me and being my voice when everyone else was telling you to do the merciful thing..." His words trail off as he sees tears running down her cheeks.

Redeemed of the guilt over the selfish decision she made, she struggles to look in Peren's eyes through the blur of tears in hers. Like a dam breaking, she presses her head into his chest and weeps.

Relaxing her head against his chest, puffy-eyed, she listens to his strong heart beating as he breathes in and out. Lifting her head after a moment, looking deep into his brown eyes, she gently brushes her lips against his.

Lifting his head up, he manages to press his lips against hers in a deep and passionate kiss. Eyes widening at his tenderness, she almost pulls back out of his reach before closing her eyes and pressing her lips harder against his, sharing every unspoken feeling between them.

Their lips linger together, only pulling back when they need to breathe. As they look into each other's eyes, Norta's cheeks flush, making her look away, embarrassed. Catching her breath, Norta's eyes wander to the window. Realising how late it's getting, she turns to Peren, and seeing the look of understanding in his eyes, she gives him a lingering final kiss before leaving, spirits high, feet gliding over the floor.

Watching her leave with a smile, Peren lays his head back and revels in the feel of her. Breathing in, he detects a delicate blend of floral and citrus notes, underscored by a warm, woody aroma. Closing his eyes, he savours her scent as he drifts off into a comforting slumber.

Closing the door behind her, Norta takes a deep breath before she heads downstairs and begins assisting her father and sister with the chores.

Waking up and rubbing the sleep from his eyes, Peren sighs and lies back against the pillow. Moments later, eyes widening in shock, he goes over what he just did. Not believing it, he does it again. Realisation dawns on him: not only can he move and feel his hand, but his whole arm. Gaping at it in disbelief, almost too scared to see whether this is some sort of dream, he manages to give himself a slap. Eyes widening further at the evidence that this is real, he can't stop grinning stupidly.

Hearing a soft knock at the door, Peren quickly puts his hand back so it looks like he hasn't used it. Poking her head in hesitantly, Norta, seeing that he is awake, moves in with lunch, skilfully closing the door with her foot as she carries the tray over to the bed. Sitting on the stool, she begins to feed him.

Glaring at Norta, he forces himself to endure spoonful after spoonful of humiliation, knowing that up until moments, ago this was his fate. When it finally ends, there is so much relief on his face that it makes Norta giggle.

Setting the tray down, she leans over and wipes his mouth with a rag before putting it on the tray. Turning back to converse, she squeals in surprise when he grabs her waist and pulls her in, planting a deep and sensual kiss on her lips. Realizing what has happened, she melts into his embrace and eagerly returns the kiss with fervour.

Shifting so she is almost straddling him, she kisses his lips, running her fingers through his hair and over his chest while Peren cups her face, marvelling in the feel of her under his touch as they kiss. In her complete focus on the way he tastes, her hands move on instinct, shifting lower and lower until they're at his waist.

Pausing when he stops feeling her touch, he opens his eyes to see what is wrong, only to find her moving further down his body. His heart is screaming *Yes!* His head is screaming *Wait! Stop!*

In a moment of realisation and panic, he halts her from going further. Looking wounded and embarrassed, she stills. As she tries to get off him, he grabs her and says, "Wait."

Flushing even further, unable to look at him, she blurts out, "Why should I? It's obvious you don't want to."

"Yes, I do!" He says it with such conviction she pauses in her struggle and looks at him. "I want to more than you know, but…" He smiles ruefully as his face turns red. "I can't feel down there yet."

Confused for a moment before she realises what he is talking about, her face on fire with embarrassment, she stutters out, "Oh, um, ok. Yeah… We should probably wait till you can feel it too."

Turning quickly, pulling out of his grip, she gathers the tray and moves out of the room hastily, leaving Peren bewildered as to her sincerity. *Girls are impossible to understand,* he thinks, letting his hand fall back to the bed and resting his head against the pillow, running over their entire interaction, questioning and second guessing everything. With his mind awhirl, sleep eludes him.

He's pulled out of his ruminations with a start as the Herb Mistress barges in, slamming the door shut without so much as a knock. Sick of his deflections while giving him a thorough examination, she demands, "Who are you, and what are you really? The time for lies is over. By all rights, you should be dead right now." Looking pointedly at his healed arm, she continues, "Not only have you stayed alive, but are recovering from something that no mortal recovers from."

Continuing when she sees the flash of concern in Peren's eyes, she says dismissively, "Don't worry; your secret will be safe with me, young stellar traveller." His eyes widen in surprise at her casual mention of his otherworldly nature.

Dismissing his worry with a wave of her hand, she says, "I know all about the wider universe, and the different ancient races." Pausing to consider him for a minute, her eyes narrow as she continues, "You're too human-like to be part of any of the more exotic races, so your race is humanoid. You're too tall and lithe to be a Dwarf. You aren't affected by the sun and do not have an unquenchable thirst for blood, so you're not a Vampyr. Unless you are somehow through and through evil—which I don't detect—you are not a Daemon." A chill runs down her spine, making her shiver at the thought. "Too thin and short for a Troll. Maybe Goblin? But I get the feeling that you aren't. That only leaves the race of the Elves."

His jaw drops in shock before he can close it. The Herb

Mistress' eyes light up as she takes it as a sign that she is right. Peren quickly shuts his mouth in an attempt to protect all races by refusing to give any information out to the humans.

"So how does an Elf—who is a figure of myth or folklore to humans—end up on a planet of humans?" Knees cracking and creaking, she lowers herself onto the stool, followed by a litany of curses. Finally settling down, she eyes him expectantly for a few seconds before her impatience gets the better of her. "Well? I'm not getting any younger, so just tell me!"

Refusing to give in to her so easily, Peren replies, "I have no idea what you're talking about. I am as human as you and Norta, and have no idea what these other… Stellar? Beings are."

Her patience shattering, she leans forward on creaky legs and demands, "Who do you think will listen to a crazy old woman?" Sighing dramatically, she splays her fingers over her heart as she continues," I swear by all that's holy, I won't tell a soul about your true identity. I will take the secret to my grave."

Glaring back at her for a few seconds, knowing that she won't leave until she has her answers, he admits the truth for the first time in his life. "I am an Elf. I don't know much about my people. I have been here all my life."

Smiling in triumph, the Mistress whispers victoriously, a little giddy, "I knew it! There was no way you could fight the Spliganders like you do without otherworldly abilities." Pausing for a minute to process this information, she continues excitedly, "So, how did you get here?"

His voice dripping with sarcasm, he responds, "On my horse, Mercy."

Waving the sarcastic comment away she repeats, clarifying, "No, how did you get here to the human world?" Leaning forward with excitement, she guesses, "Some sort of gateway, tunnel or something?"

Chuckling in relief at the fact that he can't betray his people's secrets, Peren replies, "I know nothing of my home world. All I know is that when I escaped, there was a coup going on, and millions died between the warring factions." Smirking at her with his best grin, he says, "Difference is that our wars are fought with magic, often lasting centuries if not millennia. I'm here as a refugee." Shrugging, he adds, "All I know is that if I stayed, I would have died. That's the only thing we have in common with the Goblins—we are merciless killers. You won't see us coming."

A lone eyebrow arching up in amusement, she asks, "Is that a threat, little elf?"

Struggling to keep his face blank as a small smile tugs at the corners of his mouth, Peren replies, "Maybe it is, maybe it isn't."

Turning serious, the Mistress nods in return, her expression softening. "We all carry our secrets, Peren. It's what makes us human... or Elven, in your case." As she rises to her feet, she grunts. "Damn knees." Looking at Peren, she says out of habit to the young ones, "Don't get old." Realizing her faux pas, she chuckles at herself, returning Peren's grin, and exits the room.

Seeing a very smug and satisfied Herb Mistress exiting the stairs, Norta rushes up to Peren's room, fear and worry etched on her face. Looking up as she rushes in, Peren sees a very concerned Norta move over towards him. Sitting down on the edge of the bed, she looks deeply into his eyes with a very pointed questioning look. "What did she talk to you about? She was very pleased with herself, and I have never seen her so pleased."

Struggling to keep a facade up as he feels the crushing weight of guilt, Peren is forced to lie to her. Looking into her eyes sadly, he just shakes his head and says, "A very one-sided debate about my predicament." When she glares at him, he ruefully amends his statement. "Our—our predicament!" He relaxes when her glare turns to a smile.

They spend the afternoon talking, only stopping when they are interrupted by Peren's stomach making its demands known by grumbling loudly. Bursting into laughter, Norta gets up and, heading to the door, says, "I'll get us both some dinner."

Running into Gizle as she steps into the common room, Norta is greeted with a disdainful glare from her. She hurries on before Norta has a chance to retort, whispering harshly as she rushes by, "You owe me big time!" Feeling guilty at her comment, Norta realises that she has been completely focused on Peren, leaving Gizle to cover her chores.

Rushing on, she goes to get herself and Peren dinner, but is forced to alter her plan as she comes under the watchful gaze of her father. Working with a quiet efficiency, she and Gizle manage to cover the common room and attend to all patrons quickly.

Finally allowed to get her own meal, she rushes it up to Peren, worried about the delay and his reaction, considering he is totally reliant on her. She giggles to herself at how her big strong man needs her for the simplest things.

Moving into the room, she sees that he has fallen asleep. She just stands there, enjoying watching him sleep, smiling at how beautiful he looks. Moving over as quietly as she can, she sits on the bed and puts the tray on her lap. Carefully stirring him just enough that it will take a few moments for his mind to clear, she quickly pushes the spoon of food into his mouth, gleeful at his obedience in accepting it.

As he chews, mind fog lifting, he realises what she did, and glares at her with consternation. Giving him an unapologetic smile, she tries again. This time, Peren snatches the spoon off her and begins to eat. Chuckling at this, she takes another spoon and starts to feed herself.

Once they finish and she cleans up, she climbs onto the bed at his request and snuggles him, his arm wrapped around her body as they drift off into a happy, blissful slumber. He marvels at the feeling of her in his arm before he succumbs to his weariness.

The next morning, rising early and leaving, Norta rushes to her room to try and make it look as if she spent the night there, not with Peren. Walking behind her on the way to start the chores, Gizle smiles knowingly at her sister's back.

Knocking on the door softly a few hours later, Norta pokes her head in to find Peren awake. Stopping at the way he is stupidly smiling at her; she returns a confused smile. Screaming in excitement as he moves his other hand and waves at her, she rushes in, nearly forgetting to put the tray down as she jumps on him and starts kissing his newly healed hand, happy tears running down her cheeks.

She looks up at him with teary eyes, smiling as he cups her face and wipes away the tears. Holding them to her face, she asks in a breathy whisper, "How is this possible?"

Shrugging, Peren replies with the goofiest grin he can. "Magic?"

Bursting out in a laugh, she smiles and kisses him. Not wanting to tempt fate, she ignores the nagging feeling at the back of her mind.

Focusing on other things, she gets the tray off the stool, and they both enjoy lunch together. Once they finish, Norta snuggles in with him, and with a lingering kiss, they both drift off to sleep.

Norta jumps up in shock at the door banging open and Gizle's shout of "Norta, you are needed to help with lunch!"

She kisses Peren gently on the lips before rushing out of the room toward the kitchen.

Closing his eyes to go back to sleep, he is awoken by shouting and screams, catching snatches as they get closer. "Little liar! Get back here!" He feels the vibrations feet pounding on the stairs, then the feet pounding outside his room, with what sounds like giggles and squeals of laughter from Gizle with Norta screaming behind, "Wait till I get my hands on you!" Smirking at the joke Gizle must have played on Norta, he shakes his head fondly and falls back to sleep.

Norta wakes him up a couple of hours later when she sticks her head in. Smiling at him, she moves into the room, and they both have lunch. Leaving him to sleep, she goes back to her chores.

When Norta comes in with dinner, she sees Peren absent-mindedly scratching at his chest, then rushes over and slaps his hand away. "No scratching, how do you think it will heal if you scratch at it?"

Pouting, Peren grumbles, "Fine, whatever."

Smirking at a sulking Peren, Norta realises that he has feeling back in his chest. Thinking for a few seconds on how to tell him, she decides to be mischievous by poking him hard in the chest. Moving back with a wince, Peren reflexively says, "Ow." His hand moves to the spot she poked and rubs it. "Why did you do that?"

Confused as to why she is just sitting there looking at him expectantly, he opens his mouth to question her when it dawns on him. Breaking out in a silly grin, he begins touching his chest, marvelling at the feeling of it. They spend time poking him in the chest, Norta tickling him when he doesn't stop her in time. When the novelty runs out, they get comfortable and eat a hearty meal. Feeling full and lethargic, they snuggle in each other's arms, Peren savouring the feeling of Norta against his chest as they drift off to sleep late in the night.

They wake up with a start to the heavy pounding at his door. Torach's deep commanding voice pierces the quiet morning. *"You have had enough time together! Time to get to work, Norta! We all know he is going to be ok, so you don't have to spend so much time with him! Now get to work!!"* Hearing his heavy footsteps retreat, Norta and Peren exchange amused glances before bursting into uproarious laughter. Getting up, she shares a lingering kiss with him before she leaves.

Left alone, Peren, sick of doing nothing but lying and sleeping, starts experimenting with how to move himself in bed, eventually working out that he can get into a sitting position if he grabs his small clothes and drives his elbows into the mattress.

When Norta comes in with breakfast, she nearly drops the tray in shock. Sitting on the bed is Peren, smiling up at her smugly. Rushing over to the bed, she drops the tray onto the stool, nearly spilling the food. Looking at him incredulously, she asks, "How did you manage that? *Gizle*! Get in here now!"

Waving to get her attention, Peren explains, "Gizle didn't help me. No one did. I managed this all by myself."

Crossing her arms, Norta demands, "Well, then, prove it!"

Shrugging, Peren smirks at her and says, "Sure." Moving around so that he is lying back on the bed, he winks at her and, grabbing his small clothes, proceeds to pull himself into a sitting position. Looking up at her with a very self-satisfied grin, his face dares her to question it.

Staring down at him in amazement, her heart fills with pride at his resilience.

Seeing how she looks at him with pride lifts his spirits, making him more determined than ever to fully recover.

Finally remembering to have breakfast, they eat. Smiling at him, Norta comments, "You sure do eat a lot of food."

Going red in the face from this, Peren defends his increased appetite. "Most of my energy goes into repairing my body, so I need to eat more to produce more energy for my body..." His voice trails off as he realises that she is just teasing him.

Laughing harder, she adds, "Careful, you might start getting a little pudgy." Emphasizing this, she prods his stomach. Peren only sits there, giving her dirty looks.

After the meal, Norta hops back to work, leaving Peren to work out and impress her with his latest abilities. Coming back a couple of hours later, bringing a snack for him, she says, "Thought you might be hungry and needing the extra padding." She struggles to get the words out as she bursts into laughter. Peren's only reaction is to roll his eyes and glare at her. Finishing the snack, they cuddle for a few minutes before she leaves to continue with her chores.

A few days later, with Norta's help, Peren can move around and venture outside. The townsfolk cheer and slap him on the back upon seeing him up and moving again.

A little after two weeks of waking up, Peren finds himself standing on the edge of the roof, despite Norta's concerns that he needs more rest. Antsy with anticipation, he feels relief at being able to do something instead of being cooped-up in his bed. Determined to end the plague once and for all, he gets himself psyched-up. Focusing his thoughts on the task at hand, he enters a battle-ready state.

As the Spliganders approach, giving himself one final stretch, trying to loosen any stiffness in his body, Peren springs into action. Rolling off the roof and landing amidst the creatures, he dispatches them with skill and ferocity. Being careful not to let his pride get the best of him and the need to show off, he is able to keep his movements efficient. Hours pass as he fights tirelessly, finally driving the Spliganders back as dawn breaks.

Returning to his room, Peren cleans himself and his weapons before collapsing into bed, exhausted but content. He wakes to find Norta slipping into the room with a look of relief at seeing him alive and in bed. She puts the tray of food down and they share a passionate kiss before she joins him in bed, sharing breakfast together.

As Peren sits with Norta, eating the food she's brought him, he can't help but feel overwhelmed by his feelings for her. With each bite, he savours not only the taste of the food, but also the warmth of her presence. They linger together for a while after the meal, basking in each other's company until Norta must return to her duties, leaving Peren to drift off to sleep, breathing in the scent of her.

In the days that follow, Peren falls into a routine. The nights blend together as he fights the Spliganders. Getting only partial sleep throughout each day and fighting all night starts to take its toll, forcing him to fight more defensively. Norta observes the circles under his eyes getting darker, the way he drops off to sleep the moment he hops into bed, and the way he can't keep his eyes open during meals. No matter how she brings her concerns to him, he always waves them off.

Despite him hiding his otherworldly abilities, rumours crop up about his skills, alluding to him not being fully human. Despite quashing them whenever he overhears, he only finds that the rumours become more outlandish and fanciful.

Peren's first realisation of his limits comes when he collapses from exhaustion after finishing off the last Spligander one night. Hitting the ground stuns him as a wave of black unconsciousness sweeps through. Wincing, he claws his way to the surface of consciousness from the agony in his head, along with a very nice deep-purple bruised lump on his forehead. Though he feels relief at there being no open wounds, it still is very sensitive, serving as a stark reminder for him that even Elves have limitations as to what they can do.

The next night, as Peren gets ready, he yawns as Norta enters the room. Quickly turning away to hide it, he knows she will try and talk him out of working tonight. Worried over him trying to hide his true weariness, she attempts a different tack. Moving over to him, laying a hand on his arm and asks softly, "How are you feeling?"

Stunned by this question, Peren looks up and over to her, confusion flashing on his face before it disappears. Thinking that he just hid his yawn in time, he just nods before turning away and yawning again as he continues his preparations.

Continuing along this tack, Norta adds, "I would like to personally thank you for what you have done for this town." Moving so that she is hugging him from behind, planting a soft, lingering kiss on the nape of his neck, she murmurs, "You have made me so very proud of you. The whole town is in awe of you. No one will think less of you if you take a break." Trying to encourage him further, she says, "In fact, I bet they would even think better of you for knowing your limits."

Spinning on her, Peren opens his mouth to speak, but is instead forced to stifle a yawn. Seeing his absolute weariness etched into every feature on his face, her eyes widen at underestimating how weary he truly is, knowing with a certainty that he will not make it back if he goes out there tonight. Her features become stone in their determination. Her worry peaking, she panics and demands, "You are *not* going out there tonight! You will *rest* and recover from your lack of sleep until you are ready to face them again. You have only just recovered from your near-death experience."

His features harden as he stifles another yawn, turning back and continuing with his preparations. Seeing that he is too stubborn to stop for even one night and deciding that she needs to take action to protect him, she storms out of the room and heads downstairs. Her mind races, trying to come up with a solution to her problem.

As she makes Barrarack—a bitter beverage like coffee with a very distinct aftertaste—a plan forms in her mind. Working as fast as she can, hoping to be able to get to him before he barricades his door, she rushes the drink up to him.

Opening the door after she knocks, Peren eyes her suspiciously, asking gruffly, "What do you want?"

Holding out the mug, she says, "If nothing else, please drink this."

His eyes narrow suspiciously as he looks down at the mug.

"It's just Barrarack, to give you some extra energy." Seeing his inaction, she continues, "A peace offering. I don't like us arguing."

Glad at the opening for peace, he takes it and drinks it down quickly. As he hands back the empty cup and moves to close the door, a wave of dizziness washes over him, and his senses recognise the sleeping herb Norta used the drink to mask. Bewildered and feeling betrayed, he realises too late that she has drugged him. In his final moments of consciousness before succumbing to darkness, he feels a surge of anger towards her.

With a resounding thud, Peren collapses to the ground, with Norta unable to catch him in time.

Ensuring the shutters are secured, Norta seeks her father's help to move Peren to bed and strip him. As she watches him, a pang of guilt grips her heart. She wrings her hands at what she did, hoping desperately that he will understand her reasons and forgive her.

Peren wakes abruptly, his heart pounding and adrenaline coursing through his veins. He jumps out of bed, landing in a defensive pose, muscles tensed for confrontation. As the fog of sleep lifts, he realizes he's alone, and his face reddens as he slowly relaxes his stance. The memories of what Norta did flood back, his embarrassment turning to fuming anger at her blatant disregard for his decision by drugging him.

With clenched fists and gritted teeth, he swiftly dresses and storms downstairs, his steps heavy with furious intent. Spotting Norta sweeping the common room, he strides over, his grip tight as he seizes her arm, ignoring her cries of pain as he drags her to a secluded corner. Torach and Gizle move to intervene, but the look on Norta's face halts them in their tracks.

From the heavens, looking down on the scene that is about to be played out between Norta and Peren, Ryva, the Demigoddess of Wrath, decides to intervene. Thinking about who to pick as her temporary champion, she weighs up each one's reasons. Settling on Norta, she fills her with righteous wrath. Finished in her meddling, she sits back grinning and waits to see how this will play out.

Cornering Norta, Peren opens his mouth to speak, but his words falter as he meets her gaze. Gone is the gentle girl he knows; before him stands an otherworldly figure emanating an aura of wrath, her presence commanding and fearsome. It's as though a fearsome whirlwind swirls around her, her eyes blazing with an intensity that sends a shiver down his spine. He takes an involuntary step back, overwhelmed by her power.

Pressing forward, Norta takes a step forward for Peren's every step backward, his gaze wilting under the twin liquid amber fire orbs that pierce into his very soul. Norta, imbued with the wrathful nature of the Demigoddess Ryva, pokes him hard in the chest, emphasizing each word as she bites back in a venomous downright terrifying, otherworldly voice. "Don't you dare say anything unless it's to thank me and to apologise to me for your behaviour! I did it to protect you, and you know it! You were practically falling asleep on your feet."

Shocked at this wrathful version of Norta and seeing that he is now facing something otherworldly, he has no choice but to acquiesce and accept the public humiliation he has endured. Teeth gritting in humiliation, he gives in, knowing that defiance will only make it worse for him.

Storming up the stairs, his anger crackles like lightning as he slams his door shut with a resounding crash. Its echo reverberates through the room, mirroring the tumultuous whirlwind of emotions raging within him. As he paces around his chamber, his teeth audibly grind together, and his hands clench and unclench with each step. Deep down, he knows Norta was right to act, but the sting of humiliation from her defiance against his decision and being drugged gnaws at him relentlessly, fuelling his anger and confusion. Feeling suffocated within the room by the emotions swirling with him, and unable to find an escape, he hops down into the stable yard from the roof and practices with his dagger.

Calming down after feeling the celestial goddess of wrath leave her, Norta feels bad for humiliating Peren as she did. Wanting to fix the rift between them, she makes to go after him. As she takes a step forward, a hand grabs her arm, and her father's voice makes her pause. "Wait. He needs time. Let him be."

"But, father, I shouldn't have done that. I need to go and apologise."

"No. Once he calms down, he will come to you. You need to wait for that to happen because you did what you thought was best for him. Once he calms down and thinks it over, he will see the right of it."

"But..."

"No buts. Now, go and finish your chores."

Though she's frustrated with her father, Norta can see the sense in his words. Going back to her chores, she works vigorously, trying to push thoughts of Peren out of her head. Every time he does pop up in her thoughts, it leads her to feeling frustrated. Regardless of the chasm between them, she still makes his next meal, getting Gizle to bring it up to him. Despite her desire to do otherwise, her father's words resonate with her—Peren needs to come to her to make reparations, not the other way around.

In the stable yard, Peren spends hours practicing with the dagger, his thoughts consumed by the recent debacle with Norta. Fuming over what happened, he repeats to himself, *How could I have so easily given in to her?* Shaking his head in anger at himself, he resolves, *I will not let it end this way. She will be sorry.*

Gizle arrives at Peren's door, knocking repeatedly. Losing her patience, she starts to pound harder on the door, screaming at him to open the door.

Barely making out his name being called, Peren assumes its Norta, come to continue the tirade, and ignores her, feeling smug over his revenge of not being there.

Sick of trying, Gizle dumps the tray on the ground in front of the door, making a mess, then kicks the door in frustration and storms off.

With each passing day, Norta and Peren refusing to confront each other casts a stormy shadow over the inn. He refuses to come out of his room unless it's for training in the stable yard or killing the Spliganders.

Struggling not to drown in the tumultuous sea of emotions, Norta is not only torn between being angry and worried at him, but also her guilt over her role in steering their relationship into treacherous waters.

Still seething over how Norta humiliated him, Peren is unable to focus on taking down the Spliganders during their next confrontation. Despite his skill and determination, he is vulnerable to their surprise attack, resulting in a painful ordeal as they overwhelm him with their relentless assault.

His rage reaches a boiling point as he unleashes his fury upon the Spliganders, tearing them from his body with a primal ferocity. In his frenzied state, he inflicts grievous wounds upon himself as he fights back, refusing to yield to the overwhelming odds stacked against him. With each failed attempt to free himself, his resolve only strengthens, fuelled by his anger at himself.

With a scream of defiance echoing through the chaos, Peren summons every ounce of his remaining strength for one final push. Ignoring the pain and the unending barrage of the Spliganders, he manages to explode out from a mound of writhing creatures, sending them scattering in all directions, slamming into walls, windows, doors, and posts with force, most hitting with the sound of bones crunching.

As the dust settles, he stands amidst the aftermath, battered and lightheaded from blood loss, but defiant and ready to face whatever comes next. However, his respite is short-lived as the surviving Spliganders regroup, their snarls and bared teeth signalling their intent to resume their attack with renewed ferocity.

Peren's primal instincts take over, and he launches himself into the midst of the Spliganders, his wounds oozing blood as he unleashes his pent-up anger and frustration upon them. With adrenaline coursing through his veins, he moves with lightning speed, cutting down each Spligander that dares to approach him. The ferocity of his assault manages to keep them at bay, but he can feel his strength waning with every strike.

As the inky blackness of night gradually changes to gray, a sense of impending doom fills the air. The Spliganders, sensing dawn, begin to retreat, their sinister snarls fading like the echoes of a nightmare. Despite Peren's efforts and the blood on the ground, he finds his body failing him. Each wound inflicted upon him serves as a reminder of his mortality, showing his vulnerability against such relentless foes.

With all the determination he has left, he tries to stand, his muscles straining under his injuries. His strength wanes, his vision blurs, and he soon slips into unconsciousness. The darkness envelops him like a comforting shroud, offering respite from the torment of battle and the harshness of his thoughts.

Unbarring the door, oblivious to Peren being out on the street, Norta's stomach flips as she takes in the scene before her. Corpses of Spliganders lie everywhere, their forms twisted and gutted, painting a macabre scene. The air is thick with the nauseating stench of decay, overshadowed by the inky black blood that coats everything in sight.

It takes precious moments for her to register the chaos before her, her eyes finally settling on a mound that appears eerily human amidst the carnage. With a gut-wrenching cry, she rushes forward, her heart pounding in her chest as she cradles Peren's pale head against her chest, frantically wiping away the mingled blood from his face. Her cries of anguish reverberate through the town, echoing her disbelief and despair as she clings desperately to the hope that he might still be alive, despite the chilling certainty in her heart.

Between sobs, she screams into the air, *"No! No! You promised! You said he was the cure! How can he be dead now?!"* Her voice breaks into a stream of sobs, the weight of her grief crashing down upon her as she collapses into the arms of Gizle and Torach. They too are overcome by sorrow, their own tears mingling with Norta's as they hold her close amidst the sea of mostly black.

Shuffling over to the group, the Herb Mistress mutters under her breath about the stench and the disrespect for the elderly, grumbling about having to trudge through a sea of inky black blood. Bending her already-hunched back to take a closer look at Peren, she scoffs, "Bah! He'll live. Takes more than a little blood loss to kill one like him." Her words offer a glimmer of hope amidst the despair, though they're delivered in her usual cantankerous manner. Muttering under her breath how she came all the way over and he wasn't even dead, she explains further to the bewildered Norta, "You have a stubborn one there, missy. Even when he should just give up and die, he refuses. So, no, he ain't dead, but he will be if you don't take him in, clean and dress the wounds, and get some of that broth down his gullet to help replenish the blood." With a grumble about being roused so early, the Herb Mistress shuffles away, leaving Norta with a sliver of hope and the urgent task of tending to Peren's wounds before it's too late.

With the urgent assistance of her father and sister, she swiftly carries Peren into the inn, arranging tables to form a makeshift bed. Gizle hurries to fetch water while Torach, with a swift motion of his belt knife, strips Peren of his blood-soaked clothes, discarding them in a corner. Despite the stains on his skin, Norta wastes no time, her sense of urgency palpable as she retrieves her medical pack.

Returning to Peren's side, she finds Gizle already sponging

down his wounds, the water turning a murky shade as it washes away the blood. Overwhelmed by the sight of Peren's torn and battered form, Norta takes a moment to gather herself. With a deep breath to steel herself, she slips into her role as a healer with practised ease. Directing Gizle and Torach with precision, she begins the arduous task of stitching Peren's gaping wounds, her hands steady despite the gravity of the situation.

As the hours pass, Norta works tirelessly, methodically tending to each injury with care and expertise. With each stitch, she fights to stem the flow of blood, her determination unwavering.

Finally, after what feels like an eternity, she completes her task, the last of Peren's wounds carefully closed. With a sense of relief washing over her, she gently administers the nutrient-rich broth, watching closely as Peren swallows it down, a glimmer of hope shining through the darkness that surrounds them.

As time passes, Norta diligently tends to Peren, ensuring he receives nourishment to aid in his recovery. With each feeding, she observes the gradual return of colour to his body, a tangible sign of his healing. Yet, amidst the relief, her brain finally starts to worry at a thought she has avoided till now: How can he heal so rapidly? The question gnaws at her, refusing to be ignored, despite her attempts to push it aside.

When Peren finally opens his eyes after days of unconsciousness, he finds them crusted shut. Frustration and self-directed anger surge within him as he struggles to clear his vision. He berates himself for his weakness. *No wonder she thinks she runs the show.* He doesn't want to rely on Norta's aid when he should be standing strong and independent. Determination sets his jaw as he vows to become the man she deserves, no longer content to be seen as a mere burden in her eyes.

Looking up as Norta enters the room, Peren's initial

instinct is to retreat, his face draining of colour at the sight of her. Attempting to rise from the bed, he finds himself gently but firmly held in place by her touch, her presence weighing heavily on him. With a resigned sigh, knowing that she wants to hash this out, he looks up at her expectantly.

Knowing that Peren won't say anything, she says, "We need to talk. This can't go on without us talking about it." Forced to agree, he relents to her demand to talk, noticing the bowl she carries in her other hand for the first time. Slipping back into bed, he takes the bowl and spoon from her, choosing to eat in sullen silence instead of facing the impending confrontation head-on.

Losing some of the respect she has for him as he chooses to avoid this confrontation and sick of waiting on him to answer, she asks, "Why won't you say anything?"

"You're the one who wanted to talk!"

"Come on, Peren, we need to sort this out." Sighing in frustration, she continues, "You do know that what I did was for the best, right?"

Staring at her incredulously, he spits out, "What?! How can you say that?! You drugged me! You should be apologising to me for what you did! You disrespected my decision and humiliated me in public!"

Eyes widening in shock, Norta snaps back, "You're only mad because you were humiliated! You were going to humiliate me!"

Shocked at the truth of her words, Peren sputters for a few moments, opening and closing his mouth. Refusing to let her get the upper hand, he repeats, "But you *drugged* me!"

"Because you were being stupid!"

"You don't drug people because you think they are stupid, and besides, I'm not stupid!"

"Yes, you are, and I don't drug all the stupid ones, just your stupid self!"

Going red in the face, Peren, refusing to give in, responds, "If I'm stupid, what does that make you?"

"Crazy, apparently!" Holding up her hand, Norta takes a deep breath to calm down. "This isn't getting us anywhere. Look, I am sorry for what I did; it was wrong, and it wasn't fair to you." Feeling the need to justify, she adds, "But you gave me no choice! You wouldn't listen to reason! I don't want to ever lose you!" Tears fill her eyes and her face goes red as she realises she just voiced her feelings.

Stunned at her reaction, Peren's anger disappears in an instant. *She cares for me!* Heart swelling in happiness, he thinks, *She wants to protect me, just like I have been with her.* Realising that she has been this way for some time, he feels a moment of anger at himself. *So much for being highly perceptive!* Focusing back on the present, feeling more determined, he vows, *I need to be more careful and get back to her safely. I will not let her down again!*

Standing up, he holds out his hands to her. Looking up at him, confused, she hesitantly reaches out and grabs them. Pulling her into a tight hug, Peren whispers into her ear, "I am so sorry. I should have seen it from your perspective. You were only trying to protect me." Pressing her closer to him, his voice catches as he says, "I don't ever want to lose you either."

They hold each other tightly for several moments; Norta presses her head against his warm and strong chest as he gently rests his cheek on her head as the burden of their feelings lift. Murmuring against his chest, Norta's voice breaks the silence. "I'm sorry."

Tearing up at how he hurt her, Peren whispers into her lovely, soft auburn hair, "I'm sorry too."

Norta presses a kiss against his chest as Peren presses one against the top of her head, both feeling nothing but relief and love for each other.

Parting, Peren looks down into her eyes. Coming to a decision, he says, "We cannot have a repeat of this, so what if we confronted each other in private? I will listen to you when you have something to say and will discuss my decisions with you whenever possible."

Lips quirking into a small smile, Norta just nods. Reaching up onto her toes, she kisses him. Feeling the weight of the world lift, Peren kisses her back.

As the days go by, Peren begins to realise that listening and relying on Norta is not a weakness. While he doesn't eliminate as many threats as he did during his outburst, the number of Spliganders dwindles noticeably until one night when they stop coming altogether. He descends from the roof into the common room and announces that the rodents are gone, much to the amazement and relief of the family.

Gizle is the first to recover from the shock, her joy and relief bursting forth in an excited scream. She rushes to the door and, without hesitation, unbars it, darting into the street to dance and shout in happiness.

Norta's immediate impulse is to rush out into the street to bring Gizle safely back inside, but a restraining hand from Peren and his reassuring look help to calm her.

In the home across the street, a man huddles with his family. Identifying the screams as one of the girls from the inn—whom his own children have played with—he takes a deep breath, refusing to let her die without helping. He rushes out the door, despite the cries of protests from his own family. As Gizle's elation pierces the air, the brave man rushes into the street wielding a cudgel and sweeps her up into his arms, carrying her away, prompting alarm from the shocked girl.

However, as they near the threshold of his home, the silence on the street and the change in Gizle's cries finally register with him. She manages to wriggle out of his grip and kick him hard on the shin before rushing back to her father.

Before Torach can react to this, Peren puts a restraining arm on him, indicating that he should look after his own daughter and that Peren will go and sort this out. Breathing slowly in anger, the innkeeper gives a curt nod to Peren.

Sensing that the man meant no harm, but was merely trying to protect Gizle, Peren approaches him with open hands in a gesture of peace. As he reaches the man, who is rubbing his shin from the impact of Gizle's shoe, he inquires gently, "Were you only trying to protect her?" With a nod from the man, Peren acknowledges his intention and then heads back to inform Torach of the exchange.

The weary group heads inside, exhaustion settling over them like a heavy blanket after the night's excitement. Norta follows Peren up to his room, and they collapse onto the bed in each other's arms, drifting off to a peaceful sleep, too tired to celebrate further.

FIVE

THE CAVE OF GHOSTS

The next day, word that the infestation has come to an end spreads like wildfire through Comtun, and Peren finds himself swarmed by the entire town. Despite his protests, they lift him onto their shoulders and parade him through the streets in jubilation. As they return to the inn, the crowd surges inside, catching Norta, Gizle, and Torach off-guard with the celebration. Initial concern quickly gives way to amusement as they witness the joyous spectacle.

The three of them scramble to accommodate the large group, serving food and drinks amidst the lively atmosphere. Despite sending Peren angry glares from the amount of people overrunning his inn, Torach's eyes also betray his excitement over the unexpected boon to their business. Amongst the festivities, Norta refills Peren's drink as he murmurs in protest about not finishing his contract yet. Overhearing this, she manages to catch his eye. Shaking her head, she urges him to let them celebrate.

Taking Norta's cue, Peren allows himself to be swept up in the joy of the moment, temporarily setting aside his worries.

When the sun begins to set as evening approaches, the more cautious members of the group begin to trickle away, heading back to their homes to secure them against any potential threats. Realizing the lateness of the hour, Peren rises unsteadily from his seat, weaving between tables towards the front door.

Norta manages to catch him before he stumbles, her steady hand offering support as he mumbles about the mayor and destroying some queen. Sensing his fatigue, she wraps an arm around him, guiding him gently. With a sigh of resignation, Peren collapses into her arms, surrendering to the embrace of unconsciousness.

Waking up with a start the next morning, Peren winces in agony as a sense of déjà vu washes over him, transporting him back to the morning that began this entire journey. However, there are a couple of notable differences: he's not alone in bed, and he's not in his room back at the guild, but at the Inn of the Eyeless Boar.

Stirring with his movements, Norta opens her eyes and looks up at him. Seeing him wince, she knows he has one hell of a hangover. The look on his face is so comical, a chuckle escapes her lips. Looking at her, he winces from the noise, causing her to laugh at him. When he tries to glare at her, which only serves to make him wince harder, adding to his headache, she is unable to stop her laughing, despite feeling bad for him.

Suppressing the urge to exacerbate his suffering, she whispers—though to Peren it's like she is screaming in his ear— "This is what happens when people overindulge."

Sad to be getting up, smirking knowingly at him, Norta heads down to prepare a hangover cure passed down from her mother for such occasions. Returning with the vile concoction, she helps Peren drink it down, patiently waiting for it to clear his mind before assisting him to his feet.

They shuffle into the common room as Peren's mind

gradually emerges from the fog. Seating him down, Norta serves them breakfast. As Peren eats, the fog in his mind dissipates further, and a ghost of a memory resurfaces—one involving the mayor and a queen.

Cursing himself, Peren rushes out just as Norta returns from the kitchen, looking confused at his hurried departure as he makes his way to the mayor's office.

The meeting with Mayor Jornstawn proves to be another uncomfortable and awkward conversation. Peren knows that he hasn't eradicated all the Spliganders, and he understands that the only true way to protect Comtun is to ensure that every one of them, including their queen, is eliminated.

Laying a map out on the desk, the mayor sits back down. Almost unable to cross his arms over his girthy body, he looks at Peren and demands, "Well? What now? You have your precious map."

Poring over the map, Peren states, "I am looking for a cave system that could house the entire colony of Spliganders. Including their queen."

Confused, the mayor asks, "The queen?"

Looking at him straight in the eye, enjoying having the upper hand for once, Peren says condescendingly, "Yes. You see, without its queen, a colony dies, but if you don't kill the queen, you will only delay them repopulating and coming back." When he sees the mayor looking worried, he continues, "It is said that the queen is so big that mountains look like they are specks." He smiles to himself as the mayor's face drains of its colour.

Anxious at the thought of the Spliganders returning, the mayor asks frantically, "So how do we find the queen, then?"

"The queen is said to live in a large cavern deep underground. Do you know of any cave systems that would have a large cavern?"

The mayor points with a shaky finger to three locations on the map. One to the southwest, one to the south, and one to the southeast. After scrutinizing the maps more closely and deducing the most likely route the Spliganders would take, Peren concludes that the southwestern caves are the most probable location for their nest. "I think the caves to the southwest would be the ones to check out first. They are most likely."

The mayor loses even more colour. Looking for his seat, only to realise that he is sitting, he collapses back, taking several minutes to recover from his fright.

Beckoning Peren out of the room, the scribe explains as they head to the exit, "That's where the ghost of old Kith resides, the mayor's uncle. One day, he was seen heading that way and never returned." A shiver runs down the scribe's spine as he continues, "We sent out a search party, and as they neared the caves, there was a horrible wailing. The wailing only increased as they moved closer to the cave."

Peren's scepticism flares at the revelation of a ghost inhabiting the cave. While ghosts are indeed real, the notion that it could be the spirit of old Kith feels tenuous at best.

Returning to the inn, his mind races with potential attack strategies, each one clouded by uncertainty without firsthand knowledge of the terrain. Despite his inner doubts, he resolves to investigate the southwestern caves, a sense of duty propelling him forward.

As he heads out the door towards the stables, Norta grabs his arm. Despite his protests, she drags him back to have lunch, much to the amusement of all the other patrons, which adds to his embarrassment, despite secretly enjoying her attention. Sitting down opposite him as he munches on the food, she demands, "And where do you think you're going?"

He looks up at her, confused for a minute, before

disjointed thoughts tumble out of his mouth. "Didn't I tell you? The queen? Southwestern caves?" Frowning in confusion, her eyes widen, and she shakes her head. Ordering his thoughts before spilling more nonsense, Peren clarifies. "With the Spliganders, there is a queen. Without destroying the queen, you are only delaying the rodents from coming back. After poring over the maps with the mayor, I have decided to check out the southwestern caves first, as they are most likely where the queen is hiding."

As Norta opens her mouth to say no, the memory of when she was younger comes to mind—that someone will cure the plague and soul join with her. Knowing in her heart of hearts that the man sitting opposite her must be that prophesied saviour, she takes a deep breath, knowing that he must do this, and nods in permission. Taking his hand in both of hers, she says, "Please, be careful. I can't lose you now."

Nodding solemnly, Peren replies, "I promise to be careful." Smiling at her and lifting her chin with his other hand, he adds, "Don't you know by now? I am indestructible!"

Instead of this reassuring Norta, her face starts to pale, and her eyes widen in worry. Realizing his mistake, he takes her hands in his and, looking deep into her endless, inviting pools of amber, struggling not to dive in, he amends his statement. "Sorry, that was meant to be encouraging." Looking deeper and more serious into her eyes, he adds, "I promise to be careful. I *will* come back to you in one piece."

Despite the knot in her stomach that refuses to untangle, she nods and puts on a brave face. Relaxing, Peren feels better, thinking that he managed to calm her down. Holding her hand, he finishes his lunch, revelling in the feel of her hand in his.

As Peren enters the stables, Mercy nickers in greeting. He

mimics her as he moves up to her stall, giving her a good rub on the head and some sugar cubes. As he saddles her, the weight of the impending task settles upon his shoulders. Norta's hurried approach with a small pouch of food for his journey ahead adds a bittersweet urgency to the moment as they share a deep kiss, the sweetness of their affection and parting lips masking the uncertainty of what lies ahead.

Approaching the southwestern caves a short while later, Peren is struck silent by their towering presence. Each looming shadow cast by the morning sun whispers tales of danger and mystery, sending a chill down his spine that even Mercy's steadfast presence can't dispel.

Dismounting near the yawning entrance, Peren's heart beats in sync with the darkness that seems to pulse within. His elvish senses strain against the impenetrable void, failing to discern any answers lurking beyond.

Investigating the entrance, he realises that he has no choice but to venture in either blind or with the aid of a torch. He sighs in frustration at his lack of preparation. Determined to exhaust all options, he searches the surrounding area for any other possible points of entry. Hours pass fruitlessly, and as the sun nears late-afternoon, he finds solace in the snack Norta packed for him.

Sitting in the shade, memories of shared meals with Norta flood his mind, each bite a bittersweet reminder of her absence. Finishing his snack, frustration gnaws at him as he continues his reconnaissance, the absence of a torch a constant reminder of his oversight.

As the sun bids its final farewell, Peren, feeling frustrated, reluctantly concedes that there are no other viable points of entry. Realising that the sun is going down, he rushes over to Mercy, and they both race back to the inn. Sliding off her as they enter the stables, Peren throws the reins to the stable boy, apologising for the lateness of the hour, then rushing inside so he can prepare for the night's attack. Closing the door and barricading it, he pauses as he remembers that the Spliganders aren't coming.

Shaking his head as he sighs in a mixture of relief and frustration at his own hastiness, Peren descends the stairs, his face slightly flushed with embarrassment. Entering the common room cautiously, he's met with Norta's graceful approach.

When she reaches up and kisses him on the lips, he is startled at such a public proclamation of their love, but relaxing into it and returning it after recovering moments later. They kiss with passion, Norta relieved that he's returned safe and sound. Pulling apart, she leads him by the hand to a corner table so there will be some more privacy, shooting her father a defiant glare when he frowns at her disapprovingly.

Seating him, Norta scurries off and returns with a plate piled high with tantalizing treats. She playfully slaps his hand away when he tries to sneak a bite before she sits down, her disapproving expression quickly giving way to shared laughter as they relax.

After Peren shares a beautiful meal with Norta, they part ways for the rest of the evening. Norta heads back to work, to the annoyed relief of both her sister and father, and Peren heads to his room to relax and enjoy the quiet night.

Joining him much later, Norta comes in like a whisper, hoping to surprise him, sneaking up on him as he stares out the window. "Evening, Norta," he says without turning to her, making her yelp in shock. She looks up at him indignantly, huffing as she sees his shoulders shake with laughter, demanding, "How in the hells did you hear me? I was so silent!"

Reaching out and pulling her into a hug with a deep kiss, Peren answers, "I am just that good."

Opening her mouth to demand an actual answer, she is silenced by another deep and sensual kiss. Pulling her to bed with him, Peren hopes to distract her so she doesn't demand a straight answer. They both drift into a deep, restful sleep, their bodies entwined in quiet comfort.

As the night wears on, Peren's instincts suddenly kick in. Heart racing and adrenaline pumping, he instinctively springs out of bed, weapon in hand, his mind racing to catch up with his body as he quickly readies to face whatever threat lurks outside.

Throwing open the shutters and leaping onto the roof, he's met not with cries of fear from the inhabitants, but with laughter and jubilation. Relief floods through him, mingled with a tinge of embarrassment for his overreaction. With a sheepish grin, he moves back into the room, slipping under the covers beside Norta, who stirs from her slumber. Wrapping her in his arms, they both drift back into the soothing embrace of sleep, the sounds of revelry outside now a comforting backdrop to their peaceful night.

The following morning, Peren rises early and enjoys a hearty breakfast before setting off on Mercy with Norta's lunch packed in one of his saddlebags. Despite his increased familiarity with the area, he is still struck by the ominous shadows cast by the morning sun, which evoke a sense of danger and mystery that send shivers down his spine once more.

Arriving at the entrance of the cave, he feels a surge of nervous energy as he prepares for his descent. Despite his elven senses, the darkness within the cave is impenetrable, leaving him with a queasy feeling in the pit of his stomach.

After securely tethering Mercy out of the way, Peren returns to the cave entrance with a torch and provisions, steeling himself for the unknown. His frustration builds as he struggles to light the torch, taking a deep breath, steadying himself before stepping into the void.

As he steps into the cave, he is instantly consumed by a void, an utter lack of sensation. Sight, sound, touch, even the air around him—everything vanishes in an overwhelming sense of emptiness. Disoriented and terrified, he stumbles, collapsing to the ground. The torch slips from his grasp, sputtering angrily in the darkness. Crawling toward the flickering flame, he's driven by a desperate fear that the Demigod Phyraen might reclaim his fire if he doesn't reach it in time.

Scurrying over on all fours, he grabs the torch just as it threatens to extinguish, managing to coax it back to life in the nick of time. Rising slowly into a crouch, he notes the torch is emitting such a feeble glow it barely seems to work. Creeping forward cautiously, his senses are heightened, trying but failing to catch any bit of sensory information.

Crossing the barrier, he is unprepared for the sudden overwhelming deluge of stimuli. As he falls to the ground, his scream is swallowed by the crushing wave of sensations that crashes over him, a torrent so intense it obliterates all sense of self. Every nerve in his body fires at once, drowning him in a maelstrom of pain—blistering heat, bone-chilling cold, blinding light, and suffocating darkness are all at war within him. The onslaught is so fierce that his mind can't process it; it's pure, raw agony, beyond anything a human could survive. Clutching his head, he writhes on the ground, his body convulsing as if it might tear itself apart under the strain.

Each moment stretches into an eternity of torment, until finally, mercifully, his consciousness shatters, sparing him from the unbearable anguish.

When he finally comes to, Peren's nerves still feel like they're on fire, though the intensity has diminished as his body begins to recover from the searing overload. Struggling to his feet, he gropes around in the void of pure black, unable to see. Eventually, he finds the torch. Gritting his teeth in frustration at the Demigod Phyraen for his tricks, he works on trying to light it.

After what feels like aeons, the torch splutters into a bright and powerful flame, blinding Peren as he closes his eyes too slowly to preserve his night vision. When the spots finally clear from his vision, he is amazed at the sheer size of the cavern.

Closing his mouth after an eternity, he focuses on the task at hand. A sigh escapes his lips as he realises that not only has he been unconscious for hours, but he will need to endure another trek through that empty void when he leaves shortly. Frustrated at his lack of progress, he takes a deep breath and focuses on getting back before dusk. If caught here after dark, he will undoubtedly die, especially if his senses are assaulted again. Though he wants to believe he can withstand it a second time, the chance of another overload is too great a risk.

Turning around with a determined look set on his face, Peren purposefully strides forward into the void. Before he is even completely inside, the shock of the complete loss of sensory information causes him to stumble. Managing not to fall and drop the torch this time, he creeps forward cautiously. Despite preparing himself for the overwhelming onslaught of stimuli upon exiting the void, he collapses to the ground in agony again, only a faint moan escaping his lips before he loses consciousness.

Waking up some time later, Peren winces as the pain slowly recedes. He focuses and realizes, belatedly, that the sun is saying its goodbyes before setting completely. Shaking his head to clear it, he leaps to his feet and rushes over to Mercy. When he jumps into the saddle, Mercy, sensing her master's excitement, bolts off toward the town.

SIX

THE FIELD OF STARS

When Peren arrives at the Eyeless Boar well past nightfall, Norta rushes out into the stabling yard, her embrace nearly knocking him off-balance as she showers him with kisses, feeling nothing but relief that he returned in one piece. After ensuring his well-being, she delivers a swift, stinging slap.

Though the blow isn't enough to topple Peren, he staggers under the unexpected assault. His hand instinctively rises to his cheek as he stares at Norta, shocked.

With her fists planted firmly on her hips, she stares him down, her voice tight with suppressed fury as she demands, "You were supposed to be back *hours* ago! What happened?"

Watching from behind a hay bale, the stablehand cowers, feeling sorry for Master Peren after all he has done for the town. Knowing better than to interrupt, he sneaks out as quietly as he can, whispering an apology to Mercy for leaving her saddled.

Confused at the sudden change in Norta, Peren stutters, "What? What are you talking about?"

She struts up to him, poking him hard in the chest as she raises her voice incredulously. *"What! Am! I! Talking! About?!"* Heat emanating from her flushed cheeks, she enlightens him. *"You were meant to be back hours ago!"*

Rooted to the spot, Peren is flabbergasted at her reaction, his mouth opening and closing, unable to form any words, struggling to comprehend her behaviour.

Taking this as an act of defiance, Norta steps in close and continues, *"Do you have any idea how I felt when you didn't come back on time?"*

Focusing on what she is saying for the first time, Peren demands, "What time? We never talked about a time that I had to be back by."

Further angered at his reply, she shouts, *"I shouldn't need to!"*

Peren stands his ground, "Yes you do! I can't read your mind; I need you to tell me what you need."

Norta glares at him, her voice shaking. "Fine! If you need me to spell it out—" Words tumble out as she rushes on. "We both agreed that you will be more careful and then, the next day. *The! Next! Day!* You rush off to the mayor's office so you can fight the queen! You didn't even stop to discuss it with me! You just went off on your own, being the usual thick-headed idiot you are!"

Peren stands there gawping for a few moments. Shocked at her response, thinking that she is overreacting, he asks, "Is this what you're mad about? You're mad that I went to fulfill the contract?"

Dumbfounded at his flippant response, her eyes widen, "What?! *No!* I am mad that you didn't even *think* to tell me about it! That you just went on doing what you do without a thought about how I feel!" She points sharply to herself, her finger trembling as a tear runs down her left cheek.

Defending himself, Peren replies, "You know that I am fulfilling the contract. You knew what that entailed. I didn't need to tell you about it before, so why should I now? And besides"—he holds his finger up, stalling Norta to allow himself to continue—"I am thinking about you." Looking at her pointedly before spreading his hands out, he says, "About this town! I am doing this *for* you! To protect you!"

Exasperated, Norta bites back, "What is the point of being protected when it comes at the cost of losing you? When you're out there protecting us, who will protect you?! Do you not know what it means when you *leave* and don't come back for hours on end? What it does to me?" Holding up her hand, silencing Peren, she adds, "Yes, you took on this contract and have been able to do what no one else has. But! Did you even think about the cleanup?"

She gasps in frustration when he interrupts her. "Are you upset about having to clean up the Spliganders?"

"No! You meathead! You! When *you* are injured and need to be nursed back to health! Most of the time, not knowing if you will *survive* the night!" Another tear escapes her left eye, despite her fighting back the tsunami of emotions that threatens to break free.

Stunned, Peren just stands there for a few moments, unsure of what to say to that.

Not willing to leave the silence stretch without getting everything off her chest, Norta continues, "We all get how *amazing* you are, but you forget that *some* of us care more about *you* than what you can do!"

Latching onto something, anything, Peren snaps, "You're just jealous of how popular I am! You have been here all your life, and yet no one knows who you are. I come in and within weeks, I am the most popular in all Comtun! You can't stand that I can protect your home better than you!"

They both stand there, panting and red in the face, wielding their words like swords—lunge, parry, riposte.

Spluttering with laughter, Norta fires back. "You think that I would care about that? You think I am interested in popularity? You really don't know me at all then! I *care* about what *happens* to you, Peren! Not the publicity. You can have all the fame you want! I just want a loving and caring man to share my life with!" Speaking softly, she adds, "I wanted to spend it with you." Sighing and slumping in resignation, she says, "I can see I was wrong. It certainly isn't you." Turning on her heel, she heads to the exit of the yard.

Peren stands there shocked for a few moments, thoughts flying through his mind faster than ever before, a war going on between letting her go and trying to stop her.

Reaching the threshold, Norta feels a level of disappointment, wishing deep down that he would stop her, but hating herself for believing in a stupid foretelling and feeling foolish for falling for such an ambiguous forecast. *A cure? Hah!*

Watching as she reaches the threshold, Peren feels like his heart has been torn from his body, like a black hole has opened and swallowed all the good in his life. A feeling of emptiness sets in, like life has been leeched of all its colour. A future flashes before his eyes—one without Norta in it: a world where life is meaningless to him and he no longer feels any happiness, living from one bed to the next as he fulfills the guilds contracts, not caring if he succeeded or failed, a mindless husk.

Refusing to accept this future, Peren reaches out, grabs Norta by the arm, and turns her around. It's as if all the joys and colours that just disappeared come back in an instant. Knowing that he doesn't ever want to live without her, he pulls her in and kisses her deeply on her mouth.

Shocked, she squirms as she tries to fight him off. Finally pushing him away, she opens her mouth to reprimand him.

Putting a finger against her lips, words burst from Peren's

mouth. "I am sorry. I was being petty. I should have been more considerate and discussed things with you. You are more important to me than anything in the world. You are all that's good and bright in my life. I refuse to lose that. You are the best thing that has happened to me." He adds softly, "Please don't leave me."

Standing there stunned at his confession, Norta's mouth works, but no words come out. With tears running down her cheeks and looking up into his face through her blurred vision, she sees the Peren she fell in love with. Unable to make a sound, she just hugs him and holds him tight as she lets the tears fall and sobs into his chest.

Peren's eyes tear up at seeing the look on her face as she takes in his words. When she hugs him tight and begins to sob, he loses control of his emotions and sobs into her hair.

Calming down some time later, they are pulled back into reality when Mercy whickers and stamps her foot impatiently at still being saddled. Not wanting to spend any more time in the stables, Peren looks down at Norta, and an idea forms. Reaching out and taking hold of Mercy's reins, he leads them both out of the stable.

Mounting Mercy, he helps Norta into the saddle in front of him, his arms wrapped around her waist as he holds onto the reins. Forced to push through the small crowd at the entrance to the stable yard, both of their faces flush with embarrassment, as people have clearly gathered to hear them argue.

A few of the gathered crowd slink back, embarrassed at being caught eavesdropping. Others reach up to touch their hero, admiring him and his horse. Each touch is a reminder of who overheard his confessions to Norta, making his cheeks bright red.

As they head further towards the edge of town, the noise

of the celebrations fades, allowing them to hear the rhythmic clacks of Mercy's shoes echoing off the cobblestones.

Relieved by the cloudless sky tonight, Peren is grateful for the full moon illuminating the night, allowing him to see as clearly as a human as they head into the fields outside of town.

Dismounting, he turns and helps Norta down. While Mercy grazes on the long grass, Peren pulls some blankets from the saddlebags. Handing them to Norta, he turns back to Mercy and rubs her down after he removes the saddle.

Moving a short distance away, Norta shakes out and lays the blankets down. Sitting on them, she watches how Peren's hand moves with familiarity, reminding her that being alone with Mercy had been his life before he ever stepped foot in Comtun. Wondering what that life was like, the challenges he faced, she realises that she doesn't know anything about his past.

She watches as Peren walks over to join her, settling down on the blanket. They gaze at each other silently, a soft smile on both their lips. Peren opens his mouth and begins first. "I cannot read your thoughts or subtle hints; I need you to speak them to me. If we are to be together, we need to communicate more openly."

Nodding, Norta adds, "I agree. There needs to be more discussion around things. I am so terrified of you going off to the caves." Shuddering as a cold chill travels down her spine, she says, "I worry that Old Kith will take you from me or the Spliganders. You said the queen is huge? How will you ever hope to defeat her?"

Taking her hands in his, Peren looks deeply into her eyes, "Firstly, I doubt that old Kith's ghost is still there. Secondly, I have managed to survive the Spliganders. And I will continue to do so."

Scoffing at his dismissal, she replies, "Only barely. If it wasn't for me, you wouldn't be here."

Grabbing her chin and making her look into his eyes, Peren says, "I will be forever indebted to you for what you have done for me." Looking away, she blushes at his words. He reaches out and strokes her cheek, continuing, "I *will* come back, Norta. I always have. I will never leave you alone in this world." Their eyes meet and Norta sees the conviction in his gaze.

A tear runs down her cheek as she confesses, "You aren't invincible. You *can* die. I don't think I can bear it if you do."

Feeling his heart break, he reaches out and wipes the tear away. Looking intently into her eyes, he states emphatically, "I know I am not invincible." Smiling and trying to lighten the mood, he adds, "Besides, I have you to bring me back if I need."

As she glares at him fiercely, she snaps, "No! You are not to make a joke out of this! I can't keep bringing you back if you are going to do stupid things. I can't take it. I... I don't have powers to bring you back, Peren. I can't bear losing you like this over and over!"

Dropping his smile, Peren squeezes her hand softly. "I'm sorry. I was just trying to lighten the mood. I will be careful." Snorting at him, Norta doesn't believe a word he says. Peren emphasises his point. "I *promise* I will be careful. No unnecessary risks."

Looking deep into his eyes, hers narrow suspiciously as she asks, "What would be considered as *necessary* risks?"

Mind racing, Peren flounders. "You know, ones that are necessary."

Moving so that she is kneeling right in front of him, looking him directly in the eyes, Norta presses. "Go on. Tell me what you deem as a necessary risk."

Mouth moving to try and catch up to his mind, Peren tries to placate her. "Well, for one, ensuring that the Spliganders don't come back." Wilting under her glare, he hastily adds, "You know. Ones that..." He feels himself becoming fidgety under her scrutiny. "Ones that don't lead to my death?"

Feeling that he has gotten the message, Norta nods. Peren heaves a sigh of relief that she is no longer interrogating him.

His heart lightens when he sees her smiling. Frustrated at how easily she affects his moods, he takes a deep breath. "I know that what I do is unfamiliar for you. It isn't easy, but I need you to understand and accept that this is how my life is. I need you to be there with me. I don't want to do it on my own anymore."

Nodding, Norta replies, "I know. It will just take some time to adjust. Just know that…" Looking deeply into his eyes, lacing her fingers through his, she continues, "I will never stop worrying about you."

Relieved that the air is cleared between them, Peren feels the tension dissipate. Relaxing visibly, he leans in, and as he tries to kiss her, she moves out of his reach.

Slowly opening his eyes, confused, Peren sees the look on Norta's face. Sitting back, he eyes her with concern.

"There are a couple of other things that I want to ask you."

A flicker of fear flashes in Peren's eyes, and despite how quick it disappears, Norta sees it. Masking the trembling he feels inside, he leans back on his hands as he looks at her enquiringly.

Taking a deep breath, she asks, "Where are you from? Who are your parents? Where did you grow up? Where are you travelling to?"

Eyes widening at the number of questions spilling from her mouth, Peren interrupts. "Whoa, slow down. I can only answer one at a time." Giving himself extra time to think of an answer that would satisfy her, he asks, "What was the first question?"

It spills out of her mouth in a rush. "Where are you from?" She leans forward in anticipation for the answer.

Thinking over the span of his short life, he fights to keep his mouth from smiling at the fond memories. Forcing his face into a solemn look, he answers, "I am from lots of different places. The first place I remember is Tharon. But have drifted from place to place for many years."

Norta's face pales at the name. Everyone knows the name of the place in the corrupted wastelands—how it's a free for all and the most lawless place on the continent. Looking up at him in disbelief, she asks softly, "Tharon?"

Nodding, Peren answers, "Tharon."

Feeling sick to her stomach, she reaches out a hand and, caressing his face, whispers, "I am so sorry. The stories?"

"Tame compared to what actually happens there."

Tears well in her eyes as she tries to imagine the horrors that he would have seen and been subjected to. She reaches out and squeezes his hand gently, choking out past the lump in her throat, "I am so sorry you had to go through that." Her jaw drops as he looks back at her with conflict and sadness in his eyes. "You are still going through it?"

Nodding hesitantly, Peren feels nauseous from lying so deeply to her, knowing he got out many, many years ago. "You've heard the stories of how people get sold for slavery?"

When she nods hesitantly, he feels like he is being stabbed in the heart, each look of horror and pity another thrust of the knife. He has never hated the orders to keep quiet about who he really is more than he does in this moment. For the first time in a long time, he truly hates who he is. As he opens his mouth to tell her the truth, memories come flooding back from the last time he confided to a close friend too quickly.

Her eyes widen in horror, her hands tightening around his as anguished tears start to fall down her cheeks, adding to the guilt he feels. "Are you travelling at the orders of your master?"

Thinking ahead to the possible outcomes, he decides that lying is the safest option for her and her family. If the mayor ever got wind or any proof of who he really is, then the whole town wouldn't just go after him, but Norta and her family too. Realising the risk Marizbeth is taking by having this knowledge only heightens his respect for her.

Nodding, he says, "I am on this final quest for him, then I am done. I won't have to do anything more for him."

Relieved, Norta breathes again. "Can I ask what this quest is?"

Shaking his head, he says, "I am forbidden to divulge any information about this quest to anyone. I am sorry."

Norta smiles through her tears and shakes her head. "I understand."

Still resenting himself for the lies, he decides to offer up some truth. "I never knew my parents. They were killed when I was very little."

Her heart breaks further as she imagines how they might have died at Tharon, leaving Peren to fend for himself for so many years, all alone in a cruel place. Tears stream down her face as she imagines the cruelty that he would have had to endure for so many years.

Looking up, she sees the smile Peren offers her. She marvels at how strong and resilient he must be to smile even when he has seen the worst in so many people for so long.

Wrapping her in his arms, Peren holds her tight as she is wracked with sobs, grieving for the boy who had no choice but to make himself strong. When she finally calms down, Norta looks at him with her tear-stained cheeks and reaches up. Caressing his beautiful face with her hand, she pulls him to her before kissing him tenderly.

Caught off-guard by her actions, Peren stiffens. Gasping for breath, he is suddenly overwhelmed with emotions he hasn't faced in many years.

Norta's chest tightens as she watches a tear trickle down his face, then gently kisses it away, the salty texture searing into her memory. Slowly, lovingly, she presses her lips onto his other cheek, his nose, and his chin. Moving up his face, she tenderly and protectively grazes her lips softly across his forehead and kisses him there.

Closing his eyes as she holds him tightly against her, he feels the rise and fall of her chest, her heart beating rapidly. In that moment, he is a child again, but instead of the terrible place he was, he is now warm and safe in her arms. The emotions that follow this thought almost overwhelm him. *Safe... is this what it feels like to be safe? I don't ever want to let go. My beautiful and precious Norta.*

Cupping her face with his palms, he marvels at how her face fits perfectly in his hard and calloused hands. Pressing his face into her neck, he takes in her scent, breathing it in deeply, unable to get enough of her intoxicating smell.

Drifting her hands over his clothes to his face, taking in the feel of his smooth cheeks, a thread at the back of her mind reminds her that she has never seen him shave or grow hair. Dismissing the thought as quickly as it comes, she instead focuses on the taste of his lips, the feel of his warm skin beneath her fingers. Moving her hands, she slowly traces them around his ears, sending shivers down his spine before weaving them through his silky shoulder-length brown hair.

Sliding his hands up from her face to her hair, Peren savours the taste of her in his mouth, taking in the sweet aroma of her body, the feel of her long, silky auburn hair between his fingers. Biting on her bottom lip, sucking it gently into his mouth, he feels Norta tremble against him.

Pressing her body closer, Norta cups his face in her hands as she presses her lips harder against his. Grazing her hands teasingly down to his neck, she feels his skin respond to her touch.

Pulling back slowly, she looks at him. Pausing, he opens his eyes, confused. Smiling shyly, she leans back in, kissing his neck tenderly, letting her tongue run hesitantly over his Adam's apple, nibbling gently.

Breath catching, Peren feels a shiver run from the back of his throat down his spine to his waist. Feeling the blood travel to his member, his thighs tense as he closes them slightly.

Oblivious to her effect on him, Norta's hands move slowly down to his shoulders, enjoying the rippling muscles under his shirt, her fingers caressing softly, taking in the feel of him.

Instinctively, Peren's hands slip down to her neck, completely taken over by the sensations that are bombarding his body.

Moving her hands lower to his chest, revelling in how firm it feels under her probing fingers, she slips them up to his collar and undoes the ties.

Peren is so focused on the curve of her neck, the feel of her in his mouth, the taste of her on his tongue, that he doesn't register what she does.

Sliding her hands down, she takes in the feel of his hard and firm stomach before grabbing the hem of his shirt, pulling it up as she runs her fingers along the sides of his body.

Peren first notices she is doing something other than

kissing him when she pulls back, out of his reach. Leaning forward, trying to reestablish contact, he feels his arms being lifted. Confused, he opens his eyes and meets Norta's gaze, her bright amber eyes locking with his. Instinctively, he lifts his arms, and Norta removes his shirt. Blushing at the sight of his naked torso, unhurt and unbandaged, she falls silent staring at him.

Emboldened from the way Norta looks at him, Peren reaches out and pulls her back to him. Moving her fingers, she runs them over the scant number of scars on his body as memories spring up of each stitch she made to close those gaping wounds—the hours of keeping them clean and how they held him together, keeping him from dying. Feeling him shudder beneath her fingers, she pulls back and whispers, "Does it hurt?"

Emerging from the haze of sensations, he realizes she has spoken. With a wry smile, he replies, "Not anymore."

Nodding, Norta continues to trace the scars gently, followed closely by soft kisses. Her lips brush delicately over each scar, as if trying to erase the painful memories associated with them. Peren's breath catches in his throat as her warm mouth moves across his skin, warmth spreading through him like liquid fire. He relaxes into her caresses, surrendering himself completely to the sensations she stirs within him.

His hands move down her neck to her shoulders, revelling in the feel of her soft, smooth skin beneath his calloused fingers. Pulling her closer, craving the feel of her body against his, he hears the soft sigh that escapes her lips as she presses against his bare chest. The sound sends a shiver down his spine.

He looks at Norta carefully, watching how she reacts as he reaches for the collar of her dress, slowly undoing the ties. Drawing a ragged breath, he takes in the sight of her dress falling against her body. Moving his hands slowly, he slips it from her shoulders. As it bunches around her elbows, Norta lifts her arms and slips them from her dress, allowing the material to pool at her waist.

The sight of Norta bare and smiling shyly at him, her beauty illuminated by the moonlight, is seared into Peren's memory. His hands slowly graze her, exploring the supple skin of her breasts. Cupping one, he pauses at how soft and firm it feels, how perfectly it fits into his hand. Running his thumb over her small, hardened nipple, he watches as she writhes slightly from his touch. Her movement under his stimulation arouses him, causing him to grow, his breeches getting tight and uncomfortable as he swells with need for her.

Caressing her bare skin with light, teasing pressure, he grazes his short nails gently over the tip of each nipple, sending shivers of pleasure down Norta's spine. Moving his fingers slowly up the sides of each breast, he then runs them gently down her sides, gliding them over each rib, feeling her shudder as he continues down.

Trying to focus on what she is doing, wanting him to feel the same pleasure, she copies him by running her nails gently and slowly down his stomach and over each muscle as her fingers move lower. Peren's body clenches from the shivers spreading throughout his body like wildfire.

Fighting to keep her hands from shaking, she grips the ties to his breeches. Slowly undoing them, her breath catches in her throat as her eyes wander lower to see his arousal. Her hands freeze as she takes in the bulge in his breeches, fear flashing across her face.

Taking in a shuddering breath, she continues to undo the ties. Feeling the tight, uncomfortable feeling around his waist becoming less painful, he gasps in relief, his fingers shaking along her ribs as he feels her loosening his breeches further.

Undoing the last knot, Norta takes a deep, shaky breath, her body shivering from the overwhelming sensations from Peren's grazing fingers and the sight of his breeches tenting. Determined not to back out now, she tries to slide the breeches lower, only succeeding in making them move a little bit.

Lifting his hips off the ground, Peren's muscles clench as she continues to send waves of excitement through him. Feeling him lift, she takes another breath and, gripping the breeches firmly, pulls them down.

Feeling his tip being gently scratched against the rough material, he shudders, and his thighs clench. In one quick motion, the waistband slips past the tip, and his member springs back up. Gasping in surprise at the movement, Norta gulps as she watches it twitch, her hands pausing as she takes in the sight of his member for the first time.

In all the times that she was caring for him prior, she was unable to go around that area when she was assisting. It often made the Herb Mistress snort in amusement at the blushing girl who could call down thunder, but who turned into a blushing mess at the thought of going near a naked man's shaft.

Reaching out gingerly, she timidly touches it and pulls back quickly, startled by how it seems to be moving on its own. She keeps staring at it, unable to take her eyes off this intriguing thick, twitching hose.

Feeling an urge to reach out and touch it again, she moves and wraps her hand gently around it in wonder. She looks up at Peren as she does, worrying she might be hurting him, only to relax as she sees the look of bliss and him gasping for breath as she grips his member.

Encouraged and emboldened from his reactions, she begins to explore the length of him, slowly running her fingers over his shaft, tip, and balls. Watching Peren for his reactions, she notices a liquid ooze from the tip and curiously rubs her thumb over it in circular motions, feeling its sticky warmth.

A low moan escapes his lips as she continues to pleasure him. The sound of him moaning makes her own blood rush as warmth spreads through her body, making her throb. Noticing his reactions, she begins to focus on the tip and the base of his balls, feeling his member twitching in her hands as she sends waves of pleasure through him.

Completely at the mercy of Norta's ministrations, Peren shudders and shivers as tingles course through his body. A low moan escapes his lips, reinforcing what she is seeing as bliss on his face. Slowly increasing the speed and friction, she makes him moan and groan in utter ecstasy, each sound arousing her, surprising her with how much she enjoys pleasuring him with her touch.

Every drip of fluid from the tip sliding down the shaft makes each stroke slicker, sending Peren into a state of numbing bliss. Smiling, she revels how he feels in her hands and the way his erection twitches as she plays with it.

Forcing himself from the brink, he reaches up and smiles as he stops her. The look in his eyes sends a shiver down Norta's spine; there is a hunger that she has never seen in his eyes before.

Gently pushing her till she is lying on her back, then grabbing her bunched-up dress in his hands, he slowly works it down and off her with her help when she lifts her hips. Looking down at the naked woman on display for his pleasure, he pauses and stares.

Looking up at his face, concerned at the way he is just staring at her, Norta feels panic rising as she wonders what's wrong with her body. Looking down self-consciously, she tries to work out the cause, instinctively covering up, face reddening in embarrassment at her body causing Peren discomfort.

Her hand moving in his vision pulls him out of his stupor. Looking up from her body to her face, he sees worry etched into her eyes, her cheeks bright red. Brows closing together, he looks down at where her hands are covering her body as though she is ashamed.

Gently, lovingly, Peren reaches out and pulls her hands away as he looks deeply into her eyes, reflecting the warmth and love he has for her. In a hitching and ragged voice, he mutters, "Don't cover up. You are stunning. I am overwhelmed with awe at how someone could be so beautiful."

Fear flashes in her eyes as Peren moves her hands away from her body. Looking into his eyes and feeling nothing but warmth and love from them, she reluctantly lets him continue.

Staring down at her, he is dumbfounded at the beautiful body splayed before him; his own body is at war between wanting to stare at her naked form and to bury himself deep inside her. Taking a moment to close his eyes and breathe, knowing he doesn't want to ruin this for either of them, he works on quelling the storm building between his legs.

Advice from all his guildmates comes to mind in a flood, and he tries to stop himself from smiling at some of the terrible suggestions given to him by his drunk friends many years ago.

"Now, Peren, when you take your first girl, make sure that you are on top." Food and spit were flying from Cartlan's drunk mouth as he pointed his fork at little Peren and continued, "Girls love that, especially virgins! They often get scared and try to get out of it, but you are on top, so you can make sure that they take it. Most girls say they don't like it, but deep down, they love it!"

Little Peren was just nodding and innocently storing the information away as the men sitting around the table all laughed and started throwing their own advice at him.

"Girls love it when you shove it down her throat."

"Don't forget that she wants you to just take control over her."

"Butts, girls love butt stuff." That elicits all the men to cheer.

"Force, that's what a girl loves—when a man just takes her, bends her over, and does it."

"Girls say they want the sweet things, but they are just whores underneath, waiting for the man to take them like one!"

Little Peren was trying to store all this information, but unsure how to feel, thinking to himself, *This sounds so gross.* All the men were cheering and laughing at each bit of terrible advice they were filling his impressionable mind with.

One of the few women at the guild who took a special liking to little Peren, thinking of him as her pseudo son, came over and covered up his ears. Shaking her head, she reprimanded the drunk men. "Stop filling this innocent boy with your toxic notions. Gods save all the girls you brutish lot take to bed! Tck!" Turning to look down at Peren and uncovering his ears, she whispered, "Don't listen to them. They are pigs who don't know how to treat a woman right."

As she held her hand out to him, he took it, and she led him away to his room. Sitting down on his bed, leg tucked under her, she proceeded to explain, "What a girl really wants is a man that she can rely on. Someone who is kind and patient, who cares enough to look after her, and who is willing to listen and understand her. Most of us girls just want to be held and loved by a man. If you're lucky enough to be loved, you will see that everything you give is returned twofold. That's how love is." Little Peren nodded, despite not understanding a word of what she said.

"The most important thing for a girl when you are doing

it is that you go nice and slow. Especially if they are a virgin." Smiling down at him, she continued as she tucked him in. "I will tell you more tomorrow night before bed." Kissing his forehead and whispering goodnight, she slipped out of his room.

Norta's grazing fingers along his chest pulls him out of his thoughts and, leaning forward, he kisses her deeply on the mouth before kissing his way slowly down her body. First the chin, then moving to the top of her throat before kissing his way down to the hollow base of her throat, sending shivers and shudders throughout her body.

Moving down slowly, his soft lips searing his mark on her bare skin, he makes his way between her breasts. As she arches up from the sensations, Peren quickly slides his hand behind her and pulls her closer to him. Pausing after running his lips to her left nipple, he breathes in deeply before pressing his hot, wet tongue slowly over it, teasing it into a perfect hard nub as he circles it with the tip of his tongue. The gasp from Norta brings a small smile to his face. Closing his mouth over her nipple, he sucks slowly before pulling away to flick his tongue over it again as he stares up into her eyes.

He smiles as he sees the effect his tongue has on her, the way her face looks up as her mouth is partly open, eyes closed, overwhelmed by the sensations.

Reaching out instinctively, she digs her nails into his back, pushing them in deeper as he moves off her nipple, letting the night air cool the warm nub, sending chills of pleasure down her spine.

Slowly kissing his way over to her right nipple, he gives it the same attention, torturing her with his mouth. Soft, low moans escape her lips as he continues to send wave after wave of pleasure through her from where his kisses and tongue touch her bare skin.

Working his way down to her navel, he licks her belly button, sending shivers through her body. She gasps and moans involuntarily as he licks again. Moving down lower, he kisses the small but perfect mound before slowly pushing her legs apart, grazing his fingers along her inner thighs. Kissing softly, he slows down as he feels her tense up. Running his fingers the length of each thigh, he sends waves of sensations straight to her throbbing loins.

Trying not to rush, despite every fibre of his being needing to move faster, he lowers his voice and murmurs softly, "Shall I continue?"

The air between them thick with unspoken desire, he feels the heat radiating from her skin. His heart pounds, fighting his instincts to bury himself in her.

Holding her gaze, each seeing the hesitation in both their own reflected eyes and those of each other, Peren smiles gently and whispers into her mound, "We have all the time in the world." He watches her intently as she swallows and nods.

The promise in his words hangs in the air, electrifying the space between them. He moves closer, his heart racing in anticipation. With a gentle touch that speaks volumes of his intentions, he grazes her inner thighs and watches as Norta's body arches in anticipation. Leaning in with a soft kiss, Peren smiles as she gasps his name, her fingers reaching down into his hair, holding him desperately close as her gasps slowly turns into the sweetest moans he has ever heard. Deepening the kiss, he savours the taste of her, the way her body responds to his touch and the way she gives herself fully to him. She gasps heavily and arches harder, moaning loudly as he kisses her clitoris. Looking up at her, he sees the pleasure written all over her face. Smiling, he licks her nub.

Looking up at her, he sees the pleasure written all over her beautiful, flushed face. Holding her gaze, he covers his finger in her sweet honey before sliding it up and down over her engorged nub. She grips the blanket beneath her as waves of pleasure crash through her with each movement.

Moving his mouth, he growls into her, making her shiver all over as he begins to slowly lick up and down her slit. Pulling her nub into his mouth, he begins to gently suck and nibble on it, sending uncontrollable spasms through her with each touch.

Wrapping himself tighter around her, he swallows down the sweet liquids she secretes, needing to swallow more and more of the honey pouring from her.

Looking down at her slit, he sees a small and tight hole near the base. Realising that it is way too small for him to fit, he looks at it in confusion. Deciding to prod the hole first, he coats his finger in his saliva and her sweet nectar before slowly pressing it in.

Arching back further, she moans loudly as he pushes his finger deeper into her, feeling her tighten around his finger, making it hard as he slides it in and out of her.

Slowing down, not wanting to rush it, he still wonders how he will fit in her. As he tries to fit a second finger in her, he can feel her struggle to take both of them.

Worry starts to crease his face as she tries to take both of his fingers, making him pull back slightly.

She looks up at him in confusion as he moves away from her. Feeling an unbearable ache between her legs, she opens her mouth to find out why.

He cuts before she can say anything. "I won't fit. You can't take two fingers, how are you supposed to take me?"

Overwhelmed by her need to have him in her, she shrugs and says, "It will stretch. I need you *now*." Her voice comes out strained at the end.

Trusting her, he positions himself over her, lining up his member with her entrance. Leaning in, he kisses her deeply, the world fading as they continue to kiss. Grasping his member, she helps him to push against her entrance.

As he pushes his way in, Norta gasps and winces at the size of him pushing against her, feeling some pain as her body stretches, the strange and unfamiliar feeling of pain and pleasure mingling as she tries to take him inside her. She wants him so badly and yet finds herself struggling to accommodate the size of him. A small moan of pain escapes her lips as he slowly pushes deeper.

Panicking, Peren stops. Looking down at Norta, worry written all over his face, he asks "Are you ok?"

Nodding a little, she croaks out, "Hurts."

Removing the pressure immediately, he looks down at her face worriedly.

Torn between wanting him in her and not wanting the pain, she says, "It's ok, I'm ok. I—I am—" Swallowing her embarrassment and looking away because she has not done this before, she whispers, "I—I am—a virgin."

Feeling relief, his heart fills with love and warmth at being her first. Reaching out, he turns her face to look at him. "Hey… That's ok." Going red in the face and looking away, he whispers, "Me too."

Inwardly cowering, waiting for her to mock him, he slowly opens his eyes and looks at her when she doesn't reply. He looks into her eyes filled with love and warmth, as if he has just said the most beautiful thing ever. The air between them fills with love and pride at being each other's first.

A sense of awe flows through her as she realises how rare it is to share this level of intimacy with someone who has vulnerably opened to her.

"Wh-why are you looking at me like that?" Peren stammers.

Smiling up at him, she answers, "It's our first time." Her face flushes as she continues, "That makes it all so special."

They stare lovingly into each other's eyes, lost in the moment.

Determined to be his first, she says, "Try again."

Looking down at her, initially relieved to bury himself inside her, he remembers why they stopped. "Are you sure?"

Not trusting her voice, she nods, taking a deep breath and bracing herself for the pain that will come.

Leaning down, he presses his lips against hers in a deep and passionate kiss. Putting his hand on her cheek so she looks at him, he slowly pushes against her entrance, getting slightly deeper he feels her tighten around him, sending pleasure through him, making him feel guilty as he sees the pain in her eyes.

Eventually, he gets all the way in her, both gasping at how it feels. Peren fights to stay still, waiting for the pain Norta feels to subside.

When she nods at him, he slowly pulls out and begins to move back in slowly as they whisper sweet things into each other's ears. Norta's body gradually relaxes and stretches around him, the pain replaced by an ache, a soreness that new lovers find.

Pulling out completely, Peren looks down, and shock spreads across his face as he sees blood on his shaft.

Seeing the look on his face, Norta lifts up and sees the blood coating his slick shaft. Smiling at him, she whispers, "It's okay, that's normal. It's what happens for some girls the first time they… do this." Looking down at her in disbelief, a sceptical look crosses his face before she adds reassuringly, "No, really, its ok."

Conflicted between not wanting to hurt her and the level of pleasure that he felt when he was inside her, Peren slowly reinserts himself and pushes in again, guided by Norta's voice and the sounds she makes. *Gods, the sounds she makes.* He never knew a mere whimper or a moan could make his blood rush like this.

Despite the initial pain, a feeling of pleasure that she never knew existed soon takes over, coaxing both of their bodies into a rhythm, a feeling so divine that they lose themselves in the pleasure.

The ache of euphoria increases as they come together in a union. Reaching climax with Peren deep inside of her, filling her completely, Norta feels his warmth spread within her with his seed. Kissing her tenderly on her forehead, Peren moves so that he doesn't collapse on top of her. Pulling her close into his arms and kissing her bare shoulder, he covers them both with the blanket, and they fall asleep in each other's arms.

Waking as the sky starts to lighten, Peren opens his eyes. Looking down at Norta fast asleep on his chest, her hair fallen across her face, he reaches out instinctively to move it, gently grazing her sleeping face with his fingers as he often does when he awakens. Looking down at her, a big grin breaks out on his face at the peaceful look on hers. The reflections of the setting moon illuminate her in a way he hasn't seen before. The grey light of dawn heralding the coming of the sun looks so beauti-ful today. *Wait, why am I seeing so much light? My room is never this bright,* he wonders. His eyes widen in fear as he realises they aren't in his bed. They aren't in any bed.

As he questions how they ended up here, the memories of the night before come flooding in. Remembering what they did brings a bright red flush to his face. Panicking a little, he shakes Norta awake as he starts to get up, going an even brighter crimson as he sees that not only is he naked, but they both are. As he covers up quickly, his mind races with memories and feelings from the previous night, fighting his rising panic at the hour.

Disorientated, Norta looks around, confused for a few moments. Seeing Peren, she smiles shyly up at him before trying to pull him closer. Her eyes widen as she discovers that she is naked. She gasps in shock and horror before the memories flood her mind from the previous night. Wrapping herself up in the blankets, leaving Peren to rush to his clothes naked, she gets dressed behind some nearby bushes.

As she rushes up to him hastily dressed, unable to look each other in the eyes, Peren helps Norta onto the saddled horse. Climbing up behind her, his cheeks colour at the feel of her body pressed against his. Swallowing, he heels Mercy in the ribs. Feeling the unease from her riders, Mercy bolts back towards Comtun. Thoughts of worry crash through their minds as they wonder whether or not they will be able to make it back before anyone wakes up.

When they arrive at the stable yard, the stable hand comes out, surprised to see them. Helping Norta down, Peren tells him to keep Mercy saddled and to feed her as nonchalantly as he can. Giving them a knowing grin, he leads her away.

Trying to rush inside as quietly as they can, they are caught by Gizle shouting, "Aha! And where have you two been all night?!"

Grinning at their embarrassed faces, Gizle's smile falters as the reason for their discomfort hits her. Her eyes widen in shock, and her expression quickly shifts to disgust. Blushing furiously, she bolts to her room, screaming, *Ewwwwwww!*

Torach steps out, his deep voice booming, "What's with all the screaming?" He stops short when he sees the two red-faced kids. Setting his jaw, he glares at Peren. "You better not be dragging my angel into any of your worldly mischief!"

Peren struggles to maintain a serious expression, responding in a steady, serious voice, "Yes, sir."

Torach eyes them warily before moving on, returning to his work.

The two exchange big grins, but their moment is interrupted by Torach's booming voice, making Norta jump. "Norta! Get to work!"

"Y-yes, Father," she stammers, throwing Peren a regretful look before hurrying off to her room.

Not wanting to stay under Torach's watchful glare, Peren quickly heads to his room, washes up, and dresses, making sure he's equipped for the day.

In the stable yard, as he mounts Mercy, Norta rushes up to him, handing him lunch with a quick kiss. "Be back on time today, or I'll skin your hide!" she admonishes, trying to give him her sternest glare.

But when she sees the amusement on his face, she abandons the attempt. With a playful slap on Mercy's rump, she sends the mare bolting, watching with satisfaction as Peren struggles to bring her under control. Turning on her heel, head held high, Norta walks back inside with a regal air.

Powerless to keep the grin from his face, Peren eventually calms Mercy down. Memories from the previous night flood his mind, and he finds himself reminiscing.

When he's jolted from his reverie by the sudden stillness, he blinks in shock at his surroundings. Dread builds up in his stomach as he takes in the cave entrance. Sliding to the ground, he pulls on his leather shoulder bag, which contains spare torches and food.

Stopping in front of the entrance, Peren takes a deep

calming breath, his grip tight on the torch, moving forward at speed to try and get through this void of empty nothingness as fast as possible. Despite focusing on knowing that this has to be some sort of illusion, he falls prey to the mercy of the void. Sight, sound, touch, even the air around him—everything vanishes in an overwhelming sense of emptiness. Falling to the ground instinctively, panic flows as he fears that he's lost the torch. Relief floods through him when he finds that he still has hold of it, doing his best to ensure the Demigod Phyraen doesn't snatch the flame away.

Coming to his feet, he moves swiftly to the edge of the void, passing through it as quickly as possible. Overwhelmed by the sudden torrent of senses flooding his mind, he collapses onto the ground, gasping in agony as every part of his brain is overstimulated. Despite fighting hard, he still passes out.

When he wakes a short time later, Peren's sense of time tells him that he has been unconscious for a few minutes, sending calming relief through his body. Focusing on the task at hand, he grits his teeth against the ebbing pain and unsheathes his dagger in what he imagines is a slow menacing move. Doing his best to avoid looking directly into the flames of his torch, he takes a step forward before coming to a complete stop, as the presence of unspeakable evil permeates through the air, leaving whisperings in its wake.

Goosebumps cover Peren from head to toe as terror and dread course through his veins. He struggles to calm himself, too scared to move or even blink. Forced to dig deeper than ever before, he grips his fear by the scruff of its neck and shoves it into the deepest recesses of his mind, slowly regaining control over his petrified body with focus and determination, wresting back control from the paralysing grip of terror.

Amidst the cacophony of noises echoing through the cave,

one distinct sound stands out, teasingly familiar, and yet elusive. It is as if a million Spliganders are scuttling just around the corner, their unseen presence closing in on him fast. Despite his iron grip on his fear, moments of panic slip through, but he forcefully suppresses them, delving deeper into his reserves of resilience.

Struggling to decipher the chaotic symphony assaulting his senses, he thinks, *I know there can't be more than a thousand left at most, so there's very little chance I'll be swarmed at the entrance.* Yet the strangely recognizable sound continues to perplex and taunt him as he struggles to identify it, adding an extra layer of frustration to his predicament. *Damn, I wish I could identify that noise,* he thinks, gritting his teeth.

As he moves stealthily down the main entrance, the torch burns brightly against the gloom, like a small beacon of hope in the despair of blackness. He searches through the shadows for signs of his prey. Seeing a junction up ahead on the right side of the tunnel, he slows down further and squats more. Getting to the corner, he peeks around the corner before realising that he has a torch in his hand. Grateful that the corridor is empty, he relaxes and sighs in relief.

Wanting to explore and make a mental map of the place, he walks past the opening and continues down the tunnel, coming to a dead end not far from the junction. Glad that he didn't find another tunnel, he turns around and heads back to the intersection. Peeking around the corner again, and heaving a second sigh of relief, he hugs the wall as he moves forward stealthily, knowing that moving from shadow to shadow will be useless as protection, since the Spliganders can see more clearly than he can.

Silently gliding down the tunnel like a phantom, Peren can't shake the sensation of being watched. The feeling only grows stronger the deeper he ventures into the darkness, like icy fingers crawling down his spine. Gritting his teeth, he focuses on the task at hand—eliminating the remaining Spliganders and confronting their queen. Rumours of the queen's sheer size send his mind spinning as he tries to fathom what the colossal creature might look like.

Using charcoal to mark his path, he moves deeper into the network of caves. Feeling the ominous presence of something ghostlike a few steps behind him, he turns, only to find nothing there. Warily turning back, he continues forward a few paces before sensing presence again. Using his otherworldly speed, Peren turns and finds an empty tunnel. The thought of it being old Kith has him worried for a minute. Taking a deep calming breath, he tries to dismiss it as his wild, overimaginative mind playing tricks on him.

As he continues deeper into the caves, closely followed by the feeling of malevolence, a chill starts to spread through his body. Dismissing it as his body's reaction to the eeriness of the caves, he realises a short time later the cold isn't just from this feeling, but the chilly stone surrounding him the deeper he goes.

Wrapping his already tight cloak around him tighter, he trundles forward. Constantly faced with multiple three-, four-, and even five-way forks, Peren eventually gets lost. Instead of stopping and trying to find his way back, he continues to stumble on. Turning down one tunnel, he feels nausea rise, and before he can react, he doubles over and empties his stomach to the ground.

Spitting and wiping his mouth on his sleeve, he knows he is on the right track. The stench is stronger than anything he could have imagined. Sick to his stomach, he sits down with his back against the wall, cursing his elven nose, shocked at how potent the stench is. He stays like this until his stomach stops roiling. Once he manages to acclimate somewhat to the stench—a feat he doubts he'll ever fully achieve, given the cave's poor ventilation—he presses on.

Moving deeper down the tunnel, overwhelmed by the strength of the stench, Peren pauses regularly to stop the dry retching. Choosing only the forks where the smell is the strongest keeps him on track, but he struggles to see far into the distance, despite the torch and his elven sight.

Eventually, he reaches a tunnel that seems to get smaller with each step, making him bend over in an awkward position and leave his torch behind and bag. He prays to the Demigod Phyraen to let his torch continue to burn bright. The tunnel continues to tighten until he is forced to slide along on his belly. Claustrophobia sets in as the tunnel tightens around him.

Seeing an exit ahead, Peren crawls out of the tunnel, jaw dropping in awe as he stands up in the largest cavern he has ever seen. The vast space is filled with just over a thousand Spliganders, arranged in a loose defensive pattern around their queen. The sheer size of the queen, towering hundreds of feet tall and at least half as wide, leaves him momentarily stunned. He can't comprehend how something so massive could exist, the sight before him defying all his previous notions of scale and grandeur.

A queasy rumble in the pit of his stomach reminds him that he is hungry. The sound also alerts the Spliganders to his presence. Almost as one, they look to him and begin moving forward to kill this intruder to their private sanctum.

Brandishing his dagger, excitement runs down his spine, a snarling smile twisting his face. But as the reality sinks in, he realizes he's outmatched—there will be no end to them. With no sun to aid him and no chance for rest, the frustration grinds at him. Though every part of him wants to stay and fight, he forces himself to come up with a sound strategy.

Leaping forward, he kills a few before retreating through the hole. Moving until he can stand up straight, then grabbing his bag and torch, he waits for them to pour through the opening.

Snarling at the intruder, they surge into the tunnel in pursuit. Spotting their prey at the far end, they charge toward him.

Leaping forward, Peren executes a flourish of moves and kills multiple Spliganders before retreating out of the tunnel. Moving backwards, slowly conceding ground to them, he kills one after another using the tunnels as chokepoints, taking full advantage and making them pay for each step back he takes.

Needing a break sometime later, he decides to put some distance between him and the Spliganders. Grateful that they are not strategic thinkers, he turns and runs down tunnel after tunnel, the shadows flickering as he dashes past with the torch.

Knowing he cannot keep running without eventually hitting a dead-end, he tosses the torch down a tunnel and hides in the next one, his back against the wall, breathing heavily as he waits to see what the Spliganders do.

Snarling and screeching, they rush up, and, seeing a flickering light, they all charge towards it.

Sliding down the wall to sit on the floor, panting, Peren closes his eyes for a moment in relief.

Getting his breath back, he gets to his feet. Using the obscured light to see, he moves forward and heads down a few tunnels before the light completely disappears. Continuing forward, using his hands as guides, he creeps onward, hoping that he can make it back to the entrance without getting too lost.

Given the dark, and only navigating by touch, it doesn't take long for Peren to become completely disorientated. Needing to work out his next step, he sits with his back to the wall and pulls out some food and water.

Munching on the food, he debates whether to risk using torches or continue blind. In the end, he decides that using a torch is worth the risk.

Finally getting it lit, Peren moves quickly down the tunnel, not wanting to be here any longer than he has to be. Sending a fervent prayer to the Goddess of Navigation, Arpath, to guide him safely and speedily out of the caves, he continues on.

Despite getting lost a few times, he finally stumbles across one of his marks on the tunnels. Feeling relief, he follows the markings until he makes a final left turn and reaches the cave entrance. His shoulders slump as the anxiety and tension wash away, knowing freedom is within reach. Taking a moment, he prepares for the nothingness of the void.

Moving forward at speed, he is suddenly engulfed by it. Gritting his teeth and struggling to stay on his feet, he pushes forward.

Though he is prepared for the sudden onslaught of information that will come from leaving the void, it is still not enough. As he steps out, he drops the torch, clutching his head as it screams in agony. He collapses to the ground, and a faint squeak escapes his lips before the comforting blackness of unconsciousness crashes over him.

Waking up in agony, laying there in the foetal position, he whispers his thanks to the Goddess Arpath for guiding him out safely. Slowly getting to his feet, his head pounding like a woodcutter's chopping block, he staggers toward where he left Mercy. The final tendrils of worry fade as relief washes over him—she's exactly where he left her that morning.

Moving up to her, he notices Mercy whinnying and nickering at the sight of him before resting her head on his shoulder. Surprised at her flood of affection, he breaks into a small laugh after the harrowing ordeal and gives her a good pat and rub. "I'm happy to see you too, girl." Mercy whinnies in response. Patting her along her graceful neck, he whispers, "I think we're both ready to head home, don't you?" Stowing his bag and mounting her, they head back to town.

As he enters the town, he notices people giving him looks of astonishment. He's confused and wonders what he's missed, shrugging their glances off as typical strange human behaviour until he arrives at the stable yard. Dismounting Mercy, he passes the reins to the stablehand, whose trembling fingers and pale face make it seem as though he's just seen a ghost.

Frowning, Peren pauses for a moment. Looking down and seeing that he is caked in blood and muck from the caves, he figures he must be quite a sight. Chuckling at how he must look, he heads off to the inn.

Entering the inn, he decides it's best to head to his room and clean up before Norta sees him in this sorry state and add to her worries.

"Peren Nailo! You stop right there, mister!"

Pausing with a shudder at her tone, Peren knows it's not going to be good. Turning back, desperate to try and salvage this, he gives her his best smile. "Hey, beautiful. How are you?"

"Don't you 'Hey Beautiful' me! You know how I am!"

As he opens his mouth to retort, Norta jumps in first, "*No*! You do *not* get to say a word!" Pulling in a lungful of air, she continues her tirade. "Do *you* know how long you have been gone for?" She steps forward with each word.

Peren opens his mouth again to answer, but gets cut off again. *"Three days! Three whole fucking days!"* She stabs him in the chest with her finger, underscoring her anger.

Peren flinches with each stab as his mind races at the information. *Three days?! I have been gone three whole days?* He stands there stunned for a moment as his brain absorbs this information. Realising that she is waiting for a reply, his mind races. *What do I say to her? It's not like I can brandish my dagger and chop off a few heads, like with the Spliganders. Gods! She is so mad at me. How do I salvage this?* Lifting his shoulders, he offers the only thing he can think of, which comes across more as a question than a statement. "I'm sorry?"

"You're sorry? *You're sorry?*" Completely closing the space between them, she stares him down, her eyes otherworldly little fires of amber. *"Is that all you can say?* You're sorry?" Throwing her arms up in the air, she yells, "*Oh!* Well, that's ok, then! Disappear for three *whole* days, and all you have to say is you're sorry?!"

Anger flushes her face red as her hands clench. *"Do you really think that will cover it?"*

Frustrated at not being able to express himself properly and tired of being yelled at, he opens his mouth to retort before his better sense catches on. Despite the anger flashing before him, he can see her fear underneath.

Clarity pierces through his thoughts as he sees her point of view, realising her anger is her way of letting out how scared she was. It shows her fear of losing him, of how he disappeared for three days without a word.

Pulling her into a tight embrace, he plants his lips on hers.

Her breath catches, freezing in shock. Fury ignites in her eyes as she thinks, *How dare he?!* Her anger builds in her chest, burning hot. *How dare he try to fix it with a kiss?*

Desperate to break free, she slams her hands against his chest, trying to push him away. "Let… me… go!" she hisses. When that doesn't work, she resorts to throwing her fists at him, demanding with every breath, "Let. Me. Go! Get. Your. Hands. Off. Me!"

But Peren refuses to relent. He holds her tighter,

whispering over and over between tender kisses, "I'm here. I'm here."

Her struggle is fierce, like a soldier of rage battling against him. Each swing of her anger's sword tries to push him away, yet Peren remains steadfast, blocking each attack with unwavering resolve. As her resistance weakens, the battle shifts.

Slowly, her body gives in, her fists dropping to her sides as the intensity of her anger fades. Her struggles soften, her lips returning each kiss with growing fervour.

As her anger dissipates, her fear surfaces—fear that he wouldn't come back, that she might never see her beloved again. This fear melts into profound relief that he is back, safe, and alive. The weight of her emotions—fear, relief, and everything in between—presses down on her. The dam breaks, and tears flow freely.

With each sob, she holds his face in her trembling hands and kisses him all over—his lips, cheeks, nose, and forehead—each kiss a desperate, loving punctuation. Her sobs mix with the salty taste of her tears on his lips, drawing tears to Peren's own eyes. He holds her tighter, struggling not to crumble himself under the weight of their shared relief and love.

Gripping him tightly, she chokes out between sobs and kisses, "I thought I lost you! I thought you were gone!" She shudders as she struggles to speak through the lump in her throat. "I thought you... you *died.*"

Unable to speak further, she just looks into his eyes, terrified. Peren is struck by the depth of her anguish and the shift from anger to sorrow. Seeing the pain he's caused her is unbearable. *I'd rather face a thousand enemies than see this in her eyes,* he thinks. *Fighting for my life was easier than this.* Tears flow down his cheeks as he grasps the weight of her love and his own mistakes. The pain in her eyes is a heavy reminder of the cost of his actions.

Looking down at her with love and sorrow in his eyes, he says firmly, "You can't get rid of me that easily. I will always come home to you. *Always.*"

He pulls her in for another tight hug, and they stay like that for a while.

Feeling the blood drying on his skin making his movements stiff, he looks down at her blood- and tear-streaked face. Smiling at her, he asks, "I think we both need a bath, don't you?"

Nodding, they head off to the baths. As she cleans him and patches up his scrapes, she asks tentatively, "What happened? Why were you gone for three whole days?"

Peren falls silent for a moment before responding. "I am sorry. I didn't realise that so much time had gone by. I really thought it was the same day. I lost track of time; it was pitch-black in there, and I got lost. There are a lot of tunnels in those caves. I'm sorry I didn't return sooner."

Looking into his eyes intently, she wonders, *He got lost for three whole days and thought it was the same day? How is that possible? Did he not eat or sleep? I don't understand...* Confused, she presses. "Did you eat or sleep while you were there?"

Brows touching, Peren wonders to himself, *Why is she asking this? Doesn't she believe me?* Feeling tired and defensive, he answers firmly, "Why do you need to know? I'm safe and back, isn't that all that matters?"

"Wha—what do you mean, why do I need to know?" *Why is he being so defensive? I don't understand...I just want to know how he survived in the caves.* "You were gone for three days, and you seemed to not realise it. I'm worried about how you were in there. Were you awake for whole three days?" Norta's eyes search his, filled with worry and confusion.

Exhausted and feeling like he is being interrogated, Peren

snaps, "So what if I was? What does it matter? I'm back safe now!" *Will she just stop? Why won't she drop it?*

Taken aback by his hostility over her concern, Norta frowns. "Why are you behaving like this? Can't you see that I'm just worried because you disappeared for so long and I was worrying the entire time if you were okay? It baffles me that so much time can pass without you realising, and I'm trying to understand it, that's all."

Frustrated, Peren fires back. "Can't you see that I'm fine? What's there to get? I lost track of time as I was searching the tunnels." *Geez, what is wrong with her? Why can't she just trust me and drop this? What have I done to deserve this? I just want a peaceful bath and some rest.* Standing up, he looks down on her. "Fine, don't trust me." Climbing out of the bath, he goes to dry off.

Stunned, Norta sits in the bath as Peren walks off. "This has nothing to do with trusting you! I was worried, do you not get that? You don't just disappear on people and come back after three days expecting me to just be fine with it! I just want to understand what happened! How can you not understand that?"

Getting furious now at his reaction and his rude and dismissive behaviour towards her, she continues, "You're going back to the caves, aren't you? So, what then? Am I supposed to be okay if you disappear for ten months without a word because you 'lost track of time?!'"

Gritting his teeth, too tired to think straight, Peren throws back, "*Fine!*" Storming back in and looking down at her, he says, "You want to know every little thing that happened? I had a chance to stay and fight, but I chose to come back because of you. It would have been so easy to have stayed and finished the job, but no. You made me promise to come back, and that's what I did!" *What the hells is wrong with her? Why does she need to know every little thing? I can't tell her that I nearly died at the entrance. She is bad enough.* Getting close to her face, using his hands to emphasis his words, he growls, "You know what? We are done! That's it, once I finish this contract, then I'm off, and you will never have to see me again!" Turning around, he goes to storm out of the room.

Watching in shock as he stalks off, she feels her heart sinking. A wave of devastation washes over her as she realises Peren is shutting her out. His last words echo in her mind over and over as her heart continues to break. Refusing to chase after him, she trembles, tears streaming down her face. In that moment, she understands the painful truth: she is in love with someone who doesn't recognise the hurt he causes her.

Taking his dinner in his room, Peren barely manages to eat before succumbing to sleep. The exhaustion from three sleepless days, the gruelling battle against the Spliganders, the pain from the entrance, and the argument with Norta weigh heavily on him. Finally, the enveloping darkness offers a much-needed reprieve from the turmoil he feels over his earlier words.

Hours later, he jolts awake with a pained cry, gasping for breath, drenched in sweat and tears as he reaches desperately out towards the remnants of the fading nightmare.

Norta bursts through the door, her eyes widening at the horror on his pale face. She scans the room, searching for anything that could explain his terror. "Are you okay? What happened?!" she exclaims, rushing to his side and gently placing her hand on his face, feeling the dampness of his skin. Her heart pounds at the sight of him like this. Realising he's still half-asleep, she shakes him gently, urging him to wake. "Shhh… you're okay. Everything's okay." She holds his face against her chest as she strokes his hair repeatedly, her touch meant to calm him.

The cool hand and soothing strokes brings Peren out of his terrified stupor. Looking up at Norta, he realises it was only a nightmare. She is there, safe and sound.

Through sobs, he struggles to recount what happened, his fragmented mind putting the pieces together. "I'm heading toward the caves when suddenly, the Spliganders rush past, dragging you on their backs screaming and thrashing. I charge into the caves after them and struggle to keep up with them as they go down tunnel after tunnel, unable to outrun them like I normally do. I crawl into the cavern where they took you, a cavern so big it defies imagination. In the centre of the cavern there is a beast so enormous that no words can truly capture its size. It looks like the Spliganders with some differences, and not just its size. Its features are more refined, smooth, more feminine. The rodents dump you in front of the giant beast. As she opens her maw, you frantically look around and spot me. Crying out to me, face filled with hope, you try to make your way towards me as I do the same. But, before I can get to you, the beast knocks you down and grabs you in her mouth by your legs."

Swallowing as he tries to order his chaotic mind, he continues, "Your screams fill the cavern as you thrash against her, waving me off as if trying to protect me." Tears stream down his face as he struggles to speak. "You continue to struggle, trying to get out of her grasp. I can't just let you die, so I charge forward, screaming in anger at the beast, cutting down any rodent that gets in my way. They swarm me, their attacks relentless, slowing me down. I…I am completely helpless as… as I watch." Swallowing again, he forces himself to continue. "The creature pulls you into her mouth and…" He struggles to get the words past the lump in his throat. "That sound—the terrible, awful crunch that echoes in my head with your screams."

Looking visibly ill, he presses on. "The worst part is the

silence just before the beast swallows you down. I reach out to you screaming, and I wake up."

Norta holds him tighter and, kissing the top of his head, whispers, "Its ok, I'm here, I'm safe. That will never happen, because…" Holding him at arm's length so she can look into his eyes, she says, "Because I know you will succeed in taking her down."

Taking a moment to compose himself, he nods as he takes a deep breath. Looking her deep in the eyes, he says, "I love you more than life, Norta. I am so sorry for the way I behaved earlier. I was exhausted and needed rest, but this doesn't excuse my behaviour. I don't want to lose you or for us to end. I want us to be together." Taking her hands in his, and looking into her eyes, he adds, "Forever."

Looking into his eyes, she sees the sorrow and truth in them, knowing he means every word. Though she wants to punish him for what he put her through, she knows that being petty right now would only crush the threads of love between them.

Kissing her hands, Peren caresses them gently before uttering in a voice heavy with regret, "Please forgive me, my love."

Tears in her eyes, she can only nod as she lifts her hand and cradles the side of his face and he presses his cheek against the warmth of her palm, his eyes closing with relief from her touch.

"I forgive you." Peren feels all the tension and anxiety over what he did ebb away at her reply. "But…" She pauses, stroking her thumb along his cheek until he opens his eyes and looks up at her. Gazing into them, she continues quietly, "You almost broke me with the things you said. Promise me you will never treat me like that or utter those words again. My heart cannot bear it."

Looking back into her eyes, he nods and says solemnly, "I promise."

Closing his eyes, he savours the warmth of her hand on his cheek. After a moment, he opens them again, looking deeply into hers. A knot tightens in his chest; he knows he needs to bring this up, but he's unsure how she'll take it. With a small frown, he takes a steadying breath and says cautiously, "I don't want to ruin this moment… but there's something we need to talk about."

A look of confusion comes over her face as she responds, "Yes? What is it?"

"I've spent a lot of time alone, doing what I had to do without thinking about anyone else. But now… now, there's you. I know I've made you worry, and that's on me. I need to do better, and I will. I don't want to keep causing you this kind of pain." Hesitating for a moment, he continues, "But you've got to stop too. The slapping, the yelling, poking me. I don't like it."

Taken aback, she stares at him, shocked. Appalled at how she has treated him, she clasps his hands in hers, looking into his eyes full of regret and sorrow. "I am so very sorry. I never intended to make you feel like that. I have been so worried about you, and I guess in my fear, I lash out at you. I promise to do better too."

Relief floods through him as her words dissolve the last of the tension. Leaning in with a tender smile, he gently kisses her lips. Nudging her nose with his, he whispers, "I love you."

She smiles softly, returning his kiss, then nuzzles his nose and whispers back, "I love you too."

Deciding to spend the next few days with Norta and her family, Peren mulls over different ideas on how to defeat the Spliganders, dismissing idea after idea as he tries to work out the logistics in his head, spotting impracticalities in each plan. Unwilling to sit around as he thinks, he goes and spends hours out in the stable yard, practicing his bladework. When that doesn't help, he throws himself into assisting Norta with her chores, finding himself grinning wildly when Torach or Gizle yells at them for getting distracted.

Refusing to give up, he continues running through possible solutions late into the night until exhaustion overtakes him, and he falls asleep.

Waking up the next day, still not settled on a full plan, he decides to start work on the part of the plan that he has so far: spike pit traps. Gathering sticks from the outlying fields, he starts to whittle them down into little stakes.

Whenever the inn quiets down, Norta, Torach, and Gizle sit down and help him. Sitting around a table, each whittling a stick, Torach cracks jokes, causing both Norta and Gizle to cringe, but sending Peren into fits of laughter. Encouraged by the response, he cracks even more outrageous ones. Cringing harder with each joke, Norta and Gizle beg him to stop, while Peren struggles to breathe from laughing so hard.

As Torach is opening his mouth to utter another joke, both Norta and Gizle rushes over and cover up his mouth with their hands, crying out, "No more!" Seeing the hurt look on Torach's face, though amusement dances in his eyes as he looks up at his daughters, Peren laughs even harder.

Later that night, lying in bed with Norta nestled in his arms, Peren smiles faintly as his mind drifts back to the moments he shared with them earlier. The warmth of her body against his is comforting, yet as his thoughts linger, he feels his eyes glaze over with unexpected tears. Confused, he wipes them away, trying to puzzle out his feelings, but falling asleep before he can answer these questions.

Waking up early the next day, an idea starts to form. Peren goes in search of a woodsmith and blacksmith. Finding the blacksmith first, he takes note of the location and continues to look for the woodsmith.

Finding one, he goes in and outlines his plan. After thinking for a minute, the woodsmith pulls out a charcoal pencil and draws out his understanding of what Peren wants. After a few rub-outs and redraws, they come to a workable plan. Agreeing on it, the woodsmith asks for a week to construct everything.

Heading to the blacksmith, Peren explains his needs. The blacksmith nods in understanding, and, after an in-depth conversation, he says he can have everything Peren needs in a week.

Thanking him, Peren heads back to the inn and continues to whittle away at the little stakes.

Between assisting with the chores, whittling the sticks, and spending time with Norta, the week goes by relatively quickly.

Peren heads first off to the woodsmith to get the items he requested. Impressed by the workmanship of the items, he commends him and heads off to the blacksmith's.

Handing over one of the items, the blacksmith finishes by attaching his creations to the woodsmith's. Once the creations are finished, Peren loads them onto a cart he borrows from Torach, tying the load down properly once he has collected them all, saving him from making multiple trips.

The sun hits the horizon as Peren makes his way back into the stable yard with the load. Helping the stablehand unhitch Mercy and remove the saddle, he spends some time with her, rubbing her down and feeding her.

Walking into the inn, he is met with smells of something delicious cooking for dinner. Hurrying over, he helps out before taking some for himself.

Pulling Norta aside after dinner, he sits her down. "I will

be going back to the caves tomorrow." A look of sadness covers her face as she looks away. Reaching out and tilting her head back so he can look her in the eyes, he says, "Um… That's not the bad part."

Fear grips her and clouds her features. Pushing on, Peren continues, "I will be going for a few days, a week at most. I will not be able to complete this contract if I have to keep coming back each night."

Tearing up at the thought of him being gone so long, she demands, "Why did you have to take that contract? Why couldn't you just leave it alone?"

Feeling his heart crack, Peren answers, "Because I couldn't just sit by and let them plague the town without doing something about it."

Knowing the truth of his words and loving him all the more for who he is, she sobs. "I still don't want to lose you."

"I know you don't, and I don't plan on going anywhere."

Nodding but still fearful, Norta tries to think of a solution. "I don't like you being out there all alone, so I will go with you."

Shocked at her sudden decision, Peren's mind races. *What?! She wants to go with me? Why? How?*

Taking the shocked silence as permission to continue, she adds, "That way, you won't be alone in the caves, and I can help treat any wounds then and there." She nods to herself as the plan roots in her mind. "Yes, that is what I will do." She looks up at him, eyes bright, face set in determination.

As she turns away to start preparing the food they will need to bring along, Peren grabs her by the arm and says, "Wait."

Turning back, confused at his reluctance, she opens her mouth to demand an explanation. Knowing that he better have a good reason for trying to dissuade her from coming, his mind races through different arguments he could use, rejecting them one after another.

Looking at him as he tries to think of reasons why she shouldn't join him, her face turns impatient, waiting for him to accept this decision.

He flounders at not finding any immediate reasons that would sway her. "No."

Brows touching, she asks, "'No?' what do you mean, 'No?'"

"You can't come with me."

Shocked, she stares at him for a moment. "What do you mean I can't come with you?"

"It's too dangerous. I won't have my beloved risk her life like this."

Fists resting on her hips, she speaks through gritted teeth. "Of course I'm coming! You can't stop me from coming."

Dread building up deep inside, Peren knows he must stop her, or something bad will happen to her. Taking a different approach, he gently grabs her by the shoulders. Looking deeply into her eyes, he says softly, "I love you more than life itself. If something were to happen to you, I could never forgive myself. I need you here so I have something to fight for—some*one* to fight for."

Tears welling in her eyes, she is at a loss as to what to say, looking up at him as a tear escapes and runs down her cheek.

Cupping her head in his hands, he wipes the tear away. Kissing her forehead, he pulls her into an embrace and whispers into her hair, "I need to know you are alive and safe. It allows me to not worry about you, and I can focus on the task at hand." As an afterthought, he adds, "It also means that I will also have to be careful to make sure I come home to you." Tilting her head up, he whispers as he kisses her forehead again, "I *will* come back."

Nodding, knowing deep down that he is right, she looks up into his eyes. "You come back to me, you hear?"

Smiling feeling profoundly relieved, he nods. "I will, I promise."

Leaving early in the morning, Peren kisses Norta deeply and lingeringly as they say goodbye. Arriving at the cave before sunrise, he gathers all the gear he needs and heads in, bracing himself against the disorienting effects of passing through the void.

After making several trips, Peren drops the last of the gear near the tunnel that leads to the queen. Setting up a couple of sconces to light the tunnels, he gets to work setting up the traps.

Covered in dirt, sweat, and grime from working for a few hours, Peren takes a break, retreating back to where the stench stops for something to eat.

He closes his eyes for a few minutes and wakes up feeling refreshed and hungry. After having what he deems as breakfast, he heads back to do the final checks on the traps to ensure everything is set and ready.

Then, crawling through the entrance to the cavern, Peren gets the attention of the Spliganders.

Racing back through the hole and leaping over the pits, he makes his way to the tunnel entrance. Turning around, he is ready to take on any that escape the traps.

A smile crosses his face when he hears squealing and cries as they fall into the first pit, getting skewered by the stakes in them.

Once the first pit fills up, the Spliganders run across uninjured to fall into the second pit and get skewered by the spikes in the second pit.

It doesn't take long before that pit fills up too. The Spliganders snarl as they cross and fall into the third pit. After waiting for a few moments, Peren disengages the weight that is keeping the door flap at the other end of the tunnel open, letting it swing shut, splitting and crushing any creature under it.

The third pit fills quickly, forcing Peren to step in and kill the remaining ones. Clearing out the dead Spliganders and killing any that are still alive, he resets the traps and moves to the sconced end of the tunnel, attaching the heavy weights to the rope that pulls the flap open.

When he sees no Spliganders rush through, he enters the cavern and attracts their attention again. Rushing back to the other end of the tunnel, he stands ready.

After clearing out the tunnel, and not wanting to take any unnecessary risks, he decides he will take a nap. The thought of Norta scolding him out of love brings a smile to his face. He heads back to where the stench is mostly gone, has something to eat, and falls asleep against the hard ground.

Waking up some time later, feeling refreshed, if stiff, he goes and checks on the traps before opening the tunnel up and getting the Spliganders to come after him.

Wiping the sweat and blood off his face with his filthy sleeve, he goes back and gulps down mouthful after mouthful of water.

Sitting and eating his—*lunch? Dinner?* He can't tell—he goes back and clears out the tunnel, resetting the traps.

Poking his head out into the cavern, he only sees a few Spliganders left. Feeling confident in his ability to remove the final group, he swiftly but silently moves up to the nearest one and kills it, then moves onto the next one, repeating the process until a shrill shriek reveals his presence. Abandoning stealth, he rushes around, using every ounce of his elven speed to swiftly kill the remaining few.

As he moves to head back to the tunnel to clean and prep for the queen, a reverberating scream echoes through the cavern. Peren turns to see the queen staring at him.

SEVEN

PEREN VS THE QUEEN

Covered in black, viscous blood, Peren faces the queen. Waves of dread wash over him as he sizes up the immense creature, feeling smaller than he ever has before in his life. He looks down at the dagger in his hand and lets out a hysterical chuckle, wondering how a toothpick like this could possibly take down something the size of a mountain.

Forcing himself to focus, he studies the queen again, his mind racing to absorb every detail about her. His thoughts are abruptly interrupted as the queen roars and lunges towards him. He dives out of the way, narrowly dodging the attack. Rolling to his feet, he realises that he is outmatched and needs to go away and create a plan to take down this queen. Dodging out of the way of another swipe, he thinks, *I will not just take the risk and hope that my little dagger can do something no other sword can.* Not wanting a repeat of the Brooders, and hoping that his little toothpick can cut deep enough, he looks her up and down and works out his options.

Thinking that the queen's back would be the safest place to test his dagger against her, he swiftly leaps onto her leg, attempting to climb. The queen, feeling him in her fur, retaliates, trying to bite him.

Jumping back to the ground and rolling out of the way to avoid being bitten, he rethinks his plan. Refusing to give up, he moves to her rear, hoping she can't reach him there, only to be surprised as she easily snaps at him with her powerful jaws. Realizing climbing her body is futile, a daring plan forms in his mind—a plan he dismisses as suicidal, yet can't shake as he continues evading her attacks.

With no better alternative presenting itself, Peren stands his ground as the queen strikes again. In a heart-stopping moment, she closes her jaws around him with a bone-crushing force, beginning to chew. But something is amiss, causing her to pause in confusion. It dawns on her too late as she feels a blade pierce the back of her neck.

Timing his move perfectly, Peren leaped just as the queen attempted to engulf him, landing on top of her head unnoticed. Seizing the opportunity, he descends to her neck and locates the crucial point where the brainstem meets the spine. With a swift thrust, he plunges the dagger in.

Instantly, excruciating pain engulfs him, followed by an eerie numbness spreading from his neck down. Panic grips him as he struggles to open his eyes, only to find darkness. Frantically waving and screaming, he realizes he's blinded and paralysed below the neck, his panic escalating when he recalls what transpired—a failed attempt to sever the queen's brainstem.

The queen's sudden movement sends Peren flying, crashing hard onto the ground. His left arm shatters, his ribs crack, and his pelvis and shoulder blades snap. Despite the pain, he manages to stand, clutching his mangled arm, before realizing he's no match for the queen in his current state. He hobbles toward the tunnel exit as fast as he can, hope flickering as he nears safety. When he's almost able to reach out and touch it, he dives for it, knowing this will hurt and probably break more bones. As he skids through the exit, white hot pain flares from just below his shoulder blades down his back.

With his bones shattering and tendons tearing, Peren's body crumples against the stone. Darkness beckons, urging him to surrender, but he fights against it desperately. In a last act of desperation, he taps into his healing ability to staunch the bleeding before moving out of the way just as he finally succumbs to unconsciousness, his body battered and broken in the face of overwhelming odds.

Opening his eyes against a gritty resistance, Peren panics as he realizes he's paralysed from the arms down. Memories flood back—the queen's savage attack, his futile struggle. *How can I be alive?* he thinks incredulously, astonished by his survival despite his grievous injuries. He weeps silently for the loss of his body, feeling overwhelmed by the daunting prospect of his new reality.

After hours of despair, Peren gathers himself, focusing on the immediate challenge: escaping the caves. Despite the searing pain with every movement, he uses his arms to drag himself to the tunnel exit. As he passes the traps he set earlier, the dim torchlight guides his way, reminding him of Norta and igniting a stubborn determination to survive.

Taking breaks to conserve his strength and ensure he stays on course, Peren perseveres through agonizing pain. Eventually, exhausted and hoping for some healing respite, he drifts into a restless sleep.

Upon awakening in the darkness, unable to gauge the time, he realizes the torches have burned out. Attempting to move more of his body, he's disheartened to find no improvement. Swallowing his disappointment, he continues forward with renewed resolve, praying fervently to Arpath for guidance.

Navigating the tunnels slowly, Peren hears a familiar

whisper, reminiscent of the Whispering Wood. Despite his dire situation, he laughs hysterically, finally connecting the sound to a memory. Regaining his composure, he refocuses on finding a way out, driven by thoughts of Norta and freedom.

Though hours turn into days, Peren eventually emerges from the caves, nearly overwhelmed by the sudden sensory overload. Collapsing in exhaustion, he sleeps through the urgency of needing help, awakening to the rising sun, tears of relief streaking his face.

Unable to call out to Mercy, he desperately tries to reach out to her like he has since he was little. His eyes widen in horror when there is nothing but silence on the other end. It's as if she perished in her wait. Panic grips him as he tries to scream and cry in frustration, eventually succumbing to sleep, his mind and body exhausted from the ordeal.

He is woken sometime later by the noise of humans calling out, searching for him. Relief washes over him as he hears their voices; he is saved! Overwhelmed with emotion, he weeps tears of gratitude.

It takes several minutes for the townsfolk to realize they can't find Peren. Reaching out weakly in his delirium, he manages to guide Mercy to him before falling unconscious. He doesn't hear Norta shriek in panic as she lands beside him, muttering, "Don't be dead, don't be dead." Tears stream down her face as she feels his weak pulse. Relief turns to nausea as she takes in the extent of his injuries.

With care and urgency, they load him into a wagon, Norta cradling his head in her lap, tears continuing to fall as she sees him in this state. Her mind briefly questions what will happen next; it looks so bad that he may not survive this time, and if he does, he could be burdened with permanent injuries.

Pushing aside those thoughts, she focuses on making

Peren as comfortable as possible during the bumpy ride back to town, where they hurry him into the inn. The Herb Mistress, despite her grumbling about his carelessness, immediately begins assessing and treating his injuries, setting bones back into place with firm, expert hands that cause him to wake in agonizing pain. The other women in the inn assist, holding him down as he cries out. Norta is forced to leave the room each time, as she can't bear to see him suffer.

After he's carefully transferred to his bed, Norta spends every spare moment with Peren, monitoring him closely and only reluctantly taking breaks when forced to by the other women.

The next few weeks pass in a blur as Peren heals slowly. Norta, never believing he would walk again, stays by his side, often crying in despair at the sight of his injuries. She diligently cares for him, bathing him and refusing to accept the truth, keeping his limbs active to prevent muscle atrophy.

One night, as Peren finally opens his eyes for the first time since the bones were set, he finds himself in his room at the inn with Norta sleeping on him, her head damp against his chest. Feeling just how weak he truly is, he manages to clumsily wrap his arms around her, leaning forward to kiss her head. His gesture stirs Norta awake, and for a moment, she's disoriented until she realizes what's happening. Tears of joy stream down her face as she kisses him deeply, hoping and praying hard to the Goddess of Love and Healing, Leeariah, that this isn't just some illusion or dream, that this is real, and he is awake and there with her.

However, her joy quickly turns to anger as she slaps him hard, explaining through her own tears, "You gave me such a fright. I thought you were never going to wake up." When she sees the sadness and pain in Peren's eyes at what he put her through, her anger dissipates, replaced by relief that he's awake and recovering.

Helping him sit up, Norta feeds him stew, refusing to let him move his arms in case he does more damage and making sure he eats a healthy serving after weeks of minimal food and energy spent on healing. Peren consumes enough for multiple people. Marvelling at his appetite, Norta delights in mothering him, constantly retrieving more food and drink for him, much to his chagrin.

As Peren's body heals a little more every few days, he experiences intense itching in areas he tries to scratch at, but his hand gets slapped away when Norta sees. He marvels at the sensations of feeling parts of his body that were numb before. Within a week, ignoring Norta's protests, he starts feeding himself. Resigned to seeing to his other needs he can't manage, she takes pleasure in his discomfort when assisting with some of the more intimate tasks, despite flushing at some of them.

Lying still in the room, Peren's mind churns with the echoes of his confrontation with the queen. His body aches from the wounds she inflicted, and every movement sends sharp reminders of the battle through his senses. Norta hovers nearby, her concern palpable yet restrained, her gaze flickering over Peren as she washes his limbs.

Noticing the tension between them for the first time, Peren struggles to sit up, wincing with each movement. Looking intently at her, knowing why she is acting the way she is, he reaches out and stops her from washing him. "I know you're mad at me. I can only say how sorry I am to have put you through this. It wasn't my intention; I wasn't planning on taking on the queen. I was just clearing out the Spliganders, but then the queen got between me and the exit."

"So, you thought to take on the queen, then? Why didn't you just make a break for the exit?"

"I did!"

Turning her head on its side, she glares up into his eyes.

Wilting under her unconvinced glare, he says, "I was planning to, but wanted to make sure my dagger can pierce the skin."

Closing her eyes, frustrated, she replies, "That is the worst excuse that I have ever heard, and Gizle comes up with some awful ones."

Panicking, Peren blurts out, "I'm telling the truth! I had no want of putting you through this again, I swear!"

Looking at him unconvinced, Norta retorts, "So, you got under her foot, did you?"

"What? No."

Putting her fists on her hips, she demands, "Then how did you nearly die?"

Going a little red in the face, realising how embarrassing it is, he mutters, "I climbed on her back."

Norta blinks. Hoping that she misheard, she asks, "What was that?"

Completely red in the face, Peren looks away and mutters a little louder, "I climbed on her back."

Norta is so stunned her jaw drops open. Recovering, she says, "You—*what?! How stupid are you?*" Her voice trails off, but her mouth opens and closes a few times.

Putting his hands out placatingly, Peren tries to explain. "I wasn't sure if my dagger was going to work against a beast that size. I just wanted to be sure I could take her on."

Norta didn't think she could be shocked further. She was wrong. She just stares at him, completely stunned, unable to comprehend how she could love someone so stupid.

Confused at her reaction, Peren blinks at her and says, "I thought ahead. I was being careful, and now I can plan around this information."

Frustrated at his reasoning, she bites back, "How? How could you think that was a good idea?"

Realising that she doesn't know about animal hides, Peren explains, "Not all hides are the same thickness."

Butting in, Norta snaps, "I know that!"

"So, because they are made differently, some hides are stronger than others." As she looks like she is about to explode, he rushes to add, "For example, Brooder hides."

She stares at him stunned for a moment before she makes the connection. Her mouth goes into an O shape. Her brows touch and she opens her mouth, but Peren, anticipating what she will ask next, jumps in. "Because it will be a good way to find out, and if I could easily, maybe I could end it all then and there." Shrugging, he adds, "It felt like a good idea in that moment." Looking down at himself, he chuckles. "Now, I know it wasn't the best idea I've had."

Norta shakes her head, unable to be mad at him, knowing that he took the time to think and plan instead of rushing in there like an idiot. Overcome with relief, she starts to cry.

Peren looks up at her, confused. "Why are you crying?"

Shaking her head at him as she wipes her face, she smiles. "You are such an idiot."

Completely confused, Peren just stares at her. Leaning down, she kisses him deeply. Smiling at him, she leaves feeling much better and goes back to her chores.

Peren flops back down in the bed, sighing in exhaustion. The emotional ordeal has taken more out of him than fighting Spliganders. Feeling relieved at clearing the air with Norta, he closes his eyes to rest for a minute.

A soft knock at his door startles him awake. He jumps up as Norta pops her head through. "Oh, good, you're awake," she says softly, smiling.

Returning her smile, he sits up as she closes the door behind her, holding his arms open as she goes to him. Taking her head in his hands, he kisses her deeply and tenderly on the lips. Her body responds by pushing against him more forcefully, reciprocating the kiss.

Pulling back, he looks into her eyes, scanning to see if she is okay. Finding only love and warmth, he smiles warmly and, holding his breath, tells her, "I love you."

With love and warmth in her voice, she replies, "I love you too."

Eyes widening in remembrance, she pulls back, taking out some bread and cheese. Handing them over to Peren, she says, "I thought you might be hungry." Smiling at her, he takes the bread and cheese, then motions for her to sit on the bed next to him, and they share the food, sitting so close their bodies and legs are touching.

When they finish eating, Norta wipes the crumbs onto the floor. She kisses him goodbye and heads off to continue her chores for the rest of the day.

Watching her leave, Peren feels a deep sense of peace. He sinks back onto the bed, exhaustion seeping into his bones as he reflects on the emotional exchange. Despite the weariness that weighs upon him, he finds solace in knowing that he has provided comfort to Norta during a moment of uncertainty and fear.

Slipping inside his room later, Norta sees that he is still asleep. Smiling mischievously, she sneaks up to his bed. She stands there looking down at him for a few moments, enjoying watching him sleep, thinking what she could do to him.

Before she makes a decision, the corners of his lips curl up in a smile. Unable to hold it in any longer, Peren breaks out in a huge grin and opens his eyes.

A moment of guilt crosses her face, but then she smiles down at him and, climbing on the bed, she kisses him deeply before laying her head on his chest. Gently running his fingers up and down her back, he feels her shudder under his touch. Closing her eyes, she revels in his touch and the way her body responds to it.

Her hands moving on their own, she runs them over his chest, arms, and face. Feeling him respond to her touches, she begins running her hands over more of his body. Leaning down, she kisses him deeply.

She runs her hands through his hair, up and down his back, over his arms and chest. Planting a deep loving kiss on her lips, he moves his hands over her thighs, bottom, and back, making her shiver and moan in delight.

Determined to protect Norta even more now, Peren silently vows to return safely after confronting the queen. He knows deep down he can't put her through this ordeal again. Despite his desire to end the mission quickly, he acknowledges he wouldn't stand a chance against the queen tonight.

Whispering in her ear, he assures her, "It ends soon."

Looking into Peren's eyes, Norta sees a fire she hasn't witnessed before—something almost magical and otherworldly. It fills her with both love and apprehension for what lies ahead.

Snuggling close, she pleads with Peren to wait until he's fully recovered before facing the queen. Unable to deny her, he agrees.

Over the next few days, he makes rapid progress, gaining flexibility and strength in his limbs, much to Norta's astonishment.

As the days pass, it occurs to Peren that no one has ever recorded what a queen looks like or an effective way of disposing the Spliganders. In between being in the yard practising, he starts going over all the information from the books he read and his knowledge of the Spliganders, his mind stewing over possible ways to take the queen down, actively working on the solution when he has a chance.

He is always forced to put the problem aside when in Norta's company and when he eats, as she is truly a distraction—getting great pleasure from embarrassing him, swishing her hips seductively, beaming when she sees his cheeks brighten at the way she walks. He averts his eyes as much as he can, unable to completely tear his eyes away from those swaying hips. Other patrons who notice snicker at the flirtation between them.

A few nights later, Peren manages to come up with a reasonable plan. The next morning, while Norta snuggles with him, he says, "It will end with this trip."

Looking deep into his eyes, she sees the look of fire in them, determined to finish this once and for all. Her brows touch as a new look comes over him. "What is it?"

"I'm going to need a few days in the caves again."

A look of worry crosses her face. "No, you can't. Last time, you nearly died. I will not lose you."

Looking gently into her eyes, Peren tries to convince her. "I wasn't prepared last time. I will be this time. I promise not to do something as stupid as last time. I will be better prepared this time."

She looks down at him, her brain warring with her heart over what she should do about this. Sighing in acquiescence, she nods. "Ok, but one week." Looking into his eyes, she emphasises it. "*One* week."

Agreeing, they snuggle in closer, cherishing every moment they have together before he leaves. Far too soon in Norta's opinion, he heads swiftly to the cave on Mercy, who relishes her regained freedom to run.

EIGHT

PEREN VS THE QUEEN ROUND 2

Armed with everything he needs, Peren enters the cave and begins his arduous trek towards the queen's lair. Eventually finding the tunnel that leads to the large cavern where the queen awaits, he stops for a break and runs over the plan one more time.

He gathers the necessary items, then spends hours moving stealthily around the cavern, occasionally stepping out to rest and recuperate, keeping this up for what feels like days.

After a good rest, he sneaks into the cavern and feels a wave of relief upon seeing the queen asleep. He knows he must act swiftly and quietly; starting the timer to light the torches, he moves into position.

Judging the timing, he rushes in, climbs onto her back, and targets the same spot on her neck where he previously wounded her. Despite his efforts, the dagger fails to cut deep enough, awakening the queen, who begins thrashing wildly, trying to dislodge him. Desperate to regain control, she rolls on the ground, forcing Peren to abandon his precarious position.

His mind is racing. *How much longer till the torches light?* Realizing the timer is moving too slowly, he lights the first of several torches, blasting the cavern with light that blinds him and sends the queen scurrying away, snarling. As she runs away from the light, her paws get caught in a mass of ropes and nets. With her eyes closed against the blinding light, and as Peren's adjust to the sudden brightness, he seizes the opportunity to climb back up and resume his assault on the wound.

Thrashing in response to Peren attacking her, the queen manages to move, crashing into some of the nearby torches, sending them flying across the cavern floor. As they crash into others, they knock over and land on the excess pile of rope and netting that Peren didn't use, catching fire and spreading quickly, jumping to anything that will burn, igniting the rope that has the queen tangled up.

The rope snaps as it gets eaten by the flame, freeing the queen to move more freely. Peren is so focused that he doesn't at first notice something is wrong. Only when the screeching changes from pain and anger to pain and fear does he realise something is amiss.

Looking around, he sees a lot more flame than should be coming from the torches. As he's thinking about what might have happened, the queen manages to throw him from her back. Landing in a roll, he looks around and sees light smoke rising from the ropes and netting.

A piercing scream draws his attention. Looking over to the queen, he sees thick smoke rising from her hide and smells the acrid odour of flesh and fur burning.

He watches helplessly as the queen thrashes about, consumed by fire and crashing into obstacles in a frantic attempt to extinguish the flames.

Crouching in the shadows, his heart pounding in sync with the queen's agonized cries, Peren is heartbroken by the scene. The cavern is a chaotic inferno, torches casting flickering light and heavy smoke obscuring his vision.

Determined not to let the queen suffer a lingering death by fire, he knows this is his only chance to end her misery quickly.

Taking a deep breath, he darts from his hiding place, weaving through the haze of smoke making his eyes water and breathing hard as the cavern is filled with the smoke. Managing to avoid the thrashing queen, he looks up and tries to assess what he can. Her fur is ablaze in several places; she seems to move more franticly the longer she burns.

Seeing her stumble as she gets tangled in some unburnt rope, he thinks, *It's now or never.* Leaping into the air, he lands on an untouched patch of fur and makes his way quickly up to her neck.

Dodging her desperate attempts to shake him off, he holds onto her back, gripping tightly to avoid being thrown by her convulsive movements. The intense heat sears through his clothes and stings his eyes, but he remains focused on the task at hand.

Drawing his dagger, he slashes at the soft, unprotected skin where he struck before. Each cut is meant to open the wound up, allowing him to reach deeper. Blood oozes from the wounds, mingling with his sweat and the soot as he works.

The queen roars in pain and fury, rolling and thrashing in a desperate attempt to dislodge him. Peren clings on grimly, his muscles burning from exertion and the intense heat. The smoke is suffocating him as he struggles to hang on, knowing he must finish this quickly before the queen's strength overwhelms him.

Summoning all his strength and agility, Peren makes a final, desperate lunge with his dagger, aiming for the junction where the queen's neck meets her skull. The blade sinks deeper this time, piercing through the vulnerable flesh beneath her fur. With a decisive twist, he feels the dagger sever the brain stem.

The queen crashes to the ground, and her movements cease. Peren withdraws his dagger and stumbles back from the now-lifeless mass beneath him. Smoke billows around them, and the flames from the torches dance wildly against the cavern walls.

Exhausted and singed, Peren crawls away from the queen's burning body, his hands trembling from the ordeal. He collapses against a cool rock formation, panting heavily as he watches the flames consume the remnants of both the ropes and the queen.

Feeling his skin singe, he looks down to find his clothes smouldering. In a panic, he quickly strips off and smothers them. Gingerly crawling back through the tunnel, feeling the burns he suffered along with the choking smoke, he coughs and retches with every movement. After dressing again in the smoking clothes, wincing and coughing hard, he cleans out his mouth with water before swallowing, coughing, and spitting in a fit. Feeling like his lungs are destroyed, he grabs a torch and heads out to confront the void one final time.

Gritting his teeth against the lingering pain, he packs up and mounts Mercy wearily. Adjusting himself in the saddle, trying to find a comfortable position, he glances for the final time at the ominous entrance before spurring his mount into motion. Together, they make their way back to the town, driven by a deep longing to return.

As he arrives in town, a nervous crowd gathers, eagerly awaiting news of his confrontation with the queen. Too tired and sore to acknowledge them, he ignores their stares and heads straight for the stable yard. As he dismounts Mercy, Norta rushes toward him and leaps into his arms, the force knocking him off-balance and sending them both to the ground. She plants her lips on his, and he closes his eyes, savouring the weight of her on top of him, kissing her back.

When she pulls away, he opens his eyes and sees the worry etched on her face. He offers a slight smile, his eyes roaming over her face and body, feeling himself finally relax after months of tension. Tears start to well up as he lays his head back on the ground, feeling lighter.

It's over—he's made it home.

Norta's expression shifts as the smell of the sticky, drying ichor covering Peren hits her. Her nose wrinkles in disgust as she notices the blood coating his body. Fear flickers across her face when his eyes close again, and for a moment, she hesitates, worried he's gone—but when he smiles up at her, she exhales in relief, standing up and glaring down at him in frustration.

Feeling the loss of her warmth, Peren opens his eyes gingerly and sees her standing there, arms crossed, looking indignant. Winking at her with a wince, he struggles to stand, relying on her help. Norta assists him into the inn, and, despite his weakness, he attempts to carry her toward the bathing room. He manages to lift her, but his strength falters as he approaches the tub. With a playful grin, he gives a final, unsteady push, dumping her gently into the water before he sinks to the edge, gasping slightly as he leans against the tub for support.

Norta's surprised laughter fills the room, but concern flickers in her eyes as she quickly assesses him. As she starts cleaning him, discovering the cuts and scratches scattered across his skin, her muttered scolding fills the air. Despite her relief that he's alive and safe, she fights the urge to break down in tears, focusing on patching him up.

Too exhausted to argue, Peren just shrugs and winces with each touch, closing his eyes and letting her care for him. He stays quiet about ending the plague, knowing the townsfolk outside are still waiting for news.

For now, he just wants to rest.

NINE

CELEBRATION

By nightfall, the crowd outside the inn has packed the street, all awaiting news. Convening an impromptu town meeting in the main square, the mayor sends the scribe to escort an exhausted Peren and Norta there. When the mayor spots Peren in the crowd, he breaks out in a big grin, quickly waving him up onto the stage.

With a booming voice, the mayor addresses the crowd. "Thank you all for coming. I am as eager as you to find out from the man himself how his quest went."

Filled with adrenaline from being in front of so many people, Peren feels more awake than he did minutes ago.

Gesturing to him, the mayor continues, "And now, Peren Naïlo, will you please grace us with the results of your campaign?" Stepping back, he motions for Peren to step forward.

Straightening up, Peren steps forward, and, in a very confident voice, he calls out to the crowd, "I have come back!" He pumps his fist into the air.

The cheers that come from the crowd are deafening. Waving them quiet, Peren speaks up again. "I have brought you good news and bad news!" Silencing the oohing crowd, he asks, "What would you like to hear first?"

They mostly chant, *"Good. Good. Good."*

Smiling down at them, Peren cries out, "Your plague days are over!" He pumps his fist again.

The crowd goes wild, shouting, cheering, stomping, and whistling.

It takes minutes to finally calm the crowd. One of them shouts, "And what is the bad news?"

Grinning mischievously, Peren opens his mouth and shouts, "You will be sleeping with the dogs from staying out all night away from your missuses!"

The crowd erupts even louder.

The mayor moves up and puts an arm around Peren and tries to wave them silent. Looking at him, Peren gives him a smug smirk.

Irritated at how the crowd loves Peren, the mayor smiles through his teeth at him and addresses the people. "The town is very grateful and forever indebted to you. Thank you so much for your service to this town." Clapping him on the back, the mayor turns his back to Peren and addresses the town again. "Our hero!"

As the scribe beckons Peren down from the stage, the audience all rushes towards the stage. Swarming him, they all continue to cheer and clap him on the back. Swept up, they drag him off to the inn, where they sit him down at the bar, pushing drinks in front of him before he even has a chance to finish each one. Torach comes up and says to him, "You better start chugging. Otherwise, you will fall behind."

The crowd starts to chant, *"Chug. Chug. Chug."*

Swept up in the moment, Peren gulps down drink after drink. Feeling it rush straight to his head, making him dizzy, he starts to feel nauseous in his stomach. Seeing how woozy he looks, Norta slips up to him on the other side of the bar, subtly removes the drinks, and diverts any that get poured for Peren. He looks at her with relief when he finally works out what happened.

Later, waking up, Peren tries to peel his head up from the sticky bar, only to find the room spinning. Quickly putting his head back down before his stomach empties itself, he lets out a groan.

Pushing a bucket into his lap, Norta forces his head up, quickly positioning his head in line with the bucket just as the bile rushes up and out of his mouth, narrowly missing her as he empties his stomach into the bucket.

Wiping his mouth with a rag, she helps him up to his bed. He falls asleep as soon as his head hits the pillow. Smiling down at him, Norta removes his boots, kisses his sticky forehead, and leaves him to his slumber after leaving a clean bucket in case he needs it.

Waking briefly in the night, Peren leans over the bed to empty his stomach into a nearby bucket. Feeling awful, he tries to pull the pillow off his face, but tears the fabric, and a small patch is left behind. He tosses around, trying to find a comfortable place to fall back to sleep. Giving up after a few minutes, feeling clammy and sticky, he rises up and slowly makes his way to the shutters, opening them to the cool night air. The soft breeze is like a balm on his skin. He loses track of time until the grey light of dawn breaks through.

Realizing he won't get more sleep, with a sigh, Peren cleans up the best he can before donning his boots, then quietly heads downstairs to the kitchen. Spotting him, Norta saunters over with a knowing smile, teasing him about his night. Wincing at her volume, Peren pleads with his eyes, but she revels in teasing him loudly, much to his misery.

Leading him to a table in the noisy part of the room, Norta

serves him a hearty breakfast with her hangover cure drink, holding the mug to his mouth to ensure he drinks it slowly. Despite his discomfort, she leaves him to eat alone, laughing at his reluctance.

Peren feels the effects of Norta's hangover cure halfway through his meal, gradually clearing his mind. As he glances around, he notices another person stumbling into the inn, clearly also suffering from a hangover. Observing the man's interaction with Norta at the bar, Peren recognizes the mug she places in front of him as her hangover remedy. The man gulps it down hastily, prompting Peren to realize he was made to sip it slowly.

Confused, when she comes back to clear his table, he asks, "How come you made me sip that revolting cure slowly when the guy at the bar gulped it down?"

Smiling, she responds in a firm voice, "The faster you drink it, the quicker it works. I just wanted you to experience the consequences of overindulgence." He looks up at her with hurt eyes, and she laughs at him before turning around and walking off to serve other customers.

Unable to sit idle any longer, Peren retrieves his dagger and heads to the yard for practice, aiming to dispel the remnants of his hangover and regain strength. He pushes himself until the sun dips behind the trees, leaving him glistening with sweat, panting heavily, his muscles sore and stiff.

After refreshing himself in the bath, he returns to the common room to a chorus of gratitude and cheers. Sitting down at an empty table, he orders dinner, though his stomach protests that he hasn't ordered enough. Norta notices and grins knowingly, her gaze causing Peren's cheeks to flush as he watches her walk away.

She returns, swaying her hips seductively as she takes his tray. Noticing his lingering hunger, she teases him with a mischievous glint in her eye, asking if he wants more food in a way that further embarrasses him. He can only shake his head, speechless at her playful flirtation in such a public setting.

Amused by his reaction, Norta turns away, her eyes sparkling with amusement as she leaves Peren sitting there, visibly flustered. Swinging into the kitchen, she finds Gizle looking disappointed. Without missing a beat, Gizle complains, "Why do you have to do stuff like that?"

Looking at her sister innocently, Norta replies, "Stuff like what?"

Waving to the door with a look of disgust, Gizle answers, "That!"

Laughing, Norta responds, "You mean this?" She proceeds to swish her hips seductively as she walks past Gizle, laughing harder as Gizle's cheeks heat as she becomes increasingly flustered. "You hate the lovey-dovey stuff, don't you?"

With the most disgusted look on her face, Gizle fires back, "It's gross, and ewww!" A shiver runs down her spine as she finishes her sentence.

The townspeople continue to celebrate Peren's return with fervour, their gratitude pouring forth in the form of drinks and congratulatory slaps on the back. The mayor, too, joins in the public display of admiration, his gestures seemingly generous, but stirring suspicion in Peren's mind.

Behind closed doors, however, a different dynamic unfolds. The mayor's demeanour shifts from congenial to interrogative as he relentlessly questions Peren about the extraordinary achievement he managed. Now wary and learned from previous encounters, Peren navigates the conversations with careful precision. He recognizes the mayor's intent to glean any potential advantage from their exchanges and approaches each encounter like a strategic sword fight, using words and wit as his weapons.

Skilfully avoiding divulging any significant details, he deflects the mayor's probing inquiries, often leading him in circles. He understands the stakes—the mayor's potential to exploit any slip of information—and ensures that each session ends without yielding anything substantial. Afterwards, reflecting on these verbal duels, he takes satisfaction in his ability to outmanoeuvre the mayor, safeguarding crucial information while maintaining his advantage.

Deciding that he wants to spend the rest of his life with Norta, Peren approaches Torach quietly one day and asks for permission to join souls with her.

After a long consideration, in which Torach drags out the silence to torture Peren, he finally breaks the silence.

"When I first met you, I thought, *Great, another arrogant, cocky teen who thinks he's invincible.* Then, after what you did to Gizle, I thought you were a creep," Torach says, running his fingers through his hair. "You kept proving my suspicions correct, showing how immature and arrogant you are by storming off to demand the contract for the Spliganders. When you managed to talk them into giving it to you, I really thought, *This is it. Bye-bye, arrogant kid who thinks he can do something armies struggle to accomplish.*"

Peren opens his mouth to counter, but Torach raises his hand. "Let me finish." Closing his mouth, Peren sits silently as Torach continues. "Then, that very night, you showed that you were a calculating, knowledgeable, arrogant boy." Shaking his head at the memories, he goes on. "After that first night, when you walked back in covered head-to-toe with that black blood dripping off you onto the floor, I just stood there thinking, *Damn, I was wrong.* You looked like something from the hells, yet you were steady and standing tall and proud. Then I saw the look in Norta's eyes when she beheld you, and I knew she had fallen in love with you."

Torach chuckles to himself to ease the pain. "I couldn't understand what she saw in you, an arrogant, cocky teen. But she has always seen the best in people." He stops for a moment, teary-eyed. Peren waits patiently.

Torach continues, "In that moment, I knew. I knew you were going to take her away from me. She isn't my little girl anymore; she's grown into such a beautiful woman." A tear escapes his eye and runs down his left cheek. He takes a moment to steady his voice. "But as time went on and I got to know you better, I could see you falling for her as hard as she fell for you. You've matured so much in these past months with us." Another tear escapes. He stops once more to compose himself, then turns to Peren with a deep, intense stare. "Look after her and protect her."

Peren nods solemnly. "I will, sir. To my dying breath. I promise I won't fail her and will be the man she sees me to be."

Nodding in acceptance, Torach responds, "I give you my blessing and permission to join with my daughter's soul, Peren Naïlo." He reaches out for an awkward hug, whispering, "My son."

Walking away with a surreal feeling, Peren starts to plan a way to ask Norta to join souls with him. Unable to think of anything that would sweep her off her feet, he decides on a simple, intimate way to ask.

That night, as the town continues to celebrate, Peren pulls Norta into his room, face blushing as he nervously says, "Norta, I, um…" He changes what he was about to say. "Norta, these past months…"

He's interrupted before he can continue by Norta's eyes filling with tears, and, sobbing, she chokes out, "I knew—I knew this would happen!"

Confused, not wanting to risk giving it away, Peren puts his hand on her shoulder as he asks, "What would happen?"

She pulls out of his grasp, her words coming out in a rush. "That—that you don't want me anymore. You are leaving soon and are breaking things off!"

Peren's jaw drops in shock at this, opening and closing a few times before Norta turns to rush out of the room. Moving quickly, he manages to grab hold of her and spin her back, holding her as she fights, with him repeatedly saying, "Wait. Stop. It's not what you think."

Fighting harder, Norta starts crying, mumbling, making it hard for anyone to hear, only Peren's elven ears picking up the words, but only just. "What? You are going to humiliate me in front of everyone?"

Eyes widening, Peren almost lets go, giving Norta a chance to try and break his grip. Recovering quickly, he holds her, and, looking into her eyes, he shakes her a little. "Stop! Just let me finish! You have it all wrong!"

Sniffling, she stands there glaring at him. Taking the silence as her indication to talk, he mutters, "This isn't how it was supposed to go." Shaking his head, looking into her deep liquid amber eyes, he manages to splutter out, "I don't want to let you go. Nay, I can't live without you. What I'm trying to say is... I love you!"

Norta stills further as she looks up at him. Her brows touch in confusion. "You, you...love me?"

Closing his eyes frustrated, face flushing hotter, he says, "Yes, I love you. I want to... to... join souls with you."

Norta's jaw drops in shock. Looking up at him, she stutters out, "You...you...want to join souls?"

Face red, but feeling more confident, Peren says confidently, "Yes, I do. I want to spend my life with you."

A slow smile begins to spread across her face as it sinks in. "You want to soul join. You want to soul join." Her face brightens as she repeats it over and over. Suddenly going all serious, she demands, "Have you spoken to father?"

Smiling with a nod, Peren replies, "Yes, I have, and he has given me his blessing."

She jumps into his arms, squealing, "Yes" as she plants a deep sensual kiss on his lips, which he returns vigorously.

Pulling away, breathless, Peren's eyes light up. "What if we made the announcement tonight?" He shrugs at her. "They are already together celebrating."

Looking at him, trying to find an excuse to say no, she comes up with a few optional ones, but, feeling too excited to care about them, she just nods and smiles brightly.

They head downstairs to the common room, Peren feeling drunk not only on the town's euphoria over his skills and accomplishments, but also from Norta's acceptance.

Stepping past the threshold of the common room, trembling with excitement and euphoria, Peren is unable to keep the ear-to-ear grin off his face. Seeing who stands at the threshold, the room falls silent, all eyes on them. As they step forward, the entire room erupts in cheers, raising their mugs, banging on tables, and stomping their feet in praise and thanks.

Taking time to quiet down to Peren's motions, the room slowly settles. With everyone's eyes intently on him, he opens his mouth to say a few words, but Gizle rushes up with two mugs on a tray, interrupting and distracting everyone, eliciting a chuckle at Peren's stunned face.

Recovering from the interruption, he raises his mug and addresses the room. "Thank you for all your support and hospitality." Turning to Norta with love in his eyes, he adds, "I wouldn't be here without you." Pausing until the cheering and whistling dies down, he continues, "I have another announcement to make." Looking at Norta after she elbows him, he smiles and corrects himself. "We—*we* have an announcement to make. Norta and I are now betrothed!" He's barely able to get the last word out before the room erupts with table banging, stomping, and cheering.

He empties his mug into a very empty stomach, the drink going straight to his head. Before he can move, they are besieged by everyone in the room rushing up to offer their congratulations, hugs, and back slaps. His mug is replaced by another, every mouthful making the room spin a little more as the men drag him over to the bar for many celebratory drinks.

Becoming unsteady on his stool at the bar, he constantly slides off, emptying mug after mug. They exchange lewd jokes, laughing at his inability to handle alcohol until he eventually passes out, his head thumping on the wet and sticky bar.

Waking up with a groan to a splitting headache and a spinning room, he cradles his sticky head in his hands, feeling sick. He opens his eyes when a familiar ghastly smell hits his nose like a sledgehammer, and he sees a mug placed in front of him.

Identifying the smelly drink as Norta's hangover cure, he lurches for the mug, crying out as everything spins and hurts, closing his eyes and whimpering. A breathy whisper in his ear says, "Serves you right for not watching how much you drank."

Slowly taking the mug, he gulps down the vile concoction, nearly bringing it back up. Forcing himself not to let a drop come out, he just sits there focused on not throwing up. The mug is eventually replaced with a plate of fruit, some bread, and cheese. Taking small bites when he stops feeling so queasy, he realizes just how hungry he really is.

Seeing his hunger, Norta whispers in his ear, "When did you last eat?"

Despite the fog starting to thin, he still has a splitting headache that prevents him from being able to think for long. Unable to speak without wincing in pain, he just shrugs.

"Did you even eat last night?" Norta asks, exasperation in her voice. Shrugging again in uncertainty, he focuses on the food, helping the fog to thin. Sighing in exasperation at him, Norta mutters, "No wonder you are so hungry and got so drunk."

Finishing the huge meal, he rests his head in his hands, feeling sated. Slowly turning his head to Norta, he gives her a weak smile and whispers, "Thank you."

Giving him a small glare that is ruined by a tiny smile, she takes the plate and mug away. Feeling less foggy, he slowly gets up and moves to his room, dunking his head in the washbasin, removing the sticky liquid from his face and hair. Then, flopping onto the bed, he falls into a short, deep sleep.

Opening his eyes to a knock at the door, he groggily looks at the head popping in and puts it back down, yawning. Norta comes over and kisses him on the forehead, whispering in his ear, "How are you feeling?"

"Tired," he murmurs.

Tilting her head back and laughing for a moment, she looks down at him with a huge smile. She helps him climb out of bed, and he grabs his dagger and walks out with her to the stable yard to practice and wake up more.

After sweating out any remaining alcohol in his system, he stops as the sun hits the trees. Turning to where Norta is watching him, he gives her a big cheesy grin. Heading over to her, he tries to wrap a sweaty arm around her, but she dodges his advances. Laughing, they walk side by side into the inn.

As each day passes, the revelry settles down, and Peren wakes up each morning with less of a hangover than the last. He practices with his dagger daily, working up a good sweat, pushing his limits to regain his former strength. The routine brings a sense of normality, a stark contrast to the chaos that has recently enveloped his life.

As the evenings quiet down, Torach begins to spend more time with Peren, finding solace in quiet corners or private rooms. They discuss the upcoming soul-joining ceremony, with Torach meticulously going over Peren's responsibilities and the intricate details of the ritual. Each conversation is filled with a mixture of gravity and hope, the weight of tradition resting on Peren's shoulders.

One evening, as they sit in the flickering candlelight of a secluded room, Torach leans forward, his eyes reflecting the flames. "You understand, Peren, this ceremony is not just a ritual. It's a bond—a commitment to our people and our land. You've proven your bravery, but this... this is about your heart and spirit."

Peren nods, the significance of the ceremony sinking in deeper with each word. He feels a mixture of apprehension and determination. The battle with the queen was a test of his physical limits, but this ceremony, this joining of souls, will test his inner strength and resolve.

Later that night, while Norta sleeps soundly, Peren gets up out of bed and sits on the edge of the roof, contemplating all that Torach has said and instructed. Looking at the clear night sky dotted with stars, he takes a deep breath, feeling overwhelmed about the future and insignificant amongst the heavens. Closing his eyes and letting the cool air flowing into his lungs calm him. He knows he will face the future with the same courage he had when he faced the queen.

Looking back at the window, he makes a silent vow to himself and to Norta, whose unwavering support has been his anchor: no matter what lies ahead, he will honour his commitments and protect her and his new family, cherishing the bonds that hold them all together.

TEN

SOUL-JOINING

As the days inch closer to the soul-joining, the women of the town become increasingly meticulous, fussing over every detail. They exchange sly looks and share knowing smiles with Peren, whose cheeks invariably flush bright red in response to their attention. Despite his embarrassment, he finds himself consistently being shooed away from the intimate preparations, leaving him to combat his growing nervousness by training diligently with his dagger. Unaware of how the anticipation is mounting as the significant day approaches, he immerses himself in his physical training, seeking solace in the familiar rhythm of blade against air.

Some days, he's dragged to the tailors for measurements and fittings, feeling utterly ridiculous in the elaborate garments they insist on dressing him in. The swooning seamstresses and their unceremonious handling only add to his embarrassment, and he suspects they might even be enjoying his discomfort. Despite his efforts to maintain his composure, he fails miserably.

When the morning finally arrives, Peren, sleep-deprived and anxious, finds himself yearning for the familiar trials of combat over these internal struggles. Clad in a richly embroidered brocade doublet of deep emerald, a silk shirt with billowing sleeves, and matching velvet breeches tailored to perfection, he feels utterly out of place in the elaborate ensemble chosen by the seamstresses of Comtun. A wide, finely tooled leather belt with an ornate buckle cinches the outfit, while knee-high leather boots and a luxurious cloak draped over his shoulders complete the look. Peren turns to Torach and opens his mouth to voice his complaint, but quickly thinks better of it under the innkeeper's stern gaze.

High-noted flutes fill the room, quieting down the excited chatter. Everyone turns to see Norta walking into the common room in a shimmering blue-green sleeveless dress that flows like water with every step. Her auburn hair is elegantly braided, with delicate white and lavender flowers woven throughout, forming a wreath that crowns her head. Her makeup is subtle yet striking: a touch of kohl lining her amber eyes, enhancing their brightness, and a soft blush accentuating her freckled cheeks, with a hint of rose on her lips that completes her radiant look.

The crowd parts, letting Peren see her for the first time. Knees buckling in awe, he manages to catch himself before he collapses to the ground. He's unable to take his eyes off her, even when she moves up beside him and takes his hand, intertwining her fingers with his.

Realizing that the mayor is speaking, he tears his eyes away from her and focuses on what is being said. "Before you stand two young people who have decided to join their souls together. If anyone believes there is any reason why these two should not be joined, please step forward and provide evidence."

No one steps forward, all smiling and nodding their approval. After looking at everyone in the room, the mayor turns back to Peren and Norta. "I decree, with all the people of Comtun here as my witnesses, that no one takes issue with these two being paired."

Dipping two fingers into a small bowl of blood in his left hand, the mayor speaks in a loud, clear voice as he draws two parallel lines above Peren's right eyebrow, midway up his forehead, repeating the gesture above his left eyebrow. "With the blood of Lyfe this creature has sacrificed, I connect you, Peren Naïlo, with Lyfe, opening a window to your soul," he intones solemnly. Finishing off the markings with two lines drawn down the middle of Peren's forehead from hairline to eyebrow, he then turns to Norta to repeat this part of the ritual.

Turning back to Peren, he dips his fingers into the bowl again, this time touching the right side of the bridge of Peren's nose. He speaks as he draws two lines just under the eye, stopping at the cheekbones, then repeats the gesture on the left side. "With this Lyfe's blood, I reach through the window to your soul, grasping a thread." Turning to Norta, he performs the same ritual.

Before continuing, Mayor Jornstawn takes a cloth and wipes his fingers clean. Torach moves up next to the mayor, holding two pendants. In the golden housing, two gems are seated together flawlessly to form an upside-down triangle. One is an almond-brown jasper, and the second is a mandarin garnet. The gems reflect the eye colours of Peren and Norta, and the rounded points symbolize the union of two into one, signifying that balance is key to harmony between them.

Mayor Jornstawn continues, "The rounded points not only serve to prevent the pendant from pricking the skin, but also represent that being rounded in one's own life leads to a rounded relationship."

Taking the pendant from Torach's offered left hand, Mayor Jornstawn says to Peren as he places it around his neck, "With this mythical pendant, you publicly acknowledge that you have paired your soul." Clasping the pendant around

Norta's neck at the same time, Torach smiles through tears with pride and love for his daughter.

As they were briefed before the ceremony, Peren and Norta each take the pendant around their own necks and touch the stones together. The gold housing shimmers and moves over the gems, etching and inlaying itself into a complex, intricate, unique pattern that marks their singleness merging to this union, but also the date and their pledges to each other.

Dipping his fingers in the blood again, Mayor Jornstawn turns to Peren and draws two vertical lines from the middle of his bottom lip down to the tip of his chin, then two lines from the right corner of Peren's mouth on a descending angle to his jawbone, mirroring this on the left side. Speaking while he draws in blood, he says, "With this Lyfe's blood, I attach Norta's soul thread to you." He finishes the process with Norta, then hands the bowl over to the town scribe, who provides a clean cloth to dry the blood on his fingers.

Turning to them both, Mayor Jornstawn declares, "I now pronounce you Soul-Joined. Let no one come between this bond."

Smiling into each other's eyes, they are lost in their moment, and barely hear the cheers of the crowd. As they lean in and kiss deeply, the already-shaking room gets even louder.

Breathless and with eyes filled with love, they are suddenly grabbed and dragged off for the celebrations. The entire town spills onto the streets, celebrating through the night with drink and dance.

As the sky lightens over the town, they decide it's time that the soul-joined couple seal the joining. A very drunk Peren and a slightly more sober Norta are escorted to their Joining chambers at the inn. Peren barely gets the door closed and locked before Norta leaps into his arms, thumping him against the door and devouring his mouth with hers.

He tries to carry her to the bed, stumbling and nearly falling over a few times before plopping her down. Both giggling about it, they clumsily paw at each other, managing to remove each other's clothes. Despite having seen her naked, Peren is unable to stop staring at her beautiful body hungrily. She goes red in the face and tries to cover up, thinking something is wrong with her. Before she can open her mouth, Peren leaps onto her, devouring her mouth with his, saying between kisses that she is the most beautiful woman he has ever seen.

Taking his time, he makes love to her multiple times. They both fall asleep in each other's arms, exhausted.

Slowly opening his eyes, Peren smiles as he sees a sleeping Norta wrapped up in his arms with what looks to be a contented smile on her face. Not willing to move a muscle, he just watches her as she sleeps, admiring her perfect facial features.

Eventually, she opens her eyes and looks up into his happily contented, smiling face. Closing her eyes, smiling back, and stretching with the grace of a cat, she snuggles back into his arms, angling her head to give him a soft and gentle kiss as she whispers a greeting.

Powerless to stop the loving grin on his face, he replies with the same greeting, running his fingers up and down her arm slowly and softly. He tells her that it is mid-afternoon. Moaning and giving a tired but happy yawn, she looks up to him and whispers, "I have never been so hungover in my life."

He whispers back, "Me too. Should we get some of that amazing hangover cure of yours?"

She winces as she nods. They slowly move and get dressed, sneaking out of the room to get some of the hangover cure she prepared yesterday.

Entering the common room, they find many of the villagers have passed out at the tables and bar. Quickly and quietly, they move into the kitchen as fast as their hammering heads allow. After having a couple of mugs of the cure, they look at each other ravenously. Leading her by the hand, Peren takes them back to their room, shuts the door, and locks it. As soon as he turns around, Norta pounces on him, kissing him deeply.

Stopping at the sound of dry retching, they turn to find Gizle sitting on the unmade, rumpled bed. Stomping over to the bed, Norta wipes her hungover face, grabs Gizle's arm, and starts dragging her to the door, only stopping when she threatens to scream. Still holding her arm, Norta rounds on her with a glare that could crack rocks, wincing at the movement as she demands, "What do you want?!"

Holding her arms open, Gizle simply replies with a cheeky smile, "Play with me."

Snorting, then grimacing at the pain in her head, Norta continues to drag Gizle to the door, venomously saying, "Get out and leave us!"

Pouting with her arms crossed, Gizle gives her sister the biggest sulky sad face she can. As the door shuts and she stomps away, she murmurs, "No fair."

Turning back to Peren to ask him a question, Norta barely gets her mouth open before Peren claims it with his. Stripping again, they hop into bed and make love multiple times, feeling less foggy as time goes on. Sweating and relaxing in each other's arms, they fall asleep contentedly.

A banging on the door makes them jump out of bed in complete shock. They land on the floor in a tangle of limbs. They call out to stop the banging, saying they are awake, but Gizle refuses until she is let in, banging on the door harder to emphasize her point.

They close their eyes in frustration and pain at the noise. Taking a deep breath to calm down, they untangle, and Peren staggers sleepily to the door.

As Peren unlocks the door, Norta screams out in panic, "*Stop!*" Unfortunately, the lock is disengaged, and Gizle barges into the middle of the room. Opening her mouth to say something, she just stands there gaping at her naked sister, who is trying to cover up, and a very naked, half-awake Peren. Going bright red, she runs screaming in terror from the room, waking anyone who was still asleep after her banging.

Both of them look at each other as Peren closes the door, Norta looking absolutely mortified at what just happened, her face burning hotly. Peren is mildly amused at the whole situation. Seeing his amusement, Norta's expression turns into a glare.

Seeing the glare turn back into one of shock and embarrassment, Peren gathers her into his arms, apologizing and trying to explain his amusement. Talking into her hair, he murmurs, "Just think, every time she even thinks of us, she will have that image come to mind. She will be completely embarrassed and will avoid us." Norta's lips curl up in a small smile at the memory of pure shock and humiliation of what Gizle walked into. Imagining how she will react at just the thought of either of them makes her chuckle into his chest.

Holding her back to see her reaction, Peren shakes his head internally at how women flip between moods faster than he can blink. Looking up at his incredulous face, she puts her hands on his chest and laughs heartily, kissing him deeply.

Returning her kiss, still processing how quickly she has changed moods, he shrugs it off, thinking about how happy she is right now. Thoughts of women being unpredictable flit through his mind, followed by a shocking thought: *Or is it just my Soul?* Shaking off that unbidden, hopefully incorrect thought, he moves away and says as he dresses, "We should go and eat something, my Soul." His stomach agrees with a loud grumble. His face colours at the last two words, not used to speaking in such intimate phrases.

Smiling up at him, she gets dressed and agrees, saying, "Yes, we should eat something, my Soul." She colours slightly less at the words than he did.

Dressed, they head down to the common room, holding hands, and find what appears to be every member of the town lining up for Norta's almost magical hangover cure. Smiling and shrugging up at Peren, she squeezes his hand and kisses him, then darts off to help a very obviously overwhelmed Gizle fill the mugs, which are being almost snatched out of her hands.

Sitting down in the corner, Peren observes Norta. His eyes never leave her when she comes into view. Still struggling with the thought of her being his Soul, he feels guilty about not revealing his true self to her.

The only thing stopping him are the words his master drilled into him when he was little: "Humans are fickle creatures. You cannot trust them with your deepest secrets—not unless you know them really well for many years."

In addition, Peren sees this himself, hating that he needs to wait to tell her, hoping she will forgive him for his deception.

As she's rushing around with a happy glow about her, other adults and some of the older kids give her knowing smiles, and some of the older women make very lewd comments about Peren, leaving her with a burning face each time and the women walking off laughing and chuckling.

Just as Peren is contemplating whether to break the rule ingrained in him and show her the truth, hoping for the best, he is interrupted by two older men who sit down opposite him. Not anticipating them sitting, he jumps up in a defensive position, turning the happy, playful atmosphere tense and scaring both men. They quickly hold out their empty hands to show they mean no ill will.

Taking a deep breath, Peren sits down again, the whole room relaxing as he backs down, everyone quickly busying themselves with what they were doing beforehand and sending furtive glances at the trio.

Giving the men a firm look to say not to sneak up again, Peren motions for them to speak their reason for disturbing him. After a quietly murmured apology and congratulations, they offer their heartfelt thanks for what he has done for the town, amending it to *his* town now too. Wanting to wish him the brightest happiness for the future, they offer him their wisdom on the female mind and how to interpret her meanings and signs to keep her happy. Despite disagreeing on a few of the finer points, both agree that the fastest way to be miserable is by offending her, not only through his speech, but also by misinterpreting the meanings she conveys.

By the time they leave, Peren has buried his head in his hands, trying to lessen the headache from all the undercurrent meanings and hints that he must remember.

Norta finally comes over with a tray of hot steaming porridge. As she places the bowl in front of Peren, she asks, "Are you ok? What did those men want?"

Peren mutters, "To give advice on women." As the words slip from his mouth, he peeks hesitantly through his fingers, hoping to gauge how bad this tongue lashing will be.

Fighting to keep her face neutral, Norta just stands there a little longer, making him sweat. Instead of getting mad and yelling, she sits opposite him, looks at him intently, and asks, "Like what?"

Going bug-eyed in shock at her demeanour, he just sits there spluttering for a few moments. His mind races with different strategies to safely extricate himself from this. Dismissing all of them, shoulders slumping further in defeat, he starts off with the most basic of things. "You know, like, how women can say one thing and mean something else."

Thoroughly enjoying his discomfort, she presses him further. "Oh, really? What else?" She smirks at his flustered behaviour.

Trying to come up with something less insulting, Peren draws a blank. Looking up at her, his eyes pleading, he stammers, "Th-that women always o-overreact, and that I have better things to do than waste time on petty arguments."

Giving him a scary smile, she gets up without a word and continues with her chores. Peren sits there freaking out over how calmly she reacted to the advice he was given, knowing by her farewell smile that he is in deep trouble. Not knowing what to do, he just sits there glumly, his head inventing more and more dreadful scenarios, going paler with every thought.

Looking at him out of the corner of her eye, Norta smiles internally at his imagination running wild. Leaving him to stew, she focuses on her chores.

Finishing off the meal, unable to take it any longer, Peren comes to a decision. Getting up from the table, he storms over to Norta. Grabbing her arm, he drags her upstairs to their room. Pulling the door shut with feeling, he opens his mouth to scold her on leaving him to imagine the worst.

A clap sounds through the room as Peren's face is sent turning to one side.

Turning his head back to face Norta, he glares at her tomato-red face.

Getting in his face, poking his chest hard with each word, emboldened by the Demigoddess Ryva, her voice is full of venom as she says, "Don't you ever, *ever* drag me like that again. You have no right!"

Standing his ground, Peren leans in and says with a voice

filled with promised revenge, "After earlier today, you have no right to speak to me that way! You have no right to raise your hand against me!"

Norta bites back, "Don't drag me around, and I won't slap you!"

"I wouldn't if you would stop thinking it's fun to make me sit there and imagine the worst!" The muscles in his jaw flicker as he grits his teeth in anger.

Exasperated, she says through gritted teeth, "What do you expect when you say things like that? Is that how you really think? Women overreact and that your *better things* are more important than treating women with respect?" Refusing to give Peren a chance to make some excuse, she turns towards the door, saying sadly over her shoulder, "I thought you were different. Someone who truly respected and cared for me." Sighing, she adds, "I can see that I was wrong."

Shocked at this, Peren almost doesn't stop her as she steps through the doorway. Knowing he must make it right and risking another slap to the face, he grabs her and pulls her back into the room. Shutting the door, he holds her to him tightly.

"Wh—get *off* me, Peren!" She demands as she struggles in his grip.

"Is that what you really think? That I have no respect for you or your feelings?"

Blazing, her eyes bore holes into Peren as she stops struggling. "Why else would you tell me?"

Sighing in frustration, he says, "You were never supposed to know."

Stunned for a few moments, Norta looks up at him wide-eyed. "So you were going to show me disrespect and not even tell me?"

Looking at her, understanding, he responds, "No, I wasn't

going to disrespect you. The reason why I wasn't going to tell you is because I think the advice is as useful as horse dung in dinner." Sighing in frustration, he continues, "I didn't want to upset you with that. I like it when you are smiling and happy."

Standing there gaping at what Peren said, Norta truly knows for a fact that, despite the childlike exterior, a man resides in that head of his. Feeling bad about the way she made him stew, she wraps her arms around him and, resting her head on his chest, whispers, "I am so sorry. I took it way too far. I should have known that you're not like that."

Holding her tighter, Peren says into her hair, "Yes, you did."

Confused, Norta looks up at Peren when he doesn't say anything more. Smiling down at her, he continues, "I am also sorry for dragging you up here like that."

Jaw straightening, she thinks for a moment. "Next time you want to drag me like that, tell me to come with you instead."

Nodding, he pushes her away, only to mash his lips against hers.

Pulling away, Norta heads back to work. Pausing at the threshold, she turns and sends a final smile to Peren before disappearing down the stairs.

Deciding to do some practice with his dagger, he heads down to the stable yard.

Whenever Norta can, she heads out to watch him practice. He flows from one form to the next like liquid, blocking and parrying imaginary enemies, slashing and stabbing, dispatching them with skill. She smiles hard as she watches him dance around the yard, each motion calculated and precise.

Seeing her standing there out of the corner of his eye, he starts to show off, taking on more imaginary enemies, each move more extravagant and sped up, moving faster till he is at the uppermost speed of a human. Norta laughs and claps in delight at the show, laughing even harder when, distracted, he loses focus on what he is doing, steps on a loose stone, and loses his balance. Unable to stop himself in time, he falls to the ground at speed with a loud thud.

Getting up as quickly as he can, brushing himself down, he looks at her bent over, howling in laughter, tears streaming down her face. Abashed, the corners of his lips start to curl up at how it must have looked.

Hobbling over wincing, he wraps an arm around her and lets her walk him inside as she keeps roaring in laughter at him, imagining him slipping. The look on his face as he fell keeps setting her off again and again.

Resting on his bed as he waits for Norta to bring up the evening meal, he accepts the feeling of this being the last night in Comtun, in Norta's arms. Knowing how she is likely to react, he has decided not to ruin their last night together, keeping his mouth shut.

Coming in tired, Norta strips and climbs into bed with Peren. They make love multiple times, so Peren gets little to no sleep.

Waking up, he feels a sadness deep in his bones, knowing he has to part from his beloved to continue with his original quest. Tears well up at the thought of not being able to see her face or touch her, forced to leave her behind for both his and her safety.

Holding her as close as he dares without waking her, he lets her sleep, using her as his reason for procrastination. *I will burn every part of her into my memory,* he thinks, never wanting to forget her, *and* feeling even more miserable as she stirs in his arms.

Coming out to the stable yard, Norta has a confused look on her face as she moves over to where Peren is ensuring he has everything he needs for the journey ahead. "Where are you going?" she asks as coyly as possible.

Closing his eyes, he lets the flap fall on his saddlebag. Turning around slowly, dreading this moment, he opens his mouth as her eyes widen in worry at the expression on his face. "I have to finish my quest."

A puzzled look passes over her face as she tries to remember what he said about his original quest. Her heart drops as she says falteringly, "Oh. Your master. Yes. Original quest."

Norta's face lights up as an idea forms in her head, her words coming out in a rush, trying to keep up with her racing thoughts. "I can go with you. We can do this quest together." She gets more excited as the words rush out. "I could see the world with you. We could make it our hearthbinding." Exhilarated, she starts to rush off to get packed.

Grabbing her and spinning her around, Peren makes her look at him. "You can't come with me."

Elation turns to confusion as the words sink in. Anger flashes in her eyes as she demands, "Why not?"

"It's too dangerous for you. I don't want you to get hurt." Peren's heart is melting at the look she gives him.

Grinding her teeth, she bites back, "So, you weren't going to tell me you were leaving and just go?"

Wanting to say yes more than ever, Peren takes a deep breath. "I was going to tell you now." Before Norta can finish opening her mouth, he quickly adds, "I wanted our last night together to be special, not tense with a darkness over it."

Shaking him off, she starts pacing in front of him. "So, that's it? You tell me and I stay behind? Waiting for you to return? *If* you return? How am I supposed to just let that happen? You know that will never happen. I am coming, and that's final. You can't say anything to stop me. You will wait, or even if you leave, I will chase—"

"Silverlight."

Norta pauses as he interrupts. Looking at him, confused, she demands, "What?"

"Silverlight. Thats who you are to me."

Looking pointedly at him, bracing herself, she asks, "What is that supposed to mean?!"

"You're my Silverlight, Norta, guiding me home through the dark. I will always find you. I will always come home to you."

Shocked at the words, she just stares at him, dumbfounded.

"How can I come home to you if you aren't home for me to come home to?"

Thinking for a minute, Norta asks, confused, "But isn't home wherever I am? So, if I'm with you, then aren't you are home?"

Peren opens and closes his mouth a few times before keeping it shut, his mind racing, trying to find an argument that counters hers.

"But if you die, then where will my home be? How am I to live with myself if I don't protect you?"

"And how do you think I feel?" Norta points sharply to herself. "How am *I* to live with *my*self if I am not there to protect you?"

He pleads with her. "I am begging you: please stay here. At least I will know you are safe." The corner of his mouth quirk up as he adds, "Besides, knowing that I have you to come home to will only make me fight harder to be with you." Smiling fully, he adds, "Just like I did when I lost to the queen."

"And do you remember what happened when you 'came' back to me?" Norta throws in his face. "Broken!" She continues before he can respond, "I had to be there to nurse you back to health! How can I do that if I'm not there?!"

Stumped, Peren stands there breathing hard as he processes what she said. After thinking for a minute, he tries a different tack. "What about the inn? Don't your father and little sister need you? Gizle needs her big sister."

A voice comes out from inside the inn. *"I do not! I can look after myself!"*

Turning to the inn, Norta shouts back, *"Yes, you do! You can barely feed yourself!"*

Jumping in, Peren takes this miraculous opening. "See? She does need you. You yourself said so."

Spinning on her heel to face Peren, Nora adds, "If you let me finish." She calls back over her shoulder to the inn, *"But you also need to grow up! Me being there for you all the time won't help you!"* As an afterthought, she adds, *"And quit eavesdropping, you little noblet!"*

"Make me, mischief munchkin!"

Turning to Norta, Peren adds, "Are you going to let her talk to you like that?"

Norta spins between the door and Peren, unsure of which one to scold more. Making a decision, she storms up to Peren, jamming a finger in his face. "Don't you go anywhere, mister!" Turning her back to a heavily smirking man, she struts loudly across the yard towards the door.

Moments after disappearing, there's a lot of squealing and feet banging on the floor as the girls rush through the house.

Leaning back against the stables, Peren's smile increases, knowing that the screams are Gizle having fun and hearing snatches of Norta yelling, "Get back here!" A feeling of emptiness flows through him, making him more determined than ever that Norta will stay behind. No matter what, he will not let her come with him.

Storming over to Peren and getting in his face puffing after giving Gizle a scolding, Norta opens her mouth to continue the tirade, only to hesitate at the look in his eyes. Brows coming together in confusion, she asks, "What?"

A deeply sad look comes over Peren. Feeling like he is stabbing his own heart with the dagger, he struggles to get the words past the lump in his throat, saying in a breathy whisper, "I can't take you with me, please. Knowing that you are here safe and sound with your family…" He pauses for a moment as the corners of his mouth perks up, "*Our* family. How can I take you away from your life here?" A tear runs down his cheek as he continues, "I will be there and back faster if you are here waiting for me. It will make me even more determined to come back swiftly."

Tears stream down her face as his words hit her like a physical blow. Looking back to see both her father and sister standing there in the doorway, she turns to Peren, repeating this as her mind swims.

Her bottom lip quivers as she knows that she must decide and that she will regret whatever decision she makes. For the first time in her life, she is truly stuck at a crossroads, with no clear path to the right decision.

Peren moves over to her as his heart breaks at how hard a choice this truly is for her. Wrapping her up in his arms, he kisses the top of her head. Leading her inside, he helps her to a seat. Squatting down next to her, he says in a soft voice, "You are needed here more than I need you with me. How could I live with myself if I took you with me, only to lose you on the trip? I am not talking about travelling for a few days in the sun, but a long, arduous trek through some extreme climates."

Seeing the look on her face as the words come out, Peren realises he's said the wrong thing. Norta's face becomes indignant. Sitting up straighter, she opens her mouth to voice her displeasure. He quickly continues before a word escapes her mouth. "I am not saying that you can't survive—just that why would I want to put someone I love through that?"

Closing her mouth, shocked, she stares at him, tears running down her face, shaking her head slowly, wanting to wake from this nightmare, feeling that whatever she decides, something dreadful will happen.

Moving from the chair and wrapping her arms around him, she bursts into tears, begging, "Please don't go. Stay, please, I beg you."

Tears run down his cheeks as his heart is rent in two, wishing that he had never married Norta, took the contract, fought the Spliganders, come to this town, or left the guild—wishing he could turn back time and not request to go on the quest, not feel any pain, regret, or sadness.

But one look into the eyes of his Soul, and he doesn't regret anything. The overwhelming love she has for him is pouring into his soul, filling up all the holes and cracks. Knowing that he would not ever change anything, he still knows that he needs to get all this done.

Wiping his face, he takes a deep breath and, looking into her eyes, says, "I am so sorry, my Soul. I need to do this. I will travel faster than the wind, complete this contract, and come back faster than lightning." Smiling to try and relieve some of the sombre mood, he adds, "Besides, who will keep Torach and Gizle in line if you aren't here?"

Looking back, she nods, understanding. With a thumb, he wipes away her tears and then they hug fiercely, knowing that they won't see each other for a long time. Norta whispers in his ear, "Come back to me, ok? Don't you dare not come back."

Nodding, Peren promises, "I will always come home to

you. You are my home. You have my heart. I will not fail. I will come back and see you again. This, I promise. You will see me again, and I will see you again."

Nodding against each other, they lean back and, kissing each other deeply, get up and walk hand in hand out to the stables.

Mounting Mercy, Peren leans down and gives Norta one final kiss—the kiss of promises, the kiss that this is only farewell for now, the kiss that says, "I will see you and kiss you again."

Grabbing the reins, Peren turns Mercy to face the open gate. As he passes through the gate, Norta shouts, "Be safe, my love! Come back to me! Don't make me come after you! You are my sun, my radiant sun!"

Turning in his seat as Mercy plods out onto the street, he calls, "I promise, my Soul, I will come back!"

Once the horse and rider disappear off into the distance, Norta collapses to the ground, weeping. Grieving at losing Peren, she just sits there crying.

Torach and Gizle wipe tears from their eyes and just hold her, knowing that they can't do anything to console her.

Finally helping the broken girl up, they guide her inside. As she steps up to the threshold, she takes one final look towards where Peren is heading, thinking, *I will be strong for my love. I will be here when he comes back, and I will be at the gate welcoming him home.* Gritting her teeth, she promises herself, *No more tears.*

As Peren forces himself to focus on the task at hand, tears flow down his face. Doing his best not to let any cracks show, he gives a final farewell to the town he will call home.

Edging closer to the edges of the town, he sees more and more people on the streets. Seeing him, they start to cheer, parting to give him and Mercy a path as the crowd becomes too thick to manoeuvre in. Forced to move at a crawl, Peren quickly wipes his eyes and schools his features. The crowd, thinking that he is overcome with this gathering, gives a collective "Aww." The women pull hankies from various parts and dab their eyes as they continue to praise him.

Smiling at this farewell, Peren sits up straighter and begins to wave at the crowd.

The cheering rises all through the crowd, becoming thunderous. Ears pricking up at the noise of the crowd, muscles tensing, and nostrils flaring, Mercy shifts uneasily beneath Peren. Reaching over, he pats and whispers calmly into her hear, trying to calm her down. Sceptical about being calm with all this noise, Mercy trusts him and tries to keep calm.

Finally, he arrives at the head of the crowd, where Mayor Jornstawn is standing, grinning brightly at Peren as he waves him down from Mercy.

Climbing up on the temporary stage amid the crowd cheering in a deafening chorus, Peren stands next to the mayor. Waving his hands, the mayor eventually quiets down the crowd. Turning to Peren, he gives him a big bear hug.

Addressing the crowd, the mayor calls out in a loud voice, "Thank you all for coming here today." He waves the crowd silent again. Turning to look at Peren, the mayor continues, "Peren Naïlo, the champion of Comtun, there are no words worthy of how grateful we are of what you have done for us over the past months."

Reaching out to encompass the town, the mayor says to Peren, "As representative for Comtun, I want to personally thank you for eradicating the Spligander infestation. We have all come and scrounged together this small token of our appreciation for what you have done for us all."

He waves a to a couple of men, and they come up with a

small chest. Placing it before Peren, they lift the lid, and Peren sees lots of golden and silver items, with some gems as well.

Accepting the reward, Peren gets in front of the lectern and calls out to the crowd, "I am thankful for the reward. It has been great getting to spend so much time here, getting to know you all." Lowering his head in sadness, he adds, "Unfortunately, this exciting time has come to an end. I have thoroughly enjoyed my time here with you all."

With a wave, he steps away from the lectern, allowing the mayor to step back up to the lectern and conclude the farewell. "It's a shame that you can't stay for food. We won't keep you any longer."

Shaking Peren's hand, the mayor steps out of the way, and as Peren mounts Mercy and as the crowd cheers, they leave the town behind.

ELEVEN

RIVERS TOR

As the village recedes from sight, Peren refuses to look back, finding solace in fingering his pendant. His mind is so focused on thoughts of Norta, his eyes so teared up at leaving her behind, he doesn't realise that he is nearing the Bridge of Tor.

Pulling out of his reverie, he notices long shadows stretching before him, the sun dipping below the horizon and painting the sky in deep purples and reds, a stunning backdrop to the fading day. Dismounting, Peren makes camp just off the road, near the river.

Sitting close to the fire, Peren opens one of the saddlebags, searching for food, and finds it packed full. A smile creeps across his face as his eyes well up with tears, realizing that his Soul filled it for him, thinking of his needs even when he didn't. He chuckles softly, touched by the care and warmth in every piece of food she prepared.

His heart is breaking as he wishes she was here to enjoy the meal together, but he knows deep down that it is more important that she stays safe in Comtun while he heads on this lethal quest—one in which he, a trained killer with Elven abilities, could die, let alone an inn maid.

Looking down the small incline toward the river, he picks at his light dinner, his hunger dulled by the absence of his Soul. The steady murmur of the flowing water fills the air, its soft splashes blending with the distant calls of night creatures stirring in the twilight. Though the surroundings are peaceful, the ache of loneliness gnaws at him, making the meal feel hollow.

Giving up on eating some time later, Peren rests his head against the saddle, looking up into the night sky. Despite the increasing cloud cover, many stars still shine through. Closing his eyes and finding solace in the sounds of the creatures and the river, he falls asleep.

He wakes up early the next morning to long shadows as the sky lightens. Sitting by the river, he eats breakfast as the water flows past.

Brushing the crumbs off himself, he puts his palms down on the ground and pauses when something hard comes in contact with his hand. Looking down, he sees a dirty old cracked plate.

Picking it up, some memory tugs at the back of his mind, disappearing when he pulls on it. Feeling like it has something to do with his childhood, he puts the plate back down and focuses on clearing camp and heading off.

He mounts Mercy, and they both head across the bridge. As they step off the bridge, Peren's mind is flooded with vivid memories of a story from his childhood.

A young, impoverished traveller navigates through a destitute district in a bustling city. In a corner, a beggar holds out an old, grimy, and cracked plate, ignored by passersby. Moved with compassion, the traveller shares his last morsel of food and a portion of his dwindling coins, cleans the plate, and sits with the beggar to share their meal and stories. Afterwards, he moves on, not dwelling on the encounter.

Many years later, now with grey streaks in his hair, the traveller finds himself embroiled in a battle between rival kingdoms. Despite his age, he is conscripted to the front lines and gravely wounded, left for dead among the chaos. Drifting in and out of consciousness, he glimpses an elderly beggar hobbling through the carnage, picking through the fallen.

The beggar approaches him, peers down, and simply states, "You gave me some of your last food and money, cleaned up my plate, and sat with me."

Unable to respond coherently, the traveller believes he is fading into death until the beggar transforms into a beautiful young nymph. She lays healing hands upon him, rejuvenating his wounds and granting him renewed vitality. Blessing him gratefully, she vanishes without another word, leaving him to stand on the battlefield in awe and confusion.

Confounded and unsure of his fate, he is passed from one commander to the next until he reaches the Sword-General. After an audience with the general, he is tasked with becoming an envoy between the warring kingdoms. His unique ability to unite both kings in peaceful negotiation earns him respect and a role in maintaining peace and prosperity for many years to come, until his eventual passing. Throughout his life, he becomes known for his steadfast belief: "You never know what effects your actions will have; generosity will always be rewarded."

Smiling at the memory of that childhood tale and the profound impact it had on him, Peren chuckles at its improbable nature. Despite his attempts to dismiss the similarities with the plate, he finds himself drawn back to its significance. Shrugging to himself, he crosses back over the bridge, dismounts next to the plate, and washes it clean in the cold river. Placing a large chunk of bread on it, he shakes his head at his own whimsy, remounts Mercy, and continues on his quest, fondly recalling his childhood wonder.

Hours later, he shakes his head and chuckles at himself for what he did, feeling ridiculous for such a childish whim about being blessed like the protagonist was.

Peren nibbles at some food as the sun reaches its zenith and they continue on. He finds the terrain becoming hillier the further they go, trotting up and down the grassy mounds, letting his mind wander. As it wanders to thoughts of Norta, he subconsciously pulls out the pendant and fingers it as they travel along.

As the days pass, he watches as the scenery changes around him. The beautiful, lush grasses are long gone, replaced by dull gravel. Feeling the temperatures drop as they ascend higher, he wraps his cloak tighter around him. Thick, ominous black clouds slowly choke the sky of colour, casting dark shadows across the ground.

Peren decides to find somewhere to camp for the night as the sunlight fades at an alarming rate. Spotting a cluster of boulders that offer some protection from the icy blasts of wind coming from the peaks of the mountains, he leaves Mercy to munch on some grain while he goes in search for some wood for a fire.

Disappointed, he returns emptyhanded. Wrapping himself up in his blankets, he eats a cold meal and tries to get some sleep.

Opening his eyes with a start, he finds himself surrounded by a haunting scene: walls that are constructed from skulls, bones scattered on the ground, and eerie shadows looming all around him. Quickly scanning his surroundings, he realises that he is trapped without a way to escape. The smooth skulls, each one looking familiar, giving off an aura of mockery at his attempts to climb them.

Unsheathing his dagger, he is moving forward cautiously towards a corner when he feels movement ahead of him.

Sneaking a peek around the corner, he ducks back as a

bone-chilling scream pierces the air. Ignoring his instincts to be cautious, Peren rushes through the labyrinth toward the where the scream originated.

As he runs down different paths, the moonlight casts ominous shadows that seem to morph into grotesque forms that move and start to attack him. He swipes at them with his dagger, but each time he hits them, they dissipate and reform, making them impossible for him to kill.

Abandoning his attempts to deal with them, he rushes on towards where the scream originated. Suddenly, he is in the air and crashes into one of the walls with a bone-crunching smash. Pain screams along his nerves as he struggles to get on his hands and knees, spewing out blood. Gritting his teeth, he refuses to give up.

Getting unsteadily to his feet, he faces the intangible shadow forming into a wraith in front of his eyes. Snarling at this incorporeal being, he leaps forward, diving below the attacking wraith. Rolling to his feet, running forward and ignoring the screaming pain of his body, he picks up his dagger mid-stride. Turning and facing the spirit, panting, wincing with each breath, he bottles up the pain and locks it away for later. Driven by determination, he rushes forward and swipes at the wraith.

With one final chilling, elongated wail that echoes through the air, making the hairs on the back of Peren's neck stand on end, the wraith dissipates.

Breathing heavily, Peren feels a warm liquid run down the side of his body. He looks and winces as he gingerly touches the wound. Discovering a protruding rib, he takes shallow breaths, trying to minimise the pain.

Moving forward, he dissipates any more wraiths that block his path. Reaching a clearing that he assumes is the centre, he slows, his breath catching as he takes in the sight before him.

A woman hangs suspended in the air, arms and legs outstretched, tears streaming down her face. Peren's blood runs cold as he notices a glinting upside-down triangle-shaped pendant. Focusing closer, he sees a bloody blade pressed against her throat by a menacing shadow wraith.

The wraith's taunting voice reverberates through the clearing. "Recognize her, weak, little Elf boy?"

Taking a closer look, Peren's heart sinks as he recognises her. Norta, his beloved, his soul, is hanging with agony sketched across her face. Tearing up at the sight before him, he tries to take a step forward, but finds himself unable to move.

"Ah, ah, ah! No trying to help, useless mortal."

Staring into her teary eyes, he feels helpless as his emotions rage beneath the surface.

Pulling Peren out of his rage, the wraith says in a delighted growl, "I am going to enjoy watching you lose your Soul. Just like I made her with her sister."

Blinking in confusion for a moment as the words sink in, Peren realises that there are multiple small lumps on the ground, glistening in the moonlight, just below Norta's feet.

Falling on his knees heavily in defeat, he barely hears the Wraith continuing to speak. "I very much enjoyed making that one suffer. Every time this one begged me on her knees, I went more slowly, prolonging her suffering. All she had to do was kill her little sister to stop it. But such a weak human you fell for." Forcing Peren to look into its eyes, it continues, "Will you be just as weak, Elf?"

Tears begin to stream down Peren's face as he struggles to speak past the lump in his throat. "I—I am so sorry. I couldn't protect you or Gizle, my Soul."

The wraith is chuckling at the anguish it causes in Peren, which only serves to anger him. Gritting his teeth, wiping his tears away with determination, his hand tightens around his dagger. Glaring up at the giant wraith, he spits out words laced with venom. "I will gut you so slowly, Gizle's death will seem quick."

Sneering and laughing, the wraith looks pointedly at Norta, then back to him.

Leaping forward with everything he has, Peren flies towards the wraith, which hesitates momentarily, shocked at his resolve.

In a swift and brutal motion, Peren plunges his dagger into the wraith's form, opening it from throat to navel.

As the wraith dissolves into darkness, Norta drops to the ground, lifeless. Catching her just in time, Peren lays her gently down, attempting to heal her wounds with his magic. Confusion furrows his brow as his healing attempts fail, blocked by an unknown force. Desperation creeps into his voice as he murmurs, "I'm so sorry..."

Struggling to speak, Norta manages to say, "It's okay... So, you're an Elf?" Her hand touches his cheek gently, her voice filled with understanding and acceptance, despite her pain.

Tears continue to flow down Peren's cheeks as he nods, overwhelmed by her compassion. He regrets not revealing his true nature earlier, guilt overwhelming him as he struggles to push the words past the lump in his throat. "I am. I am so sorry for not telling you, my soul."

Reaching up to wipe his tears, Norta whispers softly, "I'm sorry you didn't tell me sooner... It explains a lot."

Peren nods again, grateful for her understanding in his darkest moment. Seeing the guilt over not revealing his true nature, her eyes fill with sympathetic sadness. "I forgive you. I lo—"

Her eyes glaze over, and she breathes out for the last time.

Tears pour down Peren's cheeks as he whispers, "I love you too." Taking a deep breath, he screams his pain into the night, a sound of pure anguish echoing through the air.

Setting her down gently, he stands on shaky feet. Knowing his little slash would not have even tickled the wraith, he growls in a loud, steady voice dripping with revenge, "Come out, you coward! Come out and face me! If you're so powerful, why do you torture helpless women and children? You are nothing but a useless shadow that can only prey on the weak and defenceless!"

Rising out of the shadows, larger and more hideous than anything Peren could imagine, the wraith snarls in anger. "How dare you challenge me, mortal?! I existed before your species was even thought of and will be here long after they are gone!"

Leaping out of the way, Peren lashes out with his dagger, but the blade passes through the wraith's right arm as if through smoke. Laughing at the weak mortal, the wraith's fist connects with Peren's sternum, crushing it against his lungs and heart and sending him flying into a wall of skulls with a loud crunch. He cries out in pain as bones and ribs snap beyond their strength.

Barely able to breathe, spluttering in the bone dust disturbed by his impact, he lies there, powerless. The wraith floats over to him, a delighted snarl on its lips. "What's the matter, Elf? Can't hit shadows? Not even with that special dagger of yours?"

Struggling to his feet, crying out in pain, Peren leans against the wall of skulls and yells, "Do your worst!"

Opening its mouth, the wraith takes a bite of Peren.

The sensation of biting cold against his skin jolts him awake. He jerks upright, gasping for breath, his heart hammering in his chest, the echoes of his scream still ringing in his ears, at odds with the morning silence. The acrid taste of fear lingers on his tongue, metallic and bitter. His muscles ache, as if the phantom pain from his nightmare has followed him into the waking world.

The morning air is cold and biting, with a chill that seeps through his cloak. Each breath sends a plume of mist into the crisp air. The rough texture of the saddle beneath him is a stark contrast to the smooth, cold skulls in his dream. He can still smell the faint, musty odour of bone dust mingling with the sharp, fresh mountain air.

Rubbing the crust from his eyes, he winces at the grit beneath his fingertips, a tactile reminder of the nightmare. The memory of Norta's eyes glazing over sends a shiver down his spine, colder than the morning air.

He flops back against the saddle with a relieved sigh, realizing it was just a nightmare. His breath steadies, but the cold shivers running down his body are not entirely due to the chill. Each detail of the dream is etched vividly in his mind, like carvings on ancient stone.

He forces himself to eat a quick, cold breakfast, the food tasteless in his mouth. He cleans up the camp with mechanical efficiency, the mundane tasks a welcome distraction. Saddling Mercy, he mounts her, holding the cloak tight around him in an effort to fend off the cold and icy wind. Heeling her into a trot, he bends low over her neck, trying to keep any exposed skin covered.

As he rides, he tries to think about anything but the dream. The clinking of Mercy's hooves on the rocky ground and the distant sound of wind are soothing, but his mind keeps returning to the nightmare that was not just a nightmare.

TWELVE

GROUND THERN

Peren's heart races with the vivid memory of Norta's death, his tears freezing on his cheeks in the cold.

Suddenly, a growing whistle from above jolts him out of his horror, and he pulls Mercy aside just as a large object crashes down, creating a crater. He realizes they've arrived at Ground Thern as the loud thud and vibrations draw his full attention.

A medium-sized rock at the centre of the crater begins to vibrate violently, pulling in stones from the ground around it. Each stone snaps into place, building on the mass until, moments later, the creature takes shape—a three-foot-tall humanoid stone figure stands on two legs before them as if assessing its surroundings. Mercy snorts with worry, stepping back, her gaze locked on the strange creature.

Instinctively drawing his dagger, Peren recovers from his shock at the unbelievable and unnatural creature before him. Thinking about how he could best take on a creature like this, he only has time to blink once before the creature senses their presence, charging at them with awkwardly flailing arms.

Reacting out of instinct, Mercy turns and kicks the creature with her powerful hind legs, knocking it over with a flash as her hooves connect with the stones.

The creature quickly scrambles back to its feet, looking around in confusion before charging at them again. Mercy retaliates with another kick, and this time, several smaller pebbles go flying as the creature stumbles back. It takes longer to rise this time, the stones rearranging themselves to account for the missing fragments.

It charges at them again, and Peren begins to wonder if it has any intelligence. Mercy kicks out again, sending more fragments spraying as sparks fly from the connecting hooves. Flying back, it crumbles when it hits the ground.

Smiling at how easy it is to take these things down, Peren's turns to shock as the rock vibrates and rebuilds itself. Taking a moment to get its bearings, it turns and faces Peren and Mercy. Flailing its arms, it runs towards them again.

Mercy kicks out and sends multiple fragments flying, and it crumbles to the ground. After waiting for a few more seconds, Peren concludes that its dead. As he's letting out the breath he was holding, he hears screams emanating from the village.

Eyes wide as he realises that it wasn't the only one, he heels Mercy, and they leap into action, racing to the village.

The sight before him makes the bile rise in his throat. The same stone creatures are chasing helpless villagers, flailing arms coated in blood, leaving in their wake the cause of his nausea: piles of bodies, some moving and moaning as they die, spraying and pooling blood.

Teeth gritted in anger at the wanton slaughter, he thinks, *This is not a slaughter, but a massacre.* Mercy, feeling the horror and anger surge in her rider, moves faster towards the nearest screams.

Turning a corner, they come face to face with three of the creatures. Peren pulls on the reins, and Mercy halts.

Turning their attention to Peren, the creatures alter their path and start racing up to him. Knowing that Mercy can't take on this many, he gets her to turn around so that she can assist him. Unsheathing his dagger as he leaps to the ground, he rushes to the nearest stone creature, thrusting his dagger at it. The blade glances off as it comes into contact with some invisible barrier, sending blue sparks flying.

Frustrated, he doesn't have time to try again as the creature swings its arms at him, forcing him to dive and roll out of the way of being crushed.

Refusing to give up, he puts everything behind his next thrust and, to his shock, he pierces the barrier slightly.

Smiling at his achievement, he tries to pull the dagger out to stab again, but finds it stuck fast. The creature swings again, forcing him to dive out of the way. His instincts make him move to the right to avoid one of the other creatures from hitting him, feeling the wind from its arms as it flies past mere inches from him.

Rolling to his feet, Peren leaps forward, grabbing his dagger with everything he has and yanking it free, continuing the onslaught of this barrier. The next stab makes the whole barrier spark and flicker before the creature crumbles to the ground.

Turning to face the other two, he is panting and feeling the burn in his muscles from the exertion of attacking one. Snarling at them, he rushes towards them, putting in the same draining energy to weaken their barriers before Mercy kicks them.

By the time they are within range of Mercy, Peren is feeling exhausted, sweaty, and burned out. Between the nightmare the night before with the cold, and the strength of these barriers, he struggles to stand. The only thing that stops him from falling is his determination and the adrenaline coursing through his veins.

Kicking out, Mercy sends fragments of the first one flying. Crumpling to the ground, it doesn't so much as twitch. Turning to face the final attacking creature, Peren realizes that Mercy is in the wrong position, and it will take too long to reposition her. He takes this one down himself.

They continue through the village towards the different screams, facing and defeating creature after creature.

Struggling to stand, relying on Mercy, Peren heads towards the final scream and finds there are five of them left. Letting go of Mercy's saddle, he stands on his own. Snarling at these abominations, he rushes forward to take them on.

Seeing the threat, the five of them turn and race towards him, their flailing arms thick with blood and gore. Thrusting his dagger into the first, he manages to penetrate the barrier, but he doesn't have time to yank the blade out, as he is forced to dodge out of the way from one of the other creatures as it swings at him.

The putrid arms, missing him by a hair, crash into the one with the dagger in it, making its barrier flare up brightly. Using this to his advantage, Peren begins to bait them into attacking each other, diving out of the way just in time.

Eventually, his instincts tell him to move right, but he's unable to from momentum, and is sent flying to the right, agony shooting up his left arm as he crashes into one of the stone buildings with a bone-crunching sound.

Falling in a heap, his vision blackens from the pain shooting through his body. Fighting to stay conscious, he watches, dazed, as the creatures rush toward him. *Is this it? My end? To some stupid mindless creature?* Gritting his teeth, he vows, *No, this will not be my end! This will be theirs! I will not give up this easily.*

As he forces himself to stand up and face them, his left arm dangles uselessly by his side. Each movement sending stabs of agony up his arm, he grits his teeth and continues to attack them, having Mercy assist him in finishing them off.

When the last one crumbles, he falls to the ground, exhausted. The villagers rush in to help, but stop and gasp when they see one of the creatures rise back up.

Looking around and finding its target, the creature races towards Peren, swinging its arms at him. Peren looks up to find gore-splattered arms flying towards him. A tear escapes as pictures of his Soul come to mind, the chain of promise shattering between them. He knows this is it; he can't do anything but lie there as the arms close in.

Waiting with his eyes closed, he hears a crash. Opening them with a start, he sees the creature crash into the ground a few feet away, fragments and small pebbles flying. Looking up at Mercy, more grateful to her than ever before, he gets to his feet with the help of the villagers.

Turning and facing the creature as it rises back up, Peren snarls through gritted teeth. Using every ounce of his remaining energy to stay upright and awake, he baits it into attacking.

Managing to dodge it, he lands a powerful stab with the dagger, shattering the barrier, and the creature crumbles into a rubble of stone.

Collapsing to the ground, Peren blacks out for a few seconds before waking up with a start. As memories and pain flood his mind, he pushes himself to his feet.

He lets the villagers guide him to a step, and they assist him with bandaging up his arm, while others offer him some bread and water. Taking a slow sip, he swallows it, the water lubricating his parched and dried throat. Forcing himself, he chews on the bread, not feeling hungry, but knowing that he will need the energy to help.

As he sits there, the sounds of the wounded and the crackling of distant fires fill the air, mingling with the scent of smoke and the metallic tang of blood. He watches the villagers who helped him move on to aid others, their backs stooped with fatigue, but driven by the same relentless determination he feels. The small acts of kindness in the midst of chaos ground him, reminding him of the resilience and humanity that persist even in the darkest times.

As he continues to chew on a piece of bread, his eyes wander to the multitude of funeral pyres lighting up the darkening sky. Each flickering flame represents a life lost, a family torn apart. He feels each funeral as a personal blow, especially since most of the dead are women and children. The acrid scent of burning wood and flesh fills the air, mingling with the cries of grieving families. Mothers wail inconsolably over the small, shrouded forms of their children. Fathers, their faces etched with sorrow and defeat, kneel by the bodies of their loved ones, their shoulders heaving with silent sobs.

The sight stirs a deep ache within Peren's chest, his mind replaying the death of Norta over and over again, seeing himself powerless to save her. The weight of his own failure presses heavily on him, a constant reminder of the lives he couldn't protect.

Lost in his thoughts, he doesn't notice the tears streaming down his face until a young girl walking past tugs gently at his sleeve. Her voice is soft but clear as she asks, "Are you okay, mister?"

Her wide eyes, filled with a mix of innocence and concern, pierce through his fog of grief. The child's dirt-smudged face and tattered clothes speak volumes about the horrors she has witnessed. Her presence pulls him back to the present, and he hastily wipes his face with his dusty sleeve, forcing a smile despite the lump in his throat.

Taking a shuddering breath and wiping his face with a trembling hand, he forces a smile, though it doesn't quite reach his eyes. "Yes, I'm alright," he says, his voice cracking slightly. "How about you? Where are your parents?" His heart aches as he asks, dreading the answer.

The girl's eyes drop to the ground, and she gives a small, helpless shrug.

Her silence speaks louder than any words could, and he feels his chest tighten with a mix of sorrow and helplessness. "Do you want me to help you look for them?" he asks, his voice tinged with hope and desperation, needing to have a purpose.

He starts to rise, every movement a silent prayer that her parents are still alive. But before he can fully get to his feet, she wanders off, disappearing around a corner without a word. His heart sinks, and he feels a profound sense of loss and helplessness wash over him.

Blinking away the tears, Peren sits back down, his gaze fixed on the flickering funeral pyres as he mechanically finishes his meal. Each bite feels like a struggle against the overwhelming sorrow around him. Determined not to witness such devastation again without intervening, he pushes himself up and begins searching for the mayor, his footsteps heavy with resolve and purpose.

After asking around and being pointed in multiple directions, Peren finally tracks down the mayor. He stops, his gaze flickering in surprise as the woman introduces herself as Mayor Caril Pender. He's met powerful women before—but not in this way, openly leading a village. For a moment, he just takes her in, her steady gaze and the weight she carries as though it's second nature. Finally, he manages to ask, "You're the mayor?"

Her eyes narrow, daring him to question it further, as if challenging him to say more. The unspoken defiance in her look makes him close his mouth, unsure whether he's ever felt quite this out of his depth. Without realizing it, his fingers drift to the pendant around his neck. Her strength, her unapologetic authority, stirs something in him.

Eyes narrowing further as she looks him up and down, she demands, "Who are you, and where are you from?"

Peren's throat goes dry as she scrutinizes him. He opens his mouth to respond, but the words seem to stick, and he hesitates, caught off-guard by her intensity. The silence stretches uncomfortably, and he can feel her gaze probing him, searching for answers.

Her stare intensifies as her suspicions rise. "It was you, wasn't it? The one responsible for destroying my village!"

Jaw dropping at the accusation, Peren sputters out, his rage rising, "What? No! I was the one who saved it!" He puffs out his chest and pokes his thumb into his chest as he finishes.

Glaring through slitted eyes, Mayor Pender stares up at him, unconvinced.

Frustrated and indignant, Peren folds his arms and says through gritted teeth, "Why would I cause this terrible attack on a village that I have never been to before? I am appalled at what happened here! I was not only ambushed on my way here by one of them, but I also risked my life defeating them and protecting this village!"

Taken aback at his response, she recovers quickly. "Thank you for your assistance." Regarding him suspiciously, she demands, "So, who are you, and why are you here?"

Indignant, Peren spits out, "My name—"

Waving her arm in dismissal, she cuts him off impatiently. "Yes, yes, Pen Nails." Her eyes narrow as a thought comes to her. "But who are you *really*? And *how* did you manage to help?"

Pausing for a heartbeat, Peren realises he has done it again—stepped into a situation that he shouldn't have been able to accomplish as a human. Thinking quickly, he responds, "I am just a sell-sword that is passing through, exploring the world and offering my services to anyone who needs them."

Still unbelieving, Mayor Pender doesn't question him further. Hating sell-swords more in that moment, she asks in a clipped tone, "I suppose you want some sort of reward for your heroics?" The last word comes out in disgust.

Wincing, Peren bows slightly, doing his best to be respectful. Knowing the toll on the village, he says, "That one was for free, Milady."

The Mayor leans further forward, glaring at him, unconvinced by his tone. Backpedalling again, Peren puts his hands up placatingly and tries to explain. "Since there was no contract, I don't think it would be fair…"

Cutting in angrily, she demands, "Are you mocking me?"

Backing up, eyes wide in shock, Peren vehemently replies, "Not at all. I was just trying to show some deference to your position."

Mayor Pender fixes him with a steely gaze. "You better not be," she warns. "Now, is there anything else I can help you with?"

Before he can reply, another voice, frail yet clear, interjects. "Golems. Stone Golems, to be exact." An elderly woman leaning heavily on her stick shuffles to a stop before the two of them.

Looking over to see who spoke, Peren feels a strange sense of familiarity as he meets the old woman's gaze, though he's certain they've never crossed paths, leaving him with the odd sensation that he's seen her somewhere before. He's pulled from his thoughts as the mayor asks, "Are you sure?"

The woman nods. "Long, long ago, there were stories about these creatures, back when magic was used freely."

Brows furrowed in confusion, the mayor replies, "But magic has been outlawed since the Wolfain catastrophe, and that was a thousand years ago."

Nodding in agreement, the elder continues, "There must have been some who taught magic in secret through the ages."

Intrigued, Peren butts in. "How do you know?"

The old woman's piercing black eyes meet his. "Well, how else is someone creating golems?"

Feeling foolish at the obvious answer, Peren falls silent. The mayor gestures for the elderly woman to continue. "Magic is based on one's affinity for it. Either you can access it or you can't. It also takes someone who can access magic to unlock it for you. Whoever did this had a teacher, though the person doesn't seem very powerful."

"What do you mean, not very powerful? They nearly destroyed the entire village!" Peren and Mayor Pender exclaim in unison.

"The stories talk about armies of rock golems the size of houses running around at the command of one person."

Under his breath, Peren mutters, "Exaggerating with each telling."

Unexpectedly, the old woman hears him and responds, "True, but also not true. These stories are so old that only the oldest of us know them, and my source wasn't prone to exaggeration."

Thoroughly chastised, Peren tries to recover from his embarrassment. "What is the fastest way to destroy these stone golems?"

As if it is the most obvious thing in the world, the old woman replies, "Take out the one who is controlling them."

A curious thought crosses Peren's mind. Cringing inwardly, he asks, "Why did it end so suddenly?"

The elder replies approvingly, "Because the caster's affinity with magic is only so deep, and their well dried up. The wielder will also be very tired. It takes a huge amount of physical energy to cast and maintain those spells."

The mayor stands there, mulling over the information given to her. "How much time do we have?" she asks tentatively.

Brows angled in a frown, the old woman thinks for a few heartbeats. "I would say possibly twenty-four hours before the onslaught happens again."

Going quiet, the mayor thinks over this while Peren asks her a few more questions. "Why were the last few so difficult to kill compared to the others?"

Pausing in thought for a minute, the old woman finally says, "I cannot be completely sure, but it might be linked magic." Seeing blank stares from both the mayor and Peren, she elaborates. "There are two types of controlling magic: linked and unlinked. Think of the golem like a bucket with a hole in the bottom. Filled with water, or magic in this case, the bucket will eventually empty, and the golem will cease to exist. Unlinked magic is just like that. Linked magic is like holding that same bucket under a waterfall—the bucket never empties. Once the water source is gone, the bucket will still empty. This is what happened: the sorcerer linked with those last few golems."

Looking hopeful, Peren asks, "So, when they stopped being indestructible, it was because she ran out of magic?"

"That, or she stopped linking with them," the old woman responds. Noting the look of horror on the mayor's face, she continues, "It is most likely that she ran out of magic, as there was an end to the entire attack."

Turning to the old woman, the mayor asks, "What do you suggest?"

Pursing her lips, the old woman thinks for a few minutes. "We have two options. First, we evacuate the village and settle down somewhere new, hoping that the magic user doesn't chase after us."

The mayor feels like she is falling off a cliff into an empty, hungry abyss at the thought of leaving the place she not only grew up in, but so did many of her previous generations. Her Soul is also buried here, dragging up bittersweet memories of when he was alive. Looking at the older woman, a terrified and helpless look on her face, words slip out as her voice breaks. "H-how can we leave this place?"

Peren's heart breaks as he imagines what it must be like to have to uproot your whole life and leave behind memories move to another place. Realising that this is what most of Comtun had to do with the Spligander attacks, his mind wanders to how Norta would react to having to leave. His hand finds its way to the pendant under his tunic.

Looking at the mayor with compassion, the old woman says softly, "We must if we are to survive."

"What if they chase after us? You and others can't outrun these things." In a whisper, speaking more to herself, that anyone, the mayor asks, "What can we do?" A multitude of emotions flow across her face, from despair, to anger, to determination. Looking at the woman, hope rising, she says, "You said two options. What is the second?"

The old woman points a knobby and gnarled finger at Peren. "We send him to deal with the user."

Disbelief covers the mayor's entire face as she looks between the old woman and Peren before asking sceptically, "Him?" After the old woman nods, the mayor continues, "How can we trust a word he says?" Looking at him suspiciously again, she adds, "How can we be sure that he isn't the magic user? Trying to rob us all?"

The old woman turns to Peren. After giving him a deep, glaring appraisal, she turns to the mayor. "Do you trust me?"

The mayor nods, staring through slitted eyes at Peren.

"Then trust me when I say he isn't the one who attacked our village. He is the best shot we have at stopping this from happening again."

Staring at him a few moments longer, the mayor looks directly into his eyes, "Ok. Do *not* make me regret this."

Nodding, Peren puts his fist to his heart, and, bowing slightly, says in a solemn and serious voice, "I, Peren Naïlo, sell-sword, swear upon my blood and soul, before the gods above and below, to defend this village and its people, protecting them from this evil even with my dying breath." He maintains eye contact as he straightens.

Gasping in shock, the old woman just stares at Peren, slack-jawed. The mayor looks confused about this unusual performance by Peren and at how the old woman reacted. Looking at the old woman with a pointed questioning expression, she silently demands an explanation.

Still recovering from her shock, the old woman stammers, "That is an old binding oath. No one even makes them anymore. If the oath is broken in any way, the oath breaker is cursed for eternity, suffering for his failure, never to forget it."

As the mayor lets the words sink in, the old woman gives Peren a knowing grin, once again sending a sense of familiarity through his body. Frustrated at not knowing who she reminds him of, he turns to the mayor. "I need to see any maps you have of the area where someone could watch the village without being seen."

The old woman jumps in, "Follow me, young man. I will answer any questions you have. My limited and small knowledge about magic users is at your disposal."

Nodding, Peren turns towards the mayor. "I still want you to evacuate the village in case I cannot end this magic user. It will make my job easier knowing that everyone is going and will be out of harm's way." Leaving the mayor to the preparations, he makes a small bow, and, turning away, he assists the old woman to shuffle away.

Once out of earshot, Peren stops and turns to her. "Ok, lady, tell me who you are and why I know you."

Looking at him, confused, she says, "I have no idea—"

Gritting his teeth, Peren says, "I think you do. You also gave me a weird look back there, like you knew something. I will also know it too."

Unimpressed by his demanding tone, she narrows her eyes, her expression shifting from confusion to irritation. She meets his gaze with a challenging look that reveals a hint of defiance. Without a word, she pokes him sharply in the stomach with her stick, the impact surprisingly firm. Each word that follows resonates with a power that sends chills down his spine. "You will cease your little demands right now. I don't owe you answers, especially when you throw demands around like a child."

The muscles in Peren's jaw flicker as his rage rises at how this woman is treating him. Refusing to back down, he says intimidatingly, "I need answers to questions, and I will get them."

Meeting his stare with a spine-withering one, she fires back. "And I'm not here to cater to your whims, sell-sword. You will find that I am not that easily intimidated. If you want answers, you will ask with respect." Shoving past him with hidden strength, she continues to shuffle on her way.

Left stunned at her outburst, he clenches his fists in anger at her. Knowing that she has answers about the magic user that he needs, he forces himself to swallow his pride. Taking a calming breath, he starts after her, and, when he catches up to her, he says, "I'm sorry. You are right. I need answers about the magic user that only you seem to have."

Lifting her eyebrow at him, she says in a mocking voice, "Oh so he *can* show respect."

Muscles feather in his jaw as he struggles to keep his mouth shut.

The old woman continues her shuffle. After a few seconds, she begins to tell him about golems and magic users. "These golems are creations of earth and magic, bound by the caster's will," she begins. "Their strength and durability come from the caster's power. The more powerful the user, the more formidable the golems. They can be relentless, but they are not invincible."

Peren listens intently, supporting the woman as she continues, "The caster of these golems must be close. Linked magic requires a close proximity, though the exact range can vary. If the user's well of magic is shallow, as we suspect, they will need to rest frequently, and their power will wane quickly. There might be traces of residual magic where the golems first appeared," she adds. "But since magic has been outlawed for a millennium, no one knows these spells or has the ability to trace it back to the source."

Nodding, Peren answers, "Then I will have to do it with observation and deduction. If I can find this person and stop them, then this village will be safe." A determined look enters his gaze as he finishes speaking.

They continue on in silence as the words hang heavy in the air. When they reach her home a few minutes later, she says, "Come in, boy. I will show you the surrounds."

Nodding, Peren follows her inside, where she shows him a drawing of the surrounding landscape. Once he works out his plan of action, he turns to the woman. "Thank you so much for that. Would you like me to help you pack your things?"

Stopping abruptly, the woman realizes that Peren plans to head out and search for the magic user now, even with his injured arm. She crosses her arms, eyes narrowing with disbelief. "You're stupid if you think you're going anywhere like that," she snaps, pointing at his crushed arm. "You can barely move it, let alone fight."

Peren doesn't flinch at her words. Refusing to give into her on this, he replies, "I can, and I will. A broken arm isn't going to stop me."

She steps closer, frustration colouring her voice. "You're not invincible, Peren. You can't just march off into danger like this. You're wounded, and if you don't take care of yourself, you'll just end up dead."

He meets her gaze, unshaken. "I'm not waiting around for the golems to show up again," he says, throwing her earlier words back at her. "No one knows when they'll reappear, so the sooner I face this magic user, the better."

She glares at him, clearly irritated, but a grudging respect flickers in her eyes. With a heavy sigh, she steps back, not even attempting to argue further. "Fine," she mutters. "Be stupid, then."

But her tone softens slightly as she adds, "Just be careful. This magic user might not be powerful, but they're still dangerous. Don't underestimate them."

Peren gives her a sharp nod, his expression unreadable. "I won't."

Nodding, he leaves her house. As he heads back to where he left Mercy, he finds the villagers upset and angry, shouting at the mayor with refusals to leave their multi-generational homes.

Snapping at the villagers, the mayor says in a voice that brooks no argument, "We are leaving. It is the only safe and wise course. We will return once the sell-sword has taken care of this magic user."

Looking around at everyone as they quiet down to grumbles and mutters, she spots Peren. Waving him over to her, she calls out in a loud voice, "Here is your hero sell-sword now!"

The entire crowd turns and faces Peren. Smiling at them and taking a deep breath to give an encouraging speech, he is interrupted by them rushing him and demanding why he wants them to leave their homes and dead loved ones.

Overwhelmed, Peren can only stutter and mutter as he keeps being bombarded by their anger. Gritting his teeth, he shouts, "Be quiet!" Shocked at his outrage, the entire village stills. "That's better. Now, let me explain this in simple terms: if I cannot stop this magic user, I can give you all a head start on running. Do not let my sacrifice go to waste."

Stunned at his words, they just stand there gaping at him. One says, "Well, when you put it like that, I guess we better get packing."

"Thank you. I will do my best to ensure you all are able to return."

The villagers disperse back to their homes.

Knowing how valuable Mercy was in the last attack, Peren doesn't want to risk her in any of the upcoming dangers. He searches the village and finds her surrounded by a group of children and young teens, basking in their affection. He pauses in the shadows, a small smile tugging at his lips as he watches her revel in the attention.

After a while, he decides it's time to take Mercy away from

the crowd. Stepping into the light, he doesn't make it a dozen steps before the kids spot him. Recognizing the hero who defended their village, they rush over, surrounding him and bombarding him with questions. They beg him to show them how he fought the golems.

Peren squats down, recounting the tale of the Battle of Ground Thern, making it as entertaining as possible, with a little embellishment here and there to keep them hooked. He ends with a serious tone, but a softer delivery. "Heroism isn't about glory. It's about protecting those who can't protect themselves." The younger ones clap and rush off to play, shoving each other as they go.

Noticing some older kids lingering, Peren beckons them closer. "No matter how brave you are, there are always choices that affect others. What matters is what you do to help them," he says, pointing to the distant pyres. "Sometimes, being a hero means making sure no one has to face that."

The kids quiet down, contemplating his words, and Peren approaches Mercy, gently rubbing her side and feeding her a couple of sugar cubes, thinking to himself, *How can I keep you safe while I go deal with this horror?*

As if she can understand him, Mercy jerks her head toward the kids and gives a loud huff. Peren chuckles softly, getting her message. "Alright, I'll get them to look after you."

Calling out to the children, they turn, one grinning widely. "What now? More lessons on heroism?"

Peren laughs, shaking his head. "Sorry for the serious talk, but it's important. You'll learn that as you grow up. But that's not why I called you back." He gestures to Mercy. "I need you all to help me look after her while I go take care of something important. I can't have her with me—not with all the danger still out there."

The kids' faces light up, excitement bubbling over. "For real, mister? You want us to look after her?" one asks, eyes wide with disbelief.

Peren nods seriously. "Yes. I trust you to keep her safe."

They eagerly agree, and Peren gives them a quick rundown on how to care for Mercy, making sure they know how to feed her and keep her comfortable. As he gives her one last hug and rub, she jerks her head against his as if to say, "You come back to me."

As he hands them the reins, he says to them in a quiet voice, "Take care of her." Not sure when or if he will make it back, he knows that she is in good and capable hands.

He walks away with a heavy heart, but a clear and determined mind as the children's voices follow him, making himself a promise: *I will make them pay for every drop of blood that was spilled today.*

THIRTEEN

The Witch's Lair

Arriving at the edge of the village, Peren surveys the beginning of the valley the old woman described. The sides of the track slowly rise into smooth vertical walls that seem unwelcoming and foreboding.

With one final breath, he starts down the track with determination.

Heading further in, he keeps his eyes open for any cave entrances. About a hundred paces down the path, he comes across one on the left. Knowing it is too close to the village and the kids often play in this tiny alcove, he dismisses it and moves on, but continues to scrutinize each cave he encounters, entering and exploring them, only to find them empty and devoid of any signs of life.

As he walks, his senses sharpen, becoming more attuned to his surroundings. Missing a cave at first, he feels a strange sensation, as if something is off. Stopping, he looks back at the wall, confused. Seeing only solid rock where there should be an opening, he dismisses it as a mistake. Yet something nags at the back of his mind, urging him to reconsider. Following his gut feeling, he returns to the spot where he sensed the façade, staring up at it with a growing sense of suspicion.

Deciding to trust his instincts, he begins to climb. Gritting his teeth against the strain on his injured arm and refusing to admit defeat, he finally makes it up to the suspicious spot. As he reaches out to take a small finger hold, his entire hand goes through the rock face, causing him to lose his footing. He catches the bottom of the entrance, barely stopping himself from falling. Hanging by his fingertips, he hauls himself up, eyes watering from the pain, gripping the rock face tightly.

Using his free hand to reach up, he cautiously feels for the edges of the illusionary entrance, estimating its size. Realizing the entrance is much smaller than he had hoped, he decides to check it out, something deep inside telling him this is the magic user's entrance. Sticking his head through and back quickly, he finds no immediate danger. Climbing in, he finds the entrance quickly narrows to a small but passable crack in the wall. Knowing his warm clothing will only get caught and possibly trap him, he strips till he's only in his shirt, breeches, and boots. His skin tingles against the cold, his breath slightly fogging up as he prepares to scrape through this tunnel.

Shortening himself as much as possible, taking deep breaths, filling his blood with as much oxygen as he can, he breathes out, compressing his chest as much as possible before pushing against the small hole. *This magic user must be tiny,* he thinks wryly as he pushes himself deeper, scratching his body on the cold rock.

He takes handhold after handhold, pulling with one hand and struggling to push with the other, moving slowly through the claustrophobic space. His clothing tears on the sharp, icy rock, which slices his skin open. The only indication is the warm liquid running down his body.

As he moves into the tunnel, navigating tight turns and apparent dead ends, his neck cramps from keeping it twisted.

The deeper he goes, the less light he has to navigate by, though his sight is of little help in the narrow confines anyway. Constantly getting stuck on protruding rocks, he feels his strength waning as he smears blood along the tunnel walls.

Feeling lightheaded, a thought that this could all be a ploy to hide the real entrance crosses his mind. Desperate to be proven right, he dismisses this morbid thought and presses on, determined to trust his instincts—instincts that have saved his life more times than he can recall.

He finally stops in confusion as a flicker of hope rises in his bones. Closing his eyes for a few seconds before reopening them, he confirms that the tunnel is getting lighter; it's not his imagination or hallucinations. Tears of relief well up as he also sees that the tunnel finally widens. Slumping with exhaustion, actually able to take in a proper breath in what feels like forever, he continues on.

When the tunnel widens enough for him to move freely, he pauses to catch his breath. Looking himself over as best he can, he sees that he is bleeding from many places. If he doesn't do something soon, he will bleed out. Moving as quietly as he can, he winces as he takes his shirt off and, tearing it into strips, does his best to stem the bleeding.

Moving forward slowly, Peren reaches out with his senses, picking up the faint crackling of wood, a telltale sign of a fire nearby. Unsheathing his dagger, he feels a surge of anticipation; the tunnel exit must be just around the next corner.

He pauses, straining to detect any presence in the cavern ahead, his instincts on high alert. Only picking up on a single presence, he peeks around the corner, hoping to locate this vile thing easily. Unable to see anyone, he slips into the cavern as silent as a shadow and feels an icy chill run down his spine as he moves stealthily around the edges of the cavern, flitting from shadow to shadow.

Raeka Guro, who calls herself the Night's Shadow, has wrapped herself in blankets to keep warm despite the fire. With her eyes shut to sleep and replenish her magic, she suddenly jerks up in panic.

Wondering how anyone could have found the entrance, she slips out of bed as quietly as she can and moves into the shadows with her knife. Grateful that she stopped linking with those golems when faced with that stranger and his dagger, she moves from shadow to shadow toward the front entrance, unsure of how long she has before the target arrives.

Just as she steps out of the shadows, her second ward triggers a warning. Panicking, she leaps back into the darkness, positioning herself about halfway across the cavern.

As cautiously and quietly as possible, Peren moves into the sound-bouncing shadows, straining to look everywhere at once. With his Elven vision, he navigates swiftly, dismissing the empty shadows that surround him. Aware of the danger the magic user poses, he leverages his stealth, keen hearing, and enhanced sight to his advantage.

Finally, his target comes into view. He sizes her up, assessing her vulnerabilities, before leaping soundlessly from the shadows and swinging his dagger toward the base of her skull.

Sensing the attack from behind, Raeka blocks it just in time, barely casting a spell as the blade grazes her skin.

Frustration wells within Peren as the blade halts inches from severing her spinal column. She jumps back out of his reach, and, standing calm and confident, says, "So, you're the fancy stranger who gave me trouble and destroyed my golems."

Peren replies with a growl, giving her his biggest, smirkiest grin. "Yes, and I will destroy you the same way."

"No, you won't," she answers smugly.

A glint appears in Peren's eye, and the corners of his lips

tweak up. Taking a relaxed yet on-guard pose, he asks with every ounce of confidence he has, "Oh, yeah?"

Raeka's eyes narrow, and a smirk forms on her lips. "You think you can win against me? You have no idea what you're up against."

Peren chuckles softly. "I've faced worse. You're just another obstacle to clear."

The tension in the cavern thickens, becoming a palpable weight as both combatants size each other up with lethal intent. Peren's muscles coil, ready to strike again, while Raeka's fingers twitch, preparing another spell. The flickering firelight casts eerie shadows on the walls, heightening the sense of impending violence.

Raeka takes a step forward, her voice lilting with amusement. "You're brave, I'll give you that. But bravery? It's so ... boring," she says in a sing-song voice, as if mocking him.

"Bravery and a good blade have gotten me this far," Peren replies, gripping his dagger tightly. "Let's see if your magic can keep you alive."

He lunges, only to find himself frozen in place, bound by invisible forces.

Her laughter fills the cavern, a shrill, delighted sound. "Oh, you thought you had me! That's adorable!" She circles him like a predator playing with its food, her eyes gleaming with twisted pleasure as she looks him over. When he tries to speak, his jaw snaps shut, held by her spell. "Uh-uh," she coos, waggling a finger mockingly. "It's *my* turn to play with you."

Her face twists into a grin, her eyes alight with unhinged excitement as she leans in close. She giggles, savouring his helpless anger. "Oh, the things I could do to you," she whispers, tilting her head thoughtfully, as if considering a hundred cruel possibilities.

Deciding he needs some fixing-up, she steps close, her fingers skimming over his chest with a strange, almost intimate touch. As her fingers trace over his wounds with a disturbingly gentle touch, she hums softly. Her hands move slowly, savouring each inch of torn skin as her magic seeps into him, repairing all the damage.

Peren's pulse quickens in panic, his body immobilized and his mind racing, unable to do anything as she steps back and stares at him, her eyes glinting with a strange light. His stomach drops, panic mingling with a deeper fear as her gaze roams over him with renewed interest. He struggles against the unseen hold, muscles straining, but she only leans in closer, watching him with a curious, predatory gaze that makes his skin crawl.

She doesn't say a word at first, but just stares, her mouth curling into a smile that holds something sinister. "Oh," she whispers, almost to herself, "this just got… so much more interesting."

Peren tries to open his mouth to speak, forgetting that it is held shut by her magic. Frustration flickers in his eyes as he strains against his invisible bonds. She watches him, her expression playful, and, with a flick of her wrist, she finally releases the spell, allowing him to speak.

He narrows his eyes, unsettled, but the only reply he can muster is a sharp "*What?*"

Her only response is to examine him closer with a glint in her eyes that terrifies Peren. Refusing to give in, he cracks a gleaming smile as he asks as cockily as he can, "What? You see something you like?"

Her eyes gleam with a mad amusement, her voice dropping to a lilting murmur. "I'm just deciding what I want to do with you, now that I know what's *really* under that skin." Her fingers twitch with excitement as she circles him, occasionally muttering incoherent phrases, eyes flickering back to him as if savouring every shift of his expression.

Refusing to admit she has struck a nerve, he replies nonchalantly, "I have no idea what you are talking about."

Her eyes narrow, scrutinizing him. "You can deny it all you want, but I see it now. You're not just any warrior. You're something much more."

Peren's heart races even faster, but he maintains his composure. "You're mistaken," he says, trying to sound convincing.

Impatient with his denials, Raeka moves as close to his face as she can, her voice bubbling with an excited, almost insane energy. "I know you're an Elf. I can see through your glamour, so stop trying to deny it."

Peren shakes his head with a smug grin, forcing bravado into his words. "No, you can't. My glamour is perfect." He adopts a thoughtful expression, piecing together the links as they form in his mind. "You only changed after you healed me, so you must have seen my Elven anatomy."

In that moment, the reality crashes over him—someone else knows he is an Elf. Panic flares within him, and he struggles to maintain his cool beneath the surface.

Finally calming down, he glares at her intently, demanding, "What do you want with me?"

His cheeks flush under her unnerving gaze, and Raeka drops the pretence, her expression shifting to something serious. "I'm still figuring that out," she replies, her voice buzzing with manic energy. "I didn't expect to encounter a mythical creature; I was anticipating an exceptional fighter." Clapping her hands gleefully, she continues, "Oh, my master will be so pleased with me."

Peren stares at her, genuine fear gripping him as her eyes widen with a disturbing excitement. "Y-your master?" he stutters, his voice shaking.

"Mmhmm," she replies, nodding eagerly. As she opens her mouth to elaborate, she pauses, her focus sharpening on him as if weighing her options. A grin spreads across her face as she comes to a decision, and she begins to circle him, chanting a spell under her breath. Stopping to look up at him, she smiles and says, "That's better."

Trapped and unable to move, Peren can only stand there, realizing in horror that his glamour glyph has just been blocked, leaving her to examine his true Elf form with a frenzied curiosity.

Pulling herself together after a few moments, she resumes her animated chatter about her master. "You see, my master took me in from the streets as a child and trained me," she says, her eyes lighting up with a fervent adoration. "This is the first time my master has let me go out and have fun in the world!" Clapping her hands in delight, she beams at him. "You are my first captive."

As the realization sinks in, she gasps in awe, repeating, "My first captive is an Elf. How many can say that as their first achievement?" Turning back to Peren, her smile stretches wide, looking almost manic as she adds, "I can't wait to present you to him!"

While her words spill forth, Peren's mind races with thoughts of escape. He's only half-listening to her prattling, running through multiple scenarios in his head. Yet he keeps returning to the same grim conclusion: he knows too little about magic to devise a plan to break the bonds and free himself.

Focusing back on her voice, he attempts to engage her in conversation, hoping she might inadvertently reveal something useful. She suddenly rounds on him, fists on her hips, glaring up with a fierce expression. "You know how rude you've been, constantly interrupting me?"

"Maybe if you actually explained yourself, I wouldn't have to interrupt," he retorts, pushing against the magical force holding him.

Seemingly fed up with his defiance, she flicks her wrist, and a magical force seals his mouth shut again. He tries to grit his teeth in frustration, but he can't even grind them due to the enchantment, leaving him standing there, glaring at her with fury in his eyes.

Sighing at the newfound silence in the cavern, Raeka resumes her musing, talking to herself as if he's no longer there. "What should I do with you? Keep you as a trophy? Or perhaps as a gift for my master?" She paces back and forth, lost in thought, occasionally glancing at Peren with an unsettling mix of fascination and warped desire.

Peren's mind races, desperately searching for any weakness in her spell, any glimmer of hope to break free. But for now, he can only watch and wait, praying for a moment of distraction or a lapse in her concentration.

In the flickering light of the fire, Raeka's silhouette dances across the cavern walls, her muttering filling the air as Peren stands helplessly, ensnared by her magic. He realizes that the real struggle has only just begun, and his survival hinges on outwitting her and finding a way to escape her clutches.

Knowing she can't leave him like this, as her magic will eventually run out, Raeka begins rummaging through her belongings, searching for something to bind him with. Her voice rises with excitement as she tosses items aside. "A collar would be fitting, wouldn't it? Something pretty to mark you as mine!"

As she continues to think aloud, each scenario she conjures grows increasingly twisted, a dark thrill radiating from her words. Peren silently wishes she blocked his hearing too, not wanting to know about the grotesque possibilities she envisions.

Recognizing this as his best opportunity to flee, he strains against the magical bonds holding him, yet his efforts yield no results. Spotting her gathering a couple of items, he knows she'll return soon, and with desperation surging within him, he hurls every ounce of strength against the force, hoping to find a crack in her spell before it's too late.

To his shock, he could swear his fingers wiggle a bit. Trying again, nothing happens. Standing there, he tries to work out what was different. After multiple attempts, he still can't move a finger.

Hearing her mutter in relief at finding something that will hold him, panic flares through him again. Attempting to move his fingers, he throws everything he has at it, and, to his utter shock, his fingers move—not just wiggling, but actually moving. Throwing every bit of his willpower against her spell, he is able to clench and unclench his fist with extreme difficulty.

Flooded with relief and smiling, he quickly tries to wipe it off his face as she returns to him.

Feeling smug about what she is about to do, Raeka pauses and just happens to look up at him. Seeing an odd look on his face, she only has time to knit her brows in confusion before he throws everything he has at the spell. Tearing through it, he reaches up, grabs her by the throat, lifts her off the ground, and starts to squeeze.

Her confusion morphs into a frenzied mix of shock and twisted delight as she processes what's happening. Her eyes widen with a manic gleam, and she laughs breathlessly, the sound both terrified and exhilarated. "Oh, this is interesting!" she gasps, clawing at his hands, attempting to pry his fingers from her throat while her expression flickers between panic and gleeful insanity.

As her air supply dwindles, desperation sets in, and she

begins to plead with wide, wild eyes, offering him anything and everything to spare her life. Yet even as she claws and flails, a part of her seems almost thrilled by the chaos, lost in the exhilaration of this perilous game.

Her movements become sluggish as her body desperately fights for oxygen, her face shifting from pale to a deep purple. Tears stream down her cheeks as she stares into Peren's eyes, a mixture of fear and sadness reflected in her gaze. She pleads silently for release, her eyes slowly glazing over as she goes limp in his grip.

Holding her crushed neck in his hands, Peren finds himself transfixed, unable to look away as the life drains from her. Even after her body falls still and lifeless, he remains paralysed, trapped in this moment, unable to move a muscle or even blink.

When he finally releases her mangled neck, her body crumples to the floor like a lifeless rag doll. As he looks down at her, he feels something wither inside him—something that once brought joy and hope, now extinguished. He can't quite grasp what it was, only that it filled his world with light. Now, all that remains is a suffocating darkness, devoid of any hope or joy.

Staring down at the corpse, he notices a pool of liquid spreading across the floor. A jolt of realization hits him, and he recoils, glancing at the dark stains creeping onto his boots and breeches. Panic rises within him as he hyperventilates, unable to tear his gaze away from the lifeless form and the spots tainting his clothing.

Doubling over, he empties his stomach, vomit splattering against the ground and staining his boots and breeches further. Wiping his mouth with the back of his hand, he stumbles through the cavern, nausea churning in his gut as he grapples with the horror of what he's done—the ease with which it happened and the unsettling absence of any feeling at all.

He leans against the cold cavern wall, his breath coming in ragged gasps. The enormity of his actions crashes over him in waves, each one threatening to drown him in guilt and revulsion. Gritting his teeth in determination, he fights to suppress the thoughts. Shaking off the darkness that clings to him, he collects what he needs and turns to the entrance of the cavern.

Remembering the biting cold, the agony, and the blood he'd lost going that way before, he stops, weighing his options. *There must be more than one way out of this cavern,* he thinks. Skirting the edges of the room, he moves carefully, his eyes tracing the stone walls for any sign of another exit, anything that might lead him out without repeating his previous torment.

Returning to his starting point, frustration brews, but he refuses to accept that there's no other way out. Determined to find one, he sends out his senses, moving slowly around the cavern.

About halfway around the cave, he finds a hidden depression behind a rock outcropping that would not be found any other way. Squeezing through the gap, he finds himself in a short, narrow tunnel, his head rubbing against the ceiling. Forced to move sideways, he looks ahead and sees a vertical sliver of light.

Moving through the tunnel, he's nearly blinded by the harsh sunlight when he finally emerges into the open. Shielding his eyes with his hand until they adjust, he realizes he's standing on a rocky outcropping overlooking the village, just a short distance away. A surge of relief and satisfaction washes over him as he scans his surroundings and finds a path that heads down the mountain.

Finally making his way to the village after gathering his warm clothes, he sees some stragglers disappearing from sight in the distance. Stopping suddenly, he remembers that Raeka blocked the glyph of glamour on him. Pulling out his dagger, he manages to check and see that the glamour is working once again. He sighs in relief.

Even with his blood loss, he manages to catch up to the villagers quickly, explaining to each group he meets that it's safe to return home. As he moves onto the next group, he hears mutterings about how they could have just stayed home. Only when they mutter against the mayor does he stop and explain to them why they are wrong to blame her.

He moves swiftly through the dispersed column of people toward the front, where Mayor Pender is leading the villagers to safety. Pulling up, confused at the sight of the panting sell-sword, she asks, "You finished already?"

Trying to ignore his murder of the girl, he pushes down the haunting feelings, looking directly into her eyes. He replies, "I have, and your village is now safe once again."

Relief floods her features. Sighing out all the tense feelings she had been holding in, she beams down at him, answering in an extremely grateful voice, "Thank you very much for your help. We are all very much in your debt." Before he has a chance to open his mouth, she says, "We don't have much, but I'm sure we can come to an arrangement."

Giving her concerned face a disarming smile, he replies with a flourishing bow. "I am sure we can".

Relief flashes in her features, and, smiling fondly down at him, she calls for the villagers to return home. As mutterings and grumblings meet her new order, they turn around and start heading back to Thern.

Moving back along the column, Peren looks for the group

of young ones who should be looking after Mercy. He finds them among a large group of villagers, arguing over who gets to ride her. Seeing him approach, one of the women in the group turns towards the kids and informs them that he is back for his horse, to which they whine and groan.

When Peren arrives, they all look sad that they only had a few hours with this lovely creature. Seeing their sad faces, he says to the group, "I can see that she has been very well cared-for."

Empty-hearted, they murmur, "I guess so."

Before anyone has a chance to do anything, the woman jumps in. "Don't be like that! You all should be grateful that this stranger was willing to trust you to look after his wonderful horse."

To everyone's surprise, Mercy snorts in agreement, causing everyone to smile.

The kids turn to Peren. "Thank you, mister," they say as one before turning away.

Feeling sad that they really wanted to look after her, Peren gets an idea and looks at her questioningly. She smiles mischievously.

Taking advantage of the situation, one of the kids quietly hops into the saddle. When the others notice, they all start complaining.

The woman rubs Mercy's head as she says to Peren, "She looks like she needs regular exercise to keep her fit and healthy."

Picking up on her intentions, Peren opens his mouth, but Mercy jumps in and nods as she snorts in agreement, making Peren and the woman laugh. "Yes, she does." Looking as sad as he can, he adds, "Unfortunately, I won't be able to keep her exercise up, since I will be recovering from my injuries." Looking at her mischievously, he continues, "If only there was someone who I can pay to do it for me."

The kids light up and crowd around him, eagerly volunteering. Playing along, Peren pretends he doesn't see them and continues, "It's a shame no one wants to look after her."

The kids start shouting and bouncing, trying to get his attention. Looking down after a few more seconds, he acts surprised to see them. "Well, I guess I found her carers." They shout in jubilation, whooping and cheering.

When they get to the village, Peren watches from a distance as Mercy revels in the attention and gives each kid a ride, allowing everyone to move back in.

FOURTEEN

The Witch

That night, the village throws a feast in Peren's honour, celebrating his bravery and the safety he's brought them. Yet, haunted by the memory of Raeka's death, he slips away early, seeking solitude.

As he tries to rest, he tosses and turns, seeing the life leak out of her gaze each time he closes his eyes. Haunted by her death, he sits up in bed, wiping his face with his hand. Moving over to the basin, he washes his face before flopping back on the bed and running his damp hand through his hair, making it stick up.

Burying his head in his hands, he sighs deeply, the weight of her death pressing on him like a stone, dragging him down as though he were drowning underwater. He's taken lives before—clean, quick, detached—but somehow, this time, it's different. *Maybe it's because she was my first girl?* he thinks, the thought twisting uneasily in his mind.

Coming to a decision, he dresses quietly and slips into the cool night, retracing his path to the cavern. The shadows stretch long under the faint moonlight, and each step feels heavier than the last, as if the night itself is judging him as guilty for what he's done.

Inside the cavern, an eerie silence fills the air, making his footsteps echo softly off the walls. He finds Raeka's crumpled body just where he left it, her face now serene—an expression he never saw in her while she lived. The memory of her dying gaze flashes in his mind, and he freezes, overwhelmed by it. Falling to his knees, he begins to grieve uncontrollably, tears streaming down his cheeks as he mourns.

Finally calming down, though feeling utterly drained, Peren gathers himself and moves toward her still form. With tenderness, he cleans away the dirt and blood, smoothing her hair and straightening her clothing as best he can. Then, with a deep, steadying breath, he lifts her gently into his arms, and, cradling her against him, he carries her outside and down the mountain.

Heading off the track a ways, he gently lays her down and begins to dig a hole. At first, the motions feel mechanical, but with each shovel of earth, it's as if he's digging a hole within himself. The silence of the night is only broken by the scraping of the shovel against the ground. This is not just a burial; it's a quiet farewell to a life that could have been beautiful.

When he finishes digging, he wipes his grimy sleeve across his dirty, sweaty face. Climbing out of the hole, he moves toward Raeka's body, his legs heavy, as if each step is weighed down by boulders. Gently, almost reverently, he picks her up and carries her to the grave. With a quiet sigh, he hops into the hole, laying her down with care. He straightens her body, crossing her arms over her chest before climbing out of the grave.

Dropping to his knees, he bows his head, gazing down at her for a long moment. With a quiet whisper, he offers a short but heartfelt prayer to Twileron, the God of Death, asking for her soul's peaceful rest.

He stays like that for a while, unmoving, his gaze fixed on

her. Finally, he rises, grabbing a shovel and filling it with dirt. Standing over Raeka, he hesitates, unable to let the dirt fall. Tears flow down his face, and for a long moment, he can't bring himself to do it.

Finally, with a shaky breath, he tips the shovel, allowing the first load of earth to fall on her. After that first, excruciating moment, it becomes easier. With each shovel, his pace quickens, as if he can bury the memory of her, trying to forget she ever existed—even though deep down, he knows her dying moments will haunt him for the rest of his life.

Once she is completely buried, Peren gazes down at the mound, a hollow emptiness gnawing at him. It's more than he expected—he feels something missing, as though the weight of her short life still lingers in the air.

His legs move as if on their own accord, carrying him back to the cavern. The shadows within seem to mourn his loss, thick and heavy around him.

He searches through Raeka's belongings, each moment laced with an unsettling feeling. He shouldn't be doing this, yet his hands move without thought. And then, he finds it—the thing he hadn't known he was looking for: a frayed, well-worn neckerchief, the fabric faded from wear, as though it was once tied around her throat—that same throat he took her life from.

A sharp, jagged emotion twists in his chest. He pushes it down, forcing himself to breathe. Bringing the cloth to his face, he inhales deeply, trying to memorize the scent that lingers on it, a faint trace of her that he can never hold onto.

He trudges back to her grave, his heart heavy with guilt. Kneeling beside the mound, he carefully lays the cloth in a circle near her head. His voice barely above a breath, he whispers, "I may not know your name, but I will remember you. You deserved better."

He stays there, kneeling, until the sky begins to lighten, the first hints of dawn casting pale light over the grave. Then, with a final glance, he rises slowly, the weariness settling in his bones, and heads back to the village to clean himself up, carrying the weight of her memory with him.

FIFTEEN

THE WEIGHT OF GOODBYE

Peren is talked into staying longer than he had planned, his departure delayed by the villagers' persistent pleas and the weight of the witch he buried. Each night, his sleep is fractured by nightmares—fresh horrors that replay in his mind, with the haunting image of Norta's life slipping away in his hands replacing the face of the witch. The sensation of choking the life out of someone feels like it's suffocating his soul.

Peren often seeks the company of the old woman, drawn to her vast knowledge. She teaches him what she knows of magic while he tries to decipher what it is about her that feels so familiar.

Knowing he can't delay the farewell any longer, Peren finally prepares to say his goodbyes to the village. The children, tearful and reluctant, gather around Mercy, their hands brushing her mane one last time. Peren, his heart heavy, offers each of them a small payment as thanks for taking such good care of her.

The mayor steps forward and delivers a heartfelt farewell speech, thanking Peren for protecting the village and saving lives that would have been lost without him. The gathered villagers respond with cheers, their gratitude filling the air.

Leaving the village behind, Peren stops by the grave one last time, offering a final farewell.

Then, with a heavy heart, he mounts Mercy and continues on their journey toward Sky Thern.

SIXTEEN

SKY THERN

Two weeks pass before Peren arrives in Sky Thern at mid-afternoon. The trek has been long and exhausting, the snow reaching up to his waist in some places. Where there's no snow at all, loose pebbles threaten to make Mercy slip and injure herself. The air seems to grow colder with every step, and no matter how many coats he wears, the cold still manages to bite through, numbing his skin and chilling him to the bone.

To his surprise, he finds pastures here where shepherds tend to strange, oversized creatures—sheeplike, but much larger and woollier than anything he's seen before. Nearby, other shepherds oversee crops that somehow thrive despite the harsh, unforgiving climate.

Arriving at the village, Peren notices it's built into the peak of what must be the highest mountain in the range, with steep stone stairs everywhere and houses shuttered tight against the cold. Moving Mercy forward is nearly impossible, as he's numb and iced-over. A light but steady snowfall blurs everyone's vision, adding to the challenge.

Urging Mercy toward the nearest villager, Peren asks if there's an inn. Instead of a welcoming reply, he gets only a vague wave in one direction before the villager quickly moves on, leaving an impression of unfriendliness.

He makes his way through the village, scanning each house for any sign of an inn. At last, he spots a two-story building with a sign reading *The Melting Hoof.* He finds a stable nearby, but no stablehands in sight. After settling Mercy inside, he piles as much hay as he can into her stall to keep her warm, then gathers his saddlebags and heads into the inn.

A wave of blessed warmth greets him, radiating from two blazing fireplaces positioned on opposite sides of the common room. The room itself is nearly deserted save for a couple of patrons sitting close to the fires, nursing their mugs in silence.

Peren barely takes two steps inside before a large, stout middle-aged woman with grey hair and a perpetual squint blocks his way. With a slight bow, she greets him in a warm, sonorous voice. "Welcome to The Melting Hoof. I am inn-keeper Jain. How may I be of service to my lord?"

Returning her bow, he replies with his most disarming and warm smile. "Pleasantness to you, Mistress Jain. I'm looking for a room for a couple of nights. I've stabled my horse—hope that's all right."

With a semi-toothless smile, she tells him the price for a room—a small one on the second floor. After giving him brief directions, she heads to the kitchen to warm up some stew for him.

Following her directions, Peren finally arrives at his room. Opening the door, he takes in the cramped space: just big enough to hold a bed, a chest, and a chamber pot tucked in the corner.

Heading back down after dumping his bags on the bed, he is greeted at the bottom of the stairs by Mistress Jain, who holds a steaming bowl of stew and a spoon. With a warm gesture, she beckons him to follow, leading him to a small table in the corner. She sets the bowl down in front of him and motions for him to sit and eat.

The hot stew scalds his frozen tongue, but melts its way down his insides, slowly bringing warmth back to his numbed body. To Mistress Jain's smiling pleasure, he devours the stew in silence, pausing only to ask for a second, and then a third, helping.

Relaxing in front of the fire, warm and content after five hearty servings of stew, Peren sips on some spiced wine. Turning to Mistress Jain, he hesitates for a moment, then says, "I couldn't help but notice how quiet it is here. I met a villager outside earlier, but he didn't seem very... welcoming. Is everyone here as reserved as that?"

She laughs softly, shaking her head. "Wouldn't you be if you were stuck out there?" she replies. "I bet he just wanted to get inside as quickly as possible."

Nodding in understanding, Peren takes another sip and remains in front of the fire for a while, letting the warmth seep into his bones. Eventually, he heads up the stairs to his room. The exhaustion from his journey catching up with him, he slips into bed and falls asleep almost immediately.

A few hours later, he is roused by soft knocking. "Come in," he calls out groggily.

Mistress Jain enters, carrying a tray piled high with multiple bowls of her delicious stew. She places the tray on the chest beside the bed, her smile kind but firm. "You need to keep eating to combat the cold," she says. "Stay warm and get some rest."

With that, she exits, leaving Peren to eat and drift back to sleep.

The next morning, feeling somewhat renewed after a good

night's sleep, he takes the tray downstairs for a bowl of morning stew and spiced wine. Though his body feels restored, the experience with the nameless witch has left him numb. Hardened by the ordeal, he pushes forward with a hollow sense of calm, his energy returning, even as his emotions remain frozen.

For the next two days, he devotes himself to rest and nourishment, allowing his body the time it needs to repair itself fully and recover his strength. On the morning of his departure, he packs his things, heads downstairs to thank Mistress Jain, then saddles up Mercy and takes his leave of The Melting Hoof. Still having food left over from his Soul, he continues on while fingering his pendant as he thinks of her lovingly.

Moving down the track, Peren and Mercy are fully exposed to the brutal elements—blizzards, freezing rains, and biting winds. Huddled close to Mercy and bundled up in every layer he owns, each breath Peren exhales crystallizes in the frigid air. He knows that stopping, even briefly, could mean death from the cold, so he urges Mercy onward, step by freezing step.

The icy, treacherous path beneath them makes every movement a struggle as they trudge through relentless storms, with sheets of rain reducing visibility to nothing. The howling wind cuts through their layers of clothing, gnawing at their skin, and every breath freezes before it leaves their mouths. Peren feels the cold creeping deep into his bones, his muscles growing stiff with each hour that drags on.

Mercy struggles with every step, her hooves slipping on the slick, pebbly surface beneath the snow, her thick coat no match for the wet, freezing wind. Peren wraps himself tighter in his layers, grateful for every small break in the storm, though they're few and far between.

Day after day, they press on, exhausted and battered by the elements. The storms show no mercy—snow turning to sleet, then sleet to rain as the temperature fluctuates, turning the snow into a heavy, wet slush that clings to their feet, making each step feel like wading through molasses.

Still, they move forward, driven by the knowledge that stopping would only make their situation worse. Peren's fingers are stiff, his face numb, and the cold is beginning to feel like a part of him, yet with each step, they move closer to the end of this torment.

After what feels like an eternity, the snow begins to thin, turning to icy streams. Pushing a little further, they finally find blessed relief in a patch of land free from snow or ice. It's here, at the edge of the storm, where both rider and horse collapse, utterly spent after days of gruelling travel, the warmth of rest finally washing over them. Leaning back with his head against the saddle, Peren watches sleepily as the sun dips behind the mountains, quickly ushering in an early night.

He wakes the next morning to the blinding sun cresting the horizon, feeling more refreshed, despite the lingering exhaustion from days without rest. Deciding that both he and Mercy need a few more days to recover, he settles in, allowing them both to recover from the brutal journey.

As they continue their descent, they quickly find themselves facing the opposite problem—the heat. The sun beats down mercilessly, and soon, they're sweating harder and harder. *At least we aren't freezing,* Peren thinks wryly. Taking shelter whenever possible, they drink deeply from their dwindling water supply, only to realize they're running short not long after the last of the ice has melted. Shifting to night travel, they make better progress, pressing onward under the stars and stopping only when absolutely necessary.

Finally reaching the foot of the mountain, Peren steps onto the hot packed sand of the road, only to leap back with a cry as the intense heat sears his foot. All his preparation couldn't shield him from the scorching ground. Forced to wear his snow boots, he finds he can at least walk, though the insides quickly turn into buckets of sweat, trapping the heat.

When he tries to lead Mercy onto the sand, she rears back, snorting and whickering, reluctant to step onto the burning surface.

Realizing there's no way he or Mercy would survive more than a couple of days in their snow boots, Peren tears apart his snow clothes to fashion makeshift footwear for both of them. The uneven padding on the soles makes each step awkward and clumsy, but it's better than nothing.

With each hobbled step, Peren leads Mercy further into the desert, hoping he's on the right path toward Jarnda, a city that survives on the runoff from the Mountains of Thern.

SEVENTEEN

JARNDA

Sweltering in nothing but his breeches, Peren trudges on-ward, his footing a bit more stable now in the padded boots. His upper body is a painful shade of tomato red, peeling badly from relentless sunburn. Mercy pants heavily, sweat darkening her coat as Peren does his best to keep her cool, though both are struggling to adapt to the unforgiving desert heat after the icy chill of the mountains.

When a structure finally shimmers into view in the distance, Peren's heart fills with relief and hope. Urging Mercy forward, he continues along the road toward what must be the city. As the towering walls come into focus, he stops, momentarily awestruck, forgetting the blazing sun that is still mercilessly scorching his skin. Tilting his head back, he marvels at the sheer height of the walls—at least 500 feet high, he guesses.

His reverie is interrupted as other travellers trudge past him, all bearing the marks of the desert: sunburnt, weary, and visibly exhausted. He recalls his map—these travellers must have come from Zairedrein, the last city on the eastern road before the massive deserts of Whaern.

As the travellers head north alongside him, bound for the sanctuary of Jarnda, Peren regains his focus and presses onward, eager to escape the searing sun finally.

As the gates come into clear view, Peren joins the growing but steadily moving line of travellers, only to be jostled and cursed at by impatient strangers. His temper flares, raw from the heat and exhaustion, but he grits his teeth, focusing on Mercy and his goal of getting inside. The line inches forward as each traveller is stopped and questioned by Wall Watch soldiers at kiosks in front of the gates before being allowed entry into Jarnda.

It takes only a few minutes, but what feels like hours in the scorching sun, before Peren finally reaches one of the guards at a kiosk. The cool shade offers him some relief, and he allows himself a moment to relax as the guard offers him a much-needed drink. "Welcome to Jarnda. You look like you've travelled a long way. Where did you come from? Zairedrein?"

Shaking his head as he finishes the water the guard gave him, Peren answers, "I came from the Mountains of Thern."

Doing a double-take, the guard reevaluates Peren. "No one ever comes that way. It's far too dangerous…"

Not knowing what to say, Peren simply shrugs and offers a weary smile.

Recovering quickly, the guard nods and says, "Since it's your first time here, might I suggest the Shielded Maiden inn? It's affordable, reliable, and has complimentary services to help travellers recover, like soothing baths, sunburn relief, and massage therapy for those who've been through long journeys. They'll also help with any aches and pains, like a sore back, if you need it. Once you reach the centre of the city, cross the river, then take three lefts and a right at the hoof. Keep going, and you'll run right into it."

Thanking him, Peren steps inside the gate. The sight before him stops him in his tracks, leaving him awestruck at the bustling city—people, noise, towering buildings, and animals everywhere. Overwhelmed, he almost stumbles when a soldier shoves him and tells him to move along. Confused, he realizes that the guards at the gate are handpicked for their patience and temperament. Brushing himself off, he resumes his walk, scanning for the inn the kind guard recommended.

Sometime later, the sun sinks below the walls, plunging the city into darkness and shadows, yet the heat of the day lingers, oppressive and unyielding, making Peren sweat. As he moves through the streets, staying alert and keeping his senses sharp, he eventually reaches the heart of the city. The only reason he knows this is because he recalls the river that runs through Jarnda, feeding into a lake that stretches a short way into the desert. As he gazes at the pristine mountain-fed waters of the river, he watches small riverboats drift up and down, traversing the lake that divides the city in two.

Despite his best efforts, it takes him longer than expected to find the recommended inn. After wandering through unfamiliar streets, getting turned around more than once, and reluctantly asking for directions several times, he finally arrives at his destination—the Shielded Maiden.

Unpacking in a cool, breezy room, Peren hears a knock at the door. When he opens it, he's greeted by a girl dressed in simple, minimal clothing due to the heat. Her attire is modest, but the heat leaves little to the imagination. She speaks in a soothing, calming voice. "Good sir, you look like you could use some help. Your back doesn't look good, and I'd like to offer some relief, compliments of the inn. A warm bath and a massage could help ease your muscles and cool your body after such a long journey."

Unsure where to look, his cheeks flushing, he glances up and off into the distance, nodding awkwardly. "Thank you," he says quietly.

"Please follow me," she says, turning and leading the way.

Peren follows her down into a large underground room, and his jaw nearly drops at the sight. Water flows around the room, creating a serene atmosphere. Several travellers are being tended to by women, receiving massages or baths to ease their exhaustion. The calming sound of running water and the peaceful ambiance offer a stark contrast to the heat and chaos of the city.

Hurrying to catch up, Peren follows the woman to an empty bath, grateful for the relief it promises.

Back in his room later, lying on the bed after a satisfying meal, the sunburns on his body have dulled to a manageable discomfort. He shakes his head, still struggling to wrap his mind around the fact that only a few days ago, he was frozen solid, and now, he's nearly melting in the city heat. With his coin pouch growing lighter, he decides to seek work tomorrow to replenish his quickly dwindling supply of money.

He eventually heads down to the common room, orders dinner, and asks for some cool, refreshing mead. A couple of serving women flirt with him, but as soon as he pulls out the pendant that shows he is Soul Joined, they exchange disappointed glances and leave him be.

As it gets late and the lethargy of the day weighs on him, Peren stands, ready to retire for the night. Just as he begins to move, a man in a dark cloak sweeps in as though he knows exactly where Peren is, then calmly sits down opposite him.

Peren's instincts snap into place. He stands abruptly, hand already on his dagger, his eyes narrowing.

But the cloaked man makes no move to threaten him. Instead, he shows his unarmed hands, then stretches one out in a silent gesture for Peren to remain seated.

Warily, Peren lowers his guard just slightly, his grip still firm on the dagger, his eyes never leaving the figure. As he sits, though, he subconsciously scans the room, marking five other men in the shadows, each of them reacting almost imperceptibly as he made his move.

Sensing that he hasn't loosened his grip on his weapon, the bodyguards remain vigilant, wary of this stranger being so close to their master. Peren initially dismisses the man as a mere figure in need of protection, out of his element and no threat. But as the man moves slowly and calmly, pulling back his hood to reveal a middle-aged, wiry figure with a trimmed beard and a hollow face, Peren is immediately put off.

As the man shifts in his seat, getting comfortable, Peren realizes his mistake. The five bodyguards, despite their size, are not the real threat. There's something about this man—something that makes Peren's heart race. The feeling of danger emanating from him is far greater than anything he's felt before.

Focusing on the man rather than the bodyguards, Peren waits, trying to imitate the calm demeanour of this dangerous person.

Breaking the silence with a low chuckle, the man speaks in a calm, unremarkable tone. "Welcome to Jarnda, Peren. I trust your journey was uneventful?"

Peren's mind races as his name is spoken, but he keeps his expression neutral. Who could have told this man his name? Only a few possibilities come to mind. He mentally runs through them, but none seem to make sense. Shaking off his initial shock, he gives a small nod in response, though the man seems amused by his silence.

"There's a reason I needed to speak to you, here and now," the man continues, leaning forward slightly. "You see, there's a small matter I can't handle personally, nor can I send my men to do it."

Sensing a trap, Peren eyes the man warily, his instincts on high alert. But as the man continues, it becomes clear he's hinting at needing help. Help means a job, and a job means money—something Peren desperately needs. Slowly, he relaxes his grip on the dagger, placing his hands flat on the table. The bodyguards follow his lead, easing slightly.

Folding his arms, Peren nods for the man to continue, his expression guarded but interested. The man's smile twists into something grotesque as he continues, "There is a group of bandits hiding in the desert. They prey on weary travellers and even large caravans."

Peren reacts with a mixture of shock and confusion.

The man sees Peren's reaction and elaborates. "Yes, I've tried to infiltrate and eliminate this band myself, but they seem to know every one of my agents. The Watch made a few attempts, but only four soldiers out of a hundred returned—and they were sent as a warning. Considering how disciplined my men are, you can imagine the predicament this puts me in. I was at a loss... until I heard about someone like you in the city."

Peren's eyebrows rise in shock.

"To my associate, you look like someone who can handle himself, but you're what? Fifteen, sixteen?" The man continues when Peren doesn't correct him. "So, I'm thinking you might be able to do what my other associates couldn't—rid this city of this plague."

Sitting back, Peren realizes the man has shown too many cards. Allowing himself a small smile, Peren waits for him to reveal more.

The man smiles inwardly, thinking, *Hook, line, and sinker.* "So, my young man, will you accept this quest?" He stretches his hand out.

Peren looks from the outstretched hand to the man's face, his expression unreadable.

The man, noticing the silence, adds, "Ah yes, payment. Shall we say ten gold, plus expenses?"

Peren's jaw drops. *Ten gold. That's a fortune,* he thinks. *You could buy so much with that.* But his instincts kick in, a cold warning creeping up his spine. *Why offer so much? This feels like a trap. But... I sense he's being truthful. Ten gold is too good to be true.*

His gaze sharpens, and a small smile tugs at the corners of his lips. *Let the bartering begin.* Smiling smugly, he leans forward, arms crossed on the table. "Twenty thousand."

The man leans forward, his grin turning grotesque. "Twenty gold."

Peren raises an eyebrow, taking his time, watching the man's reaction. *He didn't flinch. That's... interesting.* After a moment of careful consideration, he replies, "Nineteen thousand and ninety."

The man freezes for just a second before bursting into laughter. "Ha! Ok, ok, you made your point. A real offer, then. Five thousand gold, plus whatever you earn on the side—expenses included."

Knowing that this is the best offer he will get, Peren grips the man's hand firmly and agrees to the deal. With a snap of the man's fingers, a lanky, skeletal man wearing new-sees—glasses—emerges, holding a parchment. He places it before the man, who skims over it quickly before dipping a quill into ink and signing his name at the bottom, then sliding the contract toward Peren.

Peren glances over the document quickly, his eyes scanning for anything that could be a trap, but then he slows down, reading more carefully to ensure nothing is overlooked. Satisfied, he signs with a smile, locking the deal in place.

As he hands the parchment to the scribe, he looks at the man, an eyebrow raised. "You knew I'd accept. How?"

"The associate who sent me the message about you has an uncanny instinct. He's almost never wrong when it comes to people."

Peren smirks, making an offhand comment. "Sounds like he'd make a great gate guard."

The man's expression tightens for a brief moment. His eyes flicker almost imperceptibly in a way that only Peren, with his elven sight, can catch.

The guard. He was one of his men. Peren's mouth slackens as the realization sinks in. He sees the man's effort to mask it, but the brief, telltale flicker betrays him. Internally, Peren curses himself for not noticing it sooner. *What are the chances that all of them are his agents? And the real watch was the one who shoved me?*

The man pauses at the threshold, turning back to Peren. "I don't have much information on them, but you'll need to gather your own intelligence. A good place to start would be the Friendly Girl tavern."

The man gives Peren directions, then offers a brief farewell before leaving with his entourage. As the door closes behind them, Peren's sharp eyes scan the group, and he realizes something: he missed two of the guards. There were actually seven of them—two who didn't react at all. *They must be his agents,* he thinks, a sense of unease settling in as the realization takes root.

Heading to his room, Peren doesn't waste time undressing. He simply falls into bed fully clothed, exhaustion overwhelming him. Within moments, he's asleep.

The next morning, Peren wakes tired, stiff, and sore. Heading downstairs, he orders breakfast, only to be stunned when the meal placed before him is the biggest he's seen since leaving the guild. He digs in, savouring every bite, but soon, the realization hits—he doesn't have enough funds to cover such a generous spread.

Turning to the serving girl, he hesitates. She offers a warm smile. "Bill's been taken care of, sir."

Peren sits back, dumbfounded. He did expect this level of treatment. With a quiet thanks, he finishes his meal quickly and heads back to bed.

Later, the woman from yesterday knocks at his door and escorts him downstairs to help heal his back. Afterward, he returns to bed and sleeps through most of the day.

When he wakes, feeling much better, he heads down for dinner. A large meal is waiting, and the same serving girl ensures he's well looked-after. Peren finishes his meal and falls into a sound sleep after climbing back into bed.

Waking up the next morning, he enjoys another hearty meal before heading out. Following the directions given to him by the mysterious man, he makes his way toward the tavern.

Entering through an unlocked door, Peren warily steps into the common room. The scene before him is a stark contrast to what he expected—scandalously clad girls, barely more than children, practicing what seems like a tryout. They appear thin and starved, their faces worn and dirty, as though life has already chewed them up and spat them out. Most look like they've come straight from the streets, just skin and bone, with no hope of a full meal in sight.

Thinking back to the cryptic words of the man who sent him here, Peren quickly realizes that this is the perfect breeding ground for scum of all kinds—a place where filth and despair mix in the shadows. He takes a steadying breath, trying to push back his discomfort at the immodesty and desperation of the scene.

He forces himself to walk forward, his eyes searching for

what he assumes is the manager. As he approaches, the manager looks him over with a critical eye. "You look like you can handle yourself," she says, not wasting any pleasantries. "You looking for work?" She nods to herself as he nods back. "Good. We're one hand short today."

Peren introduces himself, and she gives him a long, assessing look before continuing, "Think you can keep men's grubby hands off my merchandise?"

His gaze drifts to the young women being put through their paces nearby, and he realizes this place is more than just a tavern—it's a front for something darker. Gritting his teeth, he forces a casual tone. "Yeah, I can do that," he says. Pausing, he then adds, "But it'll cost you extra."

The manager's eyes narrow. "'Extra?' How much?"

"Three times the usual rate."

Her jaw drops, and a look of incredulity flashes across her face. "'Three times?' Are you mad?" She turns sharply to her guards, motioning them over with a jerk of her head. "Take this one out—he's got a real high opinion of himself."

Smiling calmly as the guards approach, Peren moves with swift precision, dispatching them in mere seconds. As the manager stares, wide-eyed and speechless, he gives a casual shrug. "Three times."

The manager sizes him up once more, clearly impressed, but reluctant. With a curt nod, she gives him his shift times and dismisses him.

After exploring the city for a few hours and resting through the hottest part of the day, Peren heads back to the tavern as dusk falls. When he steps inside, his jaw drops. He'd thought the girls' outfits during rehearsal were revealing, but now, it's worse—nothing is left to the imagination. The new girls are beet-red with embarrassment, which only makes him flush just as brightly.

After checking in with the manager, he moves to his post, scanning the crowd for any unruly types.

It isn't long before trouble finds him: a patron's voice rises above the hum of conversation as he grows increasingly handsy with the maids.

Peren approaches the man with quiet purpose and, without a word, leans in close enough to make his presence known. "Keep your hands to yourself, or I will ask you to leave," he says in a low, commanding tone.

The patron barely looks up, his dismissive sneer already in place. "Whatever, kid," he mutters, continuing to paw at the maid.

In one fluid motion, Peren grabs the man's wrist, twisting it sharply, and guides him away from the maid. His voice is even and calm, but his grip leaves no room for argument. "I don't repeat myself."

He forcefully guides the man to the exit, and as they reach the threshold, the drunkard's hand shoots to his waist, pulling out a knife with a slurred curse. The man's aim is sluggish, his movements slow and erratic from the alcohol. Peren sidesteps effortlessly, avoiding the knife with minimal effort, then quickly disarms him, twisting the blade out of his hand.

Without a word, Peren shoves the man out the door, watching him stumble as he tries to regain his balance. He slides the man's knife into his own boot, the cold steel tucked away for safety.

The drunkard's face twists with outrage. "You'll regret this," he slurs, his words thick and unfocused. "I'll come back... and kill you."

Peren gives him a slight shove, sending the man stumbling forward into the dirt. He hits the ground face-first, cutting his nose open and spilling blood into his mouth. With a pained, drunken grunt, the man struggles to get up, wiping the blood from his lips as he stumbles away, still muttering threats.

Returning to his post, Peren once again blends into the darkness, scanning the tavern for any potential troublemakers. The flickering candlelight casts long shadows across the room, and the chatter of the patrons fills the air. He remains still, watching, waiting for the slightest disruption.

As the night wears on, a few patrons grow too rowdy, their behaviour becoming more erratic with the alcohol. Peren's sharp eyes pick out the signs before it escalates, and he intervenes with the calm efficiency of someone accustomed to handling trouble.

He warns a couple of men who begin to get handsy with the maids, his voice low and firm, and they sober up just enough to back off. Another drunk tries to start an argument over a game of dice, but Peren is quick to step in, his presence alone enough to stop the fight before it can turn violent.

For the ones who don't take the hint, Peren calmly ushers them toward the door. A few try to argue or resist, but he is always one step ahead, guiding them out with little more than a firm grip and quiet words.

After Peren finishes his shift, the manager pays him exactly the amount he charged, accompanied by a begrudging growl of respect for his ability to resolve problems quickly and quietly.

Walking through the dark streets of the early morning, Peren pulls his cloak tighter around him, the familiar bite of the cold reminding him of the chill that settles in after dusk. As he nears his accommodation, his elven hearing picks up the sound of shuffling footsteps behind him. The rhythmic, uneven cadence suggests it's likely one of the drunkards from earlier. Without breaking stride, he continues walking, pretending not to notice the subtle presence shadowing him.

As he turns a corner, Peren's way is blocked by three burly men, their necks as thick as his thighs, each brandishing a club.

Calmly, he approaches them, and as he hears the footsteps stop a short distance behind him, he says into the night, loud enough for all of them to hear, "I'm really tired and just want to go to bed. How about we go our separate ways and call it a night?"

A drunken laugh breaks the silence, followed by a slurred voice. "Like hell we'll let you off that easy. You're gonna be sorry for crossing me."

Sighing, Peren offers the same suggestion a second time. After receiving only insults and refusals in response, he drops his casual demeanour, flowing into a fighting stance. His dagger stays sheathed; he doesn't need to kill anyone tonight. Facing the men, he stretches with a tired yawn. "Alright, then, let's get on with it."

Before any of them can react, he moves like a blur. He launches himself at the largest of the three, palm slamming heel-first into the man's face. There's a sickening crunch as his nose is flattened, and the man crumples to the ground, lifeless.

Crouching on the man's chest, Peren mutters with annoyance, "Didn't mean for him to die." He cranes his neck, glancing up at the other two, who are still standing in shock.

Seeing the shock on their faces slowly shift to anger, Peren responds with a shrug, which only seems to fuel their rage further. The man on the left takes a low swing, aiming to break Peren's ribs, while the one on the right swings high, ensuring that no matter how Peren moves, one of the blows will land.

Peren waits until their strikes are nearly in range. Then, he spins to his left, his right foot coming up to slam the heel into the left man's shoulder with a loud crunch that is soon overpowered by the man's high-pitched scream.

Staying low enough to avoid the high swing, Peren spins back to his right. His left palm strikes the side of the second man's knee with precision, forcing it sideways. Tendons and ligaments snap, and the man squeals in pain before collapsing face-first to the ground in agony.

The man on the left rises unsteadily to his feet. As he pulls his left hand away from his shoulder, an ugly mass of broken skin is revealed, with shards of bone jutting through and blood spurting in time with his frantic heartbeat.

Clenching his left hand into a fist, the man grits his teeth. Peren gives him a look that says, *Really?* Undeterred, the man lunges forward, acting like he has a secret weapon, and pulls a curved knife from his belt.

Staying in the defensive squat from when he crushed the other man's knee, Peren says in disbelief, "You saw what I did without a blade. Do you want to see me use one?"

The man hesitates for a split second, but then decides to take the risk, stepping forward, testing Peren's bluff, his movements semi-steady.

With an exasperated sigh, Peren springs into action. He twists in midair, using his left knee to slam into the man's left shoulder, disorienting him long enough to grab the blade. Then, in a swift motion, he drives it deep into the man's left lung, puncturing it and sliding the knife into his heart. Dark blood oozes from the wound, splattering across Peren and coating him in a mist of crimson.

The man's eyes widen in shock as the life drains from him, the realization of his fatal mistake sinking in. His eyes glaze over, and he collapses forward, the knife embedding deeper into his body as he lands.

Standing up gracefully, Peren casts a casual glance at the remaining men. The drunkard stands frozen, mouth agape, sputtering in disbelief at the carnage that has just unfolded.

With an almost bored expression, Peren shifts into a fighting stance again, his impatience evident in his voice. "Last chance."

The drunkard's eyes flicker between Peren and his fallen comrades, panic creeping into his expression. He doesn't need another warning. Realizing he's on the verge of being next, he stumbles backward, his voice shaky. "We're done here!"

The two remaining men follow suit, scrambling away in haste, their drunken bravado vanishing as they flee into the night.

Weary, Peren stumbles back to the inn, dragging himself to his room. The moment his head hits the pillow, he falls into a deep sleep.

He wakes with a start, drenched in sweat, his throat dry and cracked, his lips burning with thirst. Desperate, he grabs the pitcher of water beside his bed and drinks straight from it, the cool liquid dribbling down his chin, mingling with the sweat on his chest and soaking into the sheets.

After draining the pitcher, he pushes himself up and opens the shutters. Blinding sunlight pours into the room, followed by a cool, refreshing breeze. Squinting against the light, Peren realizes it's already mid-afternoon.

After dressing in dry clothing and washing his sweat-soaked garments in the basin, he takes a moment to clean himself, feeling a slight but welcome relief. With the worst of the heat behind him, he heads downstairs in search of food, hoping to steady his mind with a meal.

The common room is surprisingly cool, a welcome contrast to the oppressive warmth outside. It's mostly empty, the few patrons scattered around in quiet conversation. Peren moves to a table in the corner and, to his relief, is attended by the serving girl from earlier. She approaches with the same polite nod, takes his order, and disappears into the kitchen with practiced ease.

A few minutes later, she returns, placing a tray laden with food in front of him. He gives her a grateful nod and tips her generously before his attention turns to the meal before him. The assortment of meats, cheeses, and crusty bread looks inviting, but it's the unusual-looking fruits that catch his eye.

Curious about their strange shapes and vibrant colours, he picks up an oblong orange fruit, its surface smooth and firm. Without much thought, he bites into it. A burst of juice explodes across his tongue, a perfect balance of sweet and sour that catches him by surprise. He chews slowly, savouring the unexpected combination of flavours. The fruit is unlike anything he's had before, and he finds himself enjoying it more than he expected.

He quickly finishes the rest of his meal, washing it down with a drink as the warmth of the food settles in his stomach. As he finishes and stands to leave, the door to the tavern opens with a soft creak. Peren freezes for a moment as a familiar black-cloaked figure steps inside. The man's hood is low, keeping his face in shadow as he strides toward Peren's table. Without a word, he sits down across from him, his eyes glinting with that same inscrutable focus.

Peren sighs, resisting the urge to roll his eyes. Slowly, he sits back down, crossing his arms. "What now?" he mutters, his patience worn thin as he waits to see what this mysterious figure wants of him next.

Leaving the hood on for added effect, the man speaks without preamble. "I received a report early this morning of some suspicious deaths. They were seen being removed alive from the same tavern where you're working. Not to mention, some of my associates witnessed the fight."

Peren leans forward, his voice low and dangerous. "You're having me followed?"

The man gives a cold, humourless chuckle. "Of course. I don't trust you. To ensure my new asset actually proves valuable, I need to make sure he stays on task—something you seem unable to do. You're not supposed to draw attention to yourself like that."

Before the man can continue, Peren cuts him off, his tone sharp. "First of all, how dare you tail me? I'm doing exactly what you asked—I'm infiltrating their organization. Second, they attacked me, and I was defending myself. And third, how dare you lecture me about murder when you turn a blind eye to Karung's slave trade? Those serving girls are barely out of their cots, and you allow it. Don't speak to me like you're some moral authority. Not when you're this dirty."

The man's eyes narrow as he leans forward, his voice dripping with venom. "'Dirty?' You have no idea what I've done to protect this city. Don't you dare judge me, boy."

Peren's anger flares, and he spits out his words. "Then don't question my methods." Rising from his seat, he stands tall. "Now, if you'll excuse me."

Without waiting for a reply, he turns and heads to his room, the door slamming behind him as he locks it securely.

As he makes his way to the bed, a thought strikes him, and he pauses, checking the lock on the door once more, just to be sure. He stands there for a moment, considering the tension of the meeting, before moving over to the pitcher to ensure there is water in it. He sees it is full to the brim, with condensation built up on the outside.

Satisfied, he strips down to his small clothes and slips into the freshly made bed, quickly falling asleep.

As the sun touches the horizon, he wakes, dresses, has an

early dinner, and heads off to the tavern just as the last light of day fades away. Informing the manager of his arrival, he takes up his post from the night before, his cheeks flushing at the sight of the serving maids' scandalous attire.

The tavern quickly fills to capacity with both familiar faces and new ones. Peren spots a couple of troublemakers from the previous night. He glances at the manager, who shakes her head, so he keeps a watchful eye on them as they find a table.

Watching closely, Peren sees a burly man enter, followed by another, and then another, until six men sit with the troublemakers.

Not long after they start drinking, they become rowdy and begin groping the staff, so Peren slips up to them and quietly demands they either leave or keep their hands to themselves. Instead of leaving, the men become even rowdier and more invasive, forcing him to grab the largest man and lift him out of his seat. To everyone's surprise, he does this effortlessly. The man, a tower of rippling muscle, glares down at him like a hawk eyeing a mouse.

Ignoring the man's glare, Peren tightens his grip. To everyone's jaw-dropping shock, he lifts the man off the ground and carries him outside.

The tavern falls silent as everyone strains to hear the muted exchange outside. Though the words are unclear, the rising voices make it obvious that the confrontation is heated.

Moments later, the sounds of a fight break out—crunching bones and screams echo inside. The patrons watch the door intently, some placing bets on who will return.

Peren struts back in, his expression bored. Everyone stares at him, slack-jawed at his unscathed appearance. His smug look widens as he takes in the shocked crowd.

Walking up to the table of troublemakers in dead silence,

he glares at the group and points to the door. "Out," he says softly, his voice so commanding it seems to echo through the room.

The group pretends to comply, but instead of leaving, they encircle him, hands clenched into fists, glaring down at him.

Peren raises a hand. "Wait," he calls out, and the group, now gleeful, pauses. "Mistress," he continues, "do I have your permission to put these patrons down in your establishment?"

The men laugh at his audacity, cracking their knuckles in preparation for putting this stranger in his place.

After considering Peren's request, the manager calls out to the patrons, "Everyone, move the tables and chairs to make a ring for these gentlemen to fight it out."

Realizing this has escalated into a formal challenge, the group allows Peren to step out of the circle at his employer's summons. As the furniture is quietly rearranged, the manager softly asks, "How certain are you that you can defeat these guys?"

Peren meets her gaze without flinching, understanding exactly what she's setting up. He asks, "Rules?"

She raises an eyebrow, her expression one of mild amusement. "What? None."

"Then I can win this, no problem."

She whispers back, "You better, or I'm taking the losings out of your pay."

As she turns away, Peren pulls out the money bag she gave him last night. He tosses it lightly in his hand, then holds it out to her. "This is all my money. Put it on me."

She freezes for a moment, clearly surprised by his seriousness. After a brief hesitation, she shrugs and turns to the crowd. "Odds are ten to one," she announces, her voice cutting through the murmurs of the crowd. The serving maids swiftly move through the tavern, handling the bets.

As the noise of the betting dies down, Peren stands silently, his eyes locked on the six men as they form a semi-circle around him, their postures aggressive, confident. He doesn't flinch. He's already thinking ahead, waiting for the signal to attack.

As soon as the manager screams, "Fight!" Peren is already in motion, moving faster than the men can process the word. He leaps to the left, a blur of motion, and slams the heel of his right palm into the nearest man's nose with a sickening crunch. Blood bursts from the shattered nose, and the cartilage is driven into the man's brain, killing him instantly. His eyes glaze over and roll back into his head.

Without missing a beat, Peren launches off the falling body, using the momentum to spin in the opposite direction. His right elbow connects with another man's jaw, shattering it and knocking his remaining teeth free in a spray of blood. The man's eyes roll back into his head.

Peren uses the momentum to pivot, slamming his foot into the next target's left knee. The sickening snap of tendons, ligaments, and cartilage fills the air as the knee buckles sideways. The man gasps in agony, but Peren doesn't stop. Spinning again, he slams his left foot into the man's jaw with a brutal crack, snapping the man's neck.

The crowd erupts in a cacophony of screams and shouts as the bodies hit the floor, the survivors writhing in pain. Peren stands amidst the carnage, his breathing steady as he surveys the remaining men, a smirk spreading across his face. "Who's next?"

One man stands frozen, his jaw slack in disbelief at how quickly Peren has dispatched his friends. He hesitates, eyes flickering between the fallen bodies, but then, unwilling to back down, he shifts into a defensive stance, fists raised.

Peren grins, his expression one of mocking amusement at

the man's hesitation. With a fluid motion, he slips into his own stance and strikes before the man can even blink. His left hand drives into the man's stomach with brutal force, causing the man to gasp, before he follows up with a powerful uppercut. The blow shatters the man's jaw and snaps his head back with such force that it lifts him off the ground.

Peren steps back as the man flies through the air, crashing lifelessly to the floor.

The final man, still standing, is completely frozen—his eyes wide, his brain struggling to process the rapid destruction of his friends. His hands tremble, fists still clenched, but his confidence is shattered. Slowly, he begins to inch back, as if considering running, but Peren's smirk only deepens.

With a mocking shrug, Peren steps forward, closing the distance between them in a few swift strides. The man attempts a wild swing, but Peren easily dodges, his movements smooth and calculated. Grabbing the man's wrist mid-swing, he twists it sharply, eliciting a painful yelp. Before the man can react, Peren delivers a crushing knee to his abdomen, knocking the wind from him.

The man doubles over, gasping for breath, and in that moment, Peren steps behind him, locking him in a chokehold. He squeezes, the pressure cutting off the man's air supply, and within seconds, the man goes limp, his body going slack. Peren tosses him to the floor, his head hitting the ground with a sickening thud.

The tavern is utterly silent for a moment before an eruption of cheers and jeers fills the air. Peren stands tall, bloodied but unscathed, surveying the wreckage of the fight, his chest rising and falling with the adrenaline still coursing through him. The patrons look on, a mix of awe and fear on their faces, some still too stunned to move or speak.

Watching with a raised eyebrow, the manager is clearly impressed, but is masking it with her usual stern demeanour.

Resuming his spot after helping put the tables and chairs back into place, Peren leans against the bar, his eyes scanning the subdued crowd. They drink and chat, their respect for him palpable now, the tension from the fight slowly dissolving into the low hum of conversation and clinking mugs.

The tavern feels different tonight—quieter, more respectful, the usual raucous energy subdued. The air is thick with the scent of spilled ale, sweat, and something less definable, the aftermath of chaos now replaced by the calm of dominance. Candlelight flickers in the corners, casting shadows that seem to dance across the walls, mirroring the pulse of the night.

Once the tavern is empty, the manager tosses him two heavy purses. "You did great. Good thing I backed you."

Lifting the purses in thanks and nodding farewell, Peren leaves the tavern behind, heading back toward the inn with his thoughts on the night's events. As he walks, the thrill of victory and the quiet respect he earned begin to fade, replaced by a sense of weariness that grows with each step.

Deciding to take a shortcut through some dimly lit alleys, hoping to make it back faster, he turns a corner—and stops dead. Five men stand shoulder-to-shoulder in front of him, their faces patchworks of scars, their eyes glinting under the moonlight. The crude weapons in their hands—cudgels, staves, and short swords—catch the faint glow, their intent unmistakable.

Peren's instincts scream at him to avoid a confrontation, so he turns to backtrack, only to see another five men, equally armed, blocking his way. He takes a deep breath, his heart sinking as he sizes them up. They're no simple street thugs; the scars, the confidence in their stances, and the disciplined way they hold their weapons suggest experience.

Not tonight, he thinks as the fatigue of the evening settles heavily on him. Sighing with exhaustion and frustration, he yawns, shaking his head. "Are we really doing this again? You've seen what I can do unarmed. Bringing weapons won't make this end any better for you."

The men exchange uneasy glances, but shrug and raise their weapons, closing in with determined faces.

Peren sighs again, this time in resigned annoyance. Moving into a defensive stance, he mutters, "Fine. Let's get this over with. I'd like to get some sleep tonight."

Not waiting for them to make the first move, he darts toward the man farthest to the left, crouching low. With a swift, brutal strike of his right fist, he slams into the side of the man's left knee, snapping it sideways with a sickening crunch. The man's scream echoes down the alley as he collapses.

Springing to his right, Peren strikes again, his left fist delivering a mirrored blow to the next man's knee. The thug falls with a strangled shout, twisting in pain.

Peren leaps high, targeting the third attacker with a jaw-shattering uppercut, sending the man flying away, his head snapping back mid-air before he crashes onto the cobblestones.

Using his momentum, Peren swings his arms into a double-fisted strike onto the fourth man's head. The force is enough to crush the man's skull down through his spine, his body crumpling as blood and fragments of bone spray out.

Landing lightly, Peren turns to face the rest of his opponents. Behind him, the first two men are writhing on the ground, the third lies unconscious, and the fourth has already collapsed in a bloody heap. His voice low and commanding, he growls, "Go home."

The men hesitate, staring at him in shock at how quickly he dispatched four of their comrades. But then, driven by rage, they grip their weapons and charge.

Anticipating their move, Peren unsheathes his dagger, his elven reflexes launching him at the nearest man. His blade pierces through the thug's eye and deep into his brain, killing him instantly. As he pulls his dagger free, a milky liquid sprays across his face.

Pivoting with swift, practiced precision, Peren drives his dagger into the next attacker's heart with enough force to shatter ribs. As he pulls the blade free, tissue and blood spray from the wound.

The delay gives the remaining men a chance to circle around him, weapons raised. Flowing around their strikes as if they're moving in slow motion, Peren spins left, using the momentum to jump and slam his dagger into one man's neck. A spray of blood hits him and the man beside him. Continuing with the same momentum, he slashes the next man's throat, turning the air crimson.

He lands, pivoting to face the last two men. With a quick twist, he slams his knee into one man's leg, the joint shattering with a gruesome crunch as fragments of bone and cartilage spray out, blood soaking the cobblestones.

Reversing instantly, Peren leaps and buries his dagger in the last man's neck, pulling it free in a final arc of blood. The man's eyes glaze as he collapses to the ground.

Breathing heavily, exhaustion settling over him, Peren wipes his blade clean on a fallen attacker's tunic, feeling bone-weary as the sky lightens with dawn's first hints. Coated in blood, he turns and heads toward the inn. Each step is leaden with the toll of the night's brutality.

Finally reaching his room, he stumbles inside, barely managing to strip off his bloody clothes before collapsing onto the bed. The memory of the witch's death haunts him briefly, bringing a pang of fatigue and regret before exhaustion overtakes him. With his head hitting the pillow, he falls into a fitful sleep.

Back in the maze, Peren senses something is wrong. The silence feels heavier, his instincts prickling as he inches forward, only able to see a few feet ahead. Wandering through the darkness, he stumbles upon a tunnel that leads into a shadowed cave. Recognizing it, he turns, heart pounding, to leave, but an unseen force locks him in place, pulling him deeper inside.

An invisible grip forces him to look down, where he sees the decomposing body of the witch lying at his feet, the smell hitting him like a wall. He stifles a gag, then, compelled by the force, raises his head—only to meet the piercing gaze of the witch's ghost, more vivid and real than he remembers.

His face pales, all blood draining from it. "Y-you…you're dead. I-I killed you. H-how?" he stammers, his voice barely a whisper.

The witch drifts closer, her icy fingers tracing down his chest, dissolving his clothes with a single touch. "This is what happens when you kill a witch," she hisses, her voice cold, yet playful. "We come back to haunt you…until *you* die."

Peren struggles against the unseen bonds, panic rising. She clicks her tongue in mock disapproval. "Tsk, tsk. Resistance is pointless. I'm stronger here, and you have no power," she taunts, forcing him to move helplessly around the cave at her whim before pulling him back to her. She traces her fingers along his torso, laughing softly at the tension rippling beneath his skin.

No matter how hard he tries, Peren can't break free. A realization dawns—his pendant is missing. A wild, manic laugh bursts from him.

"What's so funny?" she asks, her smile faltering.

"You're in *my* mind," he spits defiantly, straining against her hold. He throws himself at the barrier binding him, but it doesn't give. He snarls, his frustration mounting.

She laughs, brushing her fingers across his chest again. "Oh, poor, naive elf. Yes, we're in your mind…but your psychic powers are nothing against mine. There's no escaping me." She smiles, savouring his helpless fury.

Peren thrashes, pouring everything he has into fighting the barrier. But as his strength drains, he's left limp, hanging in her grasp, glaring at her with fiery hatred.

Rising on her toes, she leans close to his ear and whispers, "You're mine, Peren. I can do whatever I wish with you." Her finger slides up his side, slicing his skin with a wicked edge, drawing a cry of pain from him. She drags clawed fingers down his chest and stomach, each line burning as she whispers, "I own you now. You're mine…my elven slave."

With a primal scream, Peren taps into his last reserves of willpower, throwing himself at the barrier with everything he has.

In a flash, he jolts awake, soaked with sweat, chest heaving.

A sharp sting runs down his chest and side. He pulls back the covers to find long, deep cuts exactly where the witch touched him in the dream. Shaky and still haunted by the vivid nightmare, he rises to his feet, her taunting voice echoing in his mind as he steadies himself, heart racing.

Taking slow, deep breaths, Peren steadies himself, pushing the nightmare's lingering grip aside. He washes, binds his wounds, and changes into dry clothes, casting a glance at the sweat-soaked bed before heading downstairs to the cooler air, hoping to eat and drink. The oppressive heat clings to him, and with the vivid nightmare still fresh in his mind, even the chilled ale tastes lukewarm. He scrunches up the parchment from the mysterious man, frustrated with the complaints about the bodies he's left behind, then returns to bed, though sleep only comes in fitful naps.

Finally, the restless hours lead him to a decision: he'll start looking for other work, maybe something that'll catch the attention of the sand bandits.

Watching the sunset, Peren feels some relief as the hot air cools, becoming bearable as night falls. Preparing for his shift at the tavern, he heads out into the streets. As he passes other establishments, the guards outside give him respectful nods, which he returns in kind.

Approaching the tavern unchallenged, he sighs in relief and clocks in, finding the manager to let her know he's interested in more challenging work, something fitting his skills. She nods and assures him she'll keep an eye out for opportunities.

As the tavern fills with patrons, an atmosphere of quiet respect surrounds Peren. He only needs to warn a few individuals and remove even fewer, allowing himself to become a part of the relaxed ambiance. Despite being on duty, with the girls bustling about, he finds himself enjoying the evening—the music, the laughter, and the flirtations of the older maids.

The night stretches on, and before long, the sky turns grey with the morning light. As the manager locks up, she hands Peren a purse, identical in size to the one from his first night. "Before you go, Peren, there are some men who'd like to meet you," she says, motioning for him to follow.

They make their way to a dingy office in the back. There, seated behind a large, imposing desk, is a well-built man, his presence as solid as the furniture around him. "Ah, Peren. Please, have a seat," he says, gesturing to an empty chair across from him.

Peren steps into the room, but instead of sitting, he leans against the wall, arms crossed, eyes fixed on the man. The large man shrugs at Peren's stance, but doesn't seem put off.

"Karung tells me you're a hard worker and that you can handle yourself well. She also mentioned you're looking for something more challenging."

Peren remains silent, only offering a small nod in acknowledgment.

The man raises an eyebrow, clearly unfazed by the lack of response. "I might have just the thing for you, but first, there's the small matter of your association with the shadow man."

When Peren gives him a blank stare, the man continues with a smile. "The one in the black cloak, older. He's made several attempts to infiltrate my organization. You were seen speaking with him."

The man watches Peren carefully, but the elf's expression remains unchanged.

The man calls out, and seven large, burly men squeeze into the tiny office, crowding the space like sardines in a can. The man behind the desk doesn't even flinch at the intrusion. Turning back to Peren, he narrows his eyes. "I'll only ask this once: What did he offer you?"

Peren pushes off the wall and manoeuvres through the towering figures with ease, making his way to the desk. "Sure, I met the guy. Creepy, to be honest," he starts, voice steady. "He offered me money, and I listened to his problem. Had to be something important if he was coming to me. Didn't seem like the type who gets out much anymore. He mentioned some sand bandits being a big thorn in his side."

Chuckling, he leans forward a little, the smirk on his face all too genuine. "As far as I see it, I don't care what he wants. I was just passing through, looking to make some quick coin. But when he started talking about how he'd never catch those bandits, no matter what he did, I told him I'd think about it. A couple of days later, he shows up wanting to know my answer. I told him it's not my mess to clean up. If he wants it done, he's the one who has to handle it."

The man behind the desk grins even more broadly, clearly amused. "That would explain why he came out looking pissed and frustrated." Pausing for a moment, he continues, "Seems his lackeys cleaned up your mess for you." The man places a nicely carved short sword on the desk, its edge catching the dim light. "Now, stop lying to me. Tell me what you know about us, and why you'd take his offer."

Peren forces himself to think quickly, his face betraying no emotion. After a brief pause, he responds with a plausible lie. "At that time, I hadn't agreed to anything. He didn't want me backing out, so he used pressure to try to force my hand."

The man relaxes, leaning back in his chair and nodding slowly. He waves his hand, and the others file out of the office. "Welcome to the sand bandits," he says, extending his hand.

Peren moves to shake it, replying, "Thank you, sir."

Heading back to the inn after receiving information about who to meet and where to join them out in the desert the next day, Peren feels a mix of anticipation and apprehension about his new role.

EIGHTEEN

The Sand Bandits

The next morning, Peren leaves a note with the same maid who has been serving his meals, instructing her to tell the "shadow man" that he's ready. After that, he heads out to saddle Mercy.

At the southern gate, Peren scans the area and spots the man he's meant to meet. Casually, he moves towards him. The contact wordlessly falls in behind, and they begin walking down the road.

After a while, the man signals to his horse, prompting the animal to veer off the path. Peren follows, heading into the desert as well. They meet up a few minutes later, the heat of the desert already beginning to settle on them. Wordlessly, they continue deeper into the sands.

Sensing that they may be walking in circles, Peren remains wary, scanning the landscape for any sign of a landmark.

As the sun begins to dip below the horizon, they finally arrive at camp. Despite having taken refuge under shelter during the hottest part of the day, the lingering heat has drained Peren, leaving him feeling sluggish. His muscles ache with fatigue, and, unable to resist, he falls into a deep, exhausted sleep.

The next morning, he awakens to an unsettling pitch

blackness. There's no trace of light, not even the soft glow of dawn. Confused, he tries to move, but finds himself restrained, metal cuffs binding his wrists to the ground. Panic rises within him as he tugs harder and harder at the chains, but they hold fast.

Suddenly, he hears the distinct sound of a door grinding open. He struggles to stand, his movements limited by the chains, and is immediately blinded by a harsh flood of light.

The master steps into the cell, his chuckle echoing in the empty room. "Well, well, look what we have here. You were so obvious, even a pigeon could've fooled you. Almost sad. Almost."

Fury bubbling up, Peren growls. "You will pay for this."

The man bursts into laughter, wiping tears from his eyes. "You? Escape? Never!"

With a final mocking chuckle, he turns on his heel and slams the door shut behind him. Peren screams after him, curses pouring from his mouth, but the sound is swallowed by the thick walls.

Gritting his teeth, Peren takes slow, deliberate breaths, forcing himself to calm down. The first thing he notices is the heat—it's unbearable, the air thick and oppressive. His body is drenched in sweat, and every movement feels sluggish. Ignoring his discomfort, he strains against the chains, his mind sharp despite the rising panic.

The chains are designed for humans, not elves, and after being left to rust for so long, they're starting to show their age. Peren twists his body, putting every ounce of his strength into breaking free. With a loud, agonizing screech, one of the links snaps near the base, leaving him half-freed. Though still bound by his hands and feet, he's able to shift and move slightly around the cell.

He surveys his surroundings, taking stock of the tracks in the dirt and noting the position of the sun, now climbing toward its zenith. He slides back toward the farthest corner of the cave to avoid the heat.

With grim determination, he presses the broken chain against the red-hot metal door. His fingers burn as they make contact, but he grits his teeth and bears the pain, focusing on the task at hand.

The metal door groans and screeches under the pressure as he uses the chain to weaken it gradually. The heat works in his favour now, softening the door just enough.

With a final painful push, the metal gives way with a sharp screech, the door bending and warping as it opens just wide enough for him to slip through.

Finally free of his bonds, Peren collapses onto the cooler stone floor, his limbs heavy from the heat. He curls up in the shadowy part of the cell, waiting for the sun to set. Sleep comes in fitful bursts, interrupted by the gnawing thirst and hunger that are consuming him.

As the sun dips below the horizon, the temperature starts to drop, and Peren stirs, the air finally cooling. His mind sharpens with purpose. No more waiting.

With a surge of energy, he pushes himself to his feet, the need to find the bandits driving him forward.

Night falls quickly, the clouds veiling the partial moon and casting long, shifting shadows across the dunes. Visibility is limited, but Peren keeps his senses alert, extending them outward in search of any movement or sound that might indicate the bandits' camp. With the darkness closing in around him, he proceeds cautiously, knowing his survival depends on staying hidden until the time is right to strike.

After hours of trekking across the vast sand dunes, Peren's

senses finally detect something in the distance. To his relief, the bandits haven't moved from their camp. Adjusting his course, he quickens his pace toward them, eager to strike.

As he nears the camp, he slows down, taking careful steps as he approaches the next rise. Peeking over the dune, he spots a sentry standing guard, his posture relaxed but vigilant. Moving into the sentry's blind spot, Peren expertly navigates down the small incline of the dune and begins ascending the next one. His movements are deliberate and silent, as swift as they are precise.

In the blink of an eye, Peren is upon the sentry. He drives his knife into the man's throat, immediately muffling any sound by pressing his hand firmly over the sentry's mouth. The man's body jerks as blood spills from his throat, his struggles weakening until he slumps downward, lifeless. Peren holds him until the last breath escapes, then gently lowers the sentry's body to the ground, letting the blood pool in the sand beneath him. With a flick of his wrist, he wipes the blade clean and moves toward the next sentry.

He looks up at the sky, noting with urgency that dawn is fast approaching. He has little time left to remain hidden.

Steeling himself, he heads toward the next sentry, moving with practiced stealth. He repeats the process, being careful and methodical, ensuring that no sound betrays his position.

As the last sentry falls, Peren returns to the first one he killed, silently circling back through the camp. The darkness is fading, but for now, he still has the advantage.

Staying low to the ground, he peers into the camp, assessing the layout. Most of the bandits are lying down, oblivious to his presence, but he ignores them, focusing instead on those sitting up and moving around.

Silent as a shadow, he slips between the tents, moving

closer to the nearest fire, where three men are sitting, drunk and celebrating. He approaches, moving with deadly grace, and in one fluid motion, he strikes.

The first man drops instantly as Peren severs his spine at the base of his skull. He twists his blade into the next, ripping through flesh, before snapping the neck of the third with such brutal force that the man's head swivels backward, facing the wrong way.

Without a pause, Peren moves silently to the next group, where two bandits sit by another fire, unaware of the predator in their midst.

Peren is faster than their instincts. In a blur of motion, he plunges his dagger into both of their skulls, severing the spinal cords with precision. Blood bursts from the wounds, splattering across his hand and arm. He quickly moves the bodies, arranging them to make it seem like they simply fell asleep by the fire. The sand greedily soaks up the blood that pools around them, leaving only a faint trace of what has happened.

Peren keeps his senses sharp, continuously tracking the movements of the rest of the camp. He avoids the nearby tents, focusing on the next target.

He reaches one tent, hears the soft snoring of a man within, and peers inside. The bandit is fast asleep. With the quiet stealth of a shadow, Peren covers the man's mouth, driving his dagger into his throat before quickly wiping the blood off on a nearby blanket. Then, without hesitation, he moves on to the next target.

Peren continues moving through the camp, his steps swift and silent, taking down every bandit he crosses paths with. Despite his skill and speed, the alarm is eventually raised when the dead sentries are discovered.

Now forced to rely on his heightened awareness of his

surroundings, he slows his pace, using his senses to track the movements and shifts in the air, footsteps, and even the faintest sounds. It's slower, but it keeps him on course. He moves through the camp like a shadow, his attention finely attuned to every change in the atmosphere, allowing him to slip by most of the bandits unnoticed.

His luck starts to wane, though, when a bandit stumbles upon him. The man opens his mouth to shout, but Peren is faster, his knife already slicing through the air before the alarm can escape. The bandit crumples, silent and lifeless, before he can utter a sound.

Still moving through the camp with relentless focus, Peren notices the first hints of daylight on the horizon, the sun reflecting off the shifting yellow dunes.

As he nears the last two bandits, he pauses, calculating. Then, in one fluid motion, he grabs one by the throat, the tip of his blade barely grazing the skin of the man's neck, a drop of blood running down slowly. With a steady hand, Peren pulls the bandit back a few steps, positioning him between himself and the second bandit.

Waiting for them to process their situation, he watches their faces, noting the flicker of realization as they assess their predicament. He growls hoarsely, his voice cold and menacing. "I'll only ask this once: Where is your boss?"

The bandit not in Peren's grip sneers at him, spitting in the dirt at his feet. With false bravado, he says, "Whatchya gon' do 'bout it?"

Peren's gaze hardens, and he tilts his head toward the scattered bodies around them, his eyes locking onto the bandit's. Without a word, he pushes the dagger slightly deeper into the neck of the other bandit, eliciting a pained gasp.

The bandit in Peren's grasp cries out, "Please, stop! I'll tell you wh—"

"Shut up!" the other bandit interrupts, his voice desperate. "He'll kill us either way!"

Peren nods, his voice steady and cold. "That is true. But the speed of your death depends entirely on whether you're honest. If I think you're lying, I'll make sure it's slow."

The captive bandit's eyes widen with terror as he stammers, his resolve crumbling, and opens his mouth to spill everything Peren needs to know.

In a flash of movement, the free bandit jerks his wrist, sending a knife flying toward the captive's chest. The blade cuts through the air with deadly precision, but before it reaches its mark, Peren snatches it from the air, its edge brushing perilously close to the captive bandit's heart.

Without missing a beat, Peren drops the knife and sends his dagger flying into the right knee of the free bandit. The man crumples to the ground with a scream, clutching his leg.

Turning the captive bandit to face him, Peren grips his throat tightly, his eyes locking onto the man's. The bandit, realizing that Peren usually gets what he wants, stares wide-eyed at his writhing companion. Fear edges into his voice as he begins to speak, but his words are barely coherent, a jumble of pleading and panic as he struggles to form a response.

Peren watches him silently, waiting for the moment he breaks. Seeing that the bandit needs more encouragement, he drags him over to the injured man. With a sharp yank, he pulls the knife from the bandit's knee, causing him to scream as the blade tears through cartilage, tendons, and ligaments. Before the man can recover, Peren stabs the other knee, sending a fresh wave of agony through his body. The injured bandit cries out in pain, tears filling his eyes.

Turning his gaze back to the bandit in his grasp, Peren looks at him pointedly. The captive glances between his suffering comrade and his captor, his resolve crumbling. After a long moment, he finally speaks, giving Peren the information he wants.

True to his word, Peren yanks the knife from the bandit's knee, causing fresh damage. The injured man begs, pleading for him to stop, asking him to either leave or just kill him. With a snarl, Peren shakes his head almost imperceptibly before he swiftly severs both of the man's arms at the elbows, rendering him completely incapacitated.

With wide eyes, Peren drags the captive bandit over to a nearby tent. He cuts the ropes and uses them to bind the man's hands before pulling him, tethered by the rope, toward the horses. Untying each horse, he attaches the reins to the next saddled one, finally securing the last horse to Mercy's saddle.

After eating and drinking something hearty, Peren ties the prisoner's rope to the saddle. Mounting Mercy, he calls out to the bandit behind him, "One wrong word, and I'll stab you in the foot and drag you." A grin spreads across his face as he watches the bandit's colour drain.

Peren urges Mercy forward with a nudge of his heels, leaving behind the screaming injured bandit to bleed out as he heads off to track down the master.

NINETEEN

MASTER OF THE SAND BANDITS

When they're forced to stop before the sun reaches its zenith, Peren allows the prisoner a few mouthfuls of water and a bite of hard, stale bread while he tends to the horses. The heat is already oppressive, and he knows that pushing through the peak of the day's sweltering heat would be dangerous for both them and the animals.

The prisoner, exhausted and terrified, gulps down the water, his eyes darting nervously around. Peren keeps a watchful eye on him, ready to act at the slightest sign of defiance. After tending to Mercy and the other horses, he permits himself a brief rest.

As the heat begins to dissipate, Peren urges the horses forward, keeping a steady pace. By nightfall, they reach the city's southern gate, joining the last group being interviewed before entry.

Upon seeing Peren, the associate of the "shadow man" hurries over. Noticing the blisters on Peren's skin, the associate quickly pulls him through the gate. "I need to debrief you."

Shaking his head, Peren replies, "No. I will only speak to the shadow man. But first, there is something that requires my attention. I'll meet him at our table."

With that, he leaves the associate to handle the horses and the captive, spurring Mercy into a gallop as he heads off.

Arriving outside the tavern, he leaps off Mercy and rushes around to the back, where the master's office is located. In his haste, he runs directly into two of the large bodyguards stationed there.

Recovering quickly, he unsheathes his dagger and strikes at the first man, driving the blade under his chin, through his mouth, and into his brain, killing him instantly. As the body collapses, he withdraws the dagger and uses the falling corpse as a springboard, propelling himself toward the second man. In one fluid motion, he plunges the dagger into the man's left eye, ending his life on contact.

Pulling the blade free in a spray of blood, white matter, and clear fluids, Peren lands lightly, catching the bodies to prevent them from hitting the ground with thuds, then moves cautiously into the office, where the master is engrossed in reviewing accounts.

Sensing movement, the master looks up, mumbling about being disturbed. His words die in his throat as he recognizes the figure entering the office. His face drains of colour.

Peren shuts the door behind him and steps forward, his eyes cold and unblinking. "Do you remember what I said to you?" he asks, his voice low and lethal.

The master sputters incoherently, his eyes wide with fear.

Peren steps closer, his expression darkening. "I said you will pay for this," he says, answering his own question, the words dripping with menace.

The master's gaze darts to the manacles still clamped around Peren's wrists and ankles. "How?" he manages to choke out, disbelief and terror mingling in his voice.

Playing with his dagger, Peren says nonchalantly, "I might

tell you…" He meets the master's gaze, a chilling smirk spreading across his face. "Before you die."

His voice trembling, the master sputters, "P-please, I... I beg you, h-have mercy on me."

Peren cocks his head as if considering the request. "Okay," he says, his tone deceptively calm. "I will."

Eager to feign gratitude, the master begins thanking Peren repeatedly, his words stumbling over each other. But as he rises, he slips a knife from his sleeve, thrusting it toward Peren. "You really are as dumb as a rock," he says, sneering.

Peren effortlessly dodges the attack, his movement a blur. With a swift strike, he smashes his fist into the master's wrist, snapping it with a sickening crack. The knife flies from the man's hand, landing uselessly on the floor.

Crying out in pain, the man swings with his other arm, desperate to strike Peren. Anticipating the move, he deftly sidesteps and, with a precise strike, shatters the man's other wrist with his fist. The man screams in agony, his eyes wide with horror as he stares at his now-useless, limp hands. Each twitch sends jolts of searing pain up his arms as the shards of broken bone grind against each other.

The master opens his mouth to scream for backup, but Peren is there in an instant, clamping a hand over his mouth and pressing the tip of his dagger to the man's navel. "Scream, and I'll gut you and feed you your own intestines," he growls, his voice low and deadly.

The master's face pales, his eyes wide with fear as he nods quickly. When Peren removes his hand, the man speaks, his voice shaking. "You won't get away with this. My men will come for you."

Peren tilts his head, a cold smile curling at the corner of his lips. "Do you mean your men at the camp?" he asks, his voice laced with dark amusement.

The man nods, confusion deepening in his eyes as Peren chuckles darkly. "I killed them all," he says, his tone almost casual. "All but one. He's very forthcoming with information—especially after I amputated his friend's limbs right in front of him. He's a dead man, but I promised him a swift death if he cooperated. Which he has."

The master's face pales at this revelation. Realizing he has only one card to play, he stalls for time, asking, "How did you find your way back to the camp? There must be fifteen miles between the camp and the cell."

"I walked," Peren replies with a smile. "It wasn't hard to figure out after a few minutes of studying the stars. Your sentries were useless." He chuckles darkly. "As useless as rocks."

Desperate, the master tries to reason with him. "You know what happens if I die, right? There will be a power struggle between the other clans. Wars will break out, and innocents will die. All that blood will be on *your* hands."

Peren raises an eyebrow, his voice dripping with sarcasm. "So, you want me to let you keep murdering innocents just because a war might break out between these clans?"

The man nods seriously, doing everything he can to convey the truth of his words. "Yes, exactly. It's a delicate balance, and my death will tip the scales into chaos."

Peren pauses for a moment, weighing the man's words. Then, with a quiet decision, he concludes two things: first, this isn't his city to control, and second, dealing with this mess falls squarely into the lap of the shadow man.

Dropping the master to the ground, Peren sets to work making his death memorable—slow and agonizing. Each time the man loses consciousness, he brings him back with a harsh shake and continues.

By the time the sky turns dark grey, Peren is finally done.

Wiping the blade and his face clean, he sheaths his dagger, then exits, heading toward the front, where Karung will be locking up.

As Peren reaches the front of the tavern, Karung steps out the door. Peren approaches quickly, pressing his dagger against her throat, his breath warm against her ear as he whispers, "Move inside."

Once they're inside and the door is securely locked, Peren turns to her, his tone cold. "Where are the girls?"

Karung spits in Peren's face, the act as sharp as her defiance. He pauses for a moment, a sudden memory of the witch flashing through his mind. It takes him a beat longer to shake off the thought, realizing with grim clarity that the witch was a brainwashed girl.

This woman, however, is a monster who needs to be put down.

Peren slaps her hard enough to send her flying. Crashing into a table and chairs, she crumples to the ground, groaning in pain.

He moves over to her, grabbing her by the hair and yanking her upright. She spits at him again, missing, and snarls, her voice dripping with venom. "Wait until the master hears about this. You're a dead man."

Smirking, Peren asks, "You mean the master who's in his office at the back of the tavern?"

Her face pales as she realizes what he's implying—he's already dealt with the master.

Slapping her again, Peren forces her attention back to him. "Now, tell me where the girls are kept."

Too terrified to answer, she merely points to one of the back rooms. Peren drags her along as he goes to investigate.

Throwing the door open and stepping back, Peren braces

for a trap, but relaxes a few moments later when he is faced with a room full of giggling girls. They immediately fall silent, wide-eyed at seeing Karung standing at the door, terrified of her. When they notice the blade at her neck, they gasp in fear, some of the younger ones hugging the older ones for protection.

As they see Peren's face behind her, their fear grows—he looks like a monster. But when they catch his kind expression, they remember how he used to blush whenever he spoke to them, always kind and willing to help. He has protected them, and that memory softens their fear.

Peren turns to the girls, his voice firm. "Get dressed and pack a bag of your things. I'll be back."

Closing the door behind him, he drags Karung down the hallway, checking each of the rooms. He finds various things—none of them useful. Frustrated, he finally asks, "Where are the master's bodyguards?"

Karung, trembling, nods toward a hidden door, barely noticeable.

Peren's eyes narrow. Deciding she is no longer of use to him, he moves swiftly. With a quick slash, he cuts her throat, and as her body crumples to the floor, he drags her limp form into the corner, leaving her there without a second glance.

He steps into the hidden room, where three massive bodyguards are engrossed in a game of cards. Before they can register his presence, he strikes. Two of them fall with quick jabs to the base of their skulls, blood splattering across the table.

The third bodyguard freezes, his eyes wide with shock. After a brief moment of confusion, he lets out a guttural growl and lunges forward, swinging a cudgel.

But Peren is faster. In one fluid motion, he disarms the man and steps back, snarling at the now-defenceless guard.

Spitting the words out through clenched teeth, he demands, "Where are the other two bodyguards?"

The big man shrugs indifferently, rolling his shoulders as he readies himself to attack again. Peren halts him with a raised hand, his voice cold and commanding. "The speed of your death depends on how well you answer. I could make it quick, like your friends, or slow, like your master."

Blanching at the threat, the man quickly reveals the location of the other two bodyguards. True to his word, Peren makes his death swift.

Moving on, he swiftly eliminates the last two bodyguards.

Then, rushing through the tavern, he finds various stashes of gold purses. Gathering them and putting them in his pack, he heads directly to where the girls are kept.

TWENTY

Freedom's Gift

Opening the door, Peren sees that they have all complied—most with terrified expressions, others with resigned ones. "Follow me, please," he instructs as he leaves the room.

The girls fall into an orderly line behind him, and Peren can tell this isn't the first time they've been moved from one master's property to another. His heart sinks at the thought of what these girls must have endured, but he forces himself not to dwell on it—he has no time for pity.

Moving to a spot near the door, he orders the girls to stand back. Then, after tossing a jar of oil into the room, he takes out flint and steel. His first attempt at lighting the oil fails. The second attempt is no better, the sparks falling harmlessly to the ground.

Many passersby glance at the girls and Peren, sensing something is off. They hastily quicken their pace, lowering their heads to avoid eye contact.

Finally, a spark catches, setting the oil alight. Flames spread rapidly throughout the tavern, eager to consume everything in their path.

Moving to the head of the group and leading Mercy, Peren calls out to the girls, "Follow me."

They move down the streets, each face a mixture of fear and resignation as they step into their uncertain new fate.

Turning a corner, Peren is met by five burly men, each wielding a finely crafted sword. Without breaking his stride, he eyes them coolly and says, "Get out of my way, or I'll take you down."

The leader chuckles menacingly. "You have no idea what you have done, *boy!*" Unsheathing his sword, he points it at Peren. "You're a dead man."

With that, they all advance.

Handing Mercy's reins to the nearest girl, Peren asks, "Could you please hold her?" Turning to the rest of the group, he says, "I will be right back. Stay here, please."

Pulling out his dagger, he launches himself at the men, knowing that quick work is essential and wanting to minimize bloodshed for the girls. Despite their eyes watching him, he moves swiftly, taking down each man with precision—stabbing their hearts or slitting their throats.

As the last man falls, Peren clears the path, pushing the bodies aside to create a safe passage. Moving back to the group, he takes the reins from the girl and thanks her. Waving them forward, he calls out, "Come along, girls."

They follow, their steps heavier than before, but a glimmer of relief flickers in their eyes—they know that, at least, their new master can protect them.

When they reach the inn where Peren is staying, he heads inside and approaches the innkeeper. After much haggling and arguing while the girls wait outside, looking uncomfortable and out of place, he finally strikes a deal.

A few minutes later, he steps back outside and waves the girls in. They exchange confused glances but follow him cautiously, unsure of what to expect next.

As the girls enter the inn, the maids rush to take care of them, helping the younger ones with their luggage and leading them to where baths are being prepared. The atmosphere is one of relief and cautious hope as the girls begin to unwind from their traumatic experiences.

That night, the shadow man strides in with grim determination and sits down opposite Peren. His voice dripping with fury, he demands, "What the *hells* did you do?"

Leaning forward with a snarl, Peren's eyes lock onto the man's. "You gave me a job, and I did it my way. If you didn't like it, you shouldn't have hired me. But"—he pauses, his voice tightening—"I did what you should have done years ago. Do you have any idea what those girls have been through? I will *not* carry that on my conscience."

He stands up abruptly, his eyes never leaving the man. "Now, I believe you owe me five thousand gold, and I expect it by tomorrow. I'll be gone the day after."

Peren turns to leave, but then pauses. Slowly, he turns back to face the man, his lips curling into a grim smile. "By the way, you're welcome. The sand bandits are no longer a problem—dead or scattered."

He stalks to his room, his footsteps echoing in the quiet corridor. Once inside, he sees copious purses of gold scattered on the floor—loot from the tavern, along with his winnings and earnings.

With a weary determination, he sits down and begins sorting the gold into equal piles. Each clink of a coin resonates in the silent room, a rhythmic reminder of the night's turmoil. He carefully places the sorted gold into small leather purses he'd bought earlier, already prepared for the task ahead.

Hours pass, and the night deepens. Peren's eyes grow heavy with exhaustion, the weight of his actions settling in his bones, but he forces himself to continue, each coin placed with meticulous precision, though his movements are slow with fatigue. The rhythmic sound of gold clinking against leather is the only noise in the otherwise-silent room.

His mind drifts, replaying the events of the last few days.

Finally, with the last coin placed, he climbs into bed, his muscles protesting with every movement. He pulls the covers over himself, but doesn't feel the warmth. The moment his head hits the pillow, sleep claims him, swallowing him whole in a deep, dreamless void.

Waking bleary-eyed the next morning, he carefully climbs out of bed, watching where he places his feet among the scattered purses of gold. After a quick drink and a splash of water to wash his face, he heads downstairs for breakfast. There, he is informed that his patron will no longer cover his expenses. He chuckles at this, feeling a rare lightness, his good humour intact.

He notices the absence of the girls and finds them huddled in the corners of their rooms, their eyes wide with fear. He gently beckons them downstairs, his voice low and soothing. After a few minutes of being coaxed with quiet words of reassurance and a calm presence, they finally follow him to the common room.

The innkeeper scowls as the girls enter, their dishevelled state obvious. "What have you done to these girls?" she demands, her tone sharp. She rushes around them, helping them to sit at a table while glaring back at Peren whenever she can.

Peren meets her gaze without flinching, his voice steady but firm. "I'm not responsible for their current condition," he says, "but I'll make sure they have a proper new beginning." His eyes soften as he looks at each girl, offering them a rare comforting smile.

Grumbling under her breath, the innkeeper helps the maids settle the girls and brings food to the table. When the first plate is placed in front of one of the girls, her eyes widen, thinking it's meant for the whole group. She slides it into the middle, nudging it toward the others.

But when another plate is set in front of another girl, she freezes, unsure what to do. A maid pushes the plate back to the girl.

They all look up at Peren, clearly anxious. Sensing their unease, he nods encouragingly, gesturing with his hands to show that they should eat. Slowly, the girls begin to relax and start eating, unsure but grateful.

Around midday, a rider arrives with a large purse, handing it over to Peren with a curt nod. Without a word, he rises from the table, his sudden movement causing the girls to stiffen and stand up as well, interpreting his action as a signal to follow.

Seeing their wariness, Peren pauses, offering a soft, reassuring smile. "Sit. Eat," he says, his voice steady. After a few moments, the girls cautiously lower themselves back into their seats, still unsure, but relieved to return to their meal.

Peren takes the purse and slips it into his coat, leaving the table without another word. The girls exchange glances, still unsure of what's happening, but after a brief pause, they warily return to their food.

Peren spends the afternoon carefully sorting the rest of the gold into purses. As the light starts to fade and evening approaches, he finishes his task. One purse, noticeably larger than the others, is set aside, filled to the brim with gold. With a satisfied look, he arranges the smaller purses neatly, packing them carefully before standing up.

He calls for the maids, who help him move the purses into a private room large enough to hold all of them.

Once they're inside, he goes to the girls' rooms, coaxing them to follow him into the spacious room. Though still hesitant, they feel a little bolder than before, bolstered by the kindness they've received, though some are still wary, unsure if this is just another cruel joke.

When everyone has gathered, Peren looks at them, his expression firm but kind. "This is my last night here," he says. "I'll be traveling on alone from tomorrow."

The words hang in the air, and a few of the girls start to panic, their fear of abandonment clear on their faces. They look at each other in alarm, anxiety creeping in as they worry they'll be left with another abusive master.

Peren raises a hand, calming them with a soft, steady voice. "You are not slaves anymore. I set you free." He pauses, making sure they're listening. "You no longer have to do as you're told."

Every girl gapes at him, disbelief evident on their faces, wondering if this is some cruel trick.

Finally, one girl steps forward, her voice barely above a whisper. "Master, how are we to live… without a master?"

In response to the girl's question, Peren considers her carefully, realizing the depth of their fear and uncertainty. His gaze is steady as he speaks. "Living without a master will feel strange at first," he admits, his tone softer than they've heard. "But your lives will also be yours to shape however you wish. That's what freedom means." He pauses, making sure each girl is listening, then nods toward the table near the door. "The purses there? They're filled with gold I gathered from the tavern, my earnings, and my fee for this job."

A murmur of confusion ripples through the girls, their brows knitting as they glance at each other.

Sensing their uncertainty, Peren continues. "If you

stepped out there alone, without resources, you'd likely be sold back into slavery within a week," he says, his voice carrying a note of caution. "So, I've left you with a final parting gift—enough to start fresh, on your own terms."

He stands by the door, his gaze steady as it sweeps over the room. "If you ever feel lost," he begins, his tone firm yet warm, "remember this: freedom is yours to grow into. Take it one day at a time."

Peren pauses, watching the uncertainty flicker across their faces as they wait for the other shoe to drop. "One final thing," he says, his voice growing serious. The girls tense, afraid that this will all come to an end, that this freedom is just an illusion. "I expect you to take care of each other," he continues, letting the weight of his words settle. "No girl should go without. I would have given you more if there was more to give, but what I've given is enough if you use it wisely. Be smart with the gold, be wise, and you'll be able to make it last—and even make more. I know you can do it."

He looks into their eyes one by one, making sure each girl hears and understands him. "Remember, no girl alone. You're all in this together."

He points to an older girl, offering her a reassuring smile as he waves her over. "Please, come here," he says gently.

The girl hesitates but, gathering her courage, steps forward. He asks her name and the story of how she ended up in this situation, and she whispers, "Lisselle." Her voice is barely a whisper as she briefly recounts her journey to this place. Listening intently, Peren nods, his expression softening as he places a comforting arm around her. Overcome by the flood of emotions she's held back, Lisselle breaks into sobs, clutching him tightly as her tears fall.

Once she finally calms, Peren reaches out, lifting a purse

from the table and placing it in her hands. "My parting gift to you, Lisselle," he says with quiet warmth.

Overcome with emotion, she clings to him, her gratitude spilling out between sobs as she thanks him for everything he's done. Gently, he sends her to her room to rest, watching her go with a quiet satisfaction.

One by one, he calls each girl forward, offering a few words of comfort, encouragement, and reassurance. Each girl leaves with her own purse, the weight a tangible symbol of the freedom Peren has gifted them. Late into the night, he continues, listening to their stories, sharing in their tears, and giving them each a final embrace.

At last, only one purse remains, and he hands it to the youngest girl with a tired but warm smile. With every girl cared for, he finally stands alone in the quiet room.

He turns back toward his own quarters, the weight of the night lifting just enough to let weariness settle in. As he reaches his bed, he sinks down and lets his eyes close, surrendering to a deep, untroubled sleep.

The next morning, after waking up early, Peren has a hearty breakfast. While Mercy is being saddled, Peren sorts out the expenses for himself and the girls, in addition to the provisions he requested for the next part of his journey, giving the innkeeper enough for a couple more meals for the girls, depleting most of his own purse.

As he leaves through the northern gate into the desert, he pauses after a minute. He turns back to the city, and a tear falls down his cheek as he whispers hoarsely around the lump in his throat, "Good luck, girls."

Turning back, he continues into the rising heat of the desert.

TWENTY-ONE

RIVERSDAWN

Despite pushing forward as often as possible and stopping only when absolutely necessary, it takes Peren a full week to get out of the desert. By the time he crosses the final stretch of sands, both he and Mercy are hot, tired, and irritable. Cursing under his breath, he wrestles with their footwear, finally feeling some relief as their feet touch gravel.

As the endless dunes give way to rocky, grass-patched plains, the temperature drops noticeably. He wonders if it's just his imagination or a true shift in the weather as he heads north-northeast. Feeling the change, Mercy relaxes, her familiar calm demeanour returning, while Peren, now cooled and rejuvenated, prepares himself for what lies ahead.

Slowing his pace to avoid tripping on the uneven ground, he keeps an eye out for a pond or stream to wash away the last traces of desert sand. As the day stretches on without any sign of water, his irritation grows.

Deciding to set up camp early, he brushes Mercy down with dried grass, strips off his gear, and shakes out as much sand as he can from the saddle, bridle, and his clothes. Finally, he settles in for the night, eating some of his travel rations—hard bread, dried meat, and a handful of nuts—and feeling grateful for even a small reprieve from the desert's harshness.

Waking up the next morning, Peren is relieved to find patches of green scattered along the rocky landscape, meaning Mercy finally has fresh grazing and won't have to rely on grain alone. Looking around, he finds a stream that he uses to refill his water supply, having Mercy drink her fill and then cleaning off as much of the sand as he can. Stretching out, he has a simple breakfast, appreciating the gradual change in the air's crispness as they move away from the desert. With camp packed up and Mercy saddled, they continue down the winding road that leads toward Riversdawn.

As he rides past fields, Peren notices a young farming family hard at work guiding animals and tending crops. The children pause, looking up from their tasks, and wave eagerly at him. Smiling, he lifts a hand to return the gesture, feeling a rare, unexpected warmth.

An hour further down the road, he spots a small group approaching at a steady pace, their movements purposeful and brisk.

Curiosity piqued by their hurried pace, Peren narrows his eyes, watching as the group catches sight of him. To his surprise, they manoeuvre their horses into a line across the road, creating an unmistakable barricade.

Sensing their intention, Peren reins in Mercy a few paces away, meeting their guarded expressions with a calm, steady gaze. He remains silent, relaxed, as he waits for them to make the first move, his eyes subtly assessing each rider.

A horse and rider move forward a couple of paces from the pack. The arrogance and confidence wafting off the rider leave no doubt in Peren's mind who the leader of this gang is.

Sneering, the man speaks in a haughty and condescending manner. "Gimme yer gold, I'll let yer live."

Pausing in thought while he sizes the leader up, his face impassive, Peren says in a quiet but carrying voice, "What, no tax? Just all my gold?"

The leader's arrogance grows, a gleam of excitement in his eyes. "No tax. All yer gold, and now, yer horse too."

Peren draws his dagger, its hilt catching the light. "Gonna take this too?"

A flash of greed flickers across the leader's face as his eyes lock onto the weapon. He nods eagerly. "That too," he says, his grin widening.

Peren doesn't move, his eyes cold and calculating. The leader leans forward, clearly anticipating his submission.

With a single word, Peren shatters his expectations. "No."

The leader freezes, his grin faltering. "No?" He blinks, struggling to process the unexpected response.

"No."

Sitting up straight, the leader smirks and gestures broadly to his men. "Yeh? Yer gonna stop us?"

Peren's lips curl into a small smile, the corners of his mouth twitching. "Yes, I am. In fact, I think I'll take all your gold and horses, along with any weapons you own."

The leader laughs, clearly amused by the challenge, his eyes scanning Peren for any sign of weakness. "Okay, let's do it the hard way," he says, cracking his knuckles. With a smirk, he gestures to his men. "I love the hard way."

Before the leader has a chance to make a move, Peren cuts in, offering them one final chance to leave. "There are two options: One, you let me go on my way peacefully. Two, you head home and leave banditry to the professionals."

The leader's face turns a shade of red. With a snarl, he unsheathes his sword. "Okay, yer really pissed me off now. I was only gonna take yer provisions, but now? I'll take yer life, too."

A smile plays at the corner of Peren's lips as he responds smoothly, "By all means, please try."

Before the leader can dismount, he suddenly pitches backward off his horse, crashing to the ground with a sickening thud. The rest of the bandits stare in frozen horror as they see a dagger embedded in the leader's eye.

They shift their gaze from their dead leader to Peren, confused. It seems like he hasn't moved a muscle, but they all know that is his dagger. As the realization sinks in, the bandits' faces turn pale.

Peren lets out his best, most sinister sneer. Their expressions blanch further, and instinctively, they shrink back from the malice radiating from him. Desperately, they try to urge their horses into motion, hoping to escape the malevolent force they now sense. The horses, feeling the panic of their riders, snort and rear in fear. The bandits blame Peren for their horses' frantic behaviour.

Peren raises a hand, his voice cutting through the chaos with calm authority. "Wait."

Stilling in terror, unwilling to provoke any more attacks, the bandits slowly and carefully turn their horses to face Peren. Their mounts remain restless, still shifting in unease.

In a calm, quiet voice, Peren asks, "What will you lot do now?"

One of the bandits, realizing the question is genuine, shrugs and replies with a resigned tone, "I guess we'll go home and stop playing at being bandits."

As they start to turn back around, Peren calls out once more, his voice cutting through the tension. "Wait." Turning back with fear in their eyes, the bandits look at him, their faces pale and confused. Peren, unmoved, continues, "There is one alternative that I can offer you.

"You could become the village guard," he continues, his voice firm, "protecting the people from other bandits. But to atone for the harm you've caused, you will repay every tax you took—with interest."

He raises his hand, silencing their immediate protests. "You will work honestly. When you're not on patrol, you'll find work in the village, helping with what needs doing. You will set up watches to ensure the villagers are safe. No more threatening them. You will be the first to step up and protect the people from anything that threatens their peace."

His eyes harden as he finishes, his tone carrying authority. "I charge you with the task of becoming Riversdawn's protectors."

Taking on a sinister tone that makes their blood run cold, Peren adds, "If I so much as hear a whisper, a single hint of any wrongdoing from any of you, I will hunt you down. And I'll make you beg for death. Understood?"

Too terrified to do anything but nod, the bandits cower as Peren reinforces his point, his voice cold and unwavering. "You will clear up this mess and any future ones of this nature. You will also visit every house you once taxed, and you will grovel before the owners. Apologise. Tell them you've seen the error of your ways, and pledge to each of them your personal oath to protect this village from any bandit, now and forever."

Swearing to change their ways, the bandits cautiously skirt around him and continue toward the farm he passed earlier. Doubts linger in Peren's mind, but he hopes he made the right choice.

Dismounting, he approaches the dead bandit, pulls out his dagger, and cleans it on the man's bloodstained clothes before sheathing it. He remounts Mercy, his thoughts uneasy.

As he moves deeper into the village, Peren sees the toll the bandits have taken with their cruel taxes. At the sight of him, villagers scatter, fleeing in terror and rushing into their homes, abandoning their work in their panic.

Looks of terror and resignation pass over the people Peren encounters in the street. Each of them sighs, hesitating before reaching for their coin purses to pay their tax. After the confusion with the first couple of villagers, Peren steps in with his best disarming smile. "I'm not a bandit," he says, holding up a hand to stop them as they reach for their purses. "I don't require any taxes."

Their confusion deepens, but Peren continues, adding, "The bandits have reformed. They're now the protectors of this village."

The villagers blink at him, too shocked to do much more than fumble with their coins. "W-what?" one woman stammers, her hand still hovering uncertainly over her purse.

"Trust me," Peren says, giving a small, reassuring nod. "No taxes today. Just… go on with your day. No more fear."

Still too stunned to process what's happening, most stagger forward, their minds racing to reconcile this strange encounter with the reality they know.

Even though Riversdawn is considered a small village, it takes Peren most of the day to reach the other side. This is partly due to him stopping at every passing villager to explain the changes and to purchase supplies, but mostly because of the vast size of everyone's land.

As he leaves the village behind, Peren feels a sense of relief when he reaches a wide, grassy plain. The sun is just touching the horizon, painting the sky with brilliant hues. He dismounts and sets up his camp, feeling at peace with the open space around him.

After a satisfying meal, he licks his fingers clean, his mind wandering to thoughts of the new village guard and how things went with them. He nods off to sleep in front of the fire, the cool, clear night wrapping around him and the stars winking down from above.

The next morning, he wakes feeling refreshed, the first rays of the sun peeking over the horizon. He enjoys a quiet breakfast, breaks camp, and continues on his journey towards Keyp.

TWENTY-TWO

KEYP

As the days stretch on, Peren begins to notice the air thickening with humidity and the ground growing steadily wetter beneath Mercy's hooves. Slowing their pace to avoid any missteps that could lead to injury, he feels both his mount's coat and his own clothes becoming damp with the marshland's moisture.

He recalls the map he studied so long ago, the details now coming back to him with a sense of bittersweet nostalgia. Looking around, he works out roughly where he is, and a surge of elation fills him as he realizes how close he is to his destination.

Alongside that excitement, however, the weight of anxiety presses on him—he can't help but wonder what challenges the maze will bring. Taking a slow, steady breath, he lets himself briefly indulge in a fantasy: completing the maze not just as the youngest, but as the fastest in Shadow Fang Guild history.

A sudden squelching noise pulls him from his daydream. Instantly, his senses snap to attention as he scans his surroundings for any sign of danger. He relaxes when he identifies the source—a large, shallow muddy puddle that Mercy is wading through—and lets out a quiet sigh of relief. Still, he remains alert, keeping a watchful eye on his surroundings for any potential threats.

Deciding to push through the night instead of making camp, he eats a meal made damp by the heavy humidity in the air. As the sun dips below the horizon, the stars briefly shine through before clouds quickly obscure them. He is forced to slow Mercy down even further, taking extra care to minimize the chance of her breaking a leg. He can barely see through the misty air, and with the clouds now obscuring the sky, navigating becomes even more difficult.

Despite hearing only the splashes and muffled thuds of Mercy's steps in the water, Peren's gaze remains fixed on the path ahead.

When the sun finally rises above the horizon, he is weary from the strain of focusing for so long. He sighs in frustration as the clouds drift westward, clearing the sky and blinding him with the reflected sunlight. Shielding his eyes with one hand and squinting against the glare, he turns Mercy away from the sun, trying to guide her in the right direction while the light intensifies.

The marshland's waterlogged ground makes progress slow and hazardous, with every step a reminder of the strain on Mercy's legs and hooves. Peren stops every few hours to lift her hooves from the wet earth, carefully drying them as best as he can, worried that prolonged exposure to the damp could cause injury or infection. Even though it hasn't rained, the humidity of the marshes has kept the ground soaking wet, and he can't afford for her hooves to soften or rot in the persistent dampness.

Though the journey takes longer than he had expected, Peren finally reaches a boardwalk that stretches ahead, elevated above the water. The sight of it fills him with a deep sense of relief, as Mercy no longer has to slog through the water with every step.

With the solid surface beneath them, they can travel at a more reasonable pace. The ground beneath them remains slick from the humidity, but it's a welcome change from the constant slog through marshland. Moving at a quicker pace now, Peren makes steady progress, and by the time the sun dips below the horizon, he finds himself nearing Keyp.

The entire village is built on stilts above the water, with winding paths connecting each residence and shop. As Peren dismounts Mercy, he's met with curious stares from the villagers. Confused at first, he soon realizes the reason: there are no other horses in sight. After a moment of thought, he asks one of the villagers for directions to an inn with a stable where he can spend the night.

By the time he reaches the Dry Beaver inn, it's fully dark. He's gotten lost several times in the maze-like streets of Keyp. When he finally knocks on the door, a grumpy middle-aged man with a round frame opens it. With a gruff voice, he asks, "Who disturbs my sleep?"

Bowing slightly and offering a disarming smile, Peren replies cordially, "I apologise for waking you, sir. I seek shelter for the night, both for myself and my horse."

Looking Peren and Mercy over with a critical and suspicious eye, the innkeeper growls to himself, muttering something under his breath, then spitting out a price that makes Peren flinch. He hesitates before offering a counter. After a tense few moments of back-and-forth, he negotiates a reasonably exorbitant fee. Though it's still more than he had hoped to pay, it's within his means, and he can't afford to push the matter further.

When Peren asks about a stable, the innkeeper grunts and waves him toward a small covered area beside the inn that serves as a makeshift shelter for occasional travellers. It's clear that horses are rare here; the shelter is little more than a lean-to with walls patched up to keep out some of the marsh wind. Still, it's better than leaving Mercy outside entirely.

Peren leads her over, ties her to a post, and gets to work drying her as best as he can, rubbing her coat down and carefully tending to her hooves. The cold dampness clings to the air, but the lean-to keeps the worst of it off her.

Peren heads inside. It's dimly lit, the hearth casting flickering shadows on the walls. The smell of stew and roast meat fills the air, and his stomach growls loudly at the thought of food. He quickly makes his way upstairs to his room, careful not to knock anything over in the narrow hallways. Inside his room, the bed looks lumpy and the sheets a little worn, but it's more than enough after the past few days.

He strips off his damp clothing, cleans himself as best as he can with a basin of water, and sits down to the simple meal that's waiting for him on the table. It's not much—some bread, cheese, and salted meat—but it's enough to quiet the hunger gnawing at him.

He eats in silence, his mind drifting to the journey ahead and the weight of his quest. After the long day, he finds himself growing drowsy, the warmth of the room pulling him into sleep. The bed is uncomfortable, but after everything, it's a welcome rest.

Waking the next morning to a cloudy grey sky, Peren feels a twinge of relief at the softer light—an easy reprieve from the usual harsh glare bouncing off the marsh. He rises, readies himself quickly, and heads into the common room. There, he spots the innkeeper sweeping the floors with a grumpy focus, muttering about the mud tracked in last night by Peren.

Peren pauses, offers a polite farewell and a nod of thanks, and makes his way back to Mercy's shelter. After tending to her, he checks her hooves carefully for any signs of wear from the marsh and then saddles up, leading her carefully out of Keyp as the path leads them back toward the grassy plains.

A couple of days after leaving the village, just as the grasses seem to be growing sturdier and more frequent, the boardwalk ends abruptly. Peren sighs as Mercy's hooves sink into the shallow, muddy water once more. Though she treads cautiously, he feels a pang of worry for the strain the marshland might cause her.

With a murmur of reassurance, he nudges her onward, determined to push through the wet terrain and find solid ground ahead.

TWENTY-THREE

GRASSY PLAINS

After days slogging through puddles and marshy stretches, Peren finally feels solid ground beneath Mercy's hooves as they reach the edge of the plains. The open expanse is a welcome sight, with winds sweeping through the long grasses, creating rippling waves across the landscape.

Peren lets Mercy have her head, and she breaks into a full gallop, relishing the freedom after days of careful, cautious steps. Together, they race up and down the gentle hills, the wind whipping past, carrying away the damp, stifling memory of the marshlands.

Hours later, as the sun dips low, Peren brings Mercy to a halt and sets up camp. He gazes up, enchanted by the clear night sky, where stars twinkle brightly against the vast darkness. The only disturbance in this serene place is the cold wind cutting across the open fields, making him pull his cloak tighter. Yet, despite the chill, a deep sense of peace settles over him; with each mile, he knows he's drawing closer to his goal.

As the days go by, though, apprehension builds, tingling at the edges of his nerves. His master's words echo in his mind: "This will be the toughest challenge you've ever faced—or will face."

The thought weighs heavily as he recalls his journey, his narrow escapes, and how survival often felt like a gift, not a skill. He wonders, *Will I even make it? What if I'm not good enough?* The questions linger, casting faint shadows over the bright landscape ahead, reminders of the price he's already paid to reach this point.

When he nears the edge of a massive lake stretching far into the distance, his shoulders slump as he takes in the vast, still waters with no bridge, ferry, or any visible way across. Frustration prickles at him as he realizes the lake is likely far too deep to ford. His jaw clenches as he considers his limited options, the only real choice being to go around.

Recalling the map he memorized, he visualizes the best route, tracing a path south along the shoreline. With a resigned sigh, he adjusts Mercy's reins and begins leading her southward, hoping the detour won't delay him too long.

Refusing to let the setback darken the beautifully sunny day, he focuses instead on the sun's radiance, watching the way it glints off the water and illuminates the grassy fields to his right. Setting a comfortable, steady pace, they move on until the sun retreats below the horizon. As dusk settles in, Peren makes camp, savouring a simple meal from his provisions before resting, ready to push on at first light.

Jerking awake what feels like only a moment later, he finds himself soaked to the bone from an unexpected downpour. Gritting his teeth, he covers himself as best he can against the relentless rain, choosing to push on rather than huddle in the damp.

Eventually, the downpour dwindles to a steady drizzle, casting a dark, brooding mood over the landscape. Trotting along, shivering and soaked, Peren hunkers close to Mercy, feeling the warmth of her body through the chill. Each step squelches beneath them, and the cold wind bites at his soaked clothes, testing his endurance, yet he presses forward, determined to keep moving, no matter how grim the day.

A few hours after the sky clears, Peren begins to dry out, the sun slowly working its magic on his sodden clothes.

The further south he travels along the lake, the more the landscape changes. At first, only scattered shrubs dot the horizon, but soon, they give way to dense clumps of bushes, then to small, tangled thickets.

As the days pass, the thickets grow thicker, and sparse twisted trees begin to emerge, their gnarled branches reaching for the sky. The air grows heavier, charged with an unfamiliar sense of unease. What was once an open, tranquil plain is now giving way to a dense, almost oppressive thicket of foliage. The trees become more numerous, towering over Peren as if closing in on his path.

With each step deeper into the changing landscape, an unsettling feeling stirs more strongly in his gut, a warning that the unknown lies just ahead.

TWENTY-FOUR

TURNBACK FOREST

When the trees become too tall and numerous to count, their long and dark shadows giving off an ominous feeling so thick the air could be cut with a dagger, Peren knows he has entered Turnback Forest. The very air seems to press down on him, cold and heavy with a suffocating silence.

He slows to a careful trot, every instinct within him screaming to turn back, but the path ahead calls to him, the only way forward.

Mercy, too, feels the malignant atmosphere. Her ears flatten against her head, and she rears up, snorting in panic. Her nervousness mirrors his own unease, but he forces himself to stay calm, urging her back down.

The dense canopy above blocks out the majority of the fading daylight, leaving only slivers of illumination to cut through the gloom. It feels as though the forest itself is watching them, waiting for something.

Peren reaches forward, murmuring soothing words as he pats Mercy comfortingly. "It's okay, girl," he whispers, his voice low and steady. "We'll get through this." Slowly, she begins to settle, her breathing evening out, though the unease lingers in her stance.

He urges her forward, and they continue at a cautious pace, but after a few more steps, Mercy shakes her head, snorts in terror, and rears once more, her hooves striking the air in frustration. Peren's jaw tightens, and he glances around the forest as if expecting something to jump out at them from the shadows.

Deciding it would be faster to continue on foot, Peren dismounts swiftly, carefully removing Mercy's saddle and gear. He brushes her down gently, speaking soft reassurances before letting her wander freely, though he keeps a close eye on her every movement.

"Stay safe," he whispers, giving Mercy one last pat. With a final, lingering glance at her, he dons his shoulder bag and sets off on foot, determined to push through the discomfort and the creeping sense of dread that weighs on him as he ventures deeper into the forest.

As he makes his way farther into the trees, something nags at the back of his mind—something aside from the pervasive sense of malice. It takes him some time to realize what it is: the complete absence of the usual forest sounds. There are no birds chirping, no rustling bushes from rabbits or deer, and not even the faint calls of predators. The eerie silence makes the hairs on the back of his neck stand on end.

He slips his dagger from its scabbard, the familiar weight in his hand offering a small measure of control. An unbidden memory of the Whispering Wood surfaces—how people once thought it was haunted. He smiles briefly at their ignorance, but the smile quickly fades as he grits his teeth and refocuses on the present.

The deeper he goes, the denser the foliage becomes, blocking out the sun entirely and casting the forest into a suffocating darkness that even his elven eyes cannot penetrate. With no other choice but to turn back, he gathers what little wood he can find and makes a torch. Lighting it, he steels himself before heading once again into the terrifying blackness.

His stomach growls in protest, forcing him to stop for a light snack and to rest his legs. After eating and pushing himself as far as he can into the night, he eventually makes camp, building a bright fire and preparing a meagre dinner. Yet the oppressive sense of terror lingering around him makes it hard to truly relax. Hours later, he wakes, the feeling of being watched and hunted chilling him to the core.

Cursing his inability to see without a light source, he slips deeper into the trees, hoping to shake off the unnerving feeling clinging to him. His eyes scan his surroundings for a good ambush site, and after a moment, he finds a small clearing. Planting the torch in the centre, along with his bag, he silently slips into the brush, waiting in tense silence.

Hours pass with no sign of a pursuer. Frustration mounts as he collects his belongings and tries to move on. Reaching out, as he's always done, he attempts to tap into his senses to pinpoint the presence he's been tracking, but this time, there's nothing—just an overwhelming void, as if his magic has never existed at all.

The absence claws at him, deep and suffocating. Collapsing to the ground on all fours, he trembles, feeling the emptiness consume him. Overcome with its weight, he finally weeps, the sound of his own despair echoing in the silence of the forest.

Calming down a few hours later, Peren forces himself to accept the absence of his senses, pushing the frustration to the back of his mind. He forces himself to move forward, despite the gnawing emptiness. The lack of tracks, scents, or any sign of life weighs heavily on him, but he refuses to stop.

The deeper he goes, the stronger the sense of dread

becomes. It pulses through the air, thick and suffocating, as if the forest itself were closing in on him. Still, he presses on, determined to reach his objective—whatever waits at the heart of this cursed place.

With little energy left to spare, he runs over the details of the maze in his mind, trying to focus through the exhaustion. The maze is infamous not only for testing physical endurance, but also for challenging one's mental and spiritual fortitude. Few who enter speak of their experiences, and those who survive rarely share any details, leading to some wild legends amongst the initiates and novices over what the trials could be.

Failing to shake the gnawing dread, Peren stumbles through the forest, his sleep fitful and brief. Grateful for the provisions he's stocked up on, he pushes forward.

Suddenly, he feels a shift in the air—a subtle change. The heavy dread that has been clinging to him begins to dissipate, replaced by an unsettling calmness. It's as if the suffocating atmosphere were nothing more than a figment of his imagination.

Confused and unsure, he steps back, drops the torch, and collapses onto the forest floor, the weight of the dread returning with full force. It crushes him, pulling at his chest, suffocating his thoughts. Crawling forward, he fights to escape it, and only when the dread releases him does he stop. He collapses again, finally still, lying on the ground for several minutes, too exhausted to move.

Regaining some strength, he slowly sits up, munching on a quick meal before finally giving in to the exhaustion that's weighed on him for days. He falls into a deep, dreamless sleep—the kind that truly allows his body to rest. When he wakes, refreshed and with his mind sharper, he lights the torch and rises, his gaze fixed ahead.

As he moves forward, the maze appears before him seemingly out of nowhere, its towering walls emerging from the thick forest like some ancient monolith. Its size is unsettling, far beyond what he expected, and the very air around it is thick with an oppressive, ancient presence. There's a power here, something dark and unknowable that feels akin to the witch's magic—but older, more primal.

Peren knows, without a doubt, that what lies ahead is unlike anything he's faced before.

TWENTY-FIVE

SKULL MAZE

Upon a closer look at the towering walls, Peren recoils, his stomach churning. They are made entirely of skulls, their empty eye sockets staring down at him with hollow, accusing gazes. He forces himself to look away, unwilling to let his mind dwell on the unsettling parallels between the witch's magic and this place.

Taking a steadying breath, he squares his shoulders, setting his expression with grim determination. As he approaches the maze's entrance, he notices something more: each skull bears a distinct glyph carved into its forehead, an ancient marking he can't decipher, but it's clear this is no random display.

His curiosity, stronger than his caution and revulsion, drives him to reach out and touch one of the glyphs. The moment his finger makes contact, a surge of searing energy courses through him, jolting his body as his nerves scream in agony. His back arches involuntarily, his muscles spasming violently. Flashes of chaotic, incomprehensible images dance behind his eyes—too quick, too fragmented to make sense of.

Once the surge of energy releases him, Peren stumbles back, panting, still frozen in the same pose he was in when his finger touched the skull. His body trembles, and for several minutes, he stands there, unable to move, blinking rapidly as if trying to shake off the lingering shock. His mind races, struggling to grasp what just happened, but his thoughts are muddled, disjointed. His brows furrow in confusion, a vague sense of something important slipping just beyond his reach.

Within moments, the entire ordeal vanishes from his memory, leaving him with only a blank, unsettling void where the experience should be.

Convinced that nothing significant occurred, Peren shrugs off the unsettling feeling and steps toward the entrance of the maze. The reality of his journey settles in—his quest has only just begun. He unsheathes his dagger with deliberate calm, crouching low as he moves forward.

As he steps into the maze, three things happen in quick succession. First, the sky shifts into an impenetrable indigo void free of clouds or stars, leaving him with only a few feet of visibility before a haze blurs his sight, letting him extinguish the torch. Second, an intense prickling sensation surges through the hairs on the back of his neck, so sharp it almost borders on painful. Third, the unmistakable sound of snapping underfoot freezes him in place. He looks down and recoils in horror. It's not twigs he's crushing beneath his feet, but bones—human bones.

Swallowing the surge of revulsion rising in his throat, he forces his gaze to the path ahead, squinting against the oppressive purple-blackness that obscures his vision.

As his eyes adjust, they widen in disbelief. The entire ground before him is littered with partially crushed bones. The unbroken ones are stacked along the edges, pressed up against the towering skull walls, while the centre of the path is a grisly tapestry of shattered bones, their jagged edges glinting faintly in the dim light.

Looking into the distance, Peren's eyes strain against the oppressive blackness of the maze. The path ahead stretches into nothingness, the walls of skulls casting long, foreboding shadows that seem to move in the dim light, making the silence feel suffocating. He inches over to one of the skull walls, the crunch of bones underfoot echoing off the walls. Reaching out, he feels the deep engraving of one glyph on the otherwise-smooth and perfectly placed skull. He doesn't need to try to know that there is no way anyone can scale a wall as smooth as this.

Sighing, he moves forward slowly, positive the soft crunching of bones beneath his boots is louder than it should be, wincing at each scrape.

Deeper into the maze he goes, barely breathing, until he spots an opening to his right. Hesitating, he sneaks a glance around the corner. The end of the path is barely visible, and the prickling on the back of his neck sharpens the further he ventures. He takes another cautious step, his heart hammering, until the path turns again to the right.

Peeking around the corner, he sees nothing but bones scattered across the ground. He continues creeping forward until the path abruptly ends, the looming walls of skulls surrounding him.

A haunting chuckle slices through the thick silence, sharp and unnatural. Peren freezes, his muscles locking up as the sound sends an icy chill crawling down his spine. He crouches lower, eyes scanning the corridor, desperately seeking the source of the laughter.

But there is no one. No movement. Only the oppressive stillness of the maze.

His heart racing, Peren inches closer to the dead-end wall. The chuckling grows louder, closer, vibrating through the bones and the very air around him. His eyes widen in shock as he realizes the sound is coming from the skulls themselves. The eerie laughter echoes off the walls, mocking him as if the maze itself were alive.

Peren instinctively takes a step back, his breath shallow, the hairs on the back of his neck standing on end. Backing away as quietly and quickly as he can, he retraces his steps toward the main corridor, his heart pounding in his chest. His mind races, desperately trying to rationalize the madness of this place. *This can't be real,* he thinks, his breath quickening. *I must be imagining things.*

As he moves down the corridor, faint whispers slither from the walls, each word soaked in agony. The voices recount the slow, excruciating tortures of those who have been sacrificed to the maze, their souls bound within its very structure. The gruesome details flood his mind, making him gag and swallow down bile.

But he refuses to let the horrors stop him. Steeling himself, he presses on, barely lifting his feet off the ground, his every instinct screaming to turn back.

Following the winding corridor, Peren rounds a corner, only to find himself facing a dead end. He stands there, confusion creeping into his mind, as the haunting chuckles echo around him. *How could I have possibly reached a dead end? There have been no other paths, no other turns.* The maze seems to mock him, its twisted design defying logic.

Shaking his head, Peren turns to retrace his steps. But as he does, a path suddenly opens up to his left. He stops dead in his tracks, staring in disbelief at the impossibility of it. His mind races, struggling to comprehend the absurdity. *This isn't possible. I would have seen this the first time,* he thinks fiercely, a cold knot tightening in his stomach.

Taking a deep breath, he steels himself. *I've come too far to turn back now,* he thinks, the weight of his resolve settling in. *I must keep going, no matter what.*

With renewed determination, he steps onto the newly revealed path, bracing himself for whatever horrors lie in the depths of the Skull Maze.

He focuses on the two things that keep him going: finding the exit and Norta. His hand moves instinctively to the pendant at his neck, the symbol of their Soul Joining, and he fiddles with it absentmindedly.

Moving down the path a short distance, he hears rustling up ahead. Slowing to a crawl, he inches forward to investigate the noise. As he peers around the next corner, the rustling intensifies. He creeps forward, his breath shallow, until he reaches the source.

Reaching down to move a few bones out of the way, Peren freezes as he uncovers the source of the rustling: spiders. Each one is larger than two hand spans. Hundreds, then thousands of them swarm from the rubble, rushing toward him.

His face pales as he recognizes them: Death Stingers, the deadliest spiders in existence. Just a drop of their poison on the skin is enough to kill, let alone a bite. His mind races with the horrors of their venom. *The worst part isn't the swift death—it's the poison's agonizing crawl through your body, slowly eating away at your insides, leaving you writhing in agony for days, even weeks.*

Scrambling back as fast as he can, abandoning all stealth, Peren turns and bolts down the corridor. He takes a right, then a left, then another left. He skids to a halt, his stomach dropping as he realizes he's hit a dead end. The same eerie chuckle echoes around him.

Whipping around in panic, he hears the spiders closing in, their rustling growing louder by the second. He scans the smooth, unclimbable walls, desperation gripping him. *I have to get through somehow,* he thinks, his pulse pounding. *And soon— they're almost here.*

Turning to face the oncoming swarm, Peren sprints straight at them. Timing it perfectly, he launches off a corner, propelling himself down the corridor and landing atop a cluster of spiders. Their bodies burst like overripe fruit, coating the ground—and him—in sticky, rancid goo. Fighting down nausea, he keeps running, his preternatural speed his only defence against the spiders trying to bite him. He dodges the deadly poison and slime with every step, pushing himself to stay just ahead of their reach.

Racing around corners, he uses each turn to gain momentum, finally landing on bones that crunch satisfyingly underfoot. *I never thought I'd be relieved to hear bones breaking—anything but the popping of those creatures,* he thinks.

Refusing to slow down, he charges ahead, spotting an exit to the right and darting into it as it twists left, then right. Stopping briefly to catch his breath, he stiffens as the rustling sound swells louder, as if the spiders are closing in again. The deafening chorus presses in on him for endless nerve-wracking moments until, at last, it fades.

Leaning against the wall, he savours the sudden silence, a brief relief amidst the madness.

Suddenly, he jumps forward in shock, twisting around and slashing out with his dagger. The blade connects with a skeletal arm that's reaching toward him, snapping it off and sending it clattering to the ground. He lets out a shaky breath, a slight smile tugging at his lips, despite his racing heart. *Jumping at shadows,* he thinks, knowing the maze has him on edge.

Feeling something latch onto his foot, he glances down, his confusion turning instantly to horror. Skeletal arms and hands are reaching toward him from every direction, clawing through the dust. He quickly realizes it's not only the arms and hands moving—spines, ribcages, legs, and feet are dragging themselves toward him as well, a seething mass of bones converging upon him. He stumbles back, desperate to escape the encroaching mass of skeletons.

Not only are the bones moving toward him, but they're fusing together, merging into one massive skeletal creature with multiple twisted appendages that loom high above. Peren stands there, gaping, frozen by a creature that seems to have clawed its way out of a nightmare. Powerless to move, he cranes his neck back, eyes wide, following the grotesque formation as it towers over him, inching closer with every dreadful creak and clatter of bone.

How do I fight something like this? His mind races, panic clawing at his thoughts. *I have to find a way. This can't be the end.* Swallowing hard, he steadies his breath, forcing his trembling hands to grip his dagger tighter.

Drawing a deep breath, he forces himself to be steady, tightening his grip on the dagger until his knuckles whiten. *I've faced death before,* he reminds himself fiercely. *I can do this.*

Bracing himself, he locks his gaze on the towering skeletal monstrosity, a fierce determination hardening his resolve.

The skeletal hands clawing up his legs jolt him out of his frozen state. He shoves them off and bolts, barely dodging the giant creature's reaching grasp. A guttural bellow of rage echoes down the corridor as the monstrosity hammers a massive fist onto the ground. The impact erupts into a shockwave, scattering shards of splintered bone in every direction, peppering Peren's back with stinging fragments.

The force hurls him forward, slamming him headfirst into a dead-end wall. Dazed, he takes a shaky breath, barely noticing the low, haunting chuckle reverberating from the skulls nearby.

Finally coming to his senses, Peren feels the ground rumbling as the giant creature quickens its pursuit. Panic surges through him, but his training takes over. He charges forward, dagger in hand, ducking under the creature's massive hands, narrowly dodging the first two grabs. The third swing catches him off-guard, and its fingers collide with his back, crushing bone and sending him flying through the air, his head slamming into the jagged wall of skulls. The impact sends a jolt of blinding pain through his skull, the sharp fragments biting into his skin as his vision spins. He grits his teeth, forcing himself to stay conscious, but every movement feels like he's dragging himself through a fog of agony.

Lying in a heap, Peren groans in agony, his body protesting every movement as he struggles to push himself upright. The ground beneath him vibrates with the creature's relentless steps, a constant reminder of the danger closing in. Gritting his teeth, he forces himself onto his hands and knees, desperation fuelling his every movement.

Just as he's about to rise, a massive foot strikes him from the side, sending a shock of pain through his ribs. The impact cracks bone, and he's hurled through the air, his body spinning uncontrollably until he crashes violently into the ground, bouncing off the stone like a ragdoll before finally skidding to a halt. Bones pierce his side, their jagged tips biting into flesh as he gasps, struggling to breathe through the searing pain. His face contorts in anguish, each shallow breath a battle, and he's unable to stop the flood of fear rising as the creature thunders closer, its ominous thumps shaking the very air around him.

I can't take any more of this beating, he thinks, his body screaming in protest. *I can't outrun it now.*

Ignoring the searing pain coursing through him, he pushes through, instinct and desperation taking over. With every ounce of strength left in his battered body, he scrambles beneath the creature, his hands slipping against its cold, skeletal form. Gritting his teeth, he climbs up one of its enormous legs, his fingers finding purchase on the jagged bones. His muscles burn with the effort, but he forces himself to move, determined not to become just another victim of the maze.

Finally, he reaches the creature's back, clinging to it with all his strength, his chest heaving with ragged breaths. The creature bellows in frustration, its skeletal head jerking in every direction, searching for him. But Peren's grip is like iron, his body pressed flat against the cold bone, hidden in the shadow of the beast—for the moment.

His vision blurs as blood pours from his wounds, dripping onto the creature's bones and running down its form. The blood pools and stains the ground beneath them, its metallic scent thick in the air.

Finally, the creature realizes its plaything is clinging to its back. With a growl of frustration, it begins ramming its skeletal form against the walls. The impact shakes the ground, but the walls remain steadfast, untouched by the creature's fury. Each collision sends bone shards flying, narrowly missing Peren as the creature thrashes in anger.

The force of the blows grows more erratic, and Peren's grip slips as his body is ravaged by pain. He can't hold on any longer. In a final, desperate attempt to avoid being crushed, he lets go. His body crashes to the ground with a sickening thud, the air forced from his lungs.

The creature, oblivious to the loss of its prey, continues its mindless assault. The walls remain unmoved, untouched by its violence, as the creature slams into them again and again.

But the creature itself is no match for its own power. Its bones splinter, its joints snap, and eventually, its skeletal form crumbles under the force of its own rampage, collapsing into a heap on top of Peren.

He sits there for what feels like an eternity, waiting for his body to rest, for the broken bones to shift back into place and for the shards still embedded in his side to dislodge. His every movement is slow, painful, and deliberate. He eats what little he has left, drinks sparingly, and eventually falls into a fitful sleep, waking at every imagined whisper or creaking sound around him.

When he awakens, hours—or maybe days—later, his body is sore, stiff, and battered. With a grimace, he gingerly pushes himself onto his feet, wincing with each shallow breath and feeling the tenderness of his ribs. Every motion is a reminder of how far he's pushed himself.

Shuffling forward, he retrieves his dagger, each step a silent struggle. His ribs still click and grind as they heal, the sound of his body mending more audible than he would like, but he forces himself onward, fighting against exhaustion. The provisions he's been rationing are nearly gone, burned through faster than he would've preferred, but his resolve doesn't waver. With determination, he presses forward, his heart set on survival, no matter the cost.

He briefly wonders if he'll actually survive this, the thought of his own mortality creeping into his mind. *How do humans manage to make it out of places like this?* He's left bewildered by the question, but the weight of exhaustion quickly dulls his thoughts. Too tired to dwell on it any longer, he forces his focus back to the present moment and pushes himself forward, moving down the corridor.

He turns one corner, then another. His uncanny sense of direction tells him he's backtracked, that he should have walked outside the maze's outer walls, but the reality is far different. The magic of this cursed labyrinth twists and bends reality, keeping him trapped, despite what his instincts tell him. *This maze is toying with me,* he thinks, his mind reeling from the unnatural disorientation.

Forced to ignore his usual bearings, he pushes deeper into the maze, determined to find an end, even as it plays its cruel games.

Sometimes, when he takes four right turns, he expects to be back where he started, but instead, it feels as though he's never been there before. *Magic—it has to be magic,* he thinks, pushing aside the uncomfortable thoughts creeping into his mind. He's forced to retrace his steps at dead ends, enduring the eerie, distant laughter of the skulls.

Turning a corner, he quickly backtracks, pressing himself against the cold stone wall. His mind struggles to process what his eyes just saw, even as his brain insists it can't be real.

Peeking around the corner once more, he catches another glimpse of the creature, still struggling to make sense of what he's facing.

The creature around the corner is beyond anything he could have imagined. At first, he notices its size—he thought the skeletal creature was tall, but this one dwarfs it by many feet. It's so wide that the walls of the path should be crushing it, yet somehow, it fits comfortably, with space on either side. *How is that possible?* His exhausted mind aches, struggling to make sense of it.

The second thing that grabs his attention is its eyes: hand-sized spheres perched atop narrow vertical stalks, rising above a gaping maw lined with row upon row of finger-length razor-sharp teeth, disappearing into a black void.

The creature's body is supported by six massive, thick ap-pendages, each ending in claw-like hands that scrape the ground. Above these, two enormous bird-like wings stretch, twitching slightly as the creature shifts.

Suicide, Peren thinks. It would be sheer madness to face it head-on, especially in his current state. He resolves to approach from the rear. Gritting his teeth and psyching himself up, he leaps around the corner, moving as quickly as he can without collapsing from the pain. Sliding under the beast, he rolls clear just in time to avoid a clawed leg crashing down where he was moments before.

He scrambles to his feet, but before he can fully steady himself, something lunges from above, forcing him to dive out of the way. He rolls and regains his footing a few paces away, quickly turning to face what attacked him.

Six snake-like appendages whip through the air, hissing and snapping, closing in on him. He stumbles backward, desperate to keep his distance. The creature rears up on its back four legs, its front legs rising, preparing to strike.

I can't beat this thing, Peren realizes, his body burning with exhaustion as he barely keeps ahead of its attacks. His movements are slower now, his breath ragged, each dodge more difficult than the last. *I'm not strong enough to take it down,* he thinks, gritting his teeth in frustration.

Finally, he does the sensible thing and begins to back up. The creature, sensing his retreat, hisses in triumph and surges forward, forcing Peren to evade it, giving up ground with every step. His heart pounds in his chest as he struggles to maintain his pace, but his eyes never leave the creature, scanning his surroundings for any possible escape. *I can't keep this up for much longer,* he thinks, knowing that with one misstep, he will be finished.

Turning and running, he hopes he is faster than the beast. Panic surges through him as the creature gives chase, sending vibrations through the air and ground, the hissing of its serpentine appendages close behind. *Just keep running. Don't look back,* he tells himself, pushing his body to its limits, feeling every bruise and wound with each strained breath. His legs burn, but he forces himself to keep moving, knowing that if he falters for even a moment, the creature will be on him.

After running for what feels like hours—or even days—rather than minutes, Peren finally comes to a halt, bending over with his hands on his knees, panting heavily. He takes a long gulp of water, trying to steady his breath.

When he realizes that no thumping or hissing is following, he allows himself a moment to relax, leaning against the wall. His body, exhausted beyond belief, soon drifts into a fitful stupor, his mind too tired to stay alert.

When he wakes with more pain and stiffness than before, Peren slowly drinks and eats, then falls back into a restless sleep, but it feels like only moments later when a thought jolts him awake. *Where is the sun?* It has been hours, maybe days, yet the sky remains unchanged—no hint of daylight or dusk.

Too tired to ponder it deeply, he forces himself to move forward, following the winding path that twists left and right. He retraces his steps at every dead end, the spine-chilling laughter of the skulls no longer registering, despite its growing intensity.

Peren turns a corner, and his shoulders slump in frustration and resignation as he faces an endless sea of Spliganders filling the path from wall to wall. *How much more of this can I take?* The sight of this next challenge almost breaks him, and for a moment, he wants to weep.

With a painful breath, he grits his teeth and leaps forward. Dagger in hand, he slashes left and right, cutting down the majority of them as he leaps past, using their backs as launchpads for his next strikes.

Eventually outpacing the horde of Spliganders, he continues on. Without an end in sight, he presses ahead, turning corner after corner, only to be forced to retrace his steps when he hits dead ends.

Exhausted, he slumps against the wall, taking what little comfort he can in the brief respite. He eats and drinks, the small comforts a lifeline before drifting into an unrestful slumber.

Despite the constant unease, he wakes feeling slightly refreshed. After another quick meal, he gathers what strength he has left and trudges toward the heart of the maze.

Stepping into what seems like a large clearing, Peren suspects he has finally reached the centre of the maze. He cautiously surveys his surroundings, his senses alert for any hidden dangers.

As he moves into the clearing, he blinks, momentarily disoriented by an abrupt change in the environment. His mind races, struggling to process the unfamiliar scene unfolding before him.

He finds himself in a large, opulently decorated bedroom, each surface adorned to perfection. To his right, against the wall, sits a grand, thick, and plush bed. At the foot of the bed are two cots, each holding a crying baby.

His gaze shifts, and he identifies what he assumes are the parents—royalty or perhaps incredibly wealthy nobles—fighting men in flowing cloaks with their faces obscured by hoods, wielding daggers and swords.

But then something about the scene shakes him. He realizes what makes these figures different: their movements are too graceful, too agile to be human. *Elves,* he thinks, a sudden clarity striking him as one of the nobles ducks, their hair flying up, revealing a pointed ear.

Peren's mouth hangs open in disbelief. *Another elf!* He's only ever seen two in his life—himself and his master. Though he doesn't know his parents, something deep inside tells him that these are them. The resemblance in the male's facial features is too striking to be mere coincidence.

Shocked beyond words, he barely notices one of the robed assassins sneaking up behind them. Acting purely on reflex, he flicks his dagger toward the assassin, but it passes right through the elf's form, doing no damage.

He can only watch in horror as the assassin thrusts his sword into the noble's back, piercing his heart.

The noble stares down at the protruding blade, confusion clouding his face before he slumps forward, the life draining from him as he falls to the ground with a heavy thud.

The other noble cries out in a mixture of anger and grief at the loss of her mate, her fury driving her to dispatch the remaining assassins in a flurry of swift, lethal blows.

Peren surveys the scene, his stomach twisting as he takes in the sight of the guards and servants lying lifeless in pools of blood.

The queen's gaze lingers on her fallen mate, sorrow evident in her eyes, before she rushes to the first crib, lifting a screaming baby from its confines. She presses a gentle kiss to his forehead, tears spilling down her cheeks as, in a language that Peren shouldn't understand, she whispers, "Goodbye, my darling son. May you grow up never knowing the horrors that have been visited upon us today."

Turning, she hands the baby to an elf clad in bloodstained purple robes, her composure returning, though her voice trembles as she says, "Take him to another world. Protect and train him. Don't ever return until he is ready, for they will never stop hunting him."

Holding the baby with one arm, the robed elf finishes etching symbols onto the plush bed. Peren's eyes widen as he realizes the elf is drawing in blood—similar to the glyphs that adorn the skulls in the maze. The air thickens with a sense of dread as the elf hands the baby to one of the remaining guards, then motions for the guard to step onto the bed.

As the robed elf opens his mouth to speak, a shrill scream from the queen cuts him off, breaking his concentration. Peren's heart lurches as he sees the same beast that attacked him earlier—the creature with the massive maw and snakelike tail—piercing the queen's body with one of its clawed legs. She crumples to the floor in her death throes, and Peren, in a moment of helpless desperation, reaches toward her as he cries, "Mother!"

The robed elf quickly utters something in a foreign tongue, and Peren, to his shock, understands. The words slice through the air, pushing the creature back and erecting a shimmering magical barrier.

Rushing to the second cot, the elf lifts the screaming baby and hands it to a female guard. "I don't have the time or energy to send you to another world now," he says, his voice tight with urgency. "But I will send you far away. Never stop running. Train her in the arts of the Shadow Warrior."

With a few words, the magician visibly pales as the female guard and the baby wink out of existence.

Beads of sweat form on his forehead as the elf turns to the bed, pushing a sheathed dagger and a small pouch into the other guard's hands. "Take these for him," he says urgently.

Behind him, the magic barrier trembles, the creature's powerful strikes causing it to shrink.

"Train him and protect him!" the elf commands, pressing his hand firmly onto one of the glyphs. As his finger makes contact, the spell ignites. Baby Peren instinctively grabs the pouch, shaking it with a delighted squeal, and gems spill out, their colours flashing brilliantly as they arc through the air.

In the same instant, the gems, the guard, and baby Peren himself vanish in a burst of magical energy, winking out of existence together.

With that, the vision suddenly ends, and Peren finds himself back in the clearing of the maze. Crumbling to the ground, tears streaming down his face, he weeps for the loss of his family.

Finally, he slumps against the wall, sitting on the ground, exhausted and all cried-out. After forcing himself to eat and drink, he falls into a fitful slumber, the nightmares of his childhood haunting him.

When he wakes up, the memories of his dreams and the vision flood back, causing a tear to fall down his cheek. Gritting his teeth, he wipes his nose with his sleeve, fighting to quell the storm of emotions surging within him.

As he stands and gathers his things, an unbidden thought surfaces: he has a sister. Or, at least, he *had* one. He hopes it is still the present tense, but given how ruthlessly the assassins murdered his family, he feels doubt creep in, despite his own survival.

Slowly, the pieces fall into place. He finally understands what his master has told him—and what he has left unsaid.

Trying to control the shaking anger and the desire for vengeance welling up inside him, Peren contemplates the realizations emerging in his mind.

He is, at the very least, noble by birth. He has faced the same massive, grotesque beast with the multi-snake tail. The robed elf wielded magic, just as the witch did, but on a whole new level. *Is that why they were murdered?* he wonders. But after a moment of thought, he dismisses the idea—if magic had been the cause, his family would have been executed publicly.

As his mind continues to race, Peren recognizes the guard who took him in, and, despite the human touches, he is certain that the guard is the one who trained him. Questions flood his mind: *Where was he when I lived on the streets of Tharon? And now, I understand why my master kept me in the dark for so long.* Another tear escapes, tracing a path down his cheek.

Bringing his focus back to the present, Peren remembers the task at hand: he needs to collect the Broaf flower from the centre of the clearing.

As he picks up his dagger from where it landed during the vision, a scream—laced with agony—rips through the air. Without thinking, he rushes toward the sound.

He finds a naked woman suspended in the air, her limbs stretched in an X, her head hanging down, her hair veiling her face. Standing next to her is the most hideous, disfigured, and diseased creature Peren has ever seen, its cracked smile twisted with malice. It makes perverse noises, savouring each movement as it slowly and methodically tortures and mutilates the woman's body.

Moving closer, Peren grips his dagger tightly, his knuckles white with tension as he readies himself to strike at the otherworldly evil creature, but as he draws nearer, the creature's gaze shifts, locking onto him. It lets out a spine-chilling, horrific cackle that freezes him in place, sending a shiver crawling down his spine.

In a deep and silky voice, its tone oozing into every crack of his skull, the creature murmurs, "Come closer, my jewel."

Forced to move forward against his will, Peren is drawn ever closer to the woman and the creature. When he reaches a certain point, the creature halts his movement, its twisted presence commanding his stillness. Then, with a sickening, deliberate motion, it pulls back the woman's hair, forcing her to face him.

Peren's heart stops as he recognizes her, despite the cruel disfigurement—his beloved wife, Norta. The shock paralyses him, and he can do nothing but stand frozen as she is slowly and painfully dismembered before his eyes. Each agonizing slice makes him wince and cry out in shared pain, tears streaming down both their faces. Her eyes lock with his in a silent plea for it all to end, shattering his heart, as he knows there is nothing he can do to save her.

When Norta finally succumbs, her body going limp as death claims her, Peren feels a bittersweet relief wash over him. The creature releases its hold on him, and he crumbles to the ground, unable to hold back the keening cry of pure agony that rips from his throat.

The sound of cackling suddenly cuts through his sorrow, drawing his gaze upward. His heart lurches in horror as he sees Norta, completely healed and clothed, suspended in the air again, struggling helplessly. Her eyes are wide with panic, and a chill runs through Peren as he understands the true horror unfolding before him.

The creature's voice slithers into his mind once more, cold and commanding. "My name is Fractus. You are mine."

With a jarring shift, the nightmarish scene dissolves, leaving Peren to collapse on the ground, grief-stricken. The echoes of the creature's cackling still reverberate in his mind, a haunting reminder of the soul-crushing vision he was forced to endure. His body shakes with the weight of his emotions, and he screams his anger into the oppressive silence of the maze, cursing it for the torment it has made him relive.

Slowly, painfully, he pulls himself together, each breath a

battle against the despair threatening to consume him. Determined, he rises, finds the elusive Broaf flower, plucks it with careful hands, and preserves it in a book.

Then, standing with a steady resolve, he turns towards the exit.

He follows the winding path, constantly forced to retrace his steps as the maze taunts him with dead ends. The echo of haunting cackles still lingers in his mind, sending involuntary shivers down his spine.

To his relief, he isn't faced with any challenges. Though his body aches from exhaustion, he forces himself to keep moving, taking frequent breaks to conserve his dwindling strength.

When Peren rounds the next corner, he stops dead in his tracks, his face frozen in shock as he sees Cartlan standing a few feet away. The same friend Peren thought he lost as his name is on the wall of remembrance back at the guild. For a moment, neither of them moves, their minds struggling to comprehend what they're seeing.

Then, almost instinctively, they rush toward each other, collapsing into a tight embrace, overwhelmed with joy and disbelief.

Tears well up in Peren's eyes as he pulls back slightly, still gripping Cartlan's arms. "How? We all thought you were dead…" His voice trembles, too stunned to grasp the impossible reunion fully.

Smiling through his tears, Cartlan wipes his face with a shaky hand before meeting Peren's gaze. "I thought I was too," he says, his voice catching in disbelief. "I never thought I'd see you again."

"How can this be?" Peren mutters as his brow furrows in confusion, his mind racing as a torrent of thoughts clashes in his head. He shakes his head as if trying to clear the fog.

Cartlan steps back slightly, his own expression tight with concern. "What's wrong? Why do you look like that?" he asks, voice trembling with a hint of worry. "Aren't you happy to see me?"

Another tear slips down Peren's cheek as his expression crumples, the weight of grief crashing into him. His voice just above a whisper, he says, "Your name is engraved on the Wall of Remembrance."

"I'm here, Peren. I'm alive," Cartlan replies. "I know this is... a lot. But we can leave this place together. You don't have to carry this alone anymore."

Shaking his head in disbelief, Peren whispers under his breath, his voice tinged with confusion and pain.

Cartlan frowns, stepping closer. "What did you say?"

Peren chokes on his words, his voice barely a whisper. "I said…it's not possible. No one comes back from the dead."

"You died and came back, so why can't I?" Cartlan steps forward, his eyes searching Peren's face. Gently, he takes his friend's hand, pressing it against his chest. "Can't you feel it? I'm here. I'm real. My heart is still beating, Peren."

Nodding absently, Peren feels his body stiffen as if frozen in place. A fleeting thought—a sharp, uncomfortable sensation—pricks at the edge of his mind, pulling him into focus. Slowly, a realization begins to take shape, and his pulse quickens.

Cartlan notices the subtle shift in Peren's demeanour, his eyes narrowing with understanding. Sighing deeply, he steps closer, his voice tinged with something unreadable. "What gave me away?"

"You're talking about me dying... but I didn't die until *after* I left on my quest. That was long after you failed yours."

With a sad smile, Cartlan places a hand on Peren's

shoulder. His voice a mere whisper, he says, "He did love you. And out of that love, I will make it quick."

Lightning-fast, Cartlan whips out a knife and stabs it toward Peren's heart. Caught off-guard, Peren instinctively shifts just enough to avoid the full blow, but the blade slices across the left side of his ribcage. He cries out in pain, jerking back, barely managing to escape the strike.

Frustration radiates from the Cartlan entity as it fixes Peren with a twisted, almost mocking gaze. "I was going to make this quick for you, but now…" The creature's voice turns cold, dripping with malice. "Now, I'll take my sweet time." With a sickening smirk, it licks the blood from the blade and lunges again.

Anticipating the attack, Peren sidesteps the knife with ease and drives his own dagger into Cartlan's neck. "I'm sorry, my friend," he whispers, pulling the blade free in a spray of blood.

Cartlan stumbles back, hands rising to his neck in a desperate attempt to stem the crimson fountain pouring from the wound. For a moment, confusion flickers across his face before he falls to his knees, the twisted smile never leaving his lips. His body jerks, then collapses forward, lifeless.

Crumbling to his knees, Peren lets out a raw, guttural cry of anguish, mourning the loss of his best friend. First, it was the love of his life, and now Cartlan—his only remaining tether to a life once filled with hope. Tears streak down his filthy face, his breath ragged as he wipes them away with his sleeve, leaving a streak of grime.

His chest heaves as fury boils up inside him. Squeezing his fists so tightly his knuckles turn white, he screams into the maze, the sound of his rage echoing through the silence as the weight of his torment finally overwhelms him.

Picking himself up, Peren sets his face in grim

determination. Stepping over Cartlan's lifeless body, he forces himself not to look back, each step feeling like an unbearable weight.

After navigating more twists and turns and retracing his path several times, he rounds another corner. There, standing in front of him, is yet another Cartlan, eyes wide with shock.

Peren freezes, his heart hammering in his chest, but the moment passes quickly. His instincts take over, and he rushes forward, driving his dagger deep into Cartlan's chest. "I'm so sorry, brother," he whispers through clenched teeth.

Cartlan's eyes meet his, wide with confusion as he mouths, "Why?"

Tears flood Peren's eyes, but he says nothing, lowering Cartlan gently to the ground. He wipes the blood from his dagger, his movements mechanical, before closing his friend's eyes with trembling hands. Standing over the body, he forces his legs to move, each step a battle against the grief that weighs him down.

By the time Peren faces the tenth Cartlan, he is so broken that his knees give out from beneath him. He collapses, his heart wrenching in pain as he weeps uncontrollably. His best friend's face has become a nightmare, each death more brutal than the last, and he can't bear to do it again.

Desperate, he tries to rush past, closing his eyes to the sight, praying the entity will let him go. For a long, agonizing moment, nothing happens. But then—relief. He realizes Cartlan is neither pursuing him nor appearing before him again. The haunting presence that has tormented him for what feels like an eternity finally fades away.

Sobbing in relief, the weight of everything that has happened crashes over him. He sinks to the ground, trembling, his chest heaving with raw, broken sobs.

After a long time, he dares to stop. He doesn't fight the exhaustion; he rests, allowing himself a brief, precious reprieve.

When he wakes up from a fitful, nightmare-ridden sleep, Peren's body aches as though he's been torn apart. His mind is clouded with the remnants of the horrors he's faced, the images of Cartlan's and Norta's deaths still lingering like an open wound.

The weight of his exhaustion presses down on him, but he forces himself to his feet, gritting his teeth against the sharp stinging in his ribs. His legs tremble, but he pushes forward, each step heavier than the last, as if the maze itself were trying to hold him back.

All he wants is the end of this endless torment. He doesn't know how much longer he can endure it, but he can't stop now—not when he's so close.

Each time he hits a dead end, Peren is forced to backtrack, barely registering the spine-chilling cackles of the skulls echoing through the maze. His mind is too weary to focus on their haunting sound.

As he turns a corner, his heart stops. There, looming before him, is the largest Brooder he's ever seen—its form filling the narrow passage. He holds his breath, praying it hasn't noticed him.

But, as if on cue, the creature gives a low, rumbling growl, and Peren knows it's too late.

Remembering how difficult it is to take on a Brooder even when fresh, Peren knows he can't fight now—not with his strength drained. He makes a desperate dash, leaping to the side to avoid the creature, only to freeze in shock as another Brooder appears in his path. Frustration wells up in him, but there's no time to waste.

He prepares to leap again, only to be caught off-guard by

the low growls coming from behind him. Panic surges through him as he narrowly avoids a massive claw slashing at his back. With no choice but to keep running, he sprints forward, heart pounding in his chest, barely dodging another strike as he pushes himself harder, his legs burning with the effort.

Speeding down the path, he darts around corners, sliding across the slick bones beneath him, crashing into walls that jar his already-battered body. Each movement sends a fresh wave of pain through him, the slice on his ribs leaking blood with every breath, tearing open a wound that refuses to heal. The pressure builds in his chest as every inhale makes the pain worse, choking off his strength.

Crying out in frustration and hopelessness, he turns a corner—only to slam into a dead end.

His heart sinks, the weight of his situation crashing down on him.

Turning around, Peren hears the thunderous pounding of paws and the guttural growls of the Brooders as they charge around the corner. With a desperate surge of energy, he rushes forward, managing to dodge all but one swipe. A massive claw catches him in the side, sending him flying into the wall with a sickening thud, followed by the crack of breaking bones. He crashes to the ground in a heap, his ribs screaming in protest as the pain erupts through his body. His vision blurs, and the ground spins beneath him, but he fights to stay conscious.

The Brooders howl in anticipation, circling him, their eyes glinting with hunger as they close in on their prey.

Unsteadily getting to his feet, Peren somehow manages to keep hold of his dagger, barely dodging a Brooder's gaping maw. His foot catches on one of its sharp teeth, and he's lifted into the air as the creature attempts to flip him into its mouth. In a desperate move, he adjusts midair and lands on the

Brooder's nose. The creature sneezes violently, rearing back in surprise.

Peren falls to the ground and lands on his shoulder with an echoing crack. Pain flares through his body as it aches with injuries and exhaustion, but he forces himself to rise, hobbling away as fast as his battered body will allow.

Cradling his injured shoulder, he staggers forward, desperate to put as much distance as possible between himself and the Brooders. He rushes around corners, barely keeping ahead, the time it takes the creatures to turn around the only thing saving him. His energy dwindles with every step, the strain of his battered body catching up to him.

Finally, he collapses, succumbing to darkness that swallows him whole.

When he wakes in agony to the sound of buzzing, Peren's eyes snap open to see hundreds of large wasps heading straight for him. Groaning, he pushes himself shakily to his feet, desperate to move toward the exit.

He turns corner after corner, praying he doesn't run into dead ends, but the wasps steadily close the gap. Each sting punctures his skin, injecting searing poison that tears at his muscles, forcing him to slow with every painful step.

Turning another corner, Peren spots the exit ahead and forces himself into a burst of speed. The buzzing fades further behind him, confirming that he is finally nearing his escape.

But just as he nears the exit, his foot catches on something, sending him sprawling face-first into the ground. His eyes focus on the body beneath him, and a sharp gasp escapes his lips.

He freezes, his heart sinking, then bursts into tears as he recognizes the body—his best friend, Cartlan Stracs. The *real* Cartlan Stracs.

Crawling forward, Peren barely has enough energy to

move. Knowing he can't stop to rest and eat to regain energy, he realizes this might be the end, as his body repairs itself to death. Digging out his final reserves of energy, he makes it to the exit and collapses.

Refusing to give up, he drags himself forward until the blackness washes over and takes him.

ACKNOWLEDGEMENTS

I want to express my deepest thanks to everyone who helped bring this book to life.

To my editor, Oren Eades, for their invaluable insights and careful attention to detail.

To Dave Leahey, for creating a cover that perfectly captures the essence of the story, and for his beautiful work on the maps.

To Lorna, for her exceptional work on the typography and formatting, bringing the manuscript to its final polished form.

And, of course, to you, the reader, for your support in reading this book and encouraging the next one.

Thank you all for your contributions to this journey.

9 781763 856417